Under the Beetle's Cellar

Mary Willis Walker

Under the Beetle's Cellar

WHEELER
PUBLISHING, INC.
ROCKLAND, MA

★ AN AMERICAN COMPANY ★

Published in Large Print by arrangement with
Doubleday, a division of Bantam Doubleday Dell
Publishing Group, Inc.
in the United States and Canada.

Wheeler Large Print Book Series.

Set in 16 pt. Plantin.

Library of Congress Cataloging-in-Publication Data

Walker, Mary Willis
    Under the beetle's cellar / Mary Willis Walker.
        p. cm.—(Wheeler large print book series)
        ISBN 1-56895-313-5 (pbk.)
        1. Women journalists—Texas—Fiction. 2. Kidnapping—Texas—
Fiction. 3. Cults—Texas—Fiction. 4. Large type books.
I. Title. II. Series
[PS3573.A425354U53 1996]
813'.54—dc20
                                                                      96-2292
  -   CIP

To the memory of my mother,
who would have enjoyed
all this making
of books.
Oh for a disc to the distance.

Acknowledgements

Because I seem incapable of writing a single page without stopping to ask someone for information, I am deeply grateful to those who routinely share their knowledge with me. They make research fun and writing less lonely.

Debbie Lauderdale and her fourth grade at Forest Trail Elementary School brainstormed what kids would do trapped in a bus for fifty days. Fred Askew and Glen Alyn shared their experiences in Vietnam. Joshua "JM" Logan told me the procedure for making body casts. Becky Levy consulted on art. John Hellerstedt, M.D., Norman Chenven, M.D., and Susan Wade informed me about the realities of childhood asthma.

Special Agents Nancy Houston and James Echols told me FBI stories. Gerald Adams told me more FBI stories and sparked off some wonderful ideas about a female agent. Ann Hutchison, APD Victim Services, and APD Sr. Sgt. Jack Kelley gave me information on hostage negotiating. Janice Brown at the Texas Department of Protective and Regulatory Services and Chris Douglas at Adoption Affiliates of Reproductive Services educated me on adoption procedures.

Ralph Willis offered his eighty-six years of accumulated general knowledge on all subjects. Tim Wendel gave some practical info about the world and TJ reminded me what fourth graders are like. My "muscle class" at the Hills helped on all manner of things. Susie Devening and Rebecca Bingham dredged up the worm ditty from the distant past. Amanda Walker gave unflagging Emily Dickinson consultation.

The Trashy Paperback Writers—Fred Askew, Jodi Berls, Dinah Chenven, and Susan Wade—were there helping through the whole messy process.

And Kate Miciak believed in me and edited me with enthusiasm and nit-picking attention to detail.

Thank you, all.

Under the Beetle's Cellar

"The sun turned black like sackcloth made of goat hair, the whole moon turned blood red, and the stars in the sky fell to earth, as late figs drop from a fig tree when shaken by a strong wind."

REVELATION 6:12

CHAPTER ONE

Walter Demming hadn't cried since September 2, 1968, but he sure enough felt like crying now. The lightbulb at the back had gone out while he slept, burned out most likely, leaving them with just the sixty-watt bulb that hung in the pit outside the open front door. So meager was the illumination from that one pathetic bulb, so cold and scant, it could barely be called light. Here in the middle of the bus, as Walter did his morning count, it provided just enough light to discern shapes by.

Maybe this was the way the world ended, not with the fireworks Samuel Mordecai kept ranting about, but with a simple, gradual fading of the light, a blurring of detail until everything vanished.

It would end not with a bang but a whimper.

And whimpering was exactly what Walter felt like doing. Especially when he thought about what it would feel like when that last bulb burned out, too, and cast them into utter darkness. They'd had a taste of that the day it happened. Forty-six days ago.

1

The Jezreelites had herded them into the dark barn, Walter and eleven sobbing, terrified children.

Two of the Jezreelites had put their rifles down and dragged the wooden slab to the side, revealing a raw hole in the earth. One of them walked to the barn door and flipped a switch. From inside the hole, a light glowed up. Walter stared at it. It was just an illuminated hole in the ground. He couldn't imagine that it had anything to do with him or the children he'd been driving to school.

The gunmen formed a circle around the twelve of them.

"Down you go," said one of the gunmen, pointing to the hole.

Walter had stood there uncomprehending. The children huddled around him, whining and crying.

"Bus Driver," the man said, "you go down first and help them others."

Walter had continued to stand there.

A gunman approached him; he jabbed his rifle into Walter's spine. "Do it."

So Walter had done it. He walked to the edge and looked down into the hole. He knelt and backed himself down, wondering in a distant way if he were climbing into his grave. He landed and looked around. He was standing in a rough dirt pit about four feet in diameter and six feet high. A lightbulb hung from a cord at the side of the hole.

An open bus door was the only place to go. He stepped in. The buried bus was older and more decrepit than the one they had just gotten out of, but bigger. Half of the seats had been removed, leaving an open space in the back. A hole was cut

2

in the middle of the open floor. A second dim lightbulb hung down in the back.

It was cooler by about ten degrees than it had been aboveground. And damp, like an old summerhouse after weeks of rain. The smell was musty and heavy.

But the strangest part, the worst of it, was the windows. They were black with the earth pressing in on them. Since his glasses had got broken and left behind on the road, Walter had to walk closer to look at the dirt outside the window. A thick white grub worm wiggled against the glass and a dark beetle was inching its way through a tiny burrow.

A voice from above said, "Help the others down."

Walter stood in the pit and lifted the children down, one by one. He didn't even know all their names then, but he lifted them down, one after another, delivering them to the underworld. Lucy came first, red-nosed and sobbing. Bucky dropped into his arms light as a feather, his eyes squeezed shut, his freckles vivid against blanched skin. Josh, wheezing violently, was so heavy Walter stumbled as he lifted him down. Heather clung to him like a baby monkey, wrapped her legs around him; when an impatient voice called from above, Walter had to peel her off. Sue Ellen and Sandra came clutching on to each other, whimpering. Conrad was moving his lips in silent prayer. Philip was shaking violently and he had wet his pants. Brandon's face was dark red with rage. Kim was looking around, wide-eyed and stunned. Hector was the last one. Walter knew Hector's name well because he tended to get into trouble on the bus. He was struggling against the hands pushing him from above. He pushed Walter away with his foot and jumped down, landing hard. "Ow. Shit." His lip was bleeding. At least someone had fought back.

The kids wandered into the cavity of the gutted bus and stood looking around in stunned silence.

Above them, the wood cover was slid into place over the opening. The space they stood in seemed to shrink. They were, the twelve of them, sealed into a pit with the smell of damp rotting earth. Buried alive. Walter thought it would be hard to think up something much worse.

Then it had happened: The lights had gone off.

The darkness had been so complete it had made Walter gasp. Total, absolute, end-of-the-world blackness. The darkness of the grave.

He hadn't cried then, but now, forty-six days later, he felt like making up for it. He could sit down and let it all go. Like the kids did, when it got to be too much for them. They would just sit down and sob their hearts out and afterward they'd feel all mellow for a while, their eyes red and their cheeks glowing. But if Walter did that, the kids might think he'd given up hope and then they might get more scared than they were already, which was pretty goddamned scared.

No, he wouldn't cry today. Anyway, he needed to get on with the count. Crying could wait, but the count *had* to be done–every morning, before 6 A.M. It had turned into a ritual, this counting business, but he felt that if he kept on doing it just

4

like he had been, maybe they'd all keep on being alive, just like they had been.

He squinted down at the small blurry shape curled up on the third seat from the back. In the gloom and without his glasses, all he could see from where he was standing was the silhouette of the small pale body against the torn brown vinyl seat. It was Bucky, of course–the smallest, six years old, legs skinny as a water bug's. The third seat had been Bucky's spot from the start, where he kept his white Mighty Morphin Power Ranger and the jacket he had with him that day. It was where he hummed himself to sleep at night. Lately, he had been humming himself to sleep during the day, too–or what they thought was the day, what Walter Demming's watch told him was the day, what he believed to be the day, what he told the kids was the day.

Bucky's escaping into sleep all the time was probably a sane response to a nightmare situation. Actually it was a tantalizing idea–just go to sleep and stay asleep until whatever was going to happen happened–a life that didn't actually require your presence.

Walter Demming leaned way down until his face was just inches away from the small ear. To do the count right, he needed to see some sign of movement, some sure sign that life still resided there, that Bucky had made it through another night. He watched the delicate eyelid. After a few seconds the lid quivered slightly. He kept watching until it happened again, just to be sure. Then he exhaled slowly and straightened up. Good. Bucky made eight.

He thought of something and leaned back down. The boy looked different. What was it? He studied the small, finely molded head. His hair. Yes, Bucky's dark hair had grown so shaggy it covered most of his ear. Even the cowlicks that used to stick up seemed weighted down now. In only forty-six days it had grown that much. Haircuts—one more thing to think about, or to add to his list of things he should be thinking of, but wasn't. God knows they hadn't devoted much effort to personal hygiene, but they didn't have much to work with—no hot water, no soap. He put his head closer to Bucky's and sniffed to see if Bucky smelled. He couldn't tell. He probably smelled like sin himself after all these days with no shower, but he seemed to have lost his sense of smell. At first the stench from that foul hole in the back had revolted him. Now he was slightly aware of the dank, musty, trapped air, but it didn't really offend him—proof positive that you could get accustomed to any damn thing fate threw your way. Anyway, in comparison with their other concerns, body odor and shaggy hair were just not up there at the top of the list.

And after the dream he'd had last night, dirty, shaggy kids who were alive looked pretty damn good to him. Last night he had jerked instantly awake, sweating and panicked. He had dreamt of flying past thatched cottages where tiny corpses, stiff and dry, were stacked like firewood. A new variation of the nightmare he'd had ever since Trang Loi.

Walter Demming stood up straight again and tried to keep his eyes lowered, away from the win-

6

dows, but the problem with buses was that they had windows everywhere. There was just no avoiding them, and no avoiding the black dirt pressing in against the glass. It was craziness, of course, but the dirt seemed to press harder, more relentlessly, every day, and there were moments he thought he could hear the glass creak and groan under the pressure, and the worms and beetles that tunneled right outside the windows seemed marshaling to spill in on top of them all. It made him think of that ditty the kids used to sing on the bus. The words went something like this:

Never laugh when the hearse goes by
For you may be the next to die.
They wrap you up in a dirty sheet
And put you down about six feet deep.
All goes well for about a week,
And then your coffin begins to leak.
The worms crawl in, the worms crawl out,
The worms play pinochle on your snout.

He hated it when they sang it. But he hated it more now when they didn't sing it.

He walked to the next seat and squinted down at the lumpy body curled up there. Josh. Oh, Lord, this one really worried him. He didn't need to lean over to check for signs of life here. Josh breathed in raspy gasps, his bare chest heaving with the effort. Asthma, all the kids had chorused on the first day, when Walter had thought Josh was going to strangle on his own breath, when they were all so terrified by what was happening to them it had seemed reasonable to him that one of them might just stop breathing from the terror. But on that first day Josh still had medicine left in his inhaler. The medicine had run out after the first week, and the attacks had gotten progressively more frequent and more intense. Yesterday, in the night, he'd had a choking spell that had lasted for two hours. It had turned his lips blue and made his eyes pop. The other children had wept in terror. If Walter could have one wish answered–just one–it would be to get Josh out of here and into a hospital.

Today he would make another plea for Josh's release, but trying to reason with Samuel Mordecai was like trying to reason with a whirlpool when you were caught up in its furious spinning. Everything just got swept up and flushed away in the torrent of words the man spewed out. Walter was going to have to think of something better to do or say, some better approach than he had been using.

It was silly, but he felt sure he would be able to think clearer, do better, if only he had his glasses. There was something about not being able to see well that interfered with his thought processes, made him more passive. Although, God knows, he'd rolled over and played dead even before his glasses got smashed. It had happened so damn fast. The last thing he expected early in the morning on that country road outside Jezreel, Texas, was a bunch of men with AK-47s surrounding the bus. Before he even realized what was happening, they had dragged him off the bus and smashed his glasses on the road.

Then he had simply followed their instructions.

He'd left six of his charges behind, six young children he was supposed to deliver to school. He'd left them alone on the road, as instructed. He had driven the hijacked bus with eleven whimpering kids and eight armed men to Jezreel, as instructed, even though he could barely see without his glasses.

And he hadn't done much better since then. He'd been unable to affect their situation in any way. Glasses or no glasses, today he needed to think of something new to try.

He turned to look at the seat across the aisle and, in spite of everything, the sight made him smile. Kimberly's pale red hair was swirled together with Lucy's wild brown curls. Kimberly and Lucy, nestled together like two kittens, as usual. They were both awake and starting to stir. Lucy began making a tiny mewling whine–the very noise Walter Demming had been feeling the urge to make himself. He watched as Kimberly put her arms around her friend and rocked her slowly until the whining stopped. Kimberly and Lucy–numbers ten and eleven. All accounted for, all eleven. All still alive on this, their forty-sixth day of captivity.

Behind him, the morning noises were underway–the scuffle and thumps and whines and skirmishes of kids getting up and heading to the back of the bus to the hole the Jezreelites had made for them to use as a latrine. They had cut a hole right through the bus floor and dug a pit underneath for the waste to fall into, lined it with lime. Most of the kids wouldn't use it at first. They were embarrassed by the lack of privacy and unsure how to use it. But nature took over and they had learned to squat. And there was a general agreement not to look when someone was using it. Since several of them had suffered with intestinal problems, they actually spent a lot of time sitting right next to it. It was now routine for all but Philip, who still wet his pants occasionally because he waited too long.

"Mr. Demming. Mr. Demming." Josh's raspy voice called out as it did every morning. "Is it time to get up?"

Walter checked his watch. "Quarter to six, Josh. Quarter to six in the morning." He walked back to where the boy was sitting up on the seat and reached his hand out to smooth Josh's dark blond hair. It felt greasy and damp under his palm. "It's April tenth, so the sun will be rising soon, in about fifty minutes. You could get up or rest for another half hour, Josh. They'll probably bring us something to eat pretty soon." The boy was breathing heavily; he kept both pale hands pressed to his chest.

Across the aisle, Kimberly was putting Lucy's socks on for her. Behind them, Philip Trotman still lay on the seat with his arms wrapped around his head. He'd been getting quieter and sadder each day. Walter hadn't heard a word from the boy for many days. Depression probably. Walter certainly knew the signs of depression in adults, but he wasn't sure about children. He just hadn't had enough experience with them. He was the last person in the world, the very last, who should be entrusted with eleven children. He had never had any children of his own, never wanted to; he had no younger brothers or sisters; he'd never baby-sat. He'd never even *liked* children very much. He'd only applied for the job as bus driver to augment his gardening income.

He felt pressure against his leg and looked down. Lucy was leaning against him, resting her cheek on his hip. "Hey, Lucy goosey," he said, bending down. "Sleep okay, sweetheart?"

She turned her face up to him. "Mr. Demming, how much longer is it going to be?" Her mouth turned down in a perfect red arc. "I'm hungry. My stomach hurts. I'm forgetting what my mom looks like, and Winky." Winky, Walter now knew, was her cat. "How much longer do we have to stay here?" Huge tears started to ooze out of her eyes.

He knelt down so his face was level with hers. "Honey, I don't know. Maybe five more days, but I'm not sure. I'll ask him again."

With his face close to hers he could feel the heat of her tears and her fear radiating off her skin. Her voice came out quivery and a little shrill. "But he says the world is going to end. The Beast is coming, he says." She shuddered. "I think it did end already. While we were sleeping it happened." She pointed upward. "Now there's nothing up there anymore. My mother's gone and our house. All the people are gone, just like he says. And we're left down here. And–" She stopped to gasp for air. The tears spilled down her face.

Watching the tears drip off Lucy's chin, Walter wondered where all that moisture came from. These kids never seemed to dry up. They cried and peed, cried and peed all the time, losing far more fluid than they seemed to replenish by

11

drinking from the big water jug that sat on the driver's seat.

"Lucy, honey," he said in a low voice. "Remember what I told you, our secret? He talks about all that stuff and we have to listen to him, but we don't *believe* him. He's wrong. He believes it, but he's wrong. Remember all the times we've talked about this–that he's like some phony fortune teller at a carnival who pretends to tell the future, but he doesn't know any more about it than anyone else. I promise you"–he put his hand under her chin and tipped up her wet, smeared face–"look at me, Lucy: I promise you the world has not ended." He stopped talking because she had begun to tremble. The trembling quickly accelerated into a shaking of her whole body, so violent he was afraid she would shake herself apart. He reached his arms around her and pulled her in tight, gasping at how thin she had gotten. He held on, trying to steady her, trying to hold her together, to hold himself together. He had moments of feeling the same thing she did–that there was nothing up there aboveground, no one who cared, no hope, no rescue, no nothing.

"I'm so scared," she said.

"Now listen, Lucy goosey," Walter whispered into her ear. "Picture this: Just a few feet above us, it's spring. A spring morning. Today is Monday, April tenth, and the wildflowers are out in the field up there above us–bluebonnets and pink evening primroses and the red Indian paintbrush, and my absolute favorite, the Texas prickly poppies. There are flowers everywhere, in the field and along the road. It rained a little last night, so the grass is wet and the leaves are all shiny. When the sun comes out everything will dry quickly and it will be a beautiful spring day. Your mom's at home waiting for you, and your cat, too. What's that cat's name?" he asked, even though he knew.

"Winky," she whispered in his ear.

"Yeah, Winky." He loosened his grip a little to see if she had calmed down, but the minute he relaxed, her body resumed its shuddering. He tightened his arms around her again and said, "Honey, you remember what Jacksonville does when he gets scared?"

She didn't answer.

"Remember last night when he was captured by the Barbecue Tongs and they put him in a cage?" He tried to look down at her face, but it was pressed under his arm. "He sees them building a fire and heating up the big cooking pot and he thinks maybe it's for him. He gets so scared that he starts to go all crazy, flapping his wings and hitting his head against the bars. Feathers fly around the cage and he hurts the bare skin on his head—you know, the red part where there are no feathers to protect him. Then he remembers who he is, that he is Jacksonville the turkey vulture, from Austin, Texas, and that he is on an important mission, sent by the President of the United States himself. To calm himself, he does what he always does in times of trouble. Remember?"

He drew his head back and looked down at her. She looked up and said, "He makes pictures in his head?"

"Yeah. That's right. He thinks up this beautiful picture in his head and he goes there in his mind.

Here's what he pictures: He sees himself soaring through the air with his wings spread out wide, riding high on the warm air currents that rise from the earth. He looks down at the rolling hills and lakes below. He feels so free. The wind blows through his feathers. He watches the other vultures soaring right along with him. You can do that same thing too, Lucy. But your picture would be different from Jacksonville's. Maybe something like this–picture Winky. He's lying–"

"*She*," Lucy interrupted firmly. "Winky's a girl."

"Oh, yeah. She. She's lying on your bed on a Sunday morning and she's rolling over with her paws in the air and the sun is pouring in your bedroom window warming her fur and you–"

A voice behind him said, "Mr. Demming, Philip wet himself again."

Hector Ramirez, at twelve, the oldest of the boys, stood holding a pair of wet jeans out toward Walter at arm's length. Their sharp ammonia smell made Walter's nose twitch. He slowly released his hold on Lucy, who for the moment had stopped shaking and even had a tiny smile pulling at the corners of her mouth. Walter was about to take the wet jeans when he noticed Lucy stiffen. She'd turned and was staring toward the front of the bus. He turned his head to follow her gaze, knowing what he would see. In the small black pit outside the open door, two black boots dangled in space. A sprinkle of dirt sifted down past the boots and the lightbulb began to sway on its cord.

The boots descended slowly. Long thin legs clad in tight black jeans followed, then lean hips. With a thud the boots hit packed earth and the

14

whole man appeared, filling the pit. It was a shock every time, Walter thought, even though his arrival was expected each day. It was like an alien dropping suddenly from another world. The man stood near the bulb, which swung wildly until he reached a hand up to stop it. The light illuminated the gold strands in his curly hair and glinted off the gold star earring in his left ear and the gold stubble on his cheeks, as if he'd absorbed sunshine from the world above and brought it down to the underworld.

Walter Demming had known fear before; he had lain awake nights in damp jungles waiting for attacks from an enemy he couldn't see. He had been in combat and had seen death up close. None of those events had made his stomach heave and his heart contract the way they did every time Samuel Mordecai materialized outside the bus door. Walter hoped his terror, and his loathing, didn't show. The kids all had enough of their own without his adding to it.

Samuel Mordecai stepped into the bus. He wore a white tank shirt and his long, muscled arms glistened with sweat. In his right hand he carried a Bible.

Lucy began shaking again. Walter put an arm around her shoulders and whispered into her ear, "Remember Jacksonville. You can do that, too."

Samuel Mordecai stood at the front of the buried bus and spread his arms out wide like St. Francis waiting for the birds to light on him. He smiled, flashing dazzling white teeth, but his eyes remained cloudy and intense, unmoved by what the mouth was doing. He called out in a thin twangy voice: "Lambs of God, firstborns every one, a joyful good morning to you. I come to tell of what must soon take place. The time is near. It's almost here." He closed his eyes as if in ecstasy. "Can't you just feel it, Lambs? You are the generation. You are the ones, alive and innocent when all the signs are right. The prophecies are fulfilled. Rejoice at being chosen for a role of the greatest importance in the working out of God's ultimate plan." Keeping his arms spread, Mordecai moved his fingers, inviting a response. When none came, his brilliant smile faded. His face grew stern, lips tight and thin. "Lambs," he said, "five more days! Don't it make you want to cry out in praise?"

From the back of the bus came a few small voices, Brandon and Sue Ellen murmuring, "Praise Him" and "Hallelujah."

Walter Demming, who hadn't been to church since he was fourteen, and even then had disliked public prayer, forced his lips to move, but he made no sound.

Samuel Mordecai nodded his head. "Only five more days, you sweet Lambs of God. Smile. Open your mouths and praise the name of Him, oh Him, who is gonna cause wonders beyond the imagining and terrors also. *The sun shall turn black like sackcloth made of goat hair, the whole moon shall turn blood red, and the stars in the sky shall fall to earth. The powers that are in heaven shall be shaken.*

"Our job is to prepare the way. You and me. We are the human agents for what is ripe. Now gather round for the lesson." He started walking up the aisle toward them. "Open up your ears and your

1 6

hearts to the word of God almighty, who can take one left adrift, helpless, wrapped in the cloak of the Beast and transform him into a prophet. That's the wonder He worked with me so I could be here to tell y'all and the rest of the world what is transpiring on this rebel planet."

The kids all moved like zombies to their seats. Walter knew it would be useless to try to talk to Mordecai now, when he was already rolling, so he sat, too, and resigned himself to waiting it out.

"Now you recall," Samuel Mordecai said, "we was talking about the signs that have given us to know that the end is at hand. They're all here. You see 'em every day out in the world of so-called technology. Bar codes and credit cards, TV shopping, implants, transponders, electronic transfers, cyberspace, and those so-called computer games. It was all foretold in the Book of Revelation. *'He also forced everyone, small and great, rich and poor, free and slave, to receive a mark on his right hand or on his forehead, so that no one could buy or sell unless he had the mark, which is the name of the Beast or the number of his name.'*

"I told you yesterday that I would tell you something that will amaze you, Lambs. Now, I know most of you have had enough arithmetic so you can add pretty good. So follow along. In many languages there's a code where letters of the alphabet are given numbers. Often in sixes. So A is six, B is twelve, C is eighteen, and so on. Now say we do that with our alphabet. Then we take the word "computer' and assign each letter in that word its number. Okay? You following me, Lambs? You know what that adds up to? You know what number, of all the numbers in the world, that makes?" Samuel Mordecai looked around, his eyes wide and his breathing coming hard. "Do you know what "computer' equals?"

He waited, as if expecting an answer.

Walter looked back. The kids were squirming, shaking their heads.

"You'd need pencil and paper to do the adding up, I guess. So I'm gonna just tell you." Mordecai paused again and his blue eyes were wide. "It adds up to six hundred and sixty-six. Six, six, six. Yes! The number of the Beast from the Book of Revelation. Ain't that just an amazing sign, Lambs? Don't that fill you with wonder? Just think that when all those prophecies were made two thousand years ago, the prophet John, the disciple beloved of Jesus, who wrote the Book of Revelation, could foresee the computer. John said, *"If anyone has insight, let him calculate the number of the Beast, for it is man's number. His number is 666.'* Don't that strike you with awe? The letters in "computer' add up to"–he held up six fingers and shook them in the air–"six, six, six."

Walter Demming felt his back teeth clenching tight. As the thin voice droned on and on, he turned to check the children. All of them sat perfectly still as they watched Samuel Mordecai pacing the aisle. He held his book in his left hand and stabbed the air with his right index finger, the motion jerky and so aggressive it made Walter want to reach out and break the finger off.

For the first week, he had tried to concentrate on these lessons so he could understand what Samuel Mordecai had in mind, but he soon discovered it was so crazy and repetitive he didn't need to listen. He pretended to listen, of course. He didn't want to anger the man. He looked directly at him, followed his movements with his eyes, but his mind he let float across the field of wildflowers that stretched from his house all the way to Theodora Shea's gravel driveway where her sixteen-year-old golden retriever dozed in the sun and her garden awaited his attention and the earth awaited his hands. Today he would plant geraniums, bright red geraniums–lots of them.

Lucy's sobbing brought him back. He looked over at her in the seat across from him. She was trying to hold it in, but an occasional sob escaped her.

Samuel Mordecai was shouting. "But the cowardly, the unbelieving, the vile, the murderers, the sexually immoral, those who practice magic arts, the idolators and all liars–they will all be made into blood statues on the last day! We got to go through the blood. Can't avoid it, can't go over it, can't go around it, got to go through it. If you reject the opportunity that is offered to you, woe unto you, for then you shall go to the place where the worm never dies."

Walter turned his head to check on the other kids. Bucky sat up straight with his hands folded in his lap. His eyes were shut so tight that his face was screwed up in a grimace. Philip's head had sunk into his lap. Brandon Betts was nodding and muttering under his breath.

Five more days, Walter thought–five more days of this shit and we'll all be praying for the world to end. O Lord, please help us–lately he found himself praying–him, a man who hadn't prayed even in foxholes. Whatever is going to happen, he prayed, with his eyes squeezed shut to keep the tears in, please get this over with and see us safe through it. His stomach contracted in sharp hunger pangs. But first, dear Lord, You who loved little children and incompetent sinners like myself, we sure could use some breakfast here. Oh, we sure could.

> *"We're fixing to get these new nine-digit zip codes, you know. Add this to your nine-digit Social Security number, and what does it give you? Eighteen numbers that will be your identity–that's three sixes, and the Book of Revelation prophesied it real clear–in the end days, the number 666 is gonna be stamped on people to label them as Satan's property. Don't that just bring you to your knees?"*
> SAMUEL MORDECAI,
> QUOTED BY MOLLY CATES,
> "TEXAS CULT CULTURE,"
> *LONE STAR MONTHLY*, DECEMBER 1993

CHAPTER TWO

"Beyond telling you I'm sick to death of it, I don't know how to explain it, Richard," Molly Cates said without turning away from the window.

"Try." Richard Dutton's voice retained its habitual caustic edge, even though Molly knew he was making an effort to sound warm and understanding.

She kept her eyes fixed on the tiny cars scooting along the Congress Avenue bridge in the lunch-hour traffic twenty-one stories below. "When I first got the police beat at the *Patriot,* I thought it was the world's luckiest break. I was eager for it all. Crime was an adventure, this alien subculture that sucked me in. Ever since then, for twenty-two years, I've been a regular visitor to that place." She felt the slither of dread deep in her chest. "Now I feel like a native there."

She turned around to see his reaction. The staff meeting at the Capitol Club was over, and the rest had gone back to the office, leaving Molly alone with her boss. Richard Dutton, the editor of *Lone Star Monthly,* sat with his chair pushed back from the mahogany table and stared down at his long legs stretched out in front of him.

"I've been thinking it's time for me to get out of that world," she said, her voice sounding whiny and uncertain in her ears. "I've had too much of it—a steady diet for more than twenty years. It's starting to give me bad dreams. And this horror going on in Jezreel is—" She stopped, at a loss for the end to the sentence. "Oh, Richard, I don't even want to think about it."

"But you have been thinking about it, haven't you?" He glanced up at her. "You are following the coverage."

"To avoid it you'd have to leave the planet."

"I want to understand this," he said. "Your reluctance here—is it because of your past unpleasantness with Samuel Mordecai?"

"Unpleasantness!" Just like Richard to call the most unsettling event of her journalistic career an "unpleasantness." "Let me remind you that when my cult story came out, Mordecai called and said if I didn't arrange network television time for him to respond, he would mark my soul with a bar code identifying me as one to be made into a blood statue, whatever the hell that is. For months I got preachy, barely literate letters from some of his followers who were trying to set me right. And I think he's the one who put me on the mailing list for all those right-wing religious tracts, which I am still receiving." She stopped because she was out of breath.

Richard Dutton sat up straighter in his chair. "I hear you, Molly, and I can see how strongly you feel. But you should be able to see my point of view here, too. We've got this huge story going on right in our own backyard, a story that has dominated national headlines for six weeks. The clock is ticking down on it. And we're sitting here with an unfair advantage that we aren't using. Surely you can see that."

She shook her head. "We don't have an unfair advantage. If anything, it's more like a handicap."

He clucked his tongue. "You know better than that. You appear to be the only journalist in the country who's met and interviewed Samuel Mordecai. The only one. You have a relationship with him–"

"Richard," she interrupted, "Mordecai's not someone you have a relationship with. Unless you're willing to sit for five hours at a stretch and listen to his harangues."

"But you did talk to him—for several hours and—"

"Several hours that were the worst of my life. And I include, for comparative purposes, the time the anesthetic wore off while I was having knee surgery *and* the time I went to divorce court."

Dutton laughed. "Okay. But you've already done the painful part here. You did the interview; you might as well get something out of it. And, Molly, the fact that you hated him from the start, that you saw through him, gives you—"

"Richard!" Molly had been trying to treat it lightly, but now she lost all pretense at humor. "Richard, you don't get it. I did see through him. I knew he was fanatical, and dangerous. I even suspected crimes were going on out there. When I left, I felt … *contaminated.* And what did I do? I went to the sheriff, that bumbling old Bradford County sheriff, and told him I thought Samuel Mordecai and the Hearth Jezreelites were evil and might be breaking some laws. I told him I'd felt threatened.

"He asked how they'd threatened me, and I said Mordecai had lectured and bullied me. The sheriff said it sounded like what Reverend Willard did to him every Sunday at First Baptist. Not pleasant, but not exactly against the law.

"He patted me on the head and said, "Now go on home, little lady, and leave this to me. I'll check those folks out for you, sure enough, yes, ma'am.' So I went home, good little lady that I am, and proceeded to write the story, because I had a deadline and, of course, that's the main thing—meeting deadline, right?"

"That's what we do, Molly. There's no dishonor

there. As for your other actions, they were blameless. You did what any good citizen would: You told the appropriate law-enforcement officials about your suspicions, right? What more can you expect of yourself?"

Molly groaned. The subject of Samuel Mordecai had been a sore one from the moment she met him two years earlier, and in the weeks since the school bus hijacking, it had become so agonizing that she tried not to think about him. But Mordecai was everywhere—his face, his name, his words, assaulted her from every television screen, every radio, every newspaper. It was impossible to ignore him.

Now, against her will, she saw his image: Samuel Mordecai, born Donnie Ray Grimes, standing in front of her, running his long, graceful fingers through his sun-streaked blond curls as he ranted about computers and calamity, beasts and apocalypse. It was an interview from the lowest reaches of hell. She had not gotten him to answer a single question. He just opened his mouth and started preaching, preaching and strutting, as if that was what she had come for. He gushed words at her nonstop, incoherently, ungrammatically, spewing them all over her. She made one or two feeble attempts to stop him, but on he raved. She had felt trapped and abused and mesmerized by the droning male voice that had kept her pinned to her chair far past the time she should have gotten up and walked out. There were things about that interview that still haunted her, things she had never told anyone. Finally, after enduring two hours of it, she had pushed her way out of the room and driven away from Jezreel convinced the man was dangerous.

"Molly," Richard said, "Molly, when your boss asks you a civil question, it's customary to answer him. I asked you what more could you expect of yourself?"

"Nothing. You're right, Richard. Apparently nothing more could be expected."

"Good. Now here's a problem: I get a dozen calls a day from editors and writers around the country who read your cult story and want to talk with you. They tell me they've tried to reach you, but you won't return their calls."

She had been afraid this was coming. "I know. I'm sorry about that, but I've been busy. And I didn't want to talk about it."

"I can see that. And if you want, I'll continue to field the calls so you can work. Now, I know this is distasteful, but I'd like to encourage you to go ahead and write this story. Most of your home-work for it is already done. All you need to do, really, is trot out your old interview tapes and listen to them in light of what's happened. You know how that works. You'll get interested again, in spite of your reluctance right now. You'll get caught up. You'll find some quotes and material you didn't use the first time. You can show how prophetic you were. You can follow the news as it breaks. Hell, you're doing it anyway. So just watch whatever is going to happen out there in the next five days, and write your story. You don't even need to go to Jezreel if you don't want to. I hear it's a madhouse, anyway. Just watch it all on CNN. You can do it without breaking a sweat."

"Oh, no, I can't." She held a hand out to him with the palm turned up. "Feel. It makes me sweat just to talk about it."

Richard Dutton leaned forward and rested his fingers on her damp palm. Then he looked up at her with interest. "I am amazed," he said. "I've seen you talking to serial rapists and crazed killers without batting an eye. What is it about this that rattles you so much?"

"I'm not sure," she said, knowing even as she replied that this was only half true. "He's a lunatic, but, as you say, I've known lots of lunatics, and none of them made my hands sweat." She lowered her voice because she was embarrassed by what she was about to say. "It has to do maybe with a certain power he has. Charisma. Energy. I don't know. You have to see it."

Richard leaned forward, watching her, his small deep-set eyes glowing amber the way they did when he was excited. "Just how crazy do you think Mordecai is, Molly?"

The image of him pacing the room, shouting and grabbing at his crotch as he preached, flashed before her. "Stark raving bonkers," she said. "Crazy enough to–" That old feeling of dread and disgust squeezed her stomach. "Crazy enough to do something like what happened in Waco and take those kids with him when he does it." She shook her head vigorously. "I don't want to have anything more to do with this, Richard. It's not good for me."

Molly turned back to the window and rested her forehead against the cold plate glass. She looked down at the trail that edged Town Lake and the lunch-hour joggers–tiny figures sweating it out in the midday sun so many stories below. So silly, so futile, all that. As if exercising your cardiovascular system would keep calamity at bay, as if the world were a safe place, as if we weren't all vulnerable at every breath to the random viciousness loose in it.

"Molly," Richard's voice sounded genuinely soft now, "for me this is not really about getting the story covered. Anyone on the staff could do it, and most of them would give their right arm to. But as your editor–and friend–I have a vested interest in your career. There are some realities here I want to point out. Every writer I'm aware of who has written a big breakthrough piece that vaulted her to national attention has been able to do it because of timing. It just happened that the perfect story, the very story that writer had been preparing to write all her life, came along at the exact right time, when she was primed and ready for it. That's what's happening here, Molly. Everything you have done up to now has been preparation for this one story. Surely you see that."

"Richard–"

"Just let me finish. Look at the choices you've made. You cut your teeth on street crime covering the police beat. When you came to the magazine, you gravitated to the more bizarre and high-profile crimes we tend to take on. You've been working a vein, I think–going after that dark strain, that attraction to violence we all feel but don't like to admit. And your other specialty– and this surprised me at first, when you started to take it on—has been religion, especially our own homegrown religious extremists."

He picked up a folded magazine from his stack on the table. "Listen. Some of your best work has been on this subject." He began to read from the magazine:

"'These freelance prophets flourish in Texas, as they did centuries ago in Palestine, springing up out of the sun-dried earth like mesquite, tough and tenacious as hell. They preach a gospel heavy on prophecy and apocalypse, spouting the Book of Revelation as if they had drunk it in with their mother's milk. The intensity of their charisma and their eschatology kindles in their followers a belief so passionate that it sometimes bursts into spontaneous combustion and consumes everything around it. Prophets are as native to Texas as longhorns and Stetsons.'"

Molly had to smile. It was from her piece on Texas cults. Usually it made her uncomfortable to hear something she'd written in the past read aloud, but those words still pleased her.

Richard slapped the magazine against his knee. "Jezreel and Samuel Mordecai is *your* story of a lifetime, Molly. You could win a Pulitzer." He lowered his voice. "You really could. And don't tell me that doesn't appeal to you."

"Of course it does. The prizes are hard cash, and, as usual, I need some."

"There could be a book in it, too." He rubbed his thumb and index finger together.

She sighed. "Yeah, but the problem is I don't even want to write a postcard about it. Just thinking about it makes me queasy."

"Maybe what's making your stomach queasy and your palms sweaty is something else, Molly." He lowered his eyes back to the tassels on his loafers. "Maybe it's fear. You recognize this story as the incredible opportunity it is–I know you do. Maybe it's that old female bugaboo rearing its ugly head–fear of success."

She leaned her shoulder against the window and thought about it. That hot churning in the stomach sure did feel a lot like fear. But success, by almost any definition, was something she had always wanted, wholeheartedly, unabashedly. Fame, money, recognition–she coveted them all. She deserved them and she wanted them. No, it wasn't success she feared. But she *was* afraid. She just wasn't sure what she was afraid of.

"Once you get going on it, Molly," Richard said in his most enthusiastic voice, "your old instincts will take over. Trust me."

Amazingly, she did trust him. He was a great editor with an unerring instinct for the heart of a story. And he had always had the ability to get her excited about things. Maybe this fear or timidity or repugnance or whatever it was would pass and the old thrill and obsession of pursuing a good story would take over. Maybe this *was* the story she'd been training for all her life.

"And, Molly," he added brightly, "how often do you get the chance to cover Armageddon?"

She smiled. "Only once. And you'd better meet deadline."

"And get paid up front," he said. "Here's my suggestion. Do this story. Give it your all, and when it's over, take a leave for a few months. Start another book, take up golf, go to Paris. But now is the time to do this story."

She hesitated. Maybe. Maybe it was the perfect ending to her career in writing crime. "If I do this, Richard, will you help me move on to other subjects? This may sound corny to you, but I really want to do things with more social significance than serial killers and nutty fringe religions."

He nodded. "If you still feel that way when you finish this, yes. This piece you suggested"— he looked down at his notes on the table—"these bag ladies. They'll still be with us next month, won't they?"

Molly started to collect her papers from the table and stuff them into her briefcase. She knew he was watching expectantly from under lowered lids, but she didn't say anything.

Finally he said, "So, I'll expect something brilliant on Samuel Mordecai and the Hearth Jezreelites by the twenty-ninth."

"Can I have ten pages for the homeless women in July and can I have Henry Iglesias for the photos?"

"Henry? He costs too much."

"That's because he's the best. Wait till you see what we come up with, Richard. You'll love it."

He studied her briefly. "Okay," he said. "Then I can count on you for the Jezreelites?"

Molly closed her briefcase. "Sure."

"You won't be sorry. This will be a huge story. Catch Mordecai's grandmother. Let's see where he grew up. And the bus driver. He's a Vietnam vet. What's his story? Maybe you can contrast the two men. Oh," he added casually, "I had Brenda

Natalini start some research for you. It should be on your desk."

She turned and looked at him with raised eyebrows.

"Well," he said, "I knew you'd want to hit the ground running. And Brenda lucked onto something that might be interesting. Apparently there's an old Vietnam buddy of Demming's who lives in town. Maybe you could chat him up, try to get a feel for what Demming is like."

"You speak about him in the present tense."

Richard looked up at her, surprised. "I don't think they're dead. Do you?"

Molly felt the squeezing in her stomach again. "No." She started toward the door, then stopped. "I'm interested in getting into the theology behind Mordecai. What he believes is something of a mystery even though he talks about it all the time. Even his followers aren't sure what the message is. They say it's brilliant, but they can't summarize it. I've gotten a lead on an apocalyptic scholar who had a run-in with him a few years ago."

"Molly! You've already started working on it!"

"Yes. I have actually." She gave him a smile more full of rue than humor.

She stopped in the doorway and looked back at him. "Richard, if you knew Samuel Mordecai was right and the world really was going to end in five days, would you have come to work today?"

He looked up at her with narrowed eyes for several seconds before answering. "Hmm, five days. Well, that would mean the May issue would never come out, so there would be no point in planning for it." He grinned. "And five days wouldn't give us time to get a special glossy end-of-the-world issue out. But I think I might come in anyway— you know, to talk about it, rant and complain. I'd probably tell everyone to look at the bright side, that at least the apocalypse comes before taxes are due. What about you, Molly?"

"Well, if the world really was going to end and Samuel Mordecai had predicted it, I guess I'd do exactly what I'm about to do—find out more about him and his message, sniff around the edges of belief the way I tend to do. It reminds me of what someone said should be written over the door of every church."

Richard was busy organizing his papers. "And what's that?" he asked in a bored voice.

"'Important, if true.'"

He looked up. "Well, if it is true, nonbelievers like ourselves are in deep shit."

She left thinking we might all be in deep shit anyway.

"Religion and insanity occupy adjacent territories in the mind. Historically, cults have kept up a traffic between the two."

LANCE MORROW,
TIME ESSAYIST ON JONESTOWN

CHAPTER THREE

The radio in her pickup was tuned to NPR, and the subject was the Hearth Jezreelites. Her instinct was to switch it off and drive in silence, but she couldn't make her hand reach for the button. Instead she clutched the wheel tighter and listened. It had been like that for forty-six days, ever since the bus hijacking. She didn't want to listen to the radio news updates as she drove around town, but she did. She didn't want to watch the news on television, but she did–every night, at six and ten, and sometimes in between on CNN. She didn't want to read about it in the papers, but she did read it, every word in three papers–the Austin *American-Patriot,* the New York *Times,* and the Dallas *Morning News.* Everywhere she went there was a TV or radio blaring and people were talking about it.

There was no escaping it. Richard was right– fate had come knocking on her door. But right now she felt besieged by it, as though fate were using a battering ram.

She had first heard about it like this, in her truck, as she headed to the office on the morning of February 24. A news bulletin came on:

A band of religious extremists, a cult, that lived at Jezreel, Texas, thirty miles northeast of Austin, had hijacked a school bus containing seventeen children on their way to the Joseph B. Carruth Elementary School. Molly had felt an instant rush of hot dread. The cult had to be the Hearth Jezreelites, and the leader had to be Samuel Mordecai. She remembered them all too well.

That evening some of the details had emerged on the news. Eight or nine men with rifles had stopped the bus on a rural road. They had surrounded it and dragged the driver off. Then they had boarded the bus and gone from child to child asking each one his name and age and the ages of his brothers and sisters. Six of the children had then been taken off the bus and told to lie facedown in a field. The other eleven were kept on the bus and the driver was forced to get back on and drive the bus away. The children who were left behind on the road flagged down a motorist. All were badly frightened but uninjured.

The cult leader had telephoned the Christian radio station KLTX and asked them to tape what he was about to say. First he announced that he had brought the eleven children to his compound near Jezreel, where he and his followers worshiped God and awaited the Apocalypse. In doing this, he was simply following God's orders. The children's parents would be upset, he said, but in time they would come to understand the great honor of having their children chosen to advance God's purpose.

He said federal agents and local law authorities should know that the second anyone set foot on Jezreelite property the children would be killed. He and his avenger angels were well armed and could repel any attack, but the first thing that would happen in that event would be the immediate destruction of the children and the bus driver.

He then announced that he, the Prophet Mordecai, was about to deliver the most important news anyone would ever hear: The world was going to end in fifty days, on April 14. There was still time to listen to his message and embrace salvation. For the next hour he delivered a rambling sermon about worldly corruption, the computer as the Beast of Revelation, and biblical prophecies. Over the last forty-five days excerpts from that sermon had been played and replayed hundreds of times around the world.

Today NPR's Lyle Baker was interviewing Thelma Bassett, the mother of one of the hostage children. Mrs. Bassett had emerged as the informal spokesperson for the parents. Molly had seen her interviewed several times on the TV news. As she listened to the soft twang, Molly could picture her—a rawboned young woman with limp pinkish hair and freckled milky skin. From photographs, it looked as if her eleven-year-old daughter, Kimberly, had inherited the same pink hair. Thelma Bassett was saying that she had asked the FBI to let her and some of the other parents talk to Samuel Mordecai directly. But the FBI had put her off, explaining that their highly trained hostage-negotiating team was currently in the middle of some extremely delicate discussions, and this was not the time for amateurs to get involved.

"Now, I know," Thelma Bassett drawled, "that Mr. Lattimore and the gentlemen in charge out there at Jezreel are the professionals, and I know they've been working real hard, night and day, to try to help our children. But it has been forty-six days, Mr. Baker, and we parents are craving some word of our babies. I'm just an average citizen, you know, a working woman, a mother, but I believe if I had the chance to talk to Mr. Mordecai from a mother's heart, I might have an inside track at swaying him some."

Molly had always been amazed at how fearless and articulate average citizens could be when they spoke to the media, and Mrs. Bassett was one of the best, natural and persuasive.

"Mrs. Bassett, what would you say to Samuel Mordecai if the FBI did let you speak to him?" Lyle Baker asked.

"Well, Mr. Baker, first of all I'd tell him how much we parents miss our young ones and how much we love them. Now, I've read that Samuel Mordecai had a difficult childhood, that his mother had lots of problems and he was raised by his grandmother. I'm sure sorry about that. Also, I don't believe he has any children of his own, so maybe he hasn't had the opportunity to understand how much we parents love our children and how devastated we are without them. He may not know that we can't sleep at night wondering...worrying that–" She choked, as if she'd suddenly gotten something caught in her throat. There were several ticks of silence before she resumed. "We haven't seen them or heard their voices in all this time and…we don't even know whether…"

In his smooth radio voice, Lyle Baker said, "Tell us a little about Kimberly."

"Oh, my," said Thelma Bassett, "Kimberly. Well, she's eleven now, in the fifth grade, doing real well, especially in language arts, you know–what they call reading and writing these days. She's had some trouble with mathematics–long division, fractions, but then so did I. It's in the genes maybe." She let out a half-laugh which choked off abruptly.

After some deep breaths, she began again. "Now, all I'm asking for is a chance to speak to him. I believe that sometimes experts like the negotiators who are out there talking on their phones all the time, I believe they can lose sight of some of the emotions involved, and I believe that's what I could add here–I could talk emotions to Mr. Mordecai. I'd like to tell him that I don't know about all this apocalypse business–I'll leave that to him, and to God–but I do know that it's not right to separate children from their parents. Even if the world *was* ending it's not right. *Especially* if the world was ending."

"And there are the health problems the Benderson boy has," the interviewer said.

"Yes. That is definitely something I want to talk to Mr. Mordecai about–the little boy, Joshua Benderson, who suffers from asthma. I believe if Mr. Mordecai knew how dangerous his condition is, to be without his medication, and in a stressful situation to boot, well, I believe he would let Joshua come out right now.

"Now, what I really want"–her voice turned tougher, matter-of-fact–"is not just to talk on the phone, but to walk into that compound today, and talk face to face with Mr. Mordecai. I don't fear for my own safety. I would be happy to release the government and everybody else from any responsibility for me–I'd sign anything. All I want, Mr. Baker, is to walk in there, just as a private citizen, a mother. I want to talk to Samuel Mordecai. I want to see Kim and the other children. Kim's best friend, Lucy, is in there, too, and her parents are so broke down with grief and worry they don't leave their house any more.

"All I want is to see them, to try to help, or, if worse comes to worst...I want to be there with them at the end, to share their fate, whatever it is."

Molly felt the woman's anguish right down to her toenails.

Even the interviewer sounded choked up as he thanked her and said that the FBI spokesman, Patrick Lattimore, had not been available to comment to the press about Mrs. Bassett's offer.

Molly turned off Rio Grande into the parking garage and squinted up into the shadows. She hated parking garages and avoided them whenever possible. This one was the worst–dark and so low-ceilinged she felt the need to hunch her head down into her shoulders every time she drove through. A loud fan unit made an unpleasant racket, and the ramp curved upward so sharply that twice she had scraped the tail of her pickup. If there had been any other possible place to park near the office, she would never set foot in this garage.

She pulled into her reserved space and took the elevator to a suite on the third floor where *Lone Star Monthly* had recently moved its offices, having come up in the world from the old second-floor walk-up on Brazos. Molly hated the new office because it had a marble lobby and elevators that made you feel you should be wearing panty hose.

On her desk lay a stack of phone messages and a manila folder with the name Walter Demming typed on the tab. Molly sat down and opened it. On top was the UPI photograph that had been in the *Patriot* the day after the bus had been taken by the Jezreelites. It showed a thick-chested middle-aged man dressed in a white T-shirt and jeans. He wore wire-rimmed glasses, and his graying hair was pulled back into a stubby ponytail. A solid-looking man, dependable. For the kids' sake, she hoped so.

Under his photo were small school-type photos of five of the children smiling self-consciously into the camera. Molly resisted reading their names and ages. She didn't want to get involved with them.

Before she could read the file, the phone rang. She picked it up. "Molly Cates."

"Hello, my dear, Sister Addie here." The voice was so sweet and positive, so sugary, that each time she heard it, Molly's first impulse was to hang up. There was no way she could have anything in this world in common with the owner of such a voice. "Hey, Addie," she said. "Any luck?"

"Finally. It took some doing, but I found him. He just got back from a year's sabbatical, studying prophecy in Jerusalem. That's why I hadn't been able to get him. I found him at home, unpacking. Crotchety and jet-lagged."

"Did you ask him about it?"

"I surely did. He'd heard the news over there, but only the bare outlines of it."

"Is he the one?"

"Yes. His run-in with Mr. Mordecai was several years back at the Southwest Prophecy Conference, but it's a real sore subject with him and he hates to talk about it. Also, he's scared, says Mordecai threatened him."

"Did you tell him he needs to get in touch with the FBI negotiators?"

"Yes, but he resisted. He doesn't much like the federal government."

"Neither do I. I hope you leaned on him."

"Oh, yes. I said if he didn't call them today and volunteer this information, I'd do it. He's just the sort the FBI ought to be talking with, not those Harvard Ph.D. theologians they've been consulting. Mr. Mordecai is light-years away from any mentality those consultants can get inside of. What they need is a Gerald Asquith."

"Isn't he a Ph.D., too?"

Addie laughed. "I believe his degree is an honorary one from the West Central Texas Bible College, or some such. I doubt he went to college. He's the kind of fundamentalist preacher the negotiators need if they're going to get into the mindset of a Samuel Mordecai. Asquith despises Mordecai, but he's much closer to him in worldview than those intellectuals who have been advising them. Closer to the lunatic fringe."

"Did you ask him about this Rapture of Mordecai business?"

There was a long silence, during which Molly could hear the click of knitting needles. "Maybe it's better for you to talk to Dr. Asquith yourself, sister, rather than have me filter it through my misperceptions and bad hearing."

Molly felt it–the pulsing of hot dread she'd had in her chest since this thing began. "You don't want to be the bearer of bad news."

"My dear, I'm accustomed to bearing a great deal of bad news–unfortunately. It's not that. It's just–"She stopped.

Molly was not about to let her get off the hook. "It's just what?"

"Well, you know how I am. A woman of ignorant and superstitious leanings. I guess I just don't want to form these particular words. You see I have this...Oh, I should tell it to a shrink, sister, not burden you with it."

"Go ahead. Burden me."

"Dr. Asquith says the Rapture of Mordecai is a secret oral tradition passed from one Mordecai to the next. They all have visions–that's what they call the rapture, and their doctrine they call the Heaven in Earth Vatic Gospel of the Jezreelite. It's never been written down. It's forbidden to write it down. Samuel Mordecai believes he is the latest and the last of this line."

"What is the doctrine, Addie?"

"I don't know, and if Dr. Asquith knows, he's not saying. But it has something to do with the need for human action in starting the Apocalypse."

"What sort of action?"

"Dr. Asquith says only the prophets in the direct line know, but that it's heresy and gives prophecy a bad name. He says Mordecai makes his religion up as he goes. He drafted a bill of censure to get Mordecai censured by the Council of Bible Prophecy, and that's the flap I was remembering."

"Did the Council censure him?"

"No. Mordecai resigned from the Council before they took it up. That's why they don't have a record. Dr. Asquith says Mordecai is a dangerous extremist, and that is impressive coming from a man who preaches that earthquakes are the result of gay rights demonstrations. If Mordecai hadn't resigned, Asquith would have pursued him to the ends of the earth, he says."

"Well, sounds like Dr. Asquith has some spine. It's a good thing somebody does."

"My dear girl, give yourself a break. The world is chock-full of little pockets of wickedness and nitwittery, like boils just waiting to break open and spill out their poison. You and I, because of what we do, see more of these boils than folks usually do. So we know they are there, but, sister, we are just frail creatures of very limited vision. We have no way of predicting which ones will burst open and which will not."

Molly glanced down at the newspaper photos of Walter Demming and the five children. One of them was a very small dark-haired boy with a cowlick standing straight up like a patch of weeds. Bucky DeCarlo, age six. "Oh, Addie. I knew this particular boil was festering. I had a strong hunch it would break. But I let it go."

"Molly, my dear. You couldn't have known. If

you feel responsible for the actions of every lunatic you've ever met, you'll go crazy yourself. What did you decide at your meeting? Are you going to write about this?"

"Yes."

The click of the needles stopped. "I wonder if that is the best thing for you."

"I don't know, Addie. I wonder, too. My editor thinks this is the story I've been preparing to write all my life."

"Well, maybe so. Maybe so. But what we prepare for in this life is not always what we ought to be doing. Now, I don't know what's right for you, my dear, but when I see a friend burst into tears when the television news comes on, it makes me think—"

"I was tired. I watch the news all the time without crying, Addie."

"Well, I'm sure you do. But I suspect you might need some time off. How about a rest at our church retreat in the hill country?"

"Thanks, Addie, maybe when I finish this. Is there any hope Dr. Asquith has anything in writing about this Rapture of Mordecai stuff?"

"He says he'll look for the notes he used to write the bill of censure. But remember, this was maybe seven years ago."

"I'd like to call him, Addie."

"I know. I told him and he said he'd be doing his radio show tonight—*Prophecies in the Media*. You should listen to it sometime. Station KLTX at seven."

After Addie gave her Gerald Asquith's phone number, Molly hung up and sat back in her chair thinking about the next step. She looked at the file on her desk. Under the picture, there was just one sheet with a few typed lines giving the Austin address for a man named Jacob Alesky, who was an old friend of Walter Demming, a buddy from Vietnam. Molly stuck the folder in her briefcase. She'd follow that up this afternoon if time permitted, but for now she needed to force herself to do what she had been putting off. She needed to get out her two-year-old taped interview with Samuel Mordecai and listen to it. To refresh her memory so she could try to get back inside his head—something no one in her right mind would do willingly. But here she was, about to do it.

She found on her key ring the small brass key that opened her desk file drawer. Inside were boxes of neatly labeled and dated audiotapes—all the interviews she had done over the ten years she had worked for *Lone Star Monthly*. Writers were required to keep notes and tapes for only two years, but she held on to hers much longer. Her hand went immediately to the ones she was looking for—the ones marked Samuel Mordecai I and Samuel Mordecai II. She put them on the desk and then rummaged through her bag for the tiny Sony recorder that she always carried. Before she found it, her phone rang again.

It was Stephanie in the front office. "There's a Thelma Bassett here to see you, Molly."

It took several seconds for the name to register. Oh, God. The mother, from the radio this morning. Molly's first impulse was to run. What did she want? Whatever it was, it was sure to be painful. She could say she was busy or just leaving. She really didn't have time or energy for this woman.

On the other hand, this was part of her story; sooner or later she'd want to talk to some parents. And from what she'd seen and heard, Mrs. Bassett was the best of the lot. "Okay. Send her back," Molly said.

She stood in the office doorway to wait for her. The woman appeared in the hall. She was nearly six feet tall, with broad shoulders and hips. She wore clogs and a blue denim shirtwaist dress with a silver concha belt. Her pinkish hair swayed with every move she made. Over one shoulder hung a huge canvas tote bag that looked so heavy Molly was sure she must be carrying all her files around with her–a mark of obsession. People who carry their files with them are either truly obsessed or truly terrified, or both. She knew this because there had been times in her life when she carried files around herself.

"Mrs. Bassett, hello. I'm Molly Cates." She held out her hand.

The woman clasped it in both of hers. Her eyes were a light khaki color that matched her freckles. "Thanks for seeing me without an appointment and all. Do you have a few minutes to talk?"

"Sure. Come on in." Molly led the way and gestured to the chair in front of the desk. Thelma Bassett dropped her bag with a thump. As she lowered herself into the chair, she let her eyes close for a moment. The woman was terminally exhausted, Molly thought.

"I heard you on NPR this morning," Molly told

her. "I have a daughter, too, and I can't imagine anything worse than what you are going through. I'm so sorry."

The tan-colored eyes pooled with tears, but the woman looked determined not to let them fall.

"Did you get any response from the FBI?" Molly asked.

"No. Not yet. But I'm real hopeful. That's why I came to see you, actually. To ask you a favor."

Molly sat in the chair across from her. "Well, go ahead."

"I believe Pat Lattimore and Andrew Stein are at the end of their rope–tired and discouraged."

"They sure have been looking that way on the news every night."

"I don't fault them. They have tried everything and consulted everyone who claims to know anything about how to do this. Have you been out there to the command post?"

Molly shook her head.

"Well, you can't imagine what it's like until you see it. They've got people coming in from all over the world–psychologists and psycholinguists and Bible experts and ministers and policemen and people who have been hostages and some men who teach about rescuing hostages at that FBI school up in Virginia. They've even got this psychic woman who wears a turban. But nothing works. Nothing. He just sermonizes and recites Scripture in response to anything they propose. I believe they are desperate enough to try something different." She leaned forward. "I think they're fixing to let me talk to him."

Molly must have looked skeptical, because

Thelma became defensive. "Really. I have good reason to think that. Patrick has asked me what I would say if they let me talk to him on the phone. And they look at me like they're sizing me up. I can see them thinking: Will she break down or can she carry it off?"

Molly nodded.

"I just read your article," Thelma said, "the one you wrote last year–'Texas Cult Culture.' I stayed up late last night reading it."

Molly didn't like to think about this woman sitting up in bed reading about the crazy zealotry of a man who was now in control of her daughter's fate. No wonder she looked so tired.

"What interested me most," Thelma continued, "was you mentioning that he seemed to have this…ah, contempt, I think was the word you used, for women that went back to problems with his mother."

Molly nodded. Where was this going?

"My friend says she heard you talk one time, and you said you do lots more interviewing than you use in writing, and that you tape-record everything."

"Yes." Molly felt increasingly uneasy at the direction this was taking.

"Did you do that when you interviewed Samuel Mordecai–tape-record everything?"

"Yes."

Thelma Bassett leaned forward. "Here's the thing. I want to prepare myself for when I talk to him. You must think this is a pipe dream, but I know it's going to happen. I want to make the most of it when my chance comes because it may be the only chance." A red flush darkened her cheeks. "I need to know what to say to him, how to sway him, how to get him to let those kids come home. I know that what the negotiators are doing doesn't work. I'm afraid they're fixing to attack the compound. I have a feeling about this. If I hear his voice and get to know him some ahead of time, it might help me to say the right thing." Her eyes demanded a response from Molly.

"Mrs. Bassett, I would love to help you, but if you're thinking about my tapes, that's impossible."

Thelma Bassett sat back as if stung. "Why?"

"Because they don't belong to me; they belong to the magazine." Molly wasn't actually sure that was true. She must have read the contract when she signed it, but she couldn't remember what the deal was. "Anyway, there's nothing in those tapes that will help you." She didn't say that there was another reason: she couldn't bear to have anyone else listen to them. Her interview with Samuel Mordecai had been a low point in her career, an embarrassment–definitely not something she wanted to share with anyone. And what she heard in those tapes would just scare this poor mother out of her wits. No, this was a bad idea. "It would be a waste of your time."

"You're afraid it will upset me," Thelma said, reading Molly's mind. "I appreciate that, but I already know he's a madman. Even madmen have some areas where you can get through to them. See, I have this feeling...Oh, it sounds crazy and big-talking, but I think I'm the one who can do this. I really do." Her eyes locked on to Molly's. "Please help me."

Molly felt the appeal down to her toes. The woman was in the grip of a cause and it was catching. Shit. "Well, I..."

"Does he talk about his mother on this tape?"

Molly tried to remember. "Some, but not much, I think. His mother didn't raise him. His grandmother did."

"I know. Molly, I've got this feeling. I taped that talk he did on the radio the first day and I've listened to it again and again. One of the things he keeps coming back to is how bad mothers are today, how no one should have children because the corruption of society has made mothering impossible. I want to hear what he said to you about those things: I think this is what I should talk to him about."

"This really isn't my decision," Molly said, hoping Thelma Bassett would just go away. "The tapes are not my property. I could talk to my boss tomorrow and–"

"There's no time. I need to be ready. Please. Please do this for me, for the kids. Listen with me so you can tell me what he looked like, what he was doing when he said certain things. I wouldn't pester you like this, except I can't find anyone else who's talked to him."

Molly found herself desperately searching for a way out of this. It would be like letting someone go through your garbage.

Thelma continued: "If you absolutely need to check with your boss, call him now. It's an emergency situation–we've only got five more days. Tell him there might just be some little thing that could help, could make a difference for our children. Please."

She was relentless, and shameless–exactly the way Molly would be in her circumstances. Molly sat looking at the tapes. She stood up. "I'll see if I can get him. But I don't know..." She walked to her desk phone, punched 21 for Richard's office, and hoped he wasn't there. But he picked up the phone himself on the first ring.

"Richard, Thelma Bassett is here in my office. She feels she may get a chance to talk with Mordecai and she wants to listen to the tapes of the interview I did with him. I told her the tapes belong to the magazine and that–"

"My God, Molly, I saw her on television. She's wonderful. Get to know her. Give her anything she wants."

"But what about the confidentiality of–"

"Molly, if she wants to hear them, let her."

"Right," Molly said, putting the phone down. "Okay," she said to Thelma, who was literally sitting on the edge of her chair. "I think there's about an hour and a half of tape here. Do you have time now?"

"I'll make time. Thank you." Thelma's hands were pressed together as if in prayer.

Molly slipped the first tape into the player. But she didn't start it. "I want to explain something, Thelma. This is the worst interview I ever did. It's not really an interview. He just talks on and on, and for some reason I was unable to stop him and get it back on track.... Well, you'll see."

She pushed the "play" button. The tape started with the usual static and thumps of setting up. Her own voice came on, too loud. She adjusted the volume, grimacing, as she did every time she heard her recorded voice.

On the tape she was asking about talking to some of the other cult members, especially some of the women. Before she had gotten the question out, however, Samuel Mordecai's twangy drawl took over: "Our women keep very busy here at Jezreel, you can probably see that walking through the grounds. Time spent in idle conversation is time not given over to praising the Lord or getting His work done. This is not–"

"Just a few minutes is all it would take. Maybe your wife would–"

"I told you," he said in a louder voice, "they are busy. You said you wanted to interview me. Here I am."

"What are they busy doing, Mr. Mordecai?"

"The life-affirming jobs, Miz Cates, what women are best at. They provide our food and they clean our home and they work in the garden and they also work on our construction project you saw coming in. And they train for defense, just like the men. And they study the Bible with me many hours every day–that is the most important thing we all do here at Jezreel–studying the word of God and preparing ourselves."

"Defense? How do they–"

"That is something we won't discuss today. Let me just say we are armed and able to defend ourselves fully against any attack from outside forces."

"Outside forces? Who would want to–"

"Don't be naive, Miz Cates. You know very well that agents and forces of our corrupt monster central government have been spying on us for years, looking for any excuse to attack us, just like they did to those folks in Waco. All I'm going to say about defense is that we are ready for anything. We are more ready than they were in Waco. And, like I said, even our women do their fair share. They are occupied and I speak for them."

"What about the children?" Molly's voice persisted. "You didn't mention–"

"There are no children here."

"But many of the women here are young, of–"

"Abstinence! Haven't you ever heard of abstinence, Miz Cates? Chastity. Why bring children into the world when the world is about to end? *"And woe unto them that are with child, and to them that give suck in those days.'* Matthew 24:19, Miz Cates." Mordecai laughed, and hearing it now, Molly cringed. "A child born today would not even learn to walk and talk before the end. Earth's probation is being terminated, and we will witness it all. Our period of troubles and tribulation is ending.

"Time is rushing to its end. Just listen and you can hear it. It don't sound like the flapping of angel wings, oh no. You can hear it in the squawky sounds of television and movies and rock videos, in the whir of monster computers running the world's business. You can hear it every time a credit card goes through one of them charge machines– ka-chunk–every time a bar code gets read by one of them machines they got in grocery stores–zit, zit. It's all around us, zooming around our heads, through our heads–radio waves and microwaves, Fuzzbusters and cellular phones, modems, satellite transmissions bouncing around, electrical wires everywhere, making foreign masses grow in our bodies, electronic spying devices, telephone bugs. Can't you hear it in the air? All that speed and so-called progress is the sound of time rushing to its final conclusion. I call it 'rapidation,' Miz Cates, rapidation. Just like Daniel prophesied twenty-five hundred years ago, *'Many shall run to and fro, and knowledge shall be increased.'* He was talking about our day. Have you noticed how everything gets faster every year? New computer chips calculate faster than the eye can see, airplanes break the sound barrier. It's the speeding up of time, and it was prophesied as a signpost to the end."

His voice had been building in volume and now it rose to a fierce crescendo: "All this rapidation, this running to and fro, is revving up the Apocalypse."

Underneath the relentless flow of words on the tape were the faint, yippy sounds of Molly trying to get a question in, but his mad words boiled over hers.

"And now we know it's really at hand, real soon, next year, in the spring. Next spring is when it will all finish, all the rushing madness, Miz Cates. It is coming to pass, just as it was prophesied by Ezekiel and Daniel and John. It's all written in Scripture, predicted over two thousand years ago—the earthquakes, the lawlessness and violence in the streets, the eruptions, the famines, the wars and rumors of wars, the reign of the Beast, who lives here among us. The great battle of Armageddon is coming, the Millennium, and the Judgment Day. Just read the newspaper, Miz Cates. It's all coming and we here at Jezreel are the key. It cannot happen without us. That is why I let you come in here. That is why I am talking to you. I want you to write that in your magazine. It is your job to tell it to the world. We here at Jezreel are the human agents who will spark it off."

At last Molly's voice broke through, almost yelling. "My job is to tell the truth as I see it and I need to talk with some of your members, a few women, some children, and—"

"Miz Cates, open your ears and hear. I told you our women are occupied and we don't have children here. Even if we didn't know about the end approaching, we wouldn't have children here because there are no mothers left. You must see that. They are just women, not mothers. They give birth to children and, without a thought for that child, that baby boy, they leave him, desert him, abandon him in deep waters, leave him for the hungry beast to devour. They don't care. They leave to go whoring at bars. They leave to work checking groceries at the supermarket. They leave to program computers, to service the Beast whose mark is bar codes and computer chips. You see this as well as me."

Here the noises of Molly trying to interrupt with a question were drowned out by Samuel Mordecai's voice rising to a commanding shout. "Sit down and listen. Woman, you came to hear me tell what we believe. I'm telling you. Now sit down and listen to it, the way I want to tell it, so you can write it as it should be."

Molly, hearing this on tape, felt her skin prickle as though she were covered with fire ants. She pushed the "pause" button, feeling shaky and flushed. "Thelma, this is hard for me to listen to. I feel the need to explain something here. I am not accustomed to taking orders. Actually, I can't remember a single time other than what you're hearing here where I did anything I was told to do. But something happened when I was out there at Jezreel, something extremely upsetting to me. There is this…quality about Samuel Mordecai, and you should know this if you are going to talk to him. He has this…well…I really am at a loss for words here. He has something–some force– that caused me to sit down and shut up, even though sitting down and shutting up is something I haven't done since the third grade and even then I didn't do it very well. Maybe it was fear–I *was* afraid–but usually fear makes me more aggressive…." Molly knew her words weren't conveying the insane energy and repressed violence of the man. "Anyway, I never let this sort of thing happen before."

"I think I understand it a little," Thelma said softly. "I think something like what you're describing happens to those negotiators, too, when they're talking to him on the phone. When they describe to us, the parents, what they've been trying to do, they have a hard time explaining why they never seem to be able to say what they planned to say. They get cowed, sort of scared into being quiet, even when they've planned to control the conversation. Molly, help me figure out how to prevent that from happening when I talk to him. Let's hear the rest."

Molly turned the player back on. Samuel

Mordecai's voice rambled on, unimpeded now by questions or interruptions: "We are adrift, we so-called modern men, in a river of corruption, with no life jacket, no anchor, just like I was adrift, floating helpless, no identity, abandoned by all but the cloak of the Beast enfolding me. We have no mother to take care of us, because the mother is out whoring to the false God which has risen up from the mind of man and lives embodied in the computer, that false God disguised as progress, which promises ease and wealth, but delivers chaos and–"

Thelma held a hand up. "Stop it there. Can you stop it there and replay it?"

Molly hit the "stop" button. "How far back shall I go?"

"Go back to before where he talks about how there are no more mothers."

Molly hit the reverse button. "…We have no mother to take care of us, because the mother is out whoring to the false god…"

Molly hit the "pause" button. Thelma was leaning forward raptly. "What are you thinking?" Molly asked.

"Well, that's like what he said on his KLTX talk, but he goes farther here. He sure doesn't think much of mothers. Did you know he was adopted?"

"You mean by his grandmother?"

"No. By his mother, Evelyn Grimes. Then after she adopted him, she ran off and left him with her mother, his grandmother."

Molly was surprised. "Whaaat? I never heard or read anywhere that he was adopted. Where did you hear that?"

"His grandmother told me. She called me this morning."

"She did?"

"Yes. She saw me on television and had a vision that God wanted her to call me and tell me something she'd never told anyone before. She said Donnie–that's his real name, you know, Donnie Ray Grimes–was not really her flesh-and-blood grandson. Her daughter adopted him and then ran off and she had to take him over. She also wanted to tell me she'd been praying for me and Kim every morning and that she was so sorry she just wanted to crawl into a hole."

"Really? She said her daughter adopted him?"

"Yes."

"I wonder if it's true. It hasn't appeared in any of the news coverage about him."

"Well, Miz Huff–that's the grandmother–says her daughter kept it secret. Even her friends thought she gave birth to him. So they just never talked about it. But the feeling I got was Miz Huff wants to disown him. She was in an explaining sort of mode–said she tried to do right with him, but she didn't have much money or time or support. You know, the same thing all parents seem to say at some point: I did the best I could at the time."

Molly smiled. "Yeah. Seems to me I've said that once or twice myself."

"Here's this idea I'm working on. He's real angry at mothers because his mother abandoned him–*two* mothers abandoned him, really. And Miz Huff doesn't sound like much of a mom to me. So Mordecai thinks he can just steal these kids

5 7

and use them for whatever it is he's got in mind because no one really cares." Thelma's hands rose from where they'd been resting in her lap and pressed against her chest as if she needed to hold something in. "So what if I could show him that there are mothers who love their children? What if I could show him that I am a mother who loves her child so much she will risk everything for that child? What if I walked in and offered myself, to replace Kim as a hostage? What do you think of that idea, Molly?"

Molly thought it sounded like insanity. "The negotiators would never let you do that. One of their cardinal rules is no exchanging of hostages."

Thelma's face mottled. "You don't strike me as someone who is interested in rules. I'm interested only in getting my daughter out of there alive. I don't give a fuck what their rules are."

Molly, feeling chastised, nodded. "You're right that children being abandoned by their mothers is a theme with Mordecai. It makes more sense if he was adopted–this imagery about being set adrift, like Moses. It must feel like that to be put up for adoption."

"Yes. I think so. Will you play the rest of it?" Thelma pointed at the tape player.

They sat in silence for an hour listening to the rest of Samuel Mordecai's fiery sermon about corruption and prophecies that had been fulfilled.

When it was finally over, Molly let out one shaky breath of relief and rewound the tape.

"What was he doing during this?" Thelma asked. "From the sound, he moves around all the time."

"Yes. He paces the room the whole time he's talking. Lots of energy. He gestures a lot." Molly used her index finger to stab the air. "Like that, and he tugs at his crotch and runs his fingers through his hair. He's always on the move, twitchy in the extreme. Posing like a rooster, or a rock musician. And he rarely pauses for breath, so getting a word in, even if you aren't scared and cowed like I was, is impossible. The only way is to talk right on top of his words. It's almost impossible to talk to him."

Thelma was taking it all in, nodding. "I've seen it with the negotiators." Her watch emitted a little beep and she glanced down at it. "Oh, damn. I need to run. I wouldn't go, but it's TV–Channel 33, which he watches." She rose to her feet. "Molly, may I ask you a favor?"

"Of course."

"You see now what I'm after. Would you go talk to Miz Huff for me? Ask her how I might reason with her grandson? I'd go but I have to be here. I want him to see me everywhere, on TV, in his dreams, hear me on the radio. I want him to know he can't get away from me."

"I was planning to talk to her anyway. I'd be glad to ask her that. Give me the phone number and address and I'll go tomorrow."

Thelma pulled a small red notebook out of her bag, looked up the number, and gave it to Molly along with her own phone number. "Call me when you get back."

Molly walked her to the door and, on an impulse, hugged her. Thelma was an armful, an earth mother, solid. "I'll be thinking about you,

Thelma. I don't pray, but if I did, I'd pray for you and Kim."

"I appreciate that. If you have any more ideas, call me, Molly."

Molly watched her walk down the hall, her left shoulder weighted down by the heavy bag. She sighed. Ideas—yes, she thought she just might have an idea coming up. It was just a whisper in her ear, a cold tingling in the back of her brain, nothing she could put into words yet, just that restless old feeling of an idea forming.

"And I saw an angel coming down out of heaven, having the key to the Abyss and holding in his hand a great chain. He seized the dragon, that ancient serpent who is the devil, or Satan, and bound him for a thousand years."

REVELATION 20:1-2

CHAPTER FOUR

The sound of the Bible slamming shut jarred Walter Demming back from planting geraniums in the huge terra-cotta pots on Theodora Shea's south-facing terrace. The sun had been beating down on his bare back and his fingers were sunk deep in the damp, cool earth. He returned reluctantly and found himself sweating in the stinking air of a buried bus, with eleven hungry, frightened children, listening to a madman.

"You heard it here!" Samuel Mordecai shouted.

"We're on a collision course with destiny!" In the enclosed prison of the bus his voice reverberated. He glistened with sweat; it had soaked through his shirt and darkened his hair, which curled around his face in wet ringlets. "It's clear that all this speedup of computer technology, this so-called progress–rapidation, I call it–is really a machine out of control, spinning us faster and faster–it's the *final sign* we've been waiting on.

"I know y'all was raised playing them computer games, Lambs. They got computers at y'all's school and they teach you to write book reports on them, and lots of you have one sitting on your desks at home. Looks pretty innocent, don't it? Like a toaster. But it's all part of the grand scheme, clearing the way for the Antichrist. All you have to do is look at the faces in one of them arcades where the crackle and flashing lights of so-called computer games turn young folks like yourselves into robots for the Beast. Y'all remember the prophecy from the Book of Revelation and I don't even have to open the book for this one: *"And he had power to give life unto the image of the Beast, that the image of the Beast should both speak, and cause that as many as would not worship the image of the Beast should be killed.'* It's no wonder you young ones have fallen for this false prophet. Unless someone told you, like I'm doing now, how would you know that the innocent little home computer is the way the Antichrist will control human life? And, Lambs, it was all prophesied in the Bible."

He tossed his head, flicking sweat around him. "Remember: Earth's probation terminates in five days. Ignore or disbelieve it at your own peril. Now, you can't say gosh I wish I'da known. Them that has heard and don't take heed will get stamped on the soul with the bar code that glows blue and marks them, every one, for the angel Gabriel and his avenger band to find them and make them into blood statues to rot for all eternity. Amen!"

Walter Demming checked his watch. Only two hours and ten minutes. They were getting off easy today.

Samuel Mordecai's lips curved upward in a beneficent smile, and he raised his hands in benediction, the Bible clutched in his right hand–a gesture so sanctimonious it made Walter want to leap out of his seat and attack the man, drag him to the ground and smash the expression off his face. As nutty and as incoherent as Mordecai's message was, Walter didn't question the sincerity of it. But he loathed the drama with which it was delivered.

Walter stifled the urge to attack. He got up quickly, put on his supplicant posture, and went to beseech–one more time. "Mr. Mordecai, may I have a word? Please." Walter turned away from the children and lowered his voice in the hope they wouldn't hear. "It's about Josh. He's getting sicker every day. He had an attack during the night. It almost killed him. He needs to be in a hospital. This is a matter of life and death."

Walter tried to look him in the eye, but Samuel Mordecai turned and took a step toward the door.

"Please." Walter reached out and took hold of his arm. "At the very least, send out for medication. Here"–he pulled Josh's empty inhaler out of his pocket–" this is what he needs." He pointed at the label. "See? Albuterol. Two refills left. Please." He tried to hand him the inhaler but Mordecai kept both hands behind his back. "And he should have another medication that he didn't have with him—a steroid inhaler, he says." Walter bent closer and whispered, "I'm afraid he'll die down here. We have no way to help him when he has these attacks. Please let him go home." He found himself hoping Josh would suffer an attack right now so this man could see how fearsome it was.

With a saccharine smile, Samuel Mordecai said, "Inhalers? Life and death? Mr. Bus Driver, can't you hear how foolish you sound? Here we stand at the very brink, the end of time. Stars are whirling and seas turning to blood. Listen to yourself. Forces of momentous power and glory are heaving in the heavens and you're fussing about *inhalers*. Aren't you listening?" He gestured around to include the bus and all of them. "We are gathered here to advance God's purpose, not to worry about runny noses." He turned away again.

But Walter held on to his arm. "Wait—this is no runny nose. It's a child's life and it does matter. Regardless of what is going on. You're going to come down here tomorrow and find this little boy dead and you'll be responsible for that. Then there's no turning back."

"Turning back?" Mordecai threw his head back and laughed, showing off his dimples and his even white teeth. "You think we could turn back now? I fear for you, Mr. Bus Driver. You aren't listening. Young as they are, I believe the Lambs are getting the message better than you are." He put his head so close that Walter could feel his breath. "Time. Is. Ending. Get ready."

"Okay," Walter argued, talking as fast as he could, "we're getting ready, but why can't we have some way to make hot water and steam? That would help. And we could wash in it, too. We just need a hot plate, or one of those coil things that heat water. And some instant coffee. Josh says that helps ease an attack, and citrus–a few lemons or oranges. Those aren't difficult to get. While we wait. Please. It wouldn't interfere with our...purification. And the children are hungry. Cereal isn't enough. They're losing weight. Some of them have diarrhea and stomachaches. We need some real food down here, food that kids will eat."

Mordecai tugged his arm from Walter's grip. "You figure as the world is ending we should send out to McDonald's for burgers and fries?"

The mention of burgers made Walter's mouth fill with saliva. He could feel the smooth fat beading on his tongue. "Yes, I do think so. And they keep asking how much longer we're going to be here in the bus. It's hot and stuffy and unhealthy. They need to move around, get sun and fresh air. A couple are getting real depressed and the rest are fighting all the time. Can't we just come out and stay as we are but be aboveground?"

"You're in the process of purification, Mr. Bus Driver, even if you can't feel it. We are Hearth Jezreelites–a name given to me in a living vision, a rapture, where I was taken to God and He called me by name and the name He called me by was Prophet Mordecai. Hearth is earth with an H for heaven, heaven in earth. Fifty days it takes to make

you ready. God will purify y'all through the earth."
He had been speaking into empty space. Now he
turned to look at Walter. "Also, you're down here
for your own safety. When the federal government
attacks us"–he slapped his Bible against the
driver's seat–"and, believe me, they *will* attack us,
we want you to be out of harm's way. Trust me,
this is best for you and the Lambs."

"But how much longer?"

Samuel Mordecai reached behind him and from
the back pocket of his jeans he pulled an X-acto
knife and held it up for Walter to see. "You ask
how much longer? You know the answer to that,
Mr. Bus Driver. I tell you every day." With exag-
gerated fanfare, he turned and stepped to the front
of the bus. "You have the record right here in front
of you."

He leaned over the grimy window and scraped
off one of the five Band-Aids stuck there. They
were flesh-colored with Ninja Turtles on them.
On the first day, when Samuel Mordecai had descended to welcome them, he had stuck the Band-
Aids carefully to the glass, one by one, in neat
rows, talking nonstop as he pressed each one on.
There had been fifty of them, one for each day of
what he called Earth's final Pentecost, the countdown to Apocalypse. That first day, he'd given
them what he called the daily Bible study of the
Lambs–the first of the grueling daily harangues.
When he had finally finished talking, after three
solid hours, he scraped one of the Band-Aids off
the window with a flourish.

He'd done that every day, and now there were
four left. He turned to Walter with a smile. "Four

more days is the answer, Mr. Bus Driver. Until Friday, which is Passover and Good Friday. Very good Friday."

Samuel Mordecai pushed Walter aside. He was six inches taller and his long arms rippled with muscles. Walter resolved to double his daily push-ups.

Mordecai addressed himself to the children. "Now, Lambs, I want y'all to sit around and talk, discuss what I just told you about the final signs and prophecies. Mr. Demming is going to lead you in discussion and prayer. When you've done that, Martin will come to hear what you talked about. Then he'll bring you a meal to nourish your bodies in preparation for your glorious day."

He waved his Bible. Then he stepped out of the bus into the pit. He reached his arms up the hole, and with one quick motion, he hoisted himself up. His legs undulated upward. A shower of black earth sprinkled down long after the black boots had disappeared. Then came the grating sound: the wooden platform they used to cover the hole being dragged into place.

As if all twelve had agreed on the need for total silence, no one spoke or moved. Walter sat down and closed his eyes. He'd struck out again. He was useless. He had accomplished nothing, not one thing. Each day they got closer to death–he had no doubt death was what was waiting for them on Friday–and he was unable to do a thing to change that. He couldn't even do anything to ease the kids' misery while they waited to die. He needed to figure out something else. Maybe if he got another chance to talk on the phone, he could send a message of some sort....

He heard the raspy bark of Josh's cough. He opened his eyes.

"I'm so hungry," Sandra whined. "Mr. Demming, I'm hungry."

"Martin will bring us something to eat after we talk about what he said and after we tell Martin about it. Then we can eat."

"But I'm so hungry I don't know if I can wait," Sandra said.

Walter looked at the little girl in the front seat. She was a tall, skinny eight-year-old with thick glasses, mocha-colored skin, and an Afro haircut that had, in the past six weeks, grown into a tangled bush of kinky curls. The shape of her hair in the back reminded him of the shaggy crest of the roadrunners he saw in the field behind his house. And with her long legs and tendency to tilt forward when she walked, Sandra really did look like a roadrunner. He felt the urge to sketch her and wished he had paper and pencils, but they had run out of paper six days ago, except for his emergency supply.

"I want to eat now," Sandra insisted. The earpiece of her glasses had broken off in a fight with Heather and afterward Walter had managed to hold it together with the discarded Band-Aids Mordecai dropped on the floor after scraping them off the window. Walter had molded several to form a large lump at the corner of her glasses. "I'm hungry, too, honey," Walter told her. "It sure feels bad, but maybe we need to do something to take our minds off it until Martin comes."

"Mr. Demming," Hector said, kneeling on his seat, "I was thinking. Last night when Jacksonville got caught by the Barbecue Tongs, why didn't he just fly away? You know, before they grabbed him. He saw them and all, so he could have just split."

Walter stood and turned around to face the kids. He leaned against the seat and did a head count. Eleven. The faces appeared as small pale blobs in the dimness. He took one long deep breath and let it out slowly. "Well, Hector, remember that when the Barbecue Tongs surprised him, Jacksonville was in a narrow alley. Now, you have to picture this: Jacksonville is a full-grown adult turkey vulture and when he spreads his wings out"– Walter stretched his arms out wide–"they measure six feet across. To give you an idea of how long six feet is, I am five foot nine inches tall, so Jacksonville's wingspread is three inches longer than the whole length of my body. Now, the alley he was in–you remember he got trapped in an alley in the village of Moo Goo Gai Pan–well, this alley measured only five and a half feet across. In order to fly he has to stretch his wings wide and flap them, but the alley was too narrow. And it was bricked off at one end. And of course at the other end that whole company of Tongs–three hundred of them–were waving their long iron forks and those whippy spatulas they use. So he couldn't fly or run. And of course he was outnumbered three hundred to one."

"To two," said Heather.

"No, to one, dummy." Hector reached over the seat back and gave her blond head a shove. "You never get it right, Heather-head. Lopez wasn't with him."

Walter looked at Heather to see if the shove, or the words, had got her hackles up. The child was usually quick to take offense and fight with anyone, but now she was sitting peacefully, sideways with her back against the window, legs stretched out on the seat. Walter watched her face as he spoke. "Remember, honey, Lopez was sleeping in a burrow in the jungle and couldn't wake up to go into the village with Jacksonville. He'd been eating those slumber bugs again, and they made him sleepy all the time. Now, that was a good thing—not that he was eating slumber bugs, that's bad, having a habit that dulls the senses like slumber bugs do—but it's good that he didn't get captured, too."

Heather nodded. Walter was relieved that she was not going to fight over this; he hated it when they fought and he didn't have a clue how to deal with it. He wanted them to cooperate so when the time came for them to put their emergency plan into action, they would work together effectively. He knew from his experience in Vietnam that the military was right about one thing—an effective fighting unit had to cooperate to get the job done. So he wanted desperately for them to live and work together harmoniously. Lately, when they squabbled, he felt his nerves vibrating like a high-voltage wire.

Lucy raised her hand to talk, a habit she couldn't get over, even though Walter kept telling her she didn't need to. "What happens," she asked, "after they put Jacksonville in that little cage? What was the fire for?" She was hugging her knees in to her chest, resting her chin on her knees. There was a smear of dirt on her cheek.

"Oh, well, I'll tell you all that in good time," Walter said. "But first we need to talk about what we're going to say to Martin." He paused, hoping the kids would come up with something because he hated feeding them lies; it was better, somehow, if they invented their own.

Conrad Pease, ten years old, raised his hand. He came from a devout Baptist family. His daddy was a part-time preacher, and Conrad could pray fluently at the drop of a hat. "We could just say we talked about how amazing it is that Bible prophecies made so long ago are coming true in our time and that it's amazing they predicted all the bad stuff that would happen with computers way before they were even invented. And we could say we really hope he'll tell us more about it in future lessons."

Hector Ramirez groaned. "Don't say we want him to teach us nothing more. I can't stand no more of his talking and shit."

"He's gonna do it anyways," Conrad snapped back. "No matter what we say."

"You shouldn't say that, Hector," Lucy said. "Bad word."

Brandon Betts in the last row raised his hand. His face was dark with anger. "We ought to really talk about it. People who get a chance to hear and don't listen are the ones who will get made into blood statues." His voice got higher and angrier. "We shouldn't be telling stories when we're supposed to be talking about God and all. I don't want that to happen to me, what he said about the laser knife and everything."

Everyone was quiet. Walter Demming looked at Lucy, who had pressed her hands over her ears. It was all so difficult. He had made a judgment call on the first day: to talk honestly to the kids about what he thought of Samuel Mordecai and how they should behave. They would all pretend attention and respect to him because he had power over their bodies. But his message was wrong and they would resist it. To retain their sanity. But some of the kids were breaking down under what amounted to brainwashing. Especially Brandon Betts and Sue Ellen McGregor.

"Well," Walter said, in the lowest, calmest voice he could muster, "there are two things I feel sure about, Brandon. First, the world is not going to end in four days. I promise that. It's not going to happen, so don't worry about it. The second thing I'm sure about is that none of us is going to hell. Not no way. And there's no such thing as blood statues. Now, you may be right, Brandon, that we shouldn't lie and say we've been talking about something when we haven't, but it seems to me we need some time off from this stuff. But let's discuss it. What do the rest of you think? Should we talk about what Mr. Mordecai was saying?"

There were several groans. "No. We heard enough," Hector said. "I hate that shit. I want to hear about Lopez and Jacksonville. Go on, Mr. Demming. Conrad will tell them—you know, what he just said, and the rest of us will all say uh-huh, that's right. Yeah. Amen."

There was nodding and okays all around.

Brandon sat silent with his arms crossed over his chest.

Lucy took her hands away from her ears.

Kimberly Bassett knelt on her seat. In her no-nonsense voice that made her sound more like thirty than eleven, she said, "It's settled, then. Conrad will tell them what we talked about. It's not really a lie, because we did kind of talk about it just now. Now Mr. Demming can go on with the story, okay, everyone?"

Most of the kids were nodding, as if a voice of authority had spoken and it was indeed settled. Walter studied Kimberly's snubby nose and stubborn chin. He was in awe. She was the most self-possessed person he'd ever known. How on earth did parents manage to produce such a child? She helped Walter with the younger children, and had taken Josh on as a special project. She was tender and creative in helping to relax the boy through his asthma attacks. And in a way, Walter thought, her high expectations for how responsible adults should act had been his own guide through this unfamiliar situation. He often took his lead from Kim.

"So." Walter hunkered in the aisle where all the kids could see him. "Back to Jacksonville, for those who want to listen." He paused to give those who didn't want to participate a chance to settle down where they wanted.

Several kids moved closer. Even though she didn't listen to the story, or pretended not to, Sandra stayed in her seat at the front. She had staked it out because it was closer to the light, so she could read.

Brandon Betts let out a snort of derision. He got up from the seat and stalked the aisle to the back, where he stretched his considerably thinned-down but still chunky eleven-year-old body out on the floor. He seemed to need to get as far away from the story as he could, even though it meant being closer to the stinking hole in the back. He opened his math book and started to page through it.

Philip Trotman, eyes shut, leaned his forehead against the window. Walter didn't know whether Philip listened or not. The boy never asked questions or commented or looked Walter's way during the storytelling. The remaining eight settled back in their seats, ready to listen.

Walter Demming couldn't remember having told a story before in his entire life. If he'd been asked, he would have said he was not a storyteller. Circumstances had forced him into it, or it might be more accurate to say, Kim had forced him into it, and the process had carried him along.

On that first day, after the lights went out, and the trapdoor slid shut overhead, it had been a nightmare. Kids began to scream. Then the others had picked up the panic. It grew to a chorus of sobbing, screaming, and calling out for mothers and fathers. The children milled around, bumping into one another in the dark, crying out. Underneath it all, he could hear Josh coughing and wheezing.

Walter had groped his way through the door and onto the bus, bumping into seats and panicky children. He tried to calm them with his hands. He tried to soothe with his voice, but no one could hear him over the frenzied wailing. He needed to do something, to take charge, calm them down, but he couldn't think of anything to do. As the screaming went on, he felt his own panic surging in his chest. His brain wanted to join in the screaming.

But he was the adult here, he had told himself. The only adult. These kids were going to lose their minds if he didn't do something.

"Quiet, y'all!"

A lilting girl's voice, a twangy angel-sound, had risen out of the cacophony. It lifted above the other voices and dominated. "Now, that's enough of that, y'all. Someone's gonna get hurt if we don't settle. Quiet down now, everybody. The lights will go back on, but let's all sit down together and wait. Come on up to the front. Come on. We can hold hands. Come on now. Our bus driver is going to tell us a story."

Our bus driver? That was him. He was their driver. He didn't know any stories. And even if he did, he didn't think he could tell one in the dark, in the middle of such chaos. But the voice had promised a story. And, miraculously, the promise seemed to be calming the children. They were quieting. Several screamers had stopped. The noise gradually subsided to a few sobs and whispers. There was rustling and the gentle pressure of bodies all around him in the dark.

A small hand grabbed his and held on hard. The firmness and warmth of it felt comforting. Walter squeezed back.

He opened his mouth, then cleared his throat. "Okay. Now. Find a place to sit, children," he said. "Sit down. That's right. And hold the hand of the person next to you. Good." He heard them settling down all around him in the blackness. "Everyone needs a hand to hold.

"My name is Walter Demming," he said. "I have a story to tell you. But first I'd like each of you to tell me your name and how old you are so I can sort of do a count. Okay? Just call out."

The voices came out of the darkness: "Hector Ramirez. I'm twelve, man." "Heather Yost. I'm ten, almost eleven." "Conrad Pease. Just turned ten on Tuesday." "Sue Ellen McGregor, I'm eight. How old are you, Mr. Bus Driver?"

"I'm fifty-one," Walter said, "and I'm Mr. Demming. Go on with your names, please."

The names came: Kimberly Bassett, age eleven; Lucy Quigley, age ten; Josh Benderson, age eleven; Sandra Echols, age eight; Brandon Betts, age eleven; Bucky DeCarlo, age six. Then silence fell.

Walter said, "That's only ten. There are eleven of you. Who hasn't given their name?"

There was some murmuring and a voice said, "Come on, Philip, tell him your name." There was a brief silence and finally a faint voice said, "Philip Trotman. I'm nine."

"Good," Walter said. "All twelve of us are here."

It had been his first count.

Then, still holding on to the small hand, he squatted down in the dark aisle and waited for a story to come to him. They were expecting it. He could sense the anticipation in the air. They were sitting there waiting for a story. That's what did it, he decided later—their anticipation sucked from him a story he didn't even know was there.

75

"Once upon a time," he began. "Once upon a time there was a turkey vulture who lived in Austin, Texas. His name was Jacksonville and he had a good friend named Lopez. He worried that because he was ugly no one would love him." The story began like a weak trickle, but then it flowed, and by the time the lights came back on, Jacksonville and Lopez had been given an important mission by the President of the United States, and everyone seemed calmer.

But the calm hadn't lasted long, because, when the lights came back on, Samuel Mordecai had arrived. He had dropped down into the underworld and started preaching. He had strutted up and down the aisle spouting Bible verses and doom.

Forty-six days had passed and the man was still strutting and preaching.

But at least the lights had stayed on after his first visit. That first terrifying darkness had not been repeated, though they all worried about it. Every time a bulb flickered or dimmed, they were afraid it was burning out. And there was always the possibility the Jezreelites would just flip the switch again and plunge them back into the darkness and panic of the first day.

Once he had started telling the story, it spun itself out spontaneously, as if he'd been practicing it all his life. The characters rose up and spoke. Often it felt like the story was telling itself, just passing through him. It didn't seem to be doing the kids any harm, and it filled some empty time, so he had kept it going with one installment a day, or sometimes two, if it was a particularly difficult day.

He cleared his throat. "Remember last night after the Tongs caught Jacksonville, they put him in a bamboo cage? Remember how scared he was? He fought. He beat his wings against the bars. But the cage was strong. The bars were made of thick stalks of green bamboo. And it was small–so low that he couldn't stand up straight. A turkey vulture perching is about two and a half feet tall and this cage was only two feet four inches high, so he had to keep his head bent over to one side. And when he saw what they were doing–building a fire and bringing out that huge cooking pot– you can imagine how scared he was."

Walter leaned forward as he felt the story welling up. "Now, the Tongs had never seen a vulture like Jacksonville. They have vultures in Tongaland, of course–there are vultures of one kind or another all over the world–but theirs are much smaller, only half the size, and they don't have red heads or pale yellow feet, so Jacksonville was a curiosity, a freak. Like I told you last night, they put the cage right in the middle of the village where all the people passed by. Word got around, the way it will do in a village, and everybody came to look at him. They all came–old grannies and little children, men and women, even babies who could barely walk–all day long they came by. They stared and poked him with those long forks, and they laughed.

"Jacksonville was used to people laughing at him. People often found him ugly. Now, it's real hard to get used to that. None of you would know how painful it is because you're all exceptionally handsome children, but Jacksonville knew because he'd run into it a lot. People, and other animals even, would see him and say yuck, how ugly. And they would call him bad names: buzzard or filthy buzzard, which is very insulting to a turkey vulture. And it wasn't just because of the way he looked, he knew that. Lots of people didn't like what he ate."

"Dead things," Bucky said. "He ate dead things."

"Gross!" Heather exclaimed.

"Yeah. But we eat dead things, too," Sue Ellen McGregor said. As she listened, she wove thin strands on her string box, the only one that had survived the first day's confiscation of backpacks and possibly dangerous items. She had made friendship bracelets for all the girls before Walter discovered how strong and flexible the finished products were. Now he had her making long ropelike lengths that they could use for their emergency defense plan. Everyone on the bus envied Sue Ellen's possession of the string box, even Walter, because it was such a calming activity and actually produced something useful.

"Let him tell it," Josh said. "Mr. Demming's telling it."

"Yeah," Lucy said.

Walter turned toward Sue Ellen. "That's a good point. Most of us do eat the meat of dead animals, which really isn't much different from what Jacksonville ate. But some people are grossed out by the vulture's habit of eating carrion."

"What's carrion?" Sue Ellen asked.

"Dead animals," he said, "and they're often rotting by the time the vultures find them. Of course, you and I know that vultures do a lot of good by cleaning up the roads, but still, some people just–"

Hector interrupted. "But didn't you say that Jacksonville had been trying to stop eating meat? That he was trying to become a vegetarian?" Walter had noticed that as they all got hungrier, both his story and the kids' questions turned more and more toward the subject of food. Just the mention of meat, even rotting carrion, could make his mouth water now. After forty-six days of nothing but cold cereal with a little milk and an occasional peanut butter sandwich, they were all food-crazy. It was one of the main topics of conversation: what each of them was going to eat when they got home.

"Yes, that's right, Hector," Walter said. "He'd been trying hard for several years to change his diet, but it wasn't working out very well. Jacksonville found he needed meat to keep his strength up. Flying takes lots of energy and his body craved meat even though his mind didn't like the idea of it."

"Maybe we're all going to get sick 'cause we don't get meat," Conrad said. "My mom always talks about protein and how we have to get enough."

"Yeah," Sue Ellen said, "aren't there sicknesses you get without meat?"

"Lots of people are vegetarians," Walter replied, "and they're healthy. There's protein in the cereal they give us and the milk. And lots in peanut butter." He had been surprised at how basically healthy they all had stayed on the limited diet they'd been given. It was boring as hell, but they were surviving on it.

"So," he said, getting back to the story, "Jacksonville turned out to be like all the people in the world who go on diets and can't hack it. He went back to eating whatever he could scavenge.

"Now, the Tongs were all standing around his cage talking, but Jacksonville didn't know what they were saying. See, he didn't know their language, which was Tonganese. When he saw them gathering more firewood and building up the fire under the pot, he was so scared he nearly passed out. What scared him, of course, was that it might be him that was going to get cooked in that pot.

"Then he noticed the Tongs were bringing baskets of things and dumping them into the pot, things that looked like onions and potatoes and carrots. Maybe in this village they were vegetarians. That was a hopeful idea. But then he remembered what Tong teeth looked like and he was afraid.

"And something happened that scared him even more. A bunch of Tong warriors were standing in front of his cage looking in and laughing. One of them, a big guy with a huge gut on him, did something really scary. He pointed at Jacksonville, then he stood on his tiptoes and crowed like a rooster–cock-a-doodle-doo. Then he did this with his finger." Walter stuck out his index finger and drew it slowly across his throat. "This made all the men laugh and pound their spatulas on the ground. Then they all danced around flapping their arms up and down like they were trying to fly and then they all collapsed to the ground laughing like it was the funniest thing in the world. And when they laughed you could see all their teeth, these long pointed teeth that Jacksonville found really scary. He felt like he was going to throw up.

"By now it had gotten dark and people were gathering around the fire. It looked like the whole village was coming. There was even a parade of old people with fur and feathers around their necks. Something was about to happen. Definitely.

"Then two big warriors went to a cage Jacksonville hadn't even noticed. It was on the other side of the fire. And they pulled an old man out. He was naked, and he had a long and dirty white beard. They tried to get him to stand up, but he couldn't, so they dragged him toward the pot. Jacksonville felt relieved that someone else, not him, was going to get cooked in that pot.

"But then Jacksonville saw the old man's face and he felt just awful. The man was Dr. Mortimer. You remember that the reason Jacksonville and Lopez were in Tongaland was to rescue Dr. Mortimer. He was thinner than in the picture Jacksonville had seen, but it was Dr. Mortimer.

"Jacksonville was very upset. As you can imagine. He hated to see anyone get hurt, and here was the most important person in the world about to get cooked. And you guys remember why he was so important."

"Because of the Galaxy Peace Ray," Bucky said, his thumb in his mouth.

"That's right. Dr. Mortimer was the only one in the world who knew how to make the Astral 100 Galaxy Peace Ray. He invented it. That's why the President of the United States sent Jackson-ville and Lopez to find him."

"How does it work again?" Lucy asked. "You told us at the beginning, but I forgot."

"Well, it looks like one of those old-fashioned machine guns you see in gangster movies. But when you fire it at someone, this wheel on it spins and it looks like a sparkler. It shoots out these tiny little dots of light that land on the person being shot." He pretended to shoot a machine gun at Hector in the first seat and made a machine-gun noise: "Rat-a-ta-ta! And the person starts to twinkle and they feel this strange thing happening to them—a tingle like when someone tickles the inside of your arm with their fingertips very gently. But you feel this all over your body. And then the sparks die out and they're gone and you think that's it. What you don't know is that it's changed you and the next time you feel like doing something mean or hitting someone or fighting, you get that feeling again, that tingling, and you find you couldn't possibly fight or hurt anyone.

"So here's Jacksonville feeling awful because he was hoping the person in the other cage would get cooked instead of him and that person turned out to be Dr. Mortimer—the reason Jacksonville came to Tongaland—the man who could end war forever. Jacksonville wanted to do something to save him. But he was too scared to even move. He just watched as they lifted the old man to toss him into the boiling pot.

"Then something amazing happened. Just as the Tongs were picking Dr. Mortimer up to throw him in the boiling pot, it started to rain. And not just some little rain, pitter-pat. It was like a down-pour. And it was a funny yellowish color. It put the fire right out.

"The Tongs all ran to their hootches and two big ones dragged Dr. Mortimer back to the cage and stuffed him in."

Walter stopped talking. He heard the scraping noise of the wood slab over the hole being pushed back. Every eye was focused hungrily on the pit at the bus door. First two dirty white tennis shoes appeared, and then hairy bare legs, then khaki shorts, and then Martin dropped to earth, his skinny chest and narrow shoulders heaving from the effort. As always, his thin face was stony.

"Conrad," Walter said, "will you close our discussion with a prayer?"

"Yessir. Bow your heads, please." Conrad stood and said in the solemn voice he used only for religious matters, "Dear Heavenly Father, help us to understand the message we've been given. Thank you for our many blessings and make us ever mindful of the needs of others. Amen."

"Amen," they all chorused, bringing their heads up quickly to see if Martin had brought a box of food. But he stepped into the bus empty-handed.

Sandra began to cry, and Hector called out, "Where's breakfast, man?" All eleven of them sagged in their seats.

Walter's stomach felt like it was being twisted and squeezed. He stood and approached Martin, who was the only Hearth Jezreelite other than Samuel Mordecai they had seen since the first day. "Morning," Walter said, trying to engage the man's eyes. But Martin kept his narrow, close-set

83

eyes averted. "Any chance for a little pizza or some Big Macs today?" Walter tried to inject some playfulness into his tone. "We sure deserve a break today. It would do wonders for our prayers of praise and thanksgiving."

"You're supposed to tell me what y'all talked about," Martin said. "Then I'll bring cereal."

Walter moved a little closer. "Conrad will give you a report on our discussion. But do you think we could get a new lightbulb? The one in the back burned out last night. And, Martin, we really need some hot water down here. To wash in and so we can steam Josh when he has an attack. Do you have any of those heating coils, or a hot plate, or even an electric coffeepot with an extension cord? Please, Martin, we really need that. And some soap, too." All the time he spoke, Walter was trying to get Martin to look at him, but the man refused.

"Okay," Martin said in his monotone, "who's going to tell me about your discussion?"

While Conrad gave a recitation of the theological issues they had touched on, Walter studied their captor. Martin had greasy black hair combed straight back from a narrow face. His nose was beaky and thin, his lips almost nonexistent. Several days' growth of patchy black stubble dotted his face. His expression was one of constant impatience. If Walter were to draw him as a bird it would probably be a common grackle.

It occurred to Walter that during their entire captivity Martin had come down at least twice a day, often three times, to bring them food and fresh water. By his calculations, that made well over a hundred visits. In all that time, Martin had never once looked directly at Walter or any of the children. Like a jury never looking directly at a person they were about to convict. It was the one thing, more than any other, that convinced Walter Demming that they had been condemned to death.

"'Cult' is a term outsiders use to denigrate a religious group they see as unsanctioned and extremist. But cult insiders see themselves as defenders of the one true faith and disciples of the only prophet who has a direct line to eternity."
Molly Cates, "Texas Cult Culture,"
LONE STAR MONTHLY, DECEMBER 1993

CHAPTER FIVE

The address for Jacob Alesky turned out to be Piney Haven, a trailer park off Barton Springs Road. The park had often caught Molly's attention as she drove by because it was a pocket of rural Americana from the sleepy fifties deposited right in the middle of growth-spurt Austin of the nineties. On a busy, commercial strip, flanked by trendy bars and restaurants, Piney Haven possessed an otherworldly aura of dappled light and seedy charm. An unpaved road wound through tall pecans and pines that sheltered rows of trailers which looked permanently settled into the landscape. Today, in the ninety-degree heat, the shade looked particularly cool and inviting.

She stopped at the ramshackle office and went in. A girl of around twelve was sitting on the desk reading a comic book. Her lips moved as she read.

"Hi," Molly said. "Could you tell me where Jacob Alesky lives?"

The girl didn't look up. "Like you was going, all the way back. Second from the end, green awning."

"Is he in?"

The girl looked up. "Prob'ly. He don't go out much these days." She went back to her reading. Molly thought about asking why Jacob Alesky didn't go out much anymore, but decided to let that information reveal itself. This was the sort of environment that encouraged you to relax and go with the flow.

She drove to the end of the road, admiring a cluster of vintage Airstream trailers. There was something about them that had always appealed to her—the friendly, rounded contours, the stain-less-steel luster. It made her feel nostalgic for softer, gentler times in the same way that juke-boxes and Chevy trucks from the fifties did. Like most nostalgia, she thought, it was a longing for something she'd never known.

She pulled up next to a long cream-colored trailer with a green-and-white-striped awning stretching the length of it. Under the awning, three lawn chairs and a hibachi sat on a stone terrace. Molly crossed the terrace to the door, which was propped open. She tried to peer inside, but it was too dusky for her to see anything. "Mr. Alesky," she called up into the trailer. "Are you there?"

"Who wants to know?" The deep male voice sounded prickly.

"Molly Cates wants to know. I'm from *Lone Star Monthly* magazine, Mr. Alesky. I would have called, but I couldn't find a number for you."

"That's because I don't have a number."

She glanced up at the telephone line that ran from a nearby pole to the end of the trailer and said nothing. She expected him to appear in the doorway, but nothing happened. After a long minute, she called, "Could I talk to you please, Mr. Alesky?"

"About what?"

"I hate to shout. Could you come to the door?"

She was answered with silence.

A black cat, long-haired and huge, appeared from under the trailer. It stretched and sauntered toward her. Its fur was matted and full of sticker burrs. The cat rammed its head into Molly's shin and dragged its long bedraggled body against her. Reluctantly, she squatted down and scratched it under the chin. She didn't much like cats and found this one particularly unappealing. But it was an old reporter's trick: paying attention to people's children and animals was a good way to ingratiate yourself, so she gave the beast a good scratch.

Then she glanced at the trailer door to see if she had an audience. She did. A man in a wheelchair sat there looking down at her. "Handsome cat, huh?" he said, watching her closely.

"Affectionate, anyway."

"Affectionate, yes," the man said. "He belongs to my neighbors, who aren't affectionate and who tend to forget they have a cat."

"I'm Molly Cates."

"So you said."

"Are you Jacob Alesky?"

"What remains of him." He answered with a wave of his right arm. "At your service, ma'am."

Molly's first impulse was to look away, avert her head, but she forced herself to look directly at him. He seemed to be little more than a torso propped up in the wheelchair. The doorway where he sat was in deep shadow and there was a jumble of drapery involved in his pinned-up pant legs, so she wasn't sure exactly what was there and what wasn't. There seemed to be the stump of a left thigh sticking out, but mostly he was a long torso with dangling arms. "Mr. Alesky, if this is a convenient time, I'd like to talk to you about Walter Demming."

"How did you know about me?"

"From a person who works at my magazine. She knows someone who lives here, and he told her you're an old friend of Demming's. She told me because I'm planning to write something about the Jezreel situation."

"Well," Alesky said, "the FBI found me the first week. It's taken the press somewhat longer. I figured you would eventually since Walter has become something of a celebrity." He laughed, the deep laugh of a whole man, which took her by surprise. "An unwilling celebrity, for sure. Miss Cates, you can't know how funny this is. There was never a less likely candidate for fame than Walter Demming."

"Why is that?"

"Walter took vows. When we got back from

'Nam. One of them was obscurity and another was no entanglements. He lived without a phone for twenty years. I bet he's sorry now he got one."

"Why?"

"Because phones tend to suck you into the world. He got one when he started driving the bus so they could reach him for schedule changes. And now it's gotten him into what he hated most."

"What's that?"

"Contention and violence." There was an edge to his voice. "What sort of world is it where what you try hardest to avoid is exactly what hunts you down?"

He laughed again. "I'd tell you his other vows, but I don't know you well enough."

"We could correct that situation." Molly pointed to the lawn chairs. "I could sit down, and we could drink a beer. I have a six-pack of Coors Light in a cooler in my truck. Will you join me?"

"No Shiner Bock?"

"Sorry."

He tilted his head to the side. "Okay. A beer sounds good right now. I'll come down. We'll sit on the veranda." He stretched out the word "veranda" to make it sound southern and very grand.

Molly looked at the three steps descending from the trailer door to the ground, then back at the wheelchair. She had no idea how he was going to get down.

"Don't worry about it," Alesky said. "You get the beer and I'll be right there." The wheelchair disappeared from the doorway.

Molly walked back to the truck and pulled her red Igloo out of the back seat. When she turned around, Alesky and his wheelchair were descending as if by magic on a platform she hadn't noticed to the side of the door. With a whir it lowered him to the terrace. He wheeled his chair off, came to a stop next to one of the three lawn chairs, and turned to watch her approach. With a frankly appraising gaze, he studied her hips as she moved.

She stared right back at him. He must have been a tall man, for his torso and arms were long and lanky. If his legs had matched he would have been well over six feet. His face was pitted across the forehead and along the cheeks with what looked like old acne scars and his gangly red neck was inflamed with active boil-like lumps, like a teenager's, though he was probably close to fifty. His nose was scimitar-shaped, off center and lumpy, as if it had been broken many times. His hair was just a fringe of coarse dark spikes.

"So what do you think?" he asked.

Molly sat down in the chair closest to him. She set the cooler at her feet and leaned down to open it. "I think we've got us a fine evening for sitting here in the shade and drinking a beer."

"I mean what do you think about me–the physical me?"

Molly pulled a sleek silver can of Coors out of the ice and popped the top. As she handed it to him, she looked directly into his face. Shaded by long dark lashes, his eyes were hazel. They challenged her for an answer. "I think there's more of you remaining here than got left behind," she replied.

He put the can to his lips and tipped his head back to drink. His Adam's apple bobbed as he drank. When he lowered the can, he said, "Just what is it that got left behind, do you think?"

"Well, I don't know." She looked into the fine hazel eyes. "All I can see is that there's a lot left."

"The glass-is-half-full shit." He said it pleasantly.

"Not really. I'm not that positive. It's just that I keep getting surprised by loss. I see disasters happen–to me, to other people–and I think, well, that's the end, all is lost. But then people survive and go on, and I see how much remains."

"That remains to be seen," he said with a smile.

"Mr. Alesky, could I ask you about–"

"Jake. My name is Jake."

"Jake. Good. And I'm Molly." She reached down into her bag for her notebook and laid it on her lap.

"Molly." He looked at her, nodding his head in approval. "I like that–Molly."

She thought Jake Alesky was a man who really enjoyed women and she hoped fervently that there were some women who enjoyed him back. "You and Walter Demming go way back–to Vietnam, my friend says."

He nodded. "Ancient history. If you think I'm planning to tell you anything about that, just because you brought this beer"–he held up his beer can–"you're mistaken. Why should I tell you anything about Walter? He's a real private person."

"Not anymore he's not. He was in the wrong place at the wrong time and now he's, like you said, a celebrity, even if he is an unwilling one. He's public property, and since I'm going to write something about him, it might as well be accurate. This is a chance for you to tell it straight."

He didn't answer right away. He took a long swig of his beer and kept his eyes on the cat, who had leaped up on a stump and was grooming a paw. Then he said, "Maybe. Maybe I'll tell you about him. But first, is there anything you want to ask me, something about me, before we move to Walter? Let's play a game: You get to ask me one free question and I have to answer it. Then I get to ask you one and you have to answer it."

"Jake, I don't–"

He held up a hand to stop her. "That's my fee. You want me to help you, tell you things you can write in your story. If you want to hear about Walter, you need to play the game." He pointed at the notebook resting on her lap. "But your question can't be anything that's on your notepad, like how him and me got to be friends, or whether he has a lady love. It's got to be something personal about me. And something real, something that you are sitting there wondering about."

Molly sat back and took a sip of her beer, letting it slide down slow to give her courage. He was flirting with her and in spite of everything she found it interesting. "Okay," she said. "Do I go first?"

He nodded.

"Okay," she repeated. "Okay. When you lose part of your body, like a leg, do you dream of yourself as you used to be or as you are now?"

He lowered his head and sat silent for a full minute. It was a long minute and Molly wanted to bite her tongue off. She had gone with the first impulse, what came to mind uncensored, and she had hurt him.

Finally he lifted his head. "What a fine question. I had to think about it. I dream of myself as I am now, Molly, but with a difference. A big difference. In my dreams I have no legs, but I can do things, remarkable things, that I couldn't do before. I can fly and I can do flips in the air, and I can stuff a basketball and slip through small spaces with total grace and ease." He had been looking off into space as he spoke, but now he looked Molly in the eye. "And I can fuck all night long. Anything else you want to ask me?"

She shook her head. "Now it's your turn."

He studied her, narrowing his eyes. "Okay. Here's what I want to know. When you see how this freak Mordecai gets off on publicity, don't you feel a little…sick at your stomach writing about him, giving him more of what he wants, like maybe you're encouraging him?"

It was a question that had haunted Molly throughout her long crime-writing career.

"Let me back up a little," she said. "Two years ago, after Waco, I wrote a piece on other apocalyptic cults in Texas. Samuel Mordecai was one of the cult leaders I interviewed. I chose to write about that because I've always been interested in obsession and I wanted to know what leads a person to believe something so extreme that he's willing to live and die for it. Anyway, once I got into it, I hated it. I hated him, Samuel Mordecai, and the whole crazy thing he believes in. And, beyond that, I got this crawly, unclean feeling about what was going on there in Jezreel. So in answer to your question, yes, I do worry about giving him the publicity he craves."

"So why are you writing about it again if you hated it the first time?"

"Well, *I* haven't taken a vow of obscurity. My boss thinks this will be a big story for me, so I'm doing it. Also, I am obsessed by…obsession, I guess. I don't know why."

He made a low sound of comprehension in his throat. "That sounds like an honest answer. Let me cheat here and ask a follow-up: Since you've met this guy Mordecai, you must have a feel for what's going to happen. What do you think about their chances–Walter and the kids?"

Molly felt her throat constrict; she hated to give voice to the fears that had been simmering below the surface. "I don't know. I don't know, Jake, but I'm scared. Samuel Mordecai is this…well, he's the sort of man who if he predicts the world is going to end on April fourteenth, he's not going to just sit around and watch the day pass by uneventfully and say, 'Oops, I was wrong, sorry.' *That* is just not going to happen."

Jake nodded. "But he can't make the world end, now can he?"

She shrugged.

"Oh, my. That crazy man made one hell of an impression on you, lady."

"Molly," she said.

"Molly. That crazy man made one hell of an impression on you, Molly."

"Yes. He did. He scared the shit out of me."

Jake finished his beer with a long swig, then looked down at the cooler.

"How about a beer?" she said.

"Don't mind if I do."

Molly took his empty can from his hand and replaced it with a cold one from the cooler.

"Thanks. I've been short on groceries," he said. "What do you know about Walter?"

She tossed the empty can into the cooler and closed it. "Nothing. I know what he looks like, in a newspaper photo anyway. I know he's a Vietnam veteran, he grew up in Beaumont, played football, went to Rice for two years, drives a school bus now, does some gardening. That's it." She took a long sip of her drink. "Tell me about him."

Jake looked down at his beer can for several seconds. "It's much harder to tell what someone's like when you know them real well than when you just know them a little. Ever notice that?"

"Yes. I think it's because you know all the exceptions and complexities, so it's hard to summarize. Would it help if I asked questions?"

"Well, ask a few easy ones to get me going, and we'll see."

"How did he feel about the Vietnam War?"

Jake laughed. "If that's an easy one, I'm scared about when we get to the hard stuff. How did he feel about the war? Well, Walter got to Vietnam snorting and pawing the ground. You should have seen him–this beefy, loud high school jock–a real John Wayne, the American warrior. You know. The kind that had a crew cut even before the army did it to him. Couldn't wait to show his stuff, be a real hero."

He let his eyes wander off into the dappled shade. When he brought them back into focus, he said, "Eleven months later, well, my Lord, he looked like the ghost of that warrior, and I looked like this." He glanced down at where his legs should have been. "And I believe the change in him was more dramatic than the change in me. But to answer your question, Walter started out thinking the war was necessary to teach the Commies a lesson, keep them in their place. But he ended up being the one who learned the lesson."

"What was the lesson?"

"Well, Molly, it isn't always easy to summarize these things, is it?"

"No, it certainly isn't."

"I'll try. At the Milwaukee Zoo–I'm from Milwaukee, did you know that?"

"No."

"Well, at the Milwaukee Zoo, where I used to hang out when I was a kid, in the primate house, there's a sign on a cage that says: "the most dangerous animal in the world.' When you go over to look in, there's a mirror in the cage and you see yourself reflected."

Molly nodded. "Amen," she said.

He finished off his beer with a very long swig. "Yeah. And a twenty-year-old Texas boy may be the prime example of that species."

"And that's the lesson Walter Demming learned in Vietnam?"

"One of them."

"What happened to teach him that lesson?"

He held the beer can up in his right hand and with a single squeeze crumpled it into a ball as easily as if it were a piece of paper. "*That* I'm not going to talk about," he said in a quiet voice. "So don't bother asking again."

Molly found herself making a mental note, in boldface, to do just that–ask again. When people said they absolutely would not talk about a certain subject, they usually came around to talking about it at great length. "All right," she said. "Something I was wondering about–Walter went to Rice for two years, so he must have been a good student. How come he ended up driving a bus?"

"That question disappoints me, Molly," Jake said. "It suggests a conventional turn of mind that defines a person by what he does to make a living. Anyway, he hasn't "ended up' yet–not unless as we speak he's dead."

Molly studied the man sitting next to her with renewed respect. "I agree. It is a disappointing question. I could defend myself by saying I write for an audience made up of a bunch of yuppies and they will be wondering about that. Of course I would never use that as an excuse." She smiled at him. "But I wish you'd answer the question even though it is obnoxious."

"Okay. You might say by way of explanation that after Vietnam, Walter dropped out."

"He dropped out?"

"Yeah. And in Walter's case dropping out was major, a crash, like falling from the sky and landing splat on your head. Yeah, he dropped out with a vengeance. Driving a bus is what he does to make money. It's not what he does."

"What's the real thing he does?"

"Well"–he looked at her for a moment as if he were considering something–"I could show you.

I think you'd find it interesting. But we'd have to drive out to his house."

Molly found her pulse quickening. "I'd like to." She kept her voice even.

"I have a key. I need to check on things anyway. Miss Shea is keeping an eye on the house, but I'd like to check."

"When would you like to go?"

"How about now?"

Molly checked her watch. "Oh. I can't. I have a date with my daughter in a half hour, and a telephone interview scheduled after that. Could we do it tomorrow?"

"Sure." He sounded disappointed and Molly was tempted to change her plans, but Jo Beth would be on her way already, and the phone interview with Dr. Asquith was important.

"I'm planning to drive to Elgin in the morning," she said. "How about late afternoon? I could pick you up around four."

"I'll be here," he said.

She dropped the two empty beer cans back in the cooler and closed it. "You haven't told me the other vows that Walter took."

"Let's save them for tomorrow."

"Okay." She picked up the cooler and was about to turn away when she added, "You said you were short on groceries, Jake. Tomorrow's my shopping day. Are there some things I could pick up for you?"

He looked up at her with interest. "That's a nice offer, but could we stop at a store on the way home from Walter's? Then I could do my own shopping."

She wondered how the logistics of his getting around would work. "Sure."

"And don't worry. I can get in and out on my own. I'll just need you to help with the chair."

"Okay. See you tomorrow." She turned and walked toward the truck.

"Oh, Molly," he called out, "maybe you could leave that cooler with me till tomorrow."

She took the cooler back to him, wondering if your tolerance for alcohol was lower if you had no legs.

"Set it down there on the chair, please, so I can reach it," Jake told her. "Like you said, it sure is one fine evening to sit out here in the shade and drink a beer or two."

The music seemed louder than usual and the pace faster. "Down and up," Michelle bellowed from the platform in front as she demonstrated proper squat form with her hands on her narrow hips. "Squeeze it all the way up. Imagine you're picking bluebonnets with your glutes. Down, grab it with your behind, and pull it up by the roots. Don't let your knees get past your toes. Lower it, squeeze it up. Again. *Again.*"

"Picking bluebonnets with your glutes!" Molly Cates said to her daughter. "It's illegal to pick bluebonnets–with any part of your anatomy."

"Gross," said Jo Beth Traynor, "but I wonder if it could be done. We could try. You know how people go out and take photographs of their children in the bluebonnets? Maybe–"

"Okay, feet parallel now," Michelle yelled over the thrum of the music. Glutes back and down, way down, and squeeze it up. Pick those blue-bonnets!"

Molly watched herself in the mirrored wall. It was the one time you could stare at yourself in a mirror for an hour and not feel like a total narcissist. You were supposed to use the mirror to keep checking out your form on the exercises. Over the two years she and Jo Beth had been doing this class, Molly had been watching with pleasure as her upper arms took on shape and firmness. Push-ups paying off. It wasn't hard to see why people enjoyed bodybuilding.

"Okay," Michelle yelled, "now add a pelvic thrust to it. Squat down, thrust forward, and pull-l-l up."

Molly smiled at herself in the mirror; it sure did look ridiculous. Was the fight against gravity worth this indignity?

She looked at Michelle's perfect, tanned, and muscled forty-seven-year-old legs in the orange Day-Glow very-short shorts and decided it was. Surely human vanity was one of the strongest forces in the world.

"So, Mom," Jo Beth said, "are you going to go out there to Jezreel and hang out with the barbarian hordes of reporters?"

"Definitely not. I can see it better on television."

"Dad seems really down about it. Frustrated like I've never seen him."

"Yeah, he does." Molly thought about the last time she'd seen Grady Traynor, her ex-husband and current lover. Five days ago, when he'd had a rare day off. Grady'd been stressed, angry, and exhausted. A homicide lieutenant with the Austin police, for the past six weeks he'd been on a team consulting with the FBI agents who were camped out in Jezreel trying to negotiate the release of Walter Demming and the eleven children. As the longtime head of APD's hostage-negotiating team, Grady Traynor was considered skilled and experienced in the field, but nothing had prepared him for Samuel Mordecai. In the long weeks of negotiations, they had gotten zero concessions.

"And, Mom," Jo Beth said over the throbbing music, "he's worried about leaving Copper alone so much while he's still just getting adjusted."

"Oh, God. That dog."

"Mom, he's a retired public servant." Jo Beth's eyes shone with mirth.

"He's a vicious cur, a drooling, crazed sociopath. I don't understand this. Your father has never showed the slightest interest in dogs and now in mid-life he takes on this demented beast."

"Mom, he was a hero, and they were going to kill him."

"I know, honey, but–"

"Yeah, he's developed some bad habits. So he deserves a bullet in the brain? Well, I think it's wonderful of Dad to rescue Copper and I'd really like to help, but Java and Luna have major problems with him."

"Of course they do. They're sane dogs, basically. A bit rambunctious, but–"

Michelle yelled, "Get down into those legs now, *lower!* Quads parallel to the floor."

Jo Beth bent her legs lower. "Dad was really hoping you might help out since you have that nice safe side yard and you're at home working and you could—"

"No. Jo Beth, this is unfair. I do not want a dog, any dog, but I particularly do not want *that* dog. And I really don't understand why your father committed to this."

Jo Beth smiled an indulgent smile. "Well, Mom, consider this theory of mine: Maybe Dad's trying to build a family unit and he thinks this might help knit you together."

"Whaaat?" Molly was stunned—on several levels. She didn't know where to start in refuting this wild theory. "Jo Beth, that's crazy. First of all, he doesn't want anything of the sort. Second, if he did want that, the last thing that would work is to bring a vicious attack dog into the equation. And third, he knows that, after three failed attempts at matrimony and domesticity, I've renounced both. He knows that. I will never set up housekeeping again. Not with a man. And not with a dog. Never."

"Never? If I'm remembering correctly, that's what you said last week about writing about Jezreel."

"That's different. I have to earn a living. My boss gave me an assignment and helped me to see that it makes sense for me to do it. And now that I am, I find myself getting into it. It's going to be okay."

"Well, I think the same thing would happen with Copper. He'd be fine with a little—"

"No!"

From the front of the room, Michelle was shouting out, "All right, let's go to the floor! Push-up time!"

102

Molly and Jo Beth both arranged towels on the floor and got down on their hands and knees.

"Knees apart, abs in tight, backs straight. Let's do thirty for starters," the instructor yelled over the pounding beat of salsa played in an aerobic tempo.

"Oh, God," Molly panted after three, "will this ever get any easier? And is it worth it?"

"The ultimate eschatological questions," Jo Beth said, pushing up and down with ease. "You can ask that apocalyptic radio preacher you're going to talk to later–will there be push-ups in the millennium or will all true believers have muscles given unto them without labor or sweat?"

"I'll ask him," Molly retorted. "And how about this one: Do we get new bodies when we're resurrected, or do we have to keep the same old flabby ones?"

"Well, Mom, I know this: If the world is ending in five days and we're going to get new bodies, I'd rather go out for pizza than do this crap."

"Yeah." Molly was panting so hard she could barely speak. "If he says no push-ups for believers, I'll convert on the spot."

The twangy redneck drawl over the phone immediately suggested to Molly a physical type: lean and spare, thin-lipped, squinch-eyed, and balding. "Ah am jet-lagged something awful, Miz Cates. This is not a real good time to talk. It may only be nine o'clock in Texas, but it's two A.M. in Jerusalem and mah body thinks it's still on Holy Land time and ah cain't keep mah eyes open."

"Dr. Asquith, I wouldn't bother you now

except that there's so little time left in this Jezreel matter and Addie Dodgin feels you have some important insights into Samuel Mordecai's theology."

"Any dang thing I might know about Mr. D. R. Grimes is strictly coincidental and against mah will. Miz Cates, just what is your interest in this matter?"

"I'm writing an article about Samuel Mordecai for the publication I work for and–"

"What publication is that?"

In her darkened office, Molly stretched out on the love seat. She'd been hoping he wouldn't ask. *"Lone Star Monthly."*

There was a silence, as though she'd said *Whips and Bondage.*

"Adeline didn't tell me that. You aren't the same person who wrote that story about two years back, are you?"

Molly closed her eyes. "I've written lots of stories."

"I mean that one on cults in Texas that believe in the Apocalypse."

"Yes, I did write that article."

"Well, I have to tell you, Miz Cates, as a rule I try not to argue with or insult ladies, because I honor y'all, but in my opinion, that was a sorry piece of work—un-fair, un-godly, and un-forgivable."

"In what way was it unfair, Dr. Asquith?" Molly kept her voice even.

"You made it sound like anyone who believes in biblical prophecy and the coming Apocalypse is some crazy prevert like Donnie Ray Grimes."

"That surely was not my intention, Dr.

Asquith. In the first paragraph of that article, I define the difference between a cult and a group of believers who might have a similar eschatology. I would be pleased to discuss it with you and hear your viewpoint."

"Well, that might be fruitful. I'm coming to Austin tomorrow to have a powwow with the FBI. Late afternoon. Maybe we could talk after that."

"Yes, I'd like to. What time are you likely to be finished?"

"Shall we say seven o'clock? The bar at Houston's on Spicewood Springs. How about that, ma'am?"

"That's fine. Dr. Asquith, before you go, could you tell me something about the Rapture of Mordecai?"

"Oh, were you listening to my radio show?"

"No."

"I just finished doing it live and it's carried in the Austin area, so I thought you might have. How do you know about the Rapture of Mordecai?"

"A little from my interview with him and a little from Addie Dodgin."

"Oh, Adeline…Well, I decided that I'd kept silent too long about the Jezreelites' Satan-inspired false theology. It gives prophecy a bad name."

"So you talked about that on the radio?"

"Yes, ma'am. I decided if I can tell it to the Federal Bureau of Investigation, I can tell it to the faithful."

"How do you know about this rapture business, Dr. Asquith? No one else has mentioned it."

"Like ah said. Coincidence. Accident. I made a real mistake back some seven years ago. At the

Southwest Prophecy Conference, I ran into a young man who looked like an angel come down to earth. We got friendly and one night we got ourselves inebriated. See, I don't indulge in spirits much and it's a dangerous thing when I do. Same with him, I think. His tongue was loosened up and he told me this outlandish tale about him being the Prophet Mordecai who would help jump-start the Apocalypse."

"What was the tale?"

"Oh, it's a long story. I'll tell you tomorrow when we meet. I have got to–"

"Would you just give me a summary of it now? A quick and dirty version."

He laughed. "Quick and dirty, yes, ma'am. It's an oral tradition–started during the 1830s, which you probably know was a time of great growth of sectarian invention in this country. A man named Saul Mordecai had a vision on his way to Texas–what he calls a rapture. God told Saul Mordecai he was a prophet who was to start the Apocalypse by establishing a Mordecai line. Not by giving birth, but by choosing the next prophet and telling him about this rapture he'd had and passing on what they call the Heaven in Earth Vatic Gospel of the Jezreelite–a real mouthful, huh? And heretical all the way. It was to get fulfilled in the fifth generation, and that, of course, is our current reigning Prophet Grimes, who believes he's the Messiah. It's a long, wild tale, but it has to do with fifty perfect saints of the Apocalypse and earth purification. And that's really all I know. See you tomorrow evening, Miz Cates."

Before he could get away, she said, "Dr. Asquith,

you disagree with Samuel Mordecai about this human-agency issue, but what about the rest of what he says? About the Apocalypse. Do you believe it's coming soon?"

He chuckled. "Of course. You obviously haven't read my books or my newsletters or seen my TV show. That's my message, my lifework. It's coming before the end of this millennium, within the next five years. And the strangest thing, Miz Cates, since I got back from the Holy Land last night, I've had this feeling that it's here, that it's all winding down right now. Can't you just hear it and feel it?"

"No, I can't. Describe it for me, so I can understand."

"Well, it feels like a wind blowing me toward God."

After she put the phone down, Molly shook her head and murmured into the darkness, "It's just jet lag."

"Then another sign appeared in heaven: an enormous red dragon with seven heads and ten horns and seven crowns on his heads. His tail swept a third of the stars out of the sky and flung them to the earth."

REVELATION 12:1-4

CHAPTER SIX

The house was one of those stark, tan-brick rectangles you find on the outskirts of small Texas towns. It looked like it had been made on a factory assembly line and then installed on a vacant lot that had been scraped clear of all debris. To finish it off, some toxic substance must have been sprinkled on the ground around it to ensure that nothing would grow within twenty yards—no trees, no grass, no flowers, no weeds—just dust and rocks.

Molly was ten minutes early, so she passed the place by and drove on to McDonald's. The drive to Elgin had been quicker than she had figured, and from her several phone conversations with Dorothy Huff the night before, she had gotten the impression of an elderly woman who would not like people to arrive early—or late—or maybe at all.

Once at the McDonald's drive-through window, she felt a powerful urge to order an Egg McMuffin, but managed to fight it back by reminding herself that she had already eaten breakfast and that her favorite jeans had been so hard to zip up that she'd peeled them off and worn sweatpants instead. She ordered a large coffee and sipped it sitting in her truck in the parking lot with the air conditioning going full-blast.

The night before, Molly had decided to act right away on Thelma Bassett's request. She would go see Dorothy Huff, the grandmother who had raised Donnie Ray Grimes to manhood. It was not easy to arrange. When she had called, Mrs. Huff had said she had never talked to a reporter and wasn't about to start. She had talked to the FBI, but that was her duty as a God-fearing citizen. She had washed her hands of Donnie Ray Grimes, or whatever name he chose to call himself. Anyway, she was feeling too poorly for any of this. You would think, she'd said, that people would be kind enough to leave a sick old lady alone. Then she had hung up. This was exactly the sort of rebuff that spurred Molly on. She had called Thelma Bassett and asked her to call Mrs. Huff and assure the woman that Molly was not a reporter, but a consultant who was helping Thelma to learn more about Samuel Mordecai so she might know what to say to him, when her chance came. Thelma had done this and added that since Mrs. Huff had been so gracious as to offer her help this was what she could do to help—talk to Molly. Dorothy Huff was no pushover, though; her answer was still no—until Molly promised never to write a word about Mrs. Huff. Molly also had to promise that the interview would not be stressful.

Molly leaned out of the truck to dump the undrunk half of her coffee in the gutter. How would it be possible to talk about Samuel Mordecai without it being stressful to the woman who'd raised him? she wondered.

At ten exactly she rang Dorothy Huff's door-bell. The gaunt, gray-haired woman who answered the door started speaking immediately, with no greeting or preamble. "Since you've drove all the way from Austin, I'm gonna try to get through this, but I don't know. I just don't rightly know if I'm up to it." Her words were directed several feet to the left of where Molly was standing. "Some days is worse than others." She turned and shuffled in her brown carpet slippers across the sparsely furnished living room. "The knees is just as bad as the sacroiliac today. I knowed from when I first opened my eyes before the sun come up and the pain started in so horrible I tell ya most people couldn't take it. I never should've gotten out of that bed. Anyone in their right mind, sick as I am, would've just laid there. But then the good Lord knows not everyone does their Christian duty in this world. I told that poor Mrs. Bassett I wanted to help her and she asked me to talk to you, so talk I will. I never been one to baby myself. Never had that luxury. No, ma'am. Always had too much work to get done, keeping a clean and Christian household." She stopped near a bulky gold velveteen recliner that faced a television set with a 35-inch screen. "Oh, there it is, hitting me bad— the arthritis, in both knees. Ow, Jesus. All this stress" —she waved a hand in Molly's direction— "makes it worse'n usual." She dropped into the recliner with a *ploof* sound. "Might as well take the load off, huh, Mrs...."

"Cates," Molly said. "Molly Cates." The stench of stale smoke and old cigarette butts, only slightly masked by Lysol spray, filled her nostrils, but when

Molly glanced around there was no sign of an ashtray or a cigarette pack, or even a lighter. A secret smoker. "Thank you for talking to me, Mrs. Huff. I sure am sorry to hear you're feeling poorly."

"Well, it's not like that's your headline news. Been going on a long time now, long as I can remember. But in this life you just have to take what the good Lord shovels onto you. Nothing for it but to grin and bear it." To demonstrate her fortitude, she grinned in Molly's direction. Then she relaxed in the chair and her thin lips snapped back to a pursed, sour position.

Molly fought off a sudden impulse to run to her truck and drive away. Everything about this house and this woman made her want to bolt. But Dorothy Huff, however unappealing, was surely going through hell. Molly had recently read an article by the father of a serial killer. He had written that when you're a parent, you think the worst thing in the world is to get a call in the middle of the night saying that your child has been murdered by a madman. He had learned, to his everlasting anguish, that there was something even worse. Samuel Mordecai's grandmother, the woman who had reared him, must be experiencing some of that now.

Molly looked around for a place to sit. The only option was a hard-looking brown vinyl sofa pushed against the wall. She sat on the end and said with total sincerity, "This sure must be a difficult time for you."

For the first time, Mrs. Huff looked directly at Molly. Her thin, horsey face was scored with cruel ruts that all slanted downward. "Well, honey, you

111

just don't know what difficult is. You raise up a boy best you can, teach him to be a good Christian God-fearing boy, and then something like this happens and people say behind your back, well, it must be that Dorothy Huff didn't raise him up right for him to go and do a thing like that." Her mouth tightened up so hard that her lips whitened. "Even though the boy is no blood kin of yours, and you never asked to get saddled with him."

"Mrs. Huff," Molly said, "I think most parents who have children over the age of ten understand that anything can happen when you are raising a child. There are so many influences that are outside your control."

The old woman's mouth relaxed a fraction. "Well, ain't that the truth?"

"It was so kind of you to call Thelma Bassett, Mrs. Huff. It meant a lot to her. She's a fine woman and she needs some help right now. She thinks she might get a chance to talk to…Donnie Ray. You still call him Donnie Ray?"

Mrs. Huff nodded. "When I call him anything."

"She wants to know what she might say to him that would persuade him to release the children. She thinks that maybe his being adopted might figure some way in this situation."

Dorothy Huff looked hard at Molly. "Before this goes any farther, we need to get something real clear. You know I don't talk to no newspaper or TV people or none of that kind."

"Yes, you told me on the phone. And I appreciate your—"

"Hold on, missy." She raised a bony, yellowed palm to Molly. "Just hold on with all your appreciates and such. Let's get one thing clear. You promised not to talk of this to anyone but Mrs. Bassett. I mean to no one. You clear on that?"

Molly felt bruised by the woman's bullying manner. "Yes, if that's what you want."

Dorothy Huff slapped her hands down hard on the arms of her chair. "If that's what I *want?* It's not a matter of wanting, missy. You break that promise and I'm dead, Mrs. Cates. And you, too, most likely."

"Dead?"

"Yes, ma'am, you put in the newspaper I said any of this, and I'm deader than Saturday's meat loaf."

Molly felt the force of the woman's certainty and her fear. "Who would kill you?"

"I thought you knew something about cults, Mrs. Writer Woman."

"I know something about them," Molly said.

"Then you should know that this group Donnie Ray's got hisself involved in don't cotton to people talking about their business. Ain't you wondered why there are no ex-members coming forward to tell about the group?"

Molly felt a flush of heat. She had indeed wondered about it. Two years ago when she was writing the cult article, she had searched for former Hearth Jezreelites who would talk about Samuel Mordecai and what really went on behind the fences at Jezreel. She had gotten one or two leads, but never found a willing talker at the end of those leads. And the FBI intelligence gatherers were having the same problem now.

"Like Annette." The old woman shook her

113

head. "You think she'd ever say word one about what life was like there or why she run off?"

"Annette? You mean Donnie Ray's wife— Annette Grimes?"

"Who else? Pretty little Annette."

"She isn't inside the compound?" Molly was stunned.

"Nope. She was smart. Run off while she could. Months ago. Sent me a postcard saying goodbye and thanking me for being nice to her. I was nice to her, too, always liked Annette. Too good for Donnie Ray, if you ask me."

"Where is Annette now?"

Dorothy Huff gave a snort that might have been an incipient laugh. "Who knows? She's no dummy. I suppose the Sword Hand of God might have tracked her and she's dead now."

"Sword Hand of God? Is that what he calls cult members on the outside?"

"Yes. They don't want to have all their eggs in one basket."

"Where are they, Mrs. Huff, and what do they do?"

"They're all over, probably some back in Austin where you come from. Probably some around here. They work outside and send their paychecks home to Jezreel. The main thing they do is make sure that members who get fed up and leave never talk about it." She took her index finger and slashed it across her throat.

"How do you know this?"

"I used to visit Donnie Ray and Annette at Jezreel. Back before it got to be too much for me. I heard talk."

"Why did Annette leave?"

"She just said she had to go and could never get in touch with me again, and she hoped I'd understand. And I do. I hope you do, too, Mrs. Cates."

"Yes, Mrs. Huff, I do. Nothing you tell me will go beyond me and Mrs. Bassett. I promise."

Dorothy Huff relaxed her head back onto the chair. "Well, all right, then."

"Is it true that Donnie Ray was adopted by your daughter?" Molly asked.

"Sure is. Just like I told poor Mrs. Bassett when I phoned her up."

"I'm wondering why you didn't tell anyone this before."

"Oh, mercy. Evelyn—that's my daughter—back then she didn't want people to know she couldn't have a baby on her own. Made her feel less womanly, I guess. So she went away to Austin and come back in a coupla months with this baby and claimed she had him there. I just went along with her story and it got to be a habit, I guess. We never talked about it, and no one asked."

"You didn't tell the FBI when they came to see you?"

"No, ma'am. Never thought about it."

"Is Thelma the first person you've told?"

"I guess so. What happened was I saw her on the TV set, so sweet and alone, and I had this vision I should call her and explain it all. So I did. Like you say, anything can happen with children growing up nowadays and particularly when you really don't know where they come from, I mean where they got their blood from. They could come from any sort of trash heap or even from the criminal class, and I just wanted her to know that Donnie Ray wasn't really my own kin."

"Yes, I see. Evelyn adopted him in Austin?"

"That's what she said."

"She was married at the time, wasn't she?"

"Well, sure. Back then, weren't no adoption by unmarried people like happens now with preverts and all them trash kind of people adopting these innocent little babies. Isn't that just a crime, Mrs. Cates, them homosexuals adopting babies?" The woman stopped and looked at Molly, raising her eyebrows and tipping her chin up expectantly. Molly kept her face neutral and waited it out.

Mrs. Huff went on: "No, back then you had to be married and go for interviews and have some religious background. Evelyn was married to Jimmy Grimes." A grimace of disgust twisted her face. "That man was worthless. Him and Evelyn dropped the burden on me without so much as a by-your-leave. You see, they found it was work. Raising up children is work. You're all the time spooning food into them and cleaning it up as it mucks out of them. You have to put the fear of God almighty into them to keep them on a righteous path. Yes, ma'am, you have to teach them right from wrong, clean from unclean—all them things. It is righteous work, for sure."

For the first time since she had met Samuel Mordecai, Molly felt a pang of pity for him, or, rather, for Donnie Ray Grimes, the little boy who had had no choice but to depend on this woman. She had just a glimmer why someone would grow up longing for the world to end in fire and

116

catastrophe. "So Donnie Ray lived with you from then on?"

Dorothy Huff let her head drop back on the chair, as if the subject were too heavy to support. "Yes, ma'am. Never lived a day with his mama after that. And Donnie always said, 'I want to stay right here with you, Gramma. This is my home. You take such good care of me, Gramma. Don't let my mother have me.' Well, no danger of that. She never asked for him, not once, never wanted him. He lived here with me in this house until he got to be seventeen and then he run off on me. Hardly said goodbye, never finished grade school, even, never held a real job, left all his junk here."

"His father—Jimmy Grimes—he's been dead for some years, hasn't he?"

"Oh, a long time. He got himself killed shortly after he run off." She stuck out her lower lip as if that helped her to remember. "Got drunk and run his truck off the road. It was God's judgment. Jimmy Grimes pulled it down on hisself with both hands. Sure did. He ruined my daughter, never did live up to a obligation in all his life, that man."

"And your daughter? Evelyn?" Molly had read that Evelyn Huff Grimes had turned to prostitution and died of a drug overdose.

The woman sighed. "Well. Evelyn. She stayed out there in that Las Vegas. Never wrote or called, not on my birthday or Donnie Ray's neither. She…she got sick and died. Twelve years ago. You knew that, I reckon."

Molly nodded. "I read it. Did Donnie see much of her before she died?"

"Only once in all them years. He went out there to see her one time."

"To Las Vegas? When was that?"

"About four months before she died. When he was twenty-one. Just before he started in on all that preaching and apocalypsing business. I told him not to go, but he upped and hitched out there and he come back changed, I can tell you that—full of fury, brimstone. Had him a vision, he said, and God told him to change his name to Sam-u-el Mor-de-cai. And ever since then he's been apocalypsing and doing all them cult things you read about in the newspaper."

"It sounds like you don't hold with Donnie Ray's beliefs, Mrs. Huff."

"I'm a good Christian woman. I believe every precious word the Bible says. I believe that Jesus will return to earth to judge the wicked, but the Bible says no one can know the hour or the day, not even Donnie Ray Grimes, who now says he's Sam-u-el Mor-de-cai, thank you very much. My preacher says the boy don't hold to the Bible, he goes too far into his own imaginings—always did. His religion is more Donnie Ray Grimes than our Lord Jesus Christ."

"What advice can you give Mrs. Bassett? How can she make an appeal to him?"

Dorothy Huff shrugged. "Don't matter what she says. He don't listen, anyways."

"Mrs. Huff, what can you tell me about the adoption?"

The woman put a hand up to her cheek as if she'd just been slapped. "What do you mean?"

"Well, do you know who his birth parents

are? I'd like to locate them. I think it might be helpful."

"Birth parents?" She repeated it as if she were trying to figure out the meaning. "Oh, his real folks, you mean. No. I don't know nothing about that."

"Do you know where Evelyn adopted him?"

"I already told you. She went off to Austin."

"Yes, but where in Austin? Did she mention the name of an agency? Or was it maybe a private adoption from a lawyer?"

Dorothy Huff's bony hands tightened on the arms of the chair, as if it were about to be launched into space and she needed to hold on for dear life. The veins in the backs of her hands stuck out like black worms. "She never told me nothing about that. I guess she figured I was good enough to raise up this child but not to know where he come from. When I asked to know what sort of people he come from, she said nobody knowed."

"Nobody?"

"Nobody."

"But somebody would know," Molly said, thinking aloud. "The agency, or wherever she adopted him from, might not tell her, but they would know where he came from."

"She said he was abandoned."

"Abandoned?" Molly felt the stirring of interest like an electric buzz in her chest.

"That's what she said."

Molly was almost afraid to ask the next question because if the answer was no, then this could be a dead end. "Are there some papers about the adoption somewhere?"

Mrs. Huff set her mouth into its determined downward arc. "Papers. Haven't thought about those since Donnie Ray asked me the last time." She looked down at the threadbare blue rug.

Molly waited. But the woman kept her eyes downcast until Molly couldn't stand it anymore. "*Are* there some papers, Mrs. Huff? With dates and names? Something that might help us?"

She looked up and Molly was surprised to see tears in her faded blue eyes. "Mrs. Bassett said you'd be nice and kindly and not ask me hurtful things. This is all so hard to remember."

Molly leaned forward, following her instinct to close in tight to extract information. She did not like inflicting pain, but if she needed to, she would walk over this woman's body with hobnailed boots to find out what she needed to know. "Mrs. Huff, the last thing I want to do here is hurt you with my questions, but this might really help us help those children. Do you have any papers here that relate to Donnie Ray's adoption?"

Mrs. Huff crossed her arms over her bony chest. "Well, I might have."

Molly decided to back off and approach from a different direction. "You said Donnie had asked about the papers. Did he search?"

The grooves running from Dorothy Huff's nose to her downturned mouth deepened into valleys of bitterness. "Did he? He come to me when he was seventeen and he was getting all puffed up and big for his britches, you know the way they do, and he said he wanted to find out where he come from and would I help him. I was against it. For his own good, Mrs. Cates. For his own good.

I knew for sure it would lead noplace. And even if he did find something out, it would just be trash he'd find." She let out a huge sigh. "It sure beats me why you'd go to all that trouble to find someone who didn't never want you in the first place. I told him so. And I told him it sure did hurt me bad that he wanted to find some other family, that I wasn't good enough for him."

Molly said, "It seems to be a pretty common thing among people who are adopted—wanting to make some connection with birth parents."

"I reckon. I never seen him that het up. He wanted to find his mother in the worst way. Upset him bad when it happened just like I told him and he couldn't find nothing out."

"What happened?"

"Well, he went off to Austin and run into a brick wall. See, you have to be twenty-one to see your records. He fussed and carried on trying to get me to sign, and when Donnie gets to wanting something, I can tell you there ain't many in the world can stand up to him, but I did what was best for him. And turns out I was right."

There were so many questions Molly wanted to ask, she didn't know where to begin. "What was it he wanted you to sign?"

"Oh, so he could see his records. If the parent signs, someone under twenty-one can look at them records. Evelyn was out there in Las Vegas, so he wanted me to do it. But I wasn't the mother and hadn't never adopted him, so I don't think me signing would've worked anyway, but he sure wanted me to do that." She took a deep breath from having talked so fast. "He just had to wait to twenty-one and it didn't make no difference because when the time come, there was nothing to find out. Just like I told him." She said it with grim satisfaction.

"Nothing to find out?"

"The day that boy turned twenty-one, he went back to that state adoption place and he demanded his file. Of course, it didn't tell him nothing, really, just like I told him."

"Did you see that adoption file, Mrs. Huff?"

"Well, sure. They give him a copy. He come here waving it around and carrying on. He followed me around the house, getting me to read it to him. See, he don't read so good. He kept on pushing. He wanted to find his real mother in the worst way. But the record didn't give him nothing to go on. So he took it out on me. As if I had anything to do with it. See what happens, Mrs. Cates—you do the best you can and you get blamed for everything good you done."

"It does sound unfair for him to blame you," Molly said, desperate to keep her talking. "What information was in his file?"

"Well, not much. Like Evelyn said, he was left abandoned, just hours old when he was found, throwed out like a piece of garbage."

"What was the date?"

"It was 1962. August the third."

"Who found him?"

"Some man, just passing by the creek."

"The creek?"

"Waller Creek, down there near the university, in Austin. He was floating in the creek, just like

Moses, the man said. Moses. You ever heard anything like that?"

"Floating in the creek?" Molly heard herself repeating everything like an idiot, but each revelation stunned her so much she had to check she'd heard it right.

"In one of them Styrofoam beer cooler things. Don't that beat all? Moses in a beer cooler."

Molly wasn't sure whether she believed it or not, but her entire skin surface tingled. She needed to find out more about this, much more. But there was a problem looming: Adoption records in Texas were closed; nothing short of a court order could get you access through official channels. Her only hope was right here, to extract everything there was to get from this woman. She leaned forward. "Mrs. Huff, this is very important. Do you still have that adoption file?"

Dorothy Huff's face got hard as Mount Rushmore. "Maybe."

"I'd like to read it. It might help."

"Even if I had it, it wouldn't do you no good. If he couldn't find nothing, you couldn't neither."

"Not necessarily. One of the things I do in my work is research. I'm pretty good at it, but I need some information to start me off. Do you have it?"

She looked down at her old brown slippers. "He might've left it here with his other junk, but if he found out I showed it to you, he'd have me killed, his own granny."

"Mrs. Huff, I wouldn't show it to anyone else. I'd just use it as a starting point for my research."

The woman shook her head.

"Mrs. Huff, you told Mrs. Bassett you would do anything you could to help. Well, this is how you can help her." Molly made herself add, "And little Kimberly. Those children are what's important here, aren't they?"

"Well, yes, they surely are. But I don't see how this would help them."

Molly was afraid of this question, because she wasn't sure either. But she needed to answer it because she certainly did want that file. "Well, the negotiators who are talking to Donnie Ray are having trouble communicating with him. They've tried everything they know how to do to get him to give up those children. Now they are thinking of letting Thelma Bassett and maybe some of the other parents talk to him, try to get him to see he needs to let those children go before something awful happens. If we could locate his birth mother, maybe she could talk to him, too. We need to try this. Let me look at the file, Mrs. Huff. It might make a difference. Really." It was as close to begging as she liked to get.

Dorothy Huff set her mouth in its extreme downward arc again. Molly was sure she was going to say no. "Well," she said, "it don't surprise me none that those negotiators can't talk no sense into him. I never could neither. I reckon I could take a look, see if he left it with the rest of his junk, but it ain't gonna do you no good." She struggled up out of the chair. "Oh, lordy," she moaned, teetering on scrawny legs, "I should be in bed."

Molly reached out to take her elbow. "Let me help you."

"No, no." Mrs. Huff shook her hand off. "I ain't used to no help." She walked painfully to the door that led into a hallway. "I'll look, but I don't guarantee nothing." She disappeared into a room off the hall and softly closed the door.

Feeling edgy, Molly got to her feet. If Mrs. Huff couldn't or wouldn't find the file, this search might dead-end right here. She looked out the picture window to a small stockade-fenced backyard. There wasn't so much as a blade of grass or a weed growing from the dusty earth.

She switched her attention to the room. On a table under the picture window sat one object: an acrylic square for holding photographs. There was only one picture in it—a black-haired girl with a heart-shaped face and lovely blue eyes. Annette Grimes. Molly recognized her from news photos. There was no other decoration in the room. No pictures on the wall, no photographs of Donnie Ray as a child, no books, no newspapers, no magazines. Not even a Bible. Just a big television, a sofa, a table, and the gold recliner. A motel room had more warmth.

Molly turned when she heard the shuffling tread in the hall. To her delight, Dorothy Huff carried some papers in her hand.

"All that bending down and dust is real bad for me, but here it is, for what it's worth. I surely do hope you're a woman of your word." She stuck the thin stapled sheaf out in Molly's direction.

Molly felt like kissing the yellowed hand. "Thank you, Mrs. Huff. Thelma Bassett will appreciate this and I surely do. May I keep it and send it back in a few days?" Now all she wanted to do was escape this house, and find a quiet place to sit and read the file. Of course, she should stay a while, interview this woman, listen to stories of what a burden Donnie Ray was as a baby, how wicked he was as a toddler, how unfair it had all been. The problem was, she couldn't bear to hear it. Anyway, she'd promised not to write anything about Dorothy Huff.

"Mrs. Huff, you've been very kind. I need to be getting back to Austin now." She reached out to shake the woman's hand, but Dorothy Huff had already turned and shuffled toward the door. Molly followed.

Getting into her truck, Molly felt the old tingle of the hunt vibrating through her body. She didn't want to wait until she got back to Austin to read the file, so she headed back to McDonald's, back to the drive-through window. This time she ordered an Egg McMuffin. She was in the nick of time, just minutes before the ten-thirty end to breakfast.

She parked and sipped the orange juice as she looked at the first page of the slender file. It was labeled as property of the Department of Public Welfare of Travis County, which apparently handled adoptions back in 1962. At the top it said *"Case Number 3459987—Baby Boy Waller, later named Donnie Ray Grimes."* Molly thumbed through the six pages. Her heart sank. On every page there were words blacked out. She put her Egg McMuffin, still wrapped, on the dashboard and studied the inked-out words. They were all names, last names. Someone had inked out all the important names—the name of the man who found the infant, the name of another witness who saw the man find the infant, the name of the police officer who responded to the call. She felt like banging her head against the steering wheel. If she had any hope of tracing the person who abandoned the baby, those were the names she needed.

Her first reaction was a rush of anger. That old witch Dorothy Huff had done this. But then she calmed down and decided it might have been done by the welfare department. They probably did it to keep the identity of the birth parents confidential. But in this case no one knew who the parents were, so what did it matter? Well, she certainly intended to find out. She settled back to read the file.

The story was essentially as Mrs. Huff had told her. There was a sketchy police summary describing the infant being found by a man jogging along Waller Creek. The policeman who responded to the call immediately took the infant to Brackenridge Hospital and called the county to come and take over. A caseworker's report picked up the story from there. The infant, a six-pound male, approximately five hours old, was mildly dehydrated but otherwise healthy. He spent only one day in the hospital, and was then placed in a foster family. There was a lengthy part she skimmed over about the baby's health and the financial arrangements with the foster parents.

Attached at the end were the court records concerning the termination of parental rights when the infant was two months old, and the adoption by James and Evelyn Grimes.

Molly read it through at warp speed. Then she went back and read it again, slowly. It was frustrating because with the crucial names missing it was like trying to get your footing on a glass cliff; there was nothing to grab on to. But she kept reading and got rewarded with something she'd sped over the first time: At the end of the police summary was a line saying, *"Male infant and found effects given over to the custody of Public Welfare case worker."* Found effects! Something was found with the baby? She read through the rest of the report carefully searching for any other mention of found effects, but there was none.

She looked at the Egg McMuffin on the dashboard and decided she didn't want it after all. What she needed now was some information on how adoptions like this were handled, and she didn't want to wait until she got back to Austin.

She used her car phone to get an Austin operator to look up the number for the Texas Department of Protective and Regulatory Services. Then she managed, after several tries, to get an adoption supervisor on the line.

"Susie Garcia. How can I help you?"

"This is Molly Cates, Miz Garcia. I work for *Lone Star Monthly* magazine," she said in the brisk, professional tone she assumed for extracting information from bureaucrats. It was a tone that assumed she had the right to anything she requested. "I need some information on adoption procedure for an article I'm writing and I wonder if you could help me."

"Well, I'll try, ma'am."

Molly decided to start off with something she

thought she already knew the answer to. "Miz Garcia, I know that adoption records in Texas are sealed. But what does that mean in actual practice?"

"It means that adoption records are closed to everyone except the adult adoptee and the adoptive parents."

"I see. This woman I'm writing about—she's an adult adoptee—got a copy of her file, but it has lots of names blacked out. Do you do that?"

"Of course. We have to de-identify the file before we give it to the adoptee."

"De-identify?"

"Well, yes. To protect the privacy of the birth parents."

"Yes, I see why you'd do that, but on this file, other names are blacked out, too."

"Well, ma'am, that would probably be because those people might be able to give information that could lead to exposing the identity of the birth parents."

"But in this woman's case," Molly persisted, "she was abandoned, and the parents were never found. Why would the file be de-identified if there's no identity known?"

"Well, it's our policy. I suppose it's done so that the adoptee is not even tempted to try a search. It would be a waste of time anyway. If we couldn't find the birth parents, she couldn't either."

"How hard do you look in a case like that, with an abandoned infant?"

"The law just says we are required to conduct due and diligent search. We give it a good try. If we can't find the parents after several months we go to court to have the parental

129

rights terminated so we can put the child up for adoption."

"In the meantime the child is in foster care?"

"That's right."

"What about the original file? That's not de-identified, is it?"

"Well, of course not. We keep the original in our files with all names intact, but no one is allowed to see it."

"Ms. Garcia, when an infant is abandoned, as in the case I'm writing about, your agency takes custody of the baby, right?"

"Yes."

"What happens to any clothes or items that might be left with the baby?"

"Funny you should ask. We had one just a few weeks ago. A newborn baby girl left in the Kmart parking lot with seven jars of strained prunes, a plastic nursing bottle, and a beautiful silver St. Christopher medal. What we did in that case was toss the prunes because we worried about contamination. But the medal and the bottle we gave to the foster mother when we put the baby into her care."

"Then what? The baby will get adopted, won't she?"

"If we don't find the birth parents, and we haven't so far. Oh, yes, she'll get adopted. In a flash. She's a real sweetheart."

"Then what will happen to her stuff—the bottle and the St. Christopher medal?"

"The foster mother gives it to the adoptive mother. Such objects often turn out to be very precious, you know—the only link that child has with its birth parents. So we make an effort to preserve everything we can."

"So anything abandoned with the baby would end up with the adoptive parents?"

"Yes, eventually. That's what usually happens."

"Would that have been true back in the sixties, too?"

"I imagine. I don't go back that far. This sounds interesting. What's the article about?"

"Oh, it's just the story of a woman who was adopted in the sixties and has been searching for her parents."

To prepare herself for the ordeal of another dose of Dorothy Huff, Molly fortified herself with more coffee. She decided not to phone first because she wanted to watch the woman's reaction to her questions.

When Mrs. Huff opened the door this time, she held a half-smoked cigarette between her fingers. She looked disconcerted to see Molly.

"Mrs. Huff," Molly said. "I hate to bother you again, but there's just one more favor I need to ask. I stopped at McDonald's for lunch, and I read the file there. It mentions something about the effects found with the infant. I wonder if I could take a look at them before I drive back."

Mrs. Huff assumed a quizzical look. "Effects?"

"Yes. You know, the things left with Donnie Ray when he was abandoned."

The old woman stood perfectly still, the only movement the smoke from her cigarette drifting up her arm. "It says that in the file?"

"Yes, in the police report."

Mrs. Huff turned without speaking and walked inside, wafting smoke behind her. Molly followed without being invited. She watched the woman walk to the gold chair and mash the cigarette into a coffee cup that was sitting on the arm. "Well," Dorothy Huff said with her head down, "there was the beer cooler, you know. I told you that. But it was old even then, and just one of them cheap ones you get at gas stations, and it just dried up and fell to bits some years ago. I threw it out."

Molly followed a hunch. "What about the other things?"

"You mean that thing he was wrapped in?"

"Yes." Molly's heart fluttered. "Do you still have it?"

"Just an old robe. Nothing to see."

"Will you get it for me, please?"

Dorothy Huff's face hardened into a stubborn look that worried Molly. "I really don't see—"

"Please, just let me look. It might be helpful in the search. For Mrs. Bassett and little Kimberly," she added.

Dorothy Huff sighed, but once again she turned and shuffled off. This time she was muttering something about if she'd known how much trouble all this would be, she would have stayed in bed where she belonged. She was gone longer this time and there was still nothing to look at in the living room. Except the coffee cup. Molly walked over and peered inside. There were six cigarette butts. Six in the forty minutes since Molly had left. The woman had a prodigious habit.

Finally Mrs. Huff returned carrying a flat white cardboard box about the size you'd get if you bought a sweater at Foley's. Molly wanted to grab it and run, but she stood patiently as the woman carried it across the room. She set it down on the table gingerly, as if it contained live rattlesnakes. She put her hands on the box, then paused. "Mrs. Cates, are you a saved woman?"

Molly didn't hesitate. "No, Mrs. Huff. I imagine it's a great comfort to those who are, but I seem unable to believe in anything I can't see."

Mrs. Huff nodded as if that was exactly what she'd expected to hear and raised the lid of the box. She stood aside to let Molly look inside. It was a garment made of a shiny red fabric, neatly folded. "See," she said in a hushed voice, "that's it."

"Would you take it out for me?" Molly asked.

Mrs. Huff sighed. She reached in and lifted it out. Holding it with her fingertips, she gave it a shake to open the folds. It was a kimono, clearly old, but still a vivid red. Slowly Mrs. Huff turned it to show Molly the back. Embroidered there was a huge multicolored dragon, coiled in a circle. It had lots of heads and tongues. Molly was amazed: Thirty-three years it had sat in the box and the colors were still vivid, gaudy even.

"The mark of the Beast," Dorothy Huff intoned.

A dampish, musty smell emanated from the garment. It took several seconds for Molly to make the connection. Beasts—Samuel Mordecai talked a lot about beasts. What was it he'd said? Something about being helpless and wrapped in the mantle of the Beast. My God. Was he referring to this, to being a baby wrapped in this gaudy garment and put out to die? She had assumed it was

133

metaphorical talk, images from Revelation, but it was literal. She thought about a little boy whose only connection with the mother who gave him birth was this. Her heart was thudding.

"When did Donnie Ray first see this, Mrs. Huff?" And then she asked a question she should have asked the first time she was here. "And when did he learn about the details of his abandonment and adoption?"

"Well, let me see." Dorothy Huff stuck her bottom lip out, an affectation Molly now recognized as a pose of trying to remember. "Everybody says you should tell children they been adopted early on. So I told Donnie Ray, oh, maybe when he was two or three. You know, when he could understand."

"Two or three?" Molly repeated.

"Yes, ma'am. And I showed him this. Had to warn him. You know, while there was still time."

"Warn him?"

"Yes." She shook the kimono in front of Molly's face. "About the Beast and how careful he had to be to overcome this evil sign, this early influence."

"Early influence?"

She looked at Molly with exasperation, as if she were a very slow child. "Well, you can see what with starting out life like this, marked in this terrible way, it was important for him to be careful. So when he was bad, I'd have to show him this to remind him of his inheritance. I had to warn him. Children are forgetful, so I had to do it often."

Molly didn't know if she could bear to hear more, but she said, "You'd warn him about this robe?"

"The image of the Beast, Mrs. Cates. That great dragon who waits to devour children at the moment of birth, the ancient serpent who leads the whole world astray. The Book of Revelation. You not being a Christian woman, I suppose you don't know much about them things, but the boy was born under the image of the Beast, and he needed special handling."

Molly knew she should follow up, ask about the special handling, but she didn't think she could take it right now. "Mrs. Huff, if I'm very careful, could I take this with me? I'll get it back to you with the file in a few days."

"Well..."

"It could be important for helping the children at Jezreel."

"Take it, then." She flapped a hand. "This has just wore me out. I was just fixing to lay down for a nap."

"Of course. I won't keep you. Thanks for your help, Mrs. Huff."

Molly left the house with the box under her arm.

Out on the highway, she checked to be sure her Fuzzbuster was working. Then she rolled down the windows and pushed the speedometer up to seventy. She turned on her new Rolling Stones tape with the volume at full blast—ungodly, satanic music to drive out the smell of Dorothy Huff's house, she thought, as the hot wind blew through the cab and whipped her hair wildly around her head.

"To do whatsoever is needed to help You shut down the world and this evil generation, even if it goes against all commonly held ideas of what is good and what is not good."

SAMUEL MORDECAI,
PROPHET'S PLEDGE FROM HEAVEN IN EARTH
VATIC GOSPEL OF THE JEZREELITE

CHAPTER SEVEN

Josh was wheezing, curled tight against Kim, who had her cheek pressed against his damp head. "Tell me if you want to be alone, Josh," she was saying. "I know when it's bad, you don't like anyone to be too close."

"It's okay," he gasped between wheezes. "It's okay now."

The wheezing had begun in earnest right after he'd eaten his cereal and milk. It wasn't good for Josh to drink milk, but it was all they'd been getting, so there was no choice. Josh had explained to Walter early on that milk made more mucus and that at home he drank it only occasionally. Walter had explained this to Martin and begged him to bring Josh something different. But Martin ignored the request.

It was always Martin who brought their meals, never anyone else. Twice a day he'd drop down the hole, reach up, and lift a cardboard carton down. One meal, the first of the day, was invariably cereal and milk. Sometimes the second meal was cereal and milk, too. But every second or third day the carton held peanut butter and jelly sandwiches on white bread and milk. Once a week they got a banana or an apple. They always had a jug of water that sat on the driver's seat and each of them had a plastic cup. And that was it for food and drink. For forty-seven days, it had sustained life, but they were all ready to scream from the boredom.

If you tried to design a worse situation for a kid like Josh, you couldn't do it, Walter thought. It had all the ingredients to make him sick: stuffy, bad air, a closed-in space underground, milk and cereal every day, constant stress—not just Samuel Mordecai preaching his blood statues and cataclysm all the time, not just being captives, but living in such close quarters, with all the squabbling and friction among the kids. And, of course, no medication—that was the worst thing. When Josh's yellow plastic inhaler had run out after the first week, his attacks got more severe and more frequent. In desperation Walter had filled the empty inhaler with water and got Josh to mist that into his throat. At first, the inhaler was probably picking up some residue of the medication, but by now it was straight water. Still, it seemed to give him some relief.

Now Kim held up the inhaler, which Josh always kept on the seat next to him. "Do you want another puff, Joshy?"

The boy took the inhaler, held it to his mouth, and pressed. Then he let his head loll back against Kim. She hummed to him softly. She didn't carry a tune well, but Walter thought the song was that old Cat Stevens song "Morning Has Broken." The humming seemed to soothe him. By trial and error, Kim and Walter had developed a desperate repertoire of techniques to help Josh through his breathing difficulties. The problem was they had so little to work with.

In general, they had so little. The first day down here, Martin and another man had come through the bus taking their backpacks, purses, and anything they saw that looked like it might contain dangerous or ungodly items. The only things that got left behind were the few items that happened to be out of their packs and out of sight when the confiscation occurred. And these objects had become intensely precious over the weeks—Brandon's math book; Sandra's novel, *Stuart Little;* Bucky's Mighty Morphin Power Ranger action figure; Sue Ellen's string box; Walter's towel and the pad of paper and pencil he kept under the driver's seat; Conrad's pog collection, something Walter had never seen before—little cardboard circles; Heather's packet of scrunchies for securing hair. Kim's pink comb with the little mirror on it.

The kids were amazingly inventive at figuring out ways to amuse themselves, using what they had. They were indeed the television generation; lots of their play revolved about TV shows, acting out Power Ranger scenarios and cartoon characters. One particularly therapeutic activity Walter enjoyed was watching them act out what the Power Rangers would do to the Hearth Jezreelites. Even though television shaped some of their fantasies, it seemed to Walter that when necessity arose, they had all the resourcefulness of frontier kids. They sang, invented games, squabbled, listened to his story, argued about it, and played cat's cradle and rock, paper, scissors—games he remembered from his childhood. They breathed onto the windows to fog them and played ticktacktoe. They made paper airplanes and triangles and had contests with them, keeping running scores on a sheet of paper that was now solid with numbers. Paper was at a premium. Because Walter was saving the ten sheets left on his pad for an emergency, they talked Brandon out of the index pages in the back of his math book. At first Brandon was scandalized by the suggestion that he tear a page out of a school-book, but the kids got Walter to support them in saying this was such a special situation that the school would be unlikely to punish him for defacing the book.

This morning, Conrad and Brandon sat in the doorway moving buttons they had torn off their clothes around on a checkerboard Walter had drawn on the cardboard backing from his writing pad. Heather had been braiding Sue Ellen's long black hair until they'd gotten into a fight over who had left the cup of water in the aisle to get knocked over. Hector and Lucy were playing with Conrad's pogs. Sandra read her book. When Walter asked her how many times she'd read it, her answer was that it wasn't the sort of thing you counted.

Bucky sat perched on the edge of Philip's seat trying to interest him in talking to his Power Ranger doll. Philip showed no interest in Power Rangers or anything else. He was leaning against the window, his eyes closed. Walter didn't know what to do about Philip. He hadn't gotten up from his seat today and he hadn't eaten his cereal. For at least a week, Walter hadn't heard him utter a word. He was slipping away, getting dimmer and dimmer. If they were set free today, Walter wondered, would he ever recover? Would any of them?

When Josh's wheezing finally eased, he said softly, "Hey, Mr. Demming, let's hear about Jacksonville."

"Good idea," Kim said.

"Okay," Walter said. "How about some story, kids?"

There was general agreement to have story time. Brandon stood, got some water from the thermos, and wandered to the back.

The hard-core eight gathered at the front and waited. Walter got a cup of water, too, and hunkered down in the aisle. He waited for the story to come and fill him up. The way he did it was to back up in his mind to the last installment and remember where he'd left Jacksonville. Then it felt like the story was just drawn out of him by the waiting kids. He smiled at them, sitting there waiting for him to start. It occurred to him that he enjoyed storytelling and that he'd never again have an audience as eager as this one.

"The rain," he said. "The yellow rain that came so suddenly and then just stopped. As soon as the Tongs ran back to their hootches, it stopped. Just like that. Jacksonville had never seen a rain like that. And it had been such a funny yellowish color. But he was thankful for it. Dr. Mortimer was still alive.

"But then, sitting alone in the dark, he started feeling sad and hopeless again. Nothing had really changed. Tomorrow the Tongs would just build another fire and there'd be no sudden, miraculous rain to stop it. So what difference did it make? Tonight or tomorrow—it was all the same. He thought about the big Tong warrior laughing and drawing his finger across his throat. He gave up the idea of sleeping and just sat there in his cage, scared and miserable. Waiting to die. In a way that's what life was, he thought—just waiting to die. Maybe it would be tomorrow when the sun came up, or maybe when the sun went down. But he *would* die. Jacksonville had never really felt that before: certain that he would die—sometime. It made him wonder what all the effort was for, all this searching, trying to find Dr. Mortimer. It all just ends in a cooking pot, like a carrot or a potato."

Walter paused here, alarmed by the dark direction the story had taken. This had started as an action-adventure tale to pass the time. He hadn't intended to get into all this stuff about death and dying; it had just sneaked in. Maybe it was too much for kids this young, especially kids in this situation. He walked up the aisle so he could look at them up close, see how they were taking it. He looked into the faces of the regulars: Bucky, thumb in mouth, looked in a trance. Kim sat with her legs hugged into her chest, her chin resting on her knees. Her eyes were bright with interest. Lucy was wrapping a curl around her index finger, impatient for him to go on. Josh, Hector, Heather, Conrad, and Sue Ellen all looked interested and not particularly upset. After all, these were kids who had grown up with *The Terminator* and *Nightmare on Elm Street*. These were children who had been held hostage in a buried school bus for weeks.

A buzzard fretting about death was unlikely to traumatize them any more than they already were.

He went all the way to the back where Brandon Betts lay on the floor, glowering. Tears were running down Philip's cheeks. Walter reached out and smoothed down his hair. He climbed up and sat on the back of Philip's seat so the kids in the front could see him.

"Jacksonville felt more alone than he had ever felt in his life. He watched the moon rise. It was almost full, and he was glad to have some light for company because he sure hated sitting alone in the dark.

"Then he heard footsteps. He saw this old Tong woman coming toward his cage. She was really old, with a wrinkled face.

"She came to his cage and smiled at him. Most of the Tongs have these long pointed teeth, so when they smile it's scarier than when they don't. But this woman's teeth were only a little pointed and they were very white and clean. The wrinkles around her eyes were friendly.

"But Jacksonville was nervous. The old woman looked friendly, but he'd learned to be careful. She held her hand out to the bars and made a gentle sort of clucking noise like she wanted him to come to her. But he didn't, because he was afraid. After all, she was a Barbecue Tong. And we know what they're like."

Walter paused to drink some water. He noticed Sandra was actually looking at him. He had suspected she followed the story and just pretended to be reading her book. After all, how many times could you reread *Stuart Little?*

He went on: "The woman reached her hand into the pocket of her baggy white shorts, which was what all female Tongs wear, and she pulled something out. It was shiny, like metal. Then she did something that amazed Jacksonville. She stuck her hand right into the cage, between the bars. She didn't seem afraid that he would hurt her or anything. If he had wanted to, he could have leaned forward and ripped a finger off with his beak, but she didn't seem worried about that. She dropped the shiny thing she'd taken out of her pocket onto the cage floor. She gave it a little shove toward him and pulled her hand out. Then she looked around again to see if they were still alone."

"I bet it's a gun," Bucky said, not removing his thumb from his mouth.

"No," Walter said, "actually it's not."

"A knife," Hector said.

"Nope. Not a knife either."

"Let him tell it," Lucy whined. "You're not supposed to interrupt. Go on, Mr. Demming."

"I know!" Hector shouted. "A what-do-you-call-it. Galaxy Peace Ray!"

"No," said Walter, "but wouldn't that be nice, so you could shoot the whole village into peacefulness."

"Not really," Hector said, "I'd rather shoot the bastards with an Uzi or a twelve-gauge shotgun." He laughed.

"Hector," Lucy said, "you can't talk like that. It's rude."

"Why are you such a goody-goody, Lucy? What do you think the thing is?" Hector challenged.

"I don't know." She shook her head. "A magic charm or something."

"No," Walter said, "it's not a magic charm. And I bet you're not any of you going to guess what it is. Keep trying."

"A fish," Heather called out.

"Dummy," Conrad said, "it's metal."

"No, it was *like* metal, silvery-colored," she shouted back. "Dummy yourself, Conrad."

"A hand grenade?" Conrad said.

"Nope."

"A pair of scissors," Josh said.

"Nope."

"I know! I know!" Kim yelled. "A file, like they use for jail breaks."

"Oh, Kim, that's close," Walter said. "You're getting warm."

"A file?" Heather said. "What's that?"

"Come on, Mr. Demming," Lucy urged. "Tell the story."

"Okay. Well, Jacksonville was curious, too, about what the silvery thing was, but he couldn't look right away. He was still scared of the old Tong woman. He had to keep his eye on her. She smiled again and—"

He stopped because the lightbulb started to sway on its cord. As it swayed it flickered off and on. All eyes darted to the door. In the pit, black boots appeared, long legs, and with a thud, the whole man. He burst through the bus door, with more energy than Walter had ever seen. He was wired. His body seemed to vibrate with it. His yellow hair looked electric. "Three more days, little Lambs of God!" He carried no Bible today, but a newspaper. He held it aloft. "Lookee here. The first newspaper we've seen at Jezreel in forty-seven days. We got this from them negotiators out there as part of a trade we are working out. We're going to let your bus driver here talk on the phone tomorrow. The trade is we get to share a little of our message with the world—you'd think they'd beg for that, wouldn't you? But no, they're scared to hear it."

Walter stood up. He wanted to hear the ground rules for the phone conversation. This time maybe he could do something to improve their situation.

"Sit down, Mr. Bus Driver," Samuel Mordecai commanded. "Later. Later, with all your fussing. I'm giving the lesson now."

Walter sat.

Josh began to wheeze, a series of high, desperate gasps. All the kids looked in his direction.

Samuel Mordecai narrowed his eyes as the wheezing alternated with coughing. "Get it under control, sonny boy. We haven't any time for this. I thought we'd do our lesson today out of the newspaper because, Lambs, it's all right here in the news. The signs are all present in this one edition. Look at this: war in Bosnia, war in Haiti, war in Kuwait, war in Rwanda, earthquakes in China and California, AIDS in Mexico and Africa, the European Community, a global economy controlled by computer, the Trilateral Commission, strange sightings in the heavens, debit cards, electronic transfers, movements of troops in the Middle East. Oh, Lambs, nothing is missing, nothing but us. And we will be ready in three days."

Josh let out a series of choking coughs. Mordecai

145

talked over them. "'*And ye shall hear of wars and rumors of wars. For nation shall rise against nation, and kingdom against kingdom: and there shall be famines, and pestilences, and earthquakes, in divers places.*' Matthew 24:6-7. It's all here. Lambs, this prophecy for what the world will be like at the end times could be the little summary of the news they do on this very front page. It's all happening, just like it was prophesied. It's all accomplished, just waiting for us to play our parts. Rejoice. We are the chosen human agents to—"

Josh let out some deep, desperate gasps for air.

Walter got up and went to him. Samuel Mordecai gestured for him to sit down, but he pretended not to see it. He bent down over the boy. "Water, Josh?"

"No—can't—" Josh bent forward abruptly and put his hands on his knees. He threw his head back and gulped for air.

Walter picked the inhaler up from the seat. He held it up to Josh's mouth. "Use your inhaler, honey. It helps."

Josh took it and squeezed. Walter had grown to love the *poof* sound it made because he associated it with relief. Josh handed it back to Walter and began to draw some ragged breaths.

Samuel Mordecai took a few steps down the aisle to look closer at Josh. With each step he took, Josh wheezed louder. After a few seconds Mordecai backed up and said, "We'll do the lesson later. Give sonny here a chance to get himself together."

Brandon Betts stood up. "Wait, Prophet Mordecai!" He ran to the front of the bus and

146

grabbed Mordecai's hand. "I want to come with you. I don't belong with them. I believe you, and they don't. They aren't listening like I am."

"I believe you, too." Sue Ellen stood up.

"Now, now," Mordecai said, slapping the rolled-up paper against his leg in a nervous flurry. "We'll all be together in the millennium. But you need to stay here until Friday at sundown. Then you'll have your fifty days. Fifty days for the earth to purify you." He swept his hand toward the black windows. "See the earth all around you. It is rebirthing you. Can't you feel it happening? It makes you worthy to be Lambs of God. You haveto stay here. That's where our name comes from. Hearth Jezreelites. See hearth is earth with an H, which stands for heaven, heaven in earth. And Jezreelites because Jesus trod the valley of Jezreel and I am His, His son, His prophet, His descendant."

He disengaged Brandon's hand from his arm. "You'll come with me on Friday." He pulled the X-acto knife out of his hip pocket and leaned over to the window. With a flick of the wrist, he scraped off a Band-Aid. There were three left now.

Josh's breathing had quieted, but Lucy and Bucky had begun to sob. Brandon was pleading and praying. Samuel Mordecai backed out the door. "Tend to this, Mr. Bus Driver."

Seeing him leaving, Walter was stabbed with panic. With Josh's inhaler in his hand, he bolted up the aisle. "Wait! Mordecai. You see how Josh is. This is nothing. He gets much worse attacks at night. We just need some more of his medication, an albuterol inhaler, like this one." He thrust it

147

up in front of Mordecai's face. "And maybe a steroid one for emergencies. That's all. When I talk to the negotiators, I want to ask them. I know they'll want to send one in, leave one at the gate maybe. If *I* ask for it, it won't be like you'll have to give up anything for it. Please let me. When can I talk to them?"

Samuel Mordecai turned around and pushed his wild curls back off his forehead. "There will be no asking for anything, Mr. Bus Driver, but here's something—the Lambs can send messages to their parents—one sentence per Lamb. Tomorrow. We'll come get you."

"Can I send a message, too?"

Mordecai laughed. "You'll have a minute. If you can fit it in, send a message." He turned, but Walter grabbed his arm and held up the inhaler to show him again. He opened his mouth to make another plea, too, but Samuel Mordecai reached out and took the inhaler from him. Then he stepped out the door and pulled himself up and out—quickly—a fast escape.

Walter stood stunned. He had taken the inhaler. Did that mean he was going to get it refilled? Or was he confiscating it? The one thing that actually seemed to give relief?

Walter turned back to face the chaos of the bus: Several kids were crying; Brandon and Hector were screaming at one another. Josh was gasping. Bucky was curled up into a ball, his hands pressed over his ears.

Walter stood at the front of the bus, trying to regulate his breathing. He didn't know where to start, what to do, how to calm all this down. It was chaos, total breakdown. Then Hector gave Brandon a shove that sent him reeling against one of the seats. Brandon started to scream.

"Hector, please come here," Walter barked.

Hector gave Brandon's arm a final twist and stalked up the aisle. "What?" he said, looking up into Walter's face.

"This. If Brandon believes what Mordecai is saying, that's his right. Religious freedom."

"He's like a…" He searched for the word. *"Traitor."*

"No. We're all under lots of pressure. Don't give Brandon a hard time. He's doing what he feels he has to do."

Hector lowered his voice. "I'm afraid he'll tell about our emergency plan, our rehearsals. We can't let Brandon or Sue Ellen tell him about it. Don't that worry you, man?"

"Yes. It worries me a lot. But I think Brandon's really torn apart. He's afraid Mordecai might be right."

"Mordecai's a bag of hot air. Here's what I want to do." Hector put his hand in his pocket and pulled out a red Swiss Army knife. He held it close to his chest, his back to the rest of the bus, so only Walter could see it. He opened the largest blade and whispered, "I'm sick of this shit. Why don't I stick him. Before he kills us, man. That's what he's going to do, ain't it?"

"Shhh." Walter put a finger to his mouth. "Don't scare the other kids. I don't know." He looked at the knife with keen interest. He took it from Hector and examined the blade. He ran his thumb against the cutting edge and moved the blade back and forth to see how strong it was. Then he closed it carefully and slipped it into his own pocket.

"Hey, man," Hector hissed. "It's mine. It's all I got."

"I know. But, Hector, I need to have it for the emergency plan. I've used a knife before, when I was in the army. I've used it against men. It's best for me to have it. If there's any stabbing to do, I will do it. How did you manage to hold on to it through the search?"

Hector leaned over to study the three Band-Aids. "In my Jockeys, man, and it hurt like hell." He touched one of the Band-Aids. "Three more days. Why haven't they tried to rescue us? When you talked to that FBI guy the second day he said he'd get us out, right?"

Walter nodded.

Hector's huge black eyes filled with tears. "Well, why don't they, man? Don't they know he's gonna kill us?"

It was a subject Walter had thought about endlessly. Now he squatted down, and motioned for Hector to do the same so they could talk in some privacy. Walter told the boy, "He also said our safety was the most important thing. I think they want to come rescue us, but they don't know where we are. Remember when we drove here, how big the property is, and there are lots of different buildings. I think for a rescue they need to know where we are. And from all I can figure, I suppose Mordecai threatened to kill us if they come in."

He studied the boy. At twelve, Hector Ramirez

was the most mature of the boys, and the savviest. The oldest of a family of seven, he'd had responsibilities beyond his years. His voice was already deepening and a wispy growth darkened his upper lip. Walter had found him to be quick-witted and dependable. It was probably inexcusable to burden a child with this, but he needed someone to talk to and Hector seemed like a good bet, a sturdy kid. "They probably worry that if they attack, we'll get hit in the cross fire. Or that it would take so long to find us after an attack starts that—"

Hector finished it for him: "That that scumbag will kill us."

Walter nodded. "I'm trying to think of a way to let them know where we are."

"When you talk to them tomorrow?"

"Uh-huh. Maybe try to give them some message that the Hearth Jezreelite guys wouldn't know was a message, but was."

Hector's dark eyes gleamed. "Like some secret code or something."

"Yeah, exactly. I'm working on some ideas. Hector, are you willing to let me use your message to your parents as a way to send a message?"

Hector thought for a minute. "Sure thing, man. How would you do it?"

"I'm not sure. But what would your parents do if they got a message from you that made no sense to them?"

Hector grinned. "My dad is not…well, not fast to see things that are new. But my mom, she's something else. She'd know right away what we were trying to do."

"Okay," Walter said. "But what I want to do now is get ready for what's going to happen. I need you to help. I want to practice our drills so that when it comes, we can all do our parts really fast."

"Yeah," Hector said, "I think we can do better than old Jacksonville is doing. What a dim bulb the guy is."

"Oh, I don't know," Walter said. "He may come out of it okay. Slow and steady wins the race."

Hector snorted. "Slow and steady! That don't win nothing. Don't you go to the movies, man?" He smiled his big flashing smile. "Fast and mean wins the race. That's how we gotta play it—fast and mean."

> "*As a young man I was recruited into a communal cult where we were brainwashed into following orders without thinking. They forced us to stay there and stripped us of our identities. This cult was heavily armed and very violent—the United States Army.*"
> LIEUTENANT GRADY TRAYNOR,
> AUSTIN POLICE DEPARTMENT

CHAPTER EIGHT

Seeing Grady's ancient green Mazda parked in her driveway made her pulse quicken. Molly hadn't seen him for five days, and she'd missed him—lots. Too much. She didn't bother with the garage, just pulled her truck in next to his Mazda. As she got out, she heard whimpers coming from

152

the fenced yard at the side of her town house. She walked around toward the gate. Grady's low voice floated out to her. "That's right, Copper. Good boy."

"What's he doing to be a good boy," she called over the high wood fence, "peeing on my grass?"

The gate opened for her. Grady Traynor, dressed in a gray suit that looked as if it had been slept in for several lifetimes, stood there smiling at her. His white hair and mustache looked limp and slightly greasy. The circles under his eyes had darkened alarmingly and his tan was fading fast. After forty-seven days, the standoff at Jezreel was taking a toll on him that twenty-eight years of police work, eight of it in homicide, had somehow failed to do.

He opened his arms wide and Molly stepped toward him, her heart quickening.

Before they could embrace, however, a low growl made Molly step back hastily. An enormous black dog snarled up at her, his lips drawn back to show large yellowed fangs. The coarse hair on his neck bristled and his legs were spread aggressively. His amber eyes were slits of malice.

"Goddammit, Grady. That scares me." The dog had repelled her from the start, when Grady had brought him by for the first time three months ago. He was a Belgian Malinois, Grady had informed her, though to Molly's eye he looked exactly like a German shepherd. It was an ancient working breed, Grady explained like a proud parent, bred in Europe to herd sheep and kill predators, now used almost exclusively for police and guard work.

This specimen was mostly black, but with a dusting of reddish tan on his muzzle, neck, and front legs. His long narrow muzzle had a downward bend in it about midway between the eye and the nose, and the ear on his left side had a ragged notch torn out of it.

"Sorry, Molly. I keep forgetting that he sees close contact as something he's supposed to do something about. He doesn't mean anything personal by it." He squatted down to pat the dog. "Okay, Copper. It's all right, sweetie." He rubbed his black head and chest vigorously. The dog quieted down. "See. He's a real pussycat. If you'd get to know him, you'd—"

"Grady, don't start that."

"Okay. But if you'd just keep him here for a few days, you'd see that he's—"

"No. Not for a few days. Not even a few minutes. I don't want a dog. And if I did, this dog would definitely not be the one I wanted. I think he's dangerous, a time bomb. He shows too much tooth for my taste."

"This disappoints me, Molly. I would think you'd see the challenge here."

"I've got plenty of challenges in my life. The answer was no two months ago, and it's still no. This is *your* reclamation project, Grady. I predict you'll regret it. When this animal bites someone and you get sued."

"But look at him," Grady said, still scratching the dog's chest. The dog had his eyes closed in ecstasy and his left rear leg was thumping reflexively.

"Well, you certainly have the touch." She laughed, thinking how much she'd like to get

154

Grady upstairs in bed for a few hours. "That's one thing Copper and I agree on. When do you have to be back at Jezreel?"

"Tomorrow, six A.M. We're still doing twelve hours on and twelve off."

She walked over to one of the rickety lawn chairs on the little brick terrace and sat down. "Killer schedule. After six weeks of it, it's amazing you're still standing. How's it going?"

He sat down next to her. "It's not. It's not going anywhere. It's a bust."

"Tell me."

"There's nothing to tell. Forty-seven days, Molly—a month and a half—the best negotiators in the country working round the clock, and we have gotten fucking nowhere. Andrew Stein's the guy who wrote the book on the subject. He's got thirty years' experience in talking perps out of doing insane things to hostages. He talked the Iraqi bombers out of the synagogue in Chicago; he negotiated fifty hostages out of that Colorado survivalist commune without a drop of blood getting shed. From Samuel Mordecai he can't get one kid on the telephone for ten seconds. You know what we've accomplished in forty-seven days? We got one minute with the driver on the second day. And this morning—big breakthrough—we got him to agree to let us speak to the driver again. Tomorrow, he says. For that, we give him ten minutes on KLTX radio to play his sermon tape, plus we sent in some newspapers. We also stuck some inhalers in the bag with the papers in the hope that once they're inside, he'll give them to Josh Benderson."

"Did you put listening devices in the inhalers?"

"Oh, God, Molly. We debated it all night, but if Mordecai found them, it would kill all chance of getting medication to the kid. So we didn't." He ran his hands through his hair. "That kid is seriously sick. Assuming he's still alive. For all we know, they've all been dead from day one." He said it fiercely.

"I don't think they're dead," Molly said.

Grady sighed. "Me either. Not yet."

"Have you figured out what he wants?"

"Sure. He wants an hour on network television. That's what he's really after, Molly—a worldwide satellite TV broadcast before Friday night. He wants to preach to the world."

"So let him."

"We will. Gladly. But he needs to give something in return."

"All eleven kids and the bus driver?"

"That's what we say. And they'd have to come out first." He leaned over closer to her and whispered, "Just between us, we'd settle for six kids."

"What does he say to it?"

"He doesn't answer. He rants. He says we—the negotiators—are part of the military-industrial, computer-corrupted group of world leaders he's marked to be made into blood statues. Didn't he once threaten you with that?"

"Yes. When my cult piece came out."

"So you may be wondering what blood statues are." He raised his eyebrows at her, always a dramatic gesture since they were jet black and met in the middle.

"No. But I can see you're going to tell me."

"I think it's important for you to know this. Because we—the negotiators—have not acted on his message, Mordecai has marked our souls with bar codes that emit a blue glow that can only be perceived by angels. We are not talking about just any angels here, but a team of military attack angels led by the Archangel Gabriel. When the trumpets blow on Friday, they will swoop to earth and cut our throats with heat-sealing laser knives. Then they will hang us upside down in such a way that with our arms and legs outstretched we will resemble pentagrams. And we will remain blood statues, rotting and stinking through all eternity." Grady watched her for a reaction.

"Does he—" The words stuck in Molly's throat. "Does he talk about the kids and the bus driver as being part of that corrupted group of world leaders?"

"No. He refers to them as Lambs. Damn, Molly, I'm so damned sick of his sermonizing. One of the things you count on in long hostage negotiations is the perps getting tired, but this madman shows no signs of it. We, on the other hand, are zombies. Listen to this: He says we're the captives, not him. He says we're caught between Gabriel's attack angels and his legions of cult members on the outside, what Mordecai calls his Sword Hand of God."

"Is there truth to that?" Molly asked. "Legions of cult members on the outside?"

"Not legions, but there are some and they are damned effective. It's been hard to get much intelligence. The ones we can locate who have left are terrified of talking about it."

"Are you thinking of letting some parents talk to him?"

"Mrs. Bassett. Actually, he's requested her. Saw her on television, Channel 33 news. He says he'd like to talk to her. We'll probably give it a try. She's a real persuasive lady, and we don't see how it could hurt. He also says he might let her come in and see the kids."

"Would you allow that?"

"No. An ironclad FBI rule—no one enters a hostage situation, ever, for no reason, period. But we are out of ideas, Molly, running on empty. He's just been stringing us along, buying time. I don't think he ever had the slightest intention of letting any of those kids go. I think he's got other plans for them."

"Oh, Grady."

"This leaves the door open for the HRT tactical nuts, the knuckle-walkers, to take over. They're sitting in a warehouse three miles away in their Ninja suits cleaning their assault rifles. They've had an emergency assault plan ready from day two. They're on fifteen-minute call-up and they are dieseling."

Molly had been fearing it might come to that. She groaned.

"Yeah," he continued, "giving up on negotiations probably condemns those kids to death. Eighty-six percent of the hostages who die get killed during an assault. If the bad guys don't shoot them, we do. And Mordecai has convinced us— he will kill them all the second he thinks an attack is starting. Anyway, how can we attack when we still don't know where in the compound they're being held?" He closed his eyes. "But we have no choice anymore. And we're going to lose them. Oh, Molly, it's impossible."

He let his head fall back on the chair. "I'm crisped."

She'd never before heard Grady say anything was impossible. She reached out to take his hand, but the dog, lying at his feet now, looked up and growled low in his throat. Molly drew her hand back.

She was quiet for a minute. She had been trying to decide whether to tell him about Dorothy Huff and Samuel Mordecai's adoption. It was a dilemma: Grady was a wonderful sounding board, the best person she knew to brainstorm with. And if there was a prayer of tracking down Mordecai's birth mother, she needed his help. The problem was, Grady was a cop, first and foremost. If she told him, he'd feel he had to pass it on to his boss or to the FBI.

Grady said, "Well, are you going to tell me or aren't you?"

Molly turned her head. He hadn't opened his eyes. "What?"

"Whatever it is you're agonizing over."

"If I tell you, will you promise to let me decide how to use the information?"

His eyes were open now, studying her face. "Not if it's something to do with this mess in Jezreel. Not if I think it's police business."

"Then I can't tell you. I have a feeling about this."

"Molly, don't do this. You need to tell me."

"I'm afraid the authorities will muck this up, that they won't use it right."

"Molly, my sweet, I am one of the authorities and you are the most overconfident human being I know. What makes you so sure you are better qualified to deal with whatever it is than, say, the FBI's chief negotiator, or a thirty-year police veteran like myself?"

"You're not in charge there."

"True. But they're not bad, these FBI agents. They want to negotiate the kids out and they have more experience doing that sort of thing than anyone else in the country. Some of them are assholes, but, hey, so's Samuel Mordecai."

She thought about it. "One thing I know, Grady: If I don't tell anyone, there can't be any leaks to the press."

"You are the press," he pointed out.

"No. Not in this case I'm not. This is nothing I want to write about. This information may have a much higher use."

Grady was quiet, clearly weighing it. Then he put a hand over his heart and said, "Trust me."

She leaned forward in her chair. "Did you know that Samuel Mordecai was adopted as a baby?"

The black eyebrows went up in surprise. "Evelyn Grimes was not his mother?"

"She adopted him when he was an infant."

"Says who?"

"Says his grandmother, Dorothy Huff."

He sat back in his chair. "Tell me everything."

Molly knew that when he said everything, he meant absolutely everything, with no detail omitted. So, while the dog lay panting at their feet, she told him about Samuel Mordecai's being found floating in a beer cooler in Waller Creek and about the adoption. Grady listened the way he always did, actively, and with total concentration, nodding and grunting and raising his eyebrows in astonishment.

"I have the robe and the adoption papers in my truck," she finished. "Oh, here's something else you may not know: Gramma Huff says that Annette Grimes, Mordecai's wife, is not in the compound. She left months ago and is in hiding."

"Really? She's on our list of the hundred and twenty people we think are inside." He stroked his long white mustache with his index finger. "That is mighty interesting. I would *love* to talk with Mrs. Grimes. Do you think Granny has any idea where she is?"

"No. I'm sure she doesn't. Annette wrote Dorothy Huff to say goodbye and that she'd never be able to contact her again. Apparently she's terrified for her life."

"I bet. Molly, that's important. I have to pass it on to Lattimore and Stein. We'll find her."

"Grady, here's what I've been thinking about the adoption issue. Mordecai seems desperate to know who his birth mother is. He's tried to find her and failed. It's real important to him. What if we could find his mother for him?" She watched his face to see if he was responding the way she wanted him to. "If we could do it, it could be a major bargaining chip to use with him. We'd reveal her identity, maybe let him talk to her on the phone if he'd release some kids. I haven't thought it through, but before you resort to force, this might work."

"Maybe. If we can find her. Doesn't sound like there's much to go on."

"I think I know how we could start, or how you could." She waited to see how long it would take him to figure out what she had in mind.

It took two seconds. "Oh, Molly. Do you know how difficult that would be? We weren't computerized in '62. All those incident reports are boxed up in a warehouse in South Austin. And to find it with no one knowing what we're looking for means I'd have to do the looking myself. Now, when I have no time as it is."

She gave him a wide smile. "You could do it this afternoon. Or tonight."

"Molly," he wailed, "I haven't slept in forty-eight hours. And I haven't spent any time with my dog."

Molly glanced down at the dog. Copperfield's eyes narrowed into demonic slits.

She looked back at Grady, who was grinning now. He said, "I suppose I could look for that report, if it weren't for Copper. He's going through a hard transition, Molly. He needs attention, and a stable home environment. The love of a good woman and a safe fenced yard." He leaned back in his chair and waited.

With a sinking heart, Molly looked down at the drooling muzzle and the mean amber eyes. "Oh, Christ," she said. "Not that. Anything but that."

"Everything has its price, Molly." Grady reached his arm around her shoulders, but when the dog began to growl he quickly withdrew it. "Take it or leave it."

★ ★ ★

162

They had tried to leave the dog out in the yard, but he barked nonstop. Then they let him in the house but closed him out of the bedroom. That didn't work because he howled and scratched on the door. So they let him in, which left them with the problem of how to touch one another without getting mauled. They solved it by pulling the covers up over their heads so he wouldn't see them. It seemed to work.

"This is ridiculous," Molly murmured, running her hands down Grady's bare back. "Worse than worrying the kids will walk in on you."

"He'll get used to it, Molly. Give him a little time. Actually, it may be better like this, makes it feel more illicit. Reminds me of being a kid and reading under the covers with a flashlight. Best reading I ever did."

Molly let her fingers wander all the way down the dip in his lower back and over his buttocks, still gloriously lean at fifty-two. "And just what were you reading under the covers, Lieutenant?"

"Detective magazines. Comic books. Innocent stuff."

"Detective magazines aren't so innocent. Ninety percent of all serial killers read them."

"So I guess when you grow up on them, you become either a serial killer or a cop."

"See, not innocent at all." She moved her hips slowly against his until he moaned.

Later on, she was sitting on his back massaging his shoulders.

"Yes," he said, "that knot right there. Molly, my lease is up at the end of the month."

Her hands stopped kneading. "I thought you had another year to go."

"Well, I did, but some of the residents have been complaining, so the landlord terminated it."

"Because of the dog?"

"They're so fussy. He growled once or twice in the elevator."

"Objecting to being growled at in your own elevator doesn't sound fussy to me, Grady."

"Well, I never really liked it there. And it's not a good place for a dog. No yard."

She climbed off him and stretched out next to him.

"I'll have to move," he said.

She closed her eyes.

"Molly, are you there or have you gone to sleep on me?"

"I'm here, Grady."

"If I moved in with you" —he rested the back of his hand on her stomach and slowly inched it downward—"we could read under the covers all the time."

Molly was feeling her body temperature rise, but with anxiety, not passion. She leaned over and kissed him long and warm on the lips. When they both came up for breath, she said, "I love you desperately and forever. But, Grady, I'm not cut out for domestic life. I'm a slow learner, but I do learn eventually, after three failed attempts."

He turned onto his side and pulled her tight against him. "*This* is domestic life. Right here, in bed, talking, making love. Molly, you know I don't expect you to be a wife. I just want to be close to you, see you every day, sleep next to you. So we can do this in the middle of the day, like this. I don't want you to change your life in any way."

"What's the matter with things as they are right now?" she demanded. "I love things this way. And we can do anything we want in the middle of the day now. Anyway, we tried it once and it didn't work."

"Molly, that was twenty-four years ago. We're different people now."

"I know, but—"

The phone rang.

Relieved, Molly threw off the blanket and reached for it. "Yes."

"Molly Cates?"

"Yes."

"Patrick Lattimore, Federal Bureau of Investigation."

"Yes, Mr. Lattimore. Grady is right here." She put her hand over the mouthpiece and said, "Under a blanket hiding from his dog."

"No, it's you I want to talk with," said the voice on the phone. "Miss Cates, do you know a Gerald Asquith?"

Molly sat up. "No, not really. I haven't met him. Just over the phone. We've talked."

"You had an appointment with him tonight?"

Grady sat up and gestured to her to let him listen, too.

She tilted the phone and he put his cheek next to hers.

"Yes," Molly said, "at seven."

"Well, he's not going to keep it. He's dead."

Molly's breath caught in her throat. "How?"

"He was found by a dog-walker at Pease Park,

tied upside down to a tree branch, naked. Throat cut."

"A blood statue?" she whispered.

"Yes, ma'am."

"How did you know I had an appointment with him?"

"Asquith's clothes were folded neatly nearby and in his pocket was his Day-Timer with your name and number. We had an appointment with him this afternoon. When did you talk to him?"

"Last night…around nine, I think. How would the Sword Hand of God have known about him?"

"I wondered about that, too, until I heard that Asquith did a radio show last night, one of the religious stations, and preached about the ungodly heresy of Donnie Ray Grimes." Mordecai hated being called by his old name.

"So they heard it?"

"Yeah. And Mordecai might have, too, but we're certain he can't communicate with anyone but us. I am most distressed by this, Miss Cates. It means the Hearth Jezreelites are actively at work *outside,* looking for victims. How did you learn about Asquith?"

"A friend of mine, Adeline Dodgin in Waco, knew about his past disagreements with Samuel Mordecai. She told me about him. She's the one who persuaded him to call you."

"I see. Could you give me Mrs. Dodgin's number, please?"

"Yes. I'll have to find my book. I'll give you to Grady while I look. Here." She handed the phone to Grady.

She found her address book in the kitchen and

166

got on the extension. She gave him the number. "I'm worried about her," Molly said.

"We'll check on her," Lattimore promised.

When she got back to the bedroom, Grady was sitting up against the headboard looking worried.

Molly sat next to him and slid an arm around him. From the floor came a snarling. The dog was on his feet, poised for attack. Slowly Molly withdrew her arm. "God, I couldn't live with that, Grady."

Grady wasn't paying any attention. He was staring into space. "Mordecai is lethal, he's poison. This means anyone involved in giving information to the feds is in danger. Molly, you need to be careful."

"I am always careful," she said.

He turned a skeptical look on her.

"And now I've got a chaperone." She looked down at the dog, who had settled himself next to the bed, but was watching with vigilant eyes. "So you can go out and find that police report from August 3, 1962."

"We need to talk about my lease," Grady said.

"Sure, we can talk. But let's wait until this Jezreel thing is over."

"Why?"

"Let's say I can only consider one cataclysmic event at a time."

"Of course, Christianity was once a local cult which the established church leaders and the government found threatening; they saw it as extremist, subversive, and potentially violent. History has proved them to be correct."

Molly Cates, "Texas Cult Culture,"
LONE STAR MONTHLY, DECEMBER 1993

CHAPTER NINE

The dog was sleeping on the floor outside her bedroom door. Stretched out, he was so long he blocked the entire doorway. A little pool of saliva had collected on the wood floor under his long muzzle. "Move," she said. He didn't even twitch, so she prodded his back with a bare foot. He exploded to his feet with such force she jumped back instinctively.

To cover her fear, she used her most authoritarian voice. "Copperfield, you are going out in the yard. Now." She had grown up with dogs on her daddy's ranch and had liked them well enough, but this high-strung, volatile creature was nothing like those good-natured hounds. Why on earth had she agreed to this?

The dog looked up at Molly, trembling. She walked across the living room to the sliding-glass door and pulled it open. She stood aside and said, "Out you go." The dog just stood where he was. "I said out," she said louder. He lowered his head and his tail. "Dammit. Copper, come." Very slowly the dog started toward her, one paw in front of the other, as if he were trudging through quick-sand. He walked with his big head hanging. When he reached the door he stopped. Molly took hold of his choke collar and pulled him outside. As she slid the door shut, he turned and stared up at her through the glass.

Before she reached the bedroom door again, he started barking. His barks were sharp and insistent. She whirled around. "No!" she called across the room. In answer, the dog gave one loud, abrupt bark that seemed to echo her word. "No," she shouted again. Again he barked his imitation. She turned and stomped back to the bedroom to find her shoes. Even from inside her closet the barking was deafening; it was continuous now, and intensifying. Damnation. If he went on like that, it would drive her neighbors crazy.

She slid her feet into her shoes and stalked back to the door. The dog had made a large cloudy smudge on the glass. The barking was incredibly loud and annoying. She certainly couldn't leave him outside to do that. Her neighbors in this sedate town-house complex wouldn't tolerate it. But she couldn't leave him inside either. Grady had said when left alone he tended to go on a chewing rampage. Damn.

She looked at her watch. Ten to four. She was due to pick up Jake Alesky at four, and she didn't want to keep him waiting. She looked at the dog hard, trying to stare him down. But he kept up his barking, never even drawing a breath.

Molly opened the door and the dog surged in. Tongue lolling, he ran around Molly in circles. "What am I going to do with you?" she said. The dog ran to the front door and sat staring at the door. "Well," she said, "maybe we'll try it. But don't make me sorry." She picked up his worn leather leash off the kitchen counter and slung her bag over her shoulder. "We're going out to the country, Copper. Maybe you'll run off and get lost, go feral."

Outside in the driveway, she lowered the tailgate on her pickup. Without being told to, the dog leapt up into the truck bed. He looked excited, she thought, happy even, holding his tail higher than she'd ever seen it. "Okay," she told him grudgingly. "But remember, buddy, this is an experiment. I'm watching you."

As she drove south on MoPac she checked the rearview mirror to see what he was doing. He stood with his head raised into the wind and his eyes closed. When she pulled into Piney Haven, three small children were playing behind the office. She watched the dog apprehensively. He could easily leap out and attack them, but he showed no signs of doing that. She drove back to Jake's trailer. He was sitting in his wheelchair under the green awning. He wore a clean white short-sleeved shirt, ironed and crisp, and aviator sunglasses.

Molly got out of the truck, eyeing the dog uneasily. "Sorry about the dog, Jake. I'm taking care of him for a friend and I couldn't leave him at home, so..."

Jake wheeled himself to the back of the truck and looked the dog over. "What happened to you, fellow?" he asked in a low voice.

"Oh, the ear? He's retired from the APD canine unit," Molly said. "He got beat up pretty bad, bludgeoned, actually, with a tire iron. He's a little psycho."

Jake kept studying the dog. "Well, who wouldn't be after that?" he said more to the dog than to Molly. He wheeled closer and held a hand up toward Copperfield. "Hey, fellow." The dog leaned over the side and sniffed his hand. "What's his name?"

"Copper. Short for Copperfield."

"Hey, Copper. What a good old boy you are." The dog stretched his head down and Jake scratched behind the one good ear.

"Are you ready to go?" Molly asked.

Jake gave the big dog a final pat. "All set." He rolled to the passenger door. "If you'll help with the chair, I can get myself in. A truck's a little harder because it's high, but the running board's a big help." He reached up and opened the door, wheeling backward to let it swing open.

Molly came around, feeling awkward and uncertain about how to help. He maneuvered his chair right up to the side and said, "You just hold tight to the chair so it doesn't move. And stand right there so I can brace myself against you if I need to." He gripped the arms of the wheelchair and pushed himself up so he was balanced on his stumps. "Okay, now hold tight." The veins in his arms stood out with the effort of shifting himself to the running board. Then, with one hand on the seat and another on the running board he boosted himself up, off the running board, and onto the seat. It was a lot more difficult to do than he let on. Molly wondered how you built the upper-body strength to do that.

"Wow," she said, once he was settled in the passenger seat, "I don't think I could do that if my life depended on it."

He looked down at her. "Sure you could. Being in a wheelchair makes you really strong through the arms and shoulders. Even if you don't work out, and I do." He gestured at the chair. "To fold it, just squeeze the arms together. Yeah, like that. Now you can set it in the back."

Molly folded the chair, got a tarp from the back seat, spread it out in the bed, and then with difficulty hoisted the chair into the back. By the time she climbed behind the wheel she'd worked up a sheen of sweat. She turned toward him. He was buckling the seat belt. "What's the best way to go?" she asked. "I-35?"

"Yeah. We'll take the 79 West exit toward Taylor."

They drove in silence until Molly got them through the downtown traffic. Once they were headed north on I-35, Jake said, "Tell me about the dog—how he lost his ear."

"The dog. Well, he was in the canine unit for eight years, with the same handler." Grady had told her the story—several times. "One Saturday night he and his handler were searching a field in East Austin, looking for a suspect in a 7-Eleven robbery. Copper tracked the suspect and two of his friends to a shed where they were hiding. The three suspects beat the handler to a pulp with tire irons and tried to do the same to Copper, but he managed to give as good as he got. One of the perps nearly lost an arm and the other two required numerous stitches. Copper lost half an ear.

"When the rest of the cops got to the scene, they arrested the suspects. But Copper went berserk and wouldn't let the cops or EMS get anywhere near his handler. They had their guns drawn to shoot him when one of the EMTs found a tarp. So they netted him. The handler died that night, and Copper was retired with honors. But APD policy dictates that police dogs can retire only with police families and no one in the department would take him home. No one but my friend Grady Traynor, who has never much liked dogs." She sighed. "Grady's been out at Jezreel, he's one of the negotiators. So he coerced me into taking the beast on for a few days. That's why he's in the back of my truck."

Jake turned his head to look at Copper in the back. "Is that such a problem?"

"Not if you remember never to touch anyone in his presence. When you hug someone he panics. He thinks violence is being done and considers it his responsibility to intervene."

"Must be hard on your love life."

"It would be if I had one."

"PTSD," Jake said.

"Huh?"

"Post-traumatic stress disorder. Sounds like that's what he has. Like Vietnam vets."

It seemed like an ideal segue. "You promised to tell me about Walter Demming's vows," Molly reminded him.

"Did I? Well, I might make good on that, but I can see you're someone who always turns the conversation away from yourself. I want to hear some personal contribution from you first. Tell me what you did this morning."

She laughed. "Okay. I went to talk to Samuel Mordecai's grandmother, the woman who raised him."

"What's she like?"

Molly didn't answer right away. Finally she said, "When I was about seven, I saw a play of Hansel and Gretel at the local high school. The witch was so cold and evil that I had nightmares for a year. Dorothy Huff reminds me of her."

"Oh, God," Jake said. "Can't we have any villains anymore? It seems like *everybody* got abused as a child. I suppose this means I can't hate Samuel Mordecai anymore."

"You can still hate him," she replied. "I do. But I caught a glimpse of why he's what he is. Now tell me about Walter's vows."

"Okay. You have to understand these were post-Vietnam vows. Made while he was spending time with me in the Veterans hospital. You can't imagine how angry we were." He shook his head. "No one can imagine."

"Who were you mad at?"

"Oh, our lieutenant, who was an idiot. The army, which fucked everything up. The gooks, who were braver and tougher than we were. My father, who raised me on stories of his World War II exploits, the draft board in Milwaukee that delivered me up, the American people, who didn't give a damn, the whole village of Trang Loi, the Joint Chiefs of Staff, Lyndon Johnson, Smokey the Bear, George Washington. If I'd known you then,

174

I would have been mad at you. We were just fucking furious at everything."

Molly glanced over at him. "You're right—I can't imagine."

"Yeah. Well, Walter made four vows. I told you that obscurity was one of them. The idea was never to do anything or make enough money to get noticed by the government."

"Is that why a man who went to Rice drove a school bus?"

"In part. It also allowed him time to do his real work."

"Which is?"

"You'll see when we get there."

Molly said, "The second vow was noninvolvement?"

"Yeah. No girlfriends could stay over more than one night in a row, no kids, no commitments. The third vow was never again to wear a uniform or a necktie."

Molly laughed. "For me it's panty hose. What about the fourth vow?"

"Oh, that one he's broken."

"What was it?"

"Never again to look into the barrel of a gun. It must have been an awful moment for him, like a flashback, to have been surrounded like that."

"That happened to him in Vietnam?"

Jake stared straight ahead. "No comment."

When they left the Interstate, Molly said, "We're going to go past the turnoff to Jezreel. It's right up here on the left."

"Yeah, I know. Two miles to hell."

As they passed, they looked up the rural road

marked 128. Molly had been down that road once, two years before, when she went to interview Samuel Mordecai at Jezreel. Her memory and the nonstop press coverage had since etched into her mind the compound's distinctive profile. She could draw it in her sleep—the boxlike central portion of the jerry-built wood complex, flanked by two high, round stone towers with crenellated tops and narrow slitlike gunports. Like some cheap Texas version of a medieval castle. She knew if they turned up that road, they'd see the media city, tanks and Bradley Fighting Vehicles, and a bunch of fully armed federal agents and DPS troopers at the checkpoint they'd staked out weeks ago.

"Have you been out there?" Jake asked.

"Not since I interviewed Samuel Mordecai two years ago."

"How come? Seems if you're doing a story on it, you'd want to go out and see it again."

"I see it on the TV news all the time, more than I want to."

"It's not the same thing as seeing it for yourself."

"Sounds like you'd like to go."

"Maybe so. To see what it's like. Yeah. If you decide to go, can I ride along?"

"Don't hold your breath."

Walter Demming's gravel driveway led to a tiny, ramshackle house with stained green siding and warped window frames. A trumpet vine laden with vivid orange blooms grew exuberantly up the side and over the roof. Behind the house stretched a field of wildflowers—the usual bluebonnets and Indian paintbrushes, but in the center was the densest stand of white Texas prickly poppies she'd ever seen—huge fluttery white flowers on tall stalks.

"This is beautiful," Molly breathed.

Jake was unbuckling his seat belt. "Yeah. I like it out here." He pointed to a stone barbecue on the terrace in front of the house. "Walter and me built that, out of rock we collected right around here."

Molly studied the fine rockwork and the natural way the grill seemed to grow right out of the stone terrace.

He pointed to a large white frame house just visible across the field. "That's Theodora Shea's house, Walter's real love. She does the best chocolate cake in the hemisphere."

Molly got out and opened the tailgate. Copper bounded down and started sniffing around just like a normal dog would do on an outing to the country.

She hauled Jake's wheelchair out and set it up, following his directions. Then she held it steady while he maneuvered himself into it. After he'd caught his breath, he wheeled himself toward the house.

Molly hadn't noticed the wheelchair ramp to the side of the steps until they approached the door. Jake propelled himself up it. "Walter and I did this ramp, too." He pulled a key out of his pocket, unlocked the door, and spun to the side to let Molly precede him.

The house was one big sunny room with a bed

in one corner and a kitchen in another. The rest of the room was given over to an artist's studio.

A long wooden picnic table in the center of the room was covered with cans of brushes, bottles, paints, and colored pencils—all neatly organized. On two of the walls and on three easels standing around the room hung pictures in various stages of completion. All were of birds, most of them brightly colored tropical birds.

"Lately he's been doing birds," Jake said. "In pencil."

Molly stood in the middle of the room for a minute to get the feel of Walter Demming's life. She loved to see the places where people did their work and often asked other writers to show her their offices because that seemed to be more revealing of the soul than the houses they lived in. And sometimes it seemed that just being in the workspace of someone whose work you admired might actually magically transfer to you some of their creative energy. Crazy, no doubt, but she was feeling it now as she surveyed Walter Demming's drawings.

She started to wander the room looking at pictures. The birds were all portrayed very close-up and from odd angles. These were not the usual static bird sketches, where you had a complete bird, centered on the paper, neatly grasping a twig and giving the artist its best profile. Instead you saw just part of a bird, as if you were glimpsing it flying through a frame. They were done on white textured paper with bright-colored pencils. The feathers were rendered in a distinctive cross-hatching of colors.

She'd never thought of birds as individuals before, but each of these birds had about its face and feathers the mark of idiosyncrasy; each was a bird you would be able to recognize if you saw it again. The faces were rendered in precise detail, as if the artist knew each of them intimately.

Walter Demming definitely had a style and, judging from the number of works he had going here, he was wildly productive. The feel she got was of a man who let the energy of nature swirl through him and flow out his fingertips. How would a man like that endure captivity? she wondered. Where would all that energy go?

She stopped in front of one of the easels. Arranged diagonally on the paper was the almost finished portrait of a turkey vulture. The bird was shown in profile from about mid-wing and up. The feathers of the wing and breast were rendered in a cross-hatching of brown, black, yellow, and red that shone like a dark mahogany. The naked red neck and head had isolated black hairs, prickly and assertive, growing out of them; the hooked beak seemed huge and translucent.

She was shocked to recognize the bird as Jake Alesky. Why hadn't she noticed when she'd first met him that he looked like a turkey vulture? She would never have thought of it, but now that she'd seen the resemblance, she doubted that she could ever get it out of her head. She stole a glance at him sitting across the room. Did he recognize this?

Jake was sitting in front of a completed drawing of a fluffy, assertive-looking white cockatoo with a few yellow feathers sticking up in a crest. Eyes still fixed on the picture, he said, "That's

Theodora. I wonder if she's seen this. It'll make her mad as hell if she recognizes herself." He swung his chair around so he was facing her. "How do you like Walter's work?"

"I like it very much. *Very* much."

"He's gotten really good. He always drew stuff, even back in Vietnam, but in the past year or two, he's found…oh, I guess his style, or whatever it is artists have to find. He could make some money at it if he'd get with the program."

"What program?"

"Oh, Theodora has lots of good ideas about how to sell. She got them to hang some of his stuff in the cafe over near the Crossroads up near the 128 turnoff. Occasionally someone walks in and buys one. And she thinks she might get him a show in Austin."

"How do you suppose he's managing captivity?" Molly asked.

Jake wheeled his chair to the window and looked out at the field of wildflowers. "Hating it. More than anyone I know, he hates having his freedom restricted. He hates bullies. He hates religion. He hates guns."

"What about children?" Molly asked.

Jake smiled. "I don't think he hates children, but I don't know that he likes them very much either. Other than driving that bus for a few months, I don't think he's ever had much to do with them."

"Would he be a cool head in a crisis, if it comes to it?"

"Cool?" Jake's face colored suddenly and his lips tightened. "You ask if Walter's cool? See if this fits your idea of cool—a man lying in the muck at the edge of a stinking river surrounded by seven bloody corpses, pretending to be dead while Vietcong go around checking on their handiwork. The body on one side of him, that used to be Greg Meeks, gets both ears sliced off with a bayonet. Those ears are strung on a necklace of similar objects one of the gooks is wearing. The gook then stands over Walter and looks down at his ears. He pokes at one with his bayonet. Then he moves on to Junior Carlyle, or what remains of him, lying on Walter's left. The gook leans down and cuts off Junior's ears." Jake continued to stare out at the wildflowers. His voice revealed no emotion.

"I didn't have time right then to wonder what it was about Walter's ears that didn't appeal, but I sure have thought about it since. Walter has small ears, real tight to his head, with almost no lobe. Maybe that was it. But I think it was the color. Both Meeks and Carlyle were black. I think this particular gook was specializing in black ears. While he was adding ears to his collection, Walter just lay there, his mouth and eyes full of muck. No twitching, no whining, no breathing. Is Walter a cool head? you ask me. Lady, the man's subzero."

Molly found it hard to catch her breath. "What happened then?"

"What happened then was the world ended. This freak Samuel Mordecai says the world's going to end on Friday. I know that's not true because it ended on September 2, 1968. The ears were just a tremor in the earth, a warning." He whirled his chair around. "Anyway, it's ancient history now, and not much of a subject for a pretty spring day. Let's go see Theodora. She always makes me feel like the world makes sense."

He wheeled his chair back to the door. "Let's walk on the road. It's shorter to go across the field and I can do it in my chair, but it's hard going." They both went down the ramp and Jake led the way back to the road and down to the next driveway. The house had a front porch with fat pots of red geraniums on the steps. A large golden retriever with a completely white head lay sleeping on the porch with its paws dangling down to the top step.

From around the side of the house dashed a brown-and-white spaniel, who started to yap at them. But the dog came to a sudden stop, staring at a spot behind Molly. She turned and was surprised to see that Copper had followed them. The big dog was standing with his fur bristling and his teeth bared. The spaniel turned and ran back the way it had come, disappearing around the house.

"Probably a wise move," Jake said.

The dog on the porch hadn't even opened an eye.

Molly watched Copper approach stiff-legged, growling low in his throat. "Oh, God, I left the leash in the truck." She started forward to grab the dog's collar.

Jake raised a hand. "Hold on. It'll be okay."

Reluctantly, Molly stood where she was. When Copper stepped on the first stair, growling, the old retriever opened one eye, then the other, and watched Copper approach. Then, when Copper was almost on the porch, the retriever slowly rolled over and offered its belly, paws in the air. Copper stopped and the growling died away. The erect fur flattened; he approached and sniffed the older dog's tail and belly.

Molly had been so riveted by the performance, she hadn't noticed a woman come out the door. The woman was standing still, watching the dogs with a smile of bemused interest on her face. Now she said, "Maggie could teach us all something. Sometimes pacifism works. Hey, there, Jake Alesky. I've missed you, dear heart." She walked briskly down the steps and leaned over to embrace Jake. A snarling from the porch caused her to straighten up. Copper was starting down the steps toward her.

"Oh, my," the woman said.

Molly felt a flush of embarrassment. She moved forward and grabbed Copper's collar. Her hand was shaking, but she managed to hold on and say in a firm voice, "No, Copper. Sit."

She was relieved to see him obey. "Sorry," she said. "He's not my dog. He gets confused when people have contact. He's a retired police dog, a bit unbalanced. I'm sorry."

Jake said, "Theodora, this is Molly Cates. She works for *Lone Star Monthly* and she's writing something about the Jezreel mess. I've been telling her about Walter. Molly, meet Theodora Shea."

Molly was afraid to let go of Copper's collar, so she raised her free hand and said, "It's a pleasure to meet you, Miss Shea." Theodora Shea was probably in her seventies, smooth-skinned and plump under her loose embroidered Mexican dress. Her fluffy white hair was yellowed and sticking out in places and her prominent nose curved gently. She wore white face powder. A cockatoo indeed. The resemblance made Molly smile.

"Molly, will you help me bring some chairs down from the porch so we can sit and talk a bit?" Theodora asked.

Molly looked down at Copper, who appeared to have relaxed. She took a chance and let go of his collar. Then she carried two wicker chairs from the porch and put them at the foot of the steps, one on either side of Jake's wheelchair.

Although both Jake and Molly declined the offer of refreshments, Theodora excused herself and was back in a few minutes bearing a tray with three glasses of lemonade and three huge slices of chocolate cake. She set the tray down on the bottom step and shot both dogs a warning look. "With Walter gone and the poetry group not meeting, I'm drowning in cake. You young people can help me out."

She handed icy glasses to Molly and Jake. Molly refused cake, but Jake took his plate and rested it on what lap he had, which was just large enough to support the plate.

Theodora sat down and said, "We have got to do something. Two FBI agents came to see me the second week, and I told them exactly what I thought about this madman up the road in Jezreel. All this palaver is just not going to work." She took a sip of her lemonade.

Molly noticed how moist and rich the cake looked as the forkfuls moved steadily from Jake's plate to his mouth, how fluffy the white filling in between the layers looked. "Is that whipped cream?" she asked.

"Yes." Theodora reached over to pick up a piece from the tray and hand it to Molly. "We need to snipe him and have the SWAT team move in like the wrath of God, before they have a chance to harm the hostages. I feel certain that Walter would agree with this assessment."

"They can't snipe him," Molly said with her mouth full. "He never shows himself, never even passes an uncovered window."

Theodora took a long, hard look at Molly. "How do you know that?"

"My ex-husband, Grady, is an Austin cop who's on the negotiating team."

Theodora ran her hand through her fluffy white hair. "Well. I knew you hadn't got it from the news, because I watch and read everything. Would they snipe him if they could?"

"That's a tough one. The problem is they're a civilian agency. Mordecai has never been convicted of a crime and he's not actually killing anyone right now that we know of. It's a moot point anyway since he keeps out of sight."

"What does this ex-husband of yours think is the next step?"

"They're reevaluating it," Molly said.

Theodora made a clucking noise. "Oh, come, come. You're among friends. Cut the jargon."

Molly smiled. "Okay. Every time they talk to Mordecai he reminds them that he will kill the hostages the second anyone sets foot inside his fence. The reason they haven't moved in is that they believe that. But, if you believe Mordecai's timetable, we've only got three days left now. Grady thinks it might come to SWAT, or actually

HRT is what the feds call it—Hostage Response Team. He sees them as an absolute last resort because of the high risk to the hostages, but the negotiation's gone nowhere. One problem the HRT has, though, is they don't know where on the twelve acres the hostages are."

"That's a big problem," Theodora conceded. "A big problem."

Jake was quiet. He'd already finished his cake and was going after the crumbs by mashing them onto his fork.

Theodora noticed his empty plate. She leaned over, took it from him, and handed him another one. "Oh, this is intolerable," she said, "the waiting. Doesn't it make you want to march right in there and give them what for?"

"No," Molly said, "it makes me want to run and hide until it's over."

"Me, too," Jake said.

"You say the negotiators are discouraged. I believe it. On TV that Patrick Lattimore looks close to emotional meltdown. Looks like he's giving up."

"They are discouraged."

"If that negotiator friend of yours gets to speak to Walter," Theodora said, "I'd like to send Walter a message. Ask him to send my love and tell him how much we miss him in the poetry group. We haven't done anything since he's been gone. It just doesn't feel right to go on without him. I'd like him to know we are waiting for him."

"Poetry group?" Molly asked.

"Yes. A group of us who enjoy poetry. We get together here every week. The last few months we've been reading Emily Dickinson. Oh, I just wish I could send Walter a complete Dickinson right now. He likes to memorize poetry. It's such a comfort during difficult times to have in your head when you need it."

"*Need* it?" Molly said.

"Yes. I'm afraid by now he might be running out and needs some replenishment. Don't you read poetry?"

"Almost never," Molly admitted. "I wish I did. But I can't imagine needing it. And Emily Dickinson! I have unpleasant memories of a high school anthology: "There is no frigate like a book.""

"Oh, it's such a crime the way they teach poetry in schools, especially the way they teach Dickinson. Really, she has so much to say to these alienated young people. She's very accessible. I taught English for thirty years, before I retired, and sometimes I worry that the readers of poetry are dying off one by one. I have this recurring vision that one day the very last of us will be walking home from a library with a book under her arm and keel over and that will be the end of the breed, and no one will ever know or mourn it."

Molly glanced up at the porch. The retriever was lying in the same place and Copper was lying next to her, his head resting against her flank.

"They seem to have hit it off, don't they?" Theodora said. "Maggie makes friends easily."

Jake said, "I've never seen Maggie do anything but lie right there at the top of those steps with her eyes closed."

Theodora laughed. "Maybe that's one good way

to make friends—just make space for them on your porch."

Jake handed Theodora his plate, from which he'd cleaned every crumb. "Thanks. It was delicious as usual, but we have to go. Can you keep on checking the house?"

"Sure. No trouble. Don't you worry, Jake." She turned to Molly. "Wait a minute. I'd like to give you something to take with you." She bounded up the steps and returned in a few minutes with a large tinfoil package and a fat book. She handed the package to Jake. "It would be a favor to me to get some of this out of my kitchen," she told him. The book she handed to Molly. It was *The Complete Poems of Emily Dickinson.*

"I'd appreciate it if you would give it to your negotiator friend, in case he gets a chance to send it in to Walter. Would you do that for me, please, Molly?"

Molly had to stifle a snort, thinking about Grady's response to that request. It was ludicrous. In the hierarchy of things she'd like to send in to the hostages, a book of poems by a repressed New England spinster was at the bottom of the list. Better to send them chocolate cake. "Sure," she told Theodora Shea, sticking the book in her bag.

"And I looked, and behold a pale horse: and his name that sat on him was Death, and Hell followed with him. And power was given unto them over the fourth part of the earth, to kill with sword, and with hunger, and with death, and with the wild beasts of the earth."

REVELATION 6:8

CHAPTER TEN

"You kids know what a vegetable peeler is," Walter Demming said. "Your mother has one, I bet, in the kitchen drawer. Along with all the stuff like corkscrews and garlic presses and spoons with holes—you know, the stuff she uses for cooking."

"My mom doesn't cook," Heather said. "We take home from McDonald's or sometimes Chinese." When she spoke the word "Chinese," her face glowed, as though just saying the word had filled her mouth with juicy, succulent bliss. Walter's mouth watered in response, and for an instant he tasted and smelled the chicken in hot garlic sauce from China Sea, where he and Jake often got take-out dinners, which they ate on Jake's veranda, with lots of Shiner Bock to wash it down.

"I love Chinese food." Sandra closed her book and abandoned all pretense of not listening. "Egg rolls, fried rice, sweet-and-sour pork. There's a place near us that delivers."

"My mom cooks really good," Hector said. "The best tamales. The *best.* Everybody says so. They're so good she sells them and every year she does this thing for the church where she makes hundreds of them and they raise lots of money by selling them. If I could have anything right now—other than an Uzi—it would be a huge pan of my mom's tamales. When we get out of here, my mom will have a party for us and we'll stuff ourselves with her tamales—as many as we want."

"My dad cooks," Josh said, "and I help him. We've got a couple of those vegetable peelers. We use them to peel potatoes when we're making mashed potatoes. But we leave a little skin on because my dad says it makes them more interesting. We put lots of butter and milk in them, and after you've had the mashed potatoes we make, you could never eat the boxed ones, the fake kind you like, Kim."

"You can put butter in the box kind, too, Josh," Kim said, "and salt and make them taste really good and there are no lumps."

"What I love even better than mashed potatoes," Josh said, "is fresh bread. My dad got this machine, a bread maker, for Christmas. So we make bread and we cut it while it's still hot even though you're not supposed to, and we put butter and sugar on it and it smells better than anything in the world."

A reverent and hungry silence followed.

Walter felt his stomach doing flips of desire. If they ever got out of here, the first thing he was going to do was make bread and put butter and sugar on it while it was still hot. It was the most desirable thing in the world. He looked around at the kids and thought if you could look into their heads and see what they were picturing, you would have some delectable illustrations for a cookbook.

"One sure thing," Sandra said softly, "I'm never, ever gonna eat cereal again."

"Me either," Conrad said.

"Well, anyway," Walter said, "back to the vegetable peeler. It's a thin metal thing about this long." He held his right thumb and forefinger as far apart as he could get them. "It's got a thin pointed blade with a long slot running the length of it. You use it to peel vegetables. But Jacksonville didn't understand why the old lady gave it to him. Where were the vegetables? What was he supposed—"

"For the bars," Bucky blurted out. "He's *so* dumb. It's for peeling the bamboo bars!"

Walter raised his eyebrows. "I never said Jacksonville was a genius. He's got some good traits—he's loyal and honest—but he's not what you'd call a quick thinker. It takes him a while to figure things out, Bucky. So be patient. And remember he's been under a lot of stress. Most of us don't think so well under pressure."

Boy, is that the truth, he thought. Some of us don't think at all under pressure. So far he'd been a total bust. Today, when he got on that phone, he was going to have a last chance to do something. Surely the reason the FBI had not come in to rescue them was that Samuel Mordecai had threatened to kill them if they attacked. Otherwise they would not have allowed forty-eight days to pass without doing something. You couldn't just kidnap a school bus and get away with it. And another problem was that they probably didn't know where the kids were being held. That made a rescue difficult in a place as big and spread out as this compound had looked to him. If he could just let the FBI know where they were and what he would promise to do during a rescue, it might help. He'd also like to let them know that if they didn't come in, he and the kids were dead for sure. But it was risky and he only had one minute to do it. It all depended on—

"Mr. Demming! Earth to Mr. Demming!" The twangy girl's voice interrupted his train of thought. Walter looked around. It was Kim, trying to call him back to the story, always there, from the start, to point out to him how responsible adults should behave. "Mr. Demming, are you okay?"

"Oh, sure. Sure. Sorry. I was thinking about something else. Where was I, Kim?"

"Jacksonville was trying to figure out how to use the vegetable peeler."

"Oh, yeah. He kept looking at it, trying to figure it out. It was an old vegetable peeler—they last forever—it's a kitchen utensil you only need one of in a lifetime. It had a little rust on the blade part, but it looked plenty sharp. After a while he remembered a friend of his peeling carrots and then he looked at the green bamboo bars, and slowly he got the idea. Maybe he could scrape the bars. Maybe he could peel enough away so he could escape. Maybe he could do it now, in the dark, before morning."

Josh let out some dry, hacking coughs that sounded ominous. Walter paused, worried the coughs might lead to an attack. After a few seconds, however, Josh recovered, and nodded that he was all right.

Walter continued: "He picked the peeler up with

his claw and tried to peel one of the bamboo bars. But the peeler just slid off. It didn't do anything. See, vultures don't have strong claws like hawks and eagles because they're scavengers who don't usually kill their prey. But their beaks are very strong. So Jacksonville tried using his beak instead to hold the peeler. That worked better. After a few minutes he made some progress. He had a long way to go, but he was a hard worker and he kept on scraping. While he worked, he thought about Lopez. He wondered where he was.

"You kids have probably been wondering, too. Where has Lopez been all this time? Last time we saw him, he'd burrowed into a hill outside the town after eating too many slumber bugs.

"Well, Lopez finally woke up after about twenty-four hours of sacking out. He remembered Jacksonville had said he was going to go into Moo Goo Gai Pan. So Lopez headed on into town. His progress was pretty slow because armadillos tend to shuffle along with their noses plowing the ground. Even when they're hurrying, armadillos are slow. They're even slower than we human beings, and by the standards of the animal world, we are pretty darn slow."

Conrad laughed. "That's why you always see them squished on the road. Ugh."

"Roadkill." Sue Ellen wrinkled her nose.

"Road pizza," Hector said.

"Highway hamburger!" Heather called. "Great green gobs of greasy, grimy gopher guts!"

"Blasted armadillo butts," Josh chimed in. "Mutilated monkey meat."

"Dirty turkey vulture feet," Walter sang.

They all laughed uproariously. Walter thought the laughter was the most beautiful sound in the world. He hadn't heard much of it lately. He wished he could sing and tell jokes, make up songs, entertain them, but he couldn't. His story would have to do.

"On his way to town, Lopez came to this neighborhood where giant anteaters lived. These are cousins of the armadillo—they're both edentates—but anteaters are much bigger, and they have long hollow noses, really long. And claws that are awesome. And when Lopez set eyes on the female anteaters, well, he just couldn't believe it. They were so big and glossy. And they had these long, plumy tails that swayed when they walked. He loved looking at them."

Hector and Kim laughed.

"And the anteaters were all eating slumber bugs—they had camped out next to a huge hill that was just chock-full of them. Also, they were drinking cheap wine from jugs. They had a huge supply of that, too."

Walter stopped. He kept getting lost, forgetting where he was in the story. His mind kept wandering back to the phone call he was going to make. Martin said it would happen around ten and they would come get him right before that. Now it was almost nine and he wanted to go into a corner and practice some more. He wanted to have some time alone to be silent and get prepared. This was the last chance. He tried to imagine what was going on aboveground, but he had so little to go on.

"Mr. Demming. Earth to Mr. Demming. Go on," Lucy said.

"Right. Now…Let's see. Were we talking about Lopez? He knew he should be looking for Jacksonville, but one of the females invited him to visit awhile. And one thing led to another. Lopez ate slumber bugs, he drank wine, he kissed the female anteaters, and he fell asleep again. When he woke up it was dark and he felt really guilty about Jacksonville. So he asked around. Had anyone seen a vulture of Jacksonville's description? Someone told him about the Tongs capturing a buzzard and dragging him off.

"Lopez didn't know what to do. He was scared to go into the Tong camp alone, so he got the anteaters to go along with him—for protection. He bribed them. He promised if they came and helped him rescue his buddy, he would buy them some more wine. So they all went to the Tong camp. It was dark and they saw the fire, so they crept up to it and looked through the bushes. In the firelight they saw the big pot boiling and all the Tongs gathered in a circle around poor Dr. Mortimer.

"Now Lopez knew they were going to have to do something right quick if they were going to save the doctor. He had to come up with a plan. What he did was this: He told all the giant anteaters to suck wine up into their long snouts and spray it out. But that plan didn't work because the anteaters had already drunk all the wine, every drop. So he had to figure out something else.

"Now, it happened that all the anteaters who'd come with him were boys. The girls had all gone to bed. So here's what Lopez did: He got the anteaters to line up. There were lots of them and they'd all drunk so much wine they were full of it.

195

He counted to five and at the same time they all peed on the Tongs. Long streams of pee."

Walter stopped because the kids were laughing. It was a cheap shot. After forty-eight days with this age group, he knew how popular bathroom jokes were.

Hector said through his laughter, "That's great. I thought Lopez had something to do with it."

"Didn't the Tongs know it was pee?" Heather asked. "You can smell it."

"Well, they noticed that it was different from normal rain and that's one of the things that scared them. But it smelled more like wine because that was what they'd been drinking." Walter knew he wasn't making any sense. He was barely able to concentrate now, thinking about the phone call coming up.

"My mom drinks wine," Heather said, "and even when she says she hasn't been, I know she has because I can smell it. Was it red or white wine?"

"It was white wine," Walter told her. "Tongs don't use alcohol at all, so they really aren't familiar with its smell the way you are, Heather."

Walter looked at his watch. He couldn't concentrate. He was just too preoccupied to go on. His head was churning with anxieties. If only he knew what was happening aboveground. Martin spoke of the negotiators as if they were just a part of everyday life. So maybe there had been ongoing conversation during these endless days. His only contact with the negotiators, the only reason he knew for sure they were out there, had been the half-minute conversation the second day. If you could call what they'd had a conversation. Walter had read, at gunpoint, a statement Mordecai handed him: "'My name is Walter Demming. The eleven children are with me. We are all safe and being taken care of. Samuel Mordecai is in charge here. He has an important message for the world.'"

A voice had said, "Mr. Demming, I'm Andrew Stein of the Federal Bureau of Investigation. We are doing everything we can to secure your release. The safety of you and the children is our primary concern. What can we—" At that point Samuel Mordecai had taken over the phone and Walter had been dragged back to the barn through a wooden corridor. Then they pulled the wooden slab aside and shoved him back down into the buried bus. That was the only time he'd been aboveground in forty-eight days. The only time he'd heard a voice from the outside world.

Surely by now the FBI knew that Mordecai was no negotiator. The man had his own agenda and it didn't include letting them go. Walter had vague recollections of news items about hostage situations and the Waco standoff. There was something in Utah and something in California, he thought, but he couldn't remember the details. So what were the negotiators thinking of?

Walter had been awake all night thinking about the negotiators, wondering how smart they were, wondering if what he was going to try was worth the risk. He was going to try to tell them they were all underground, in the barn. He was going to try to tell them that they should attack and he would keep the kids down and safe for as long as it took. But it would work only if the people on the receiving end of his message were creative in trying to figure it out, only if they went to the trouble of talking to the important people in his life—Jake and Theodora. Certainly they would locate Jake. But Theodora? He just didn't know.

"Mr. Demming, are you all right?" Kim asked. "I guess that's all for today, huh?"

"Yes." He looked up at the kids. "I'm sort of preoccupied, thinking about the phone call. I could use a little quiet time to get myself ready. I want to give your messages just right."

"Mr. Demming," Conrad said, "I want to change my message. Can I do some more?"

"No. Remember, we timed it at one minute. You can change what you've got if it's the same length."

"Oh, I guess not then. I was just thinking. When we were talking about food, I got to thinking about the fried liver my mom—"

"Liver!" Sandra grimaced. "Barf."

"Mr. Demming," Lucy said, "what happens if we get rescued before you finish the story?"

Walter held up two fingers as though he were taking the Boy Scout oath. "I promise you this, Lucy goosey, if we get rescued before I finish, I'll get you all together and do it later. Maybe when Hector's mom has us over for tamales."

Ten minutes later, as Walter was reading over the twelve messages for the hundredth time, the wooden cover scraped back and they all looked toward the pit. "It's time!" Martin's head appeared upside down next to the bulb at the bus door. "Come on, Bus Driver. I'll give you a hand up."

"Okay." Walter stood up. He folded his paper and tucked it into his shirt pocket. He glanced toward the empty fourth seat where he'd stuffed the knife inside a rip and deep under the padding for safekeeping. "I won't be long," he said, looking around at the kids.

Hector came up close and gave him a little punch in the chest. "Good luck, man." He stood on his tiptoes and whispered into Walter's ear, "This is going to work for us, I know it. The FBI's real smart. I seen it in that movie *The Silence of the Lambs*. They'll figure it out."

Walter tried to smile. What he was planning to do seemed so ridiculous. He was taking a big risk for something that seemed impossibly unrealistic, as ephemeral as moonbeams.

As he walked up the aisle to the door, each of the kids except Philip reached out to touch him. Walter stopped and took each hand in turn, engulfing each smaller hand in both of his and squeezing. It was as if he were receiving from each of them a surge of power and confidence. By the time he got to the door, he felt all things were possible.

"Each time a new cultic prophet bursts to public attention, we dismiss him as a violent eccentric making a guest appearance from the lunatic fringe. But these religious wild men have a long and continuous history in the United States; they speak not to some momentary discontent or aberration, but to persistent American pain and alienation that expresses itself in a yearning for a holy community under the protection of an old-fashioned patriarch."

MOLLY CATES, "TEXAS CULT CULTURE,"
LONE STAR MONTHLY, DECEMBER 1993

CHAPTER ELEVEN

He called just after midnight. "How's my dog?"

Molly had been asleep for less than an hour. She turned over and looked down at the floor where the dog lay in the pale spill from the nightlight—a huge dark shape stretched out next to her bed. Earlier, she'd closed the door to keep him out of the bedroom, but he'd kept her awake whining and scratching on the door, so eventually she'd relented and let him in.

"At least he doesn't smell bad," she said, her voice hoarse with sleep. She reached down to pat his head. "I hope he doesn't have fleas."

"Not Copper," Grady said.

"We went out to the country. He made a friend—a senile golden retriever—but he nearly killed her first."

"Ah," he said. "You're bonding with him. I can tell."

She sat up and leaned against the headboard. "You found something."

"You sound sleepy. What are you wearing?"

"Oh, so this is one of those calls."

"Uh-huh. What have you got on?"

"Chanel No. 5 and the radio." She laughed. "I think I'll come over and see my dog."

"Come. But first tell me what you've found."

"Lots of dust, pill bugs, a few spiders—and you know how I feel about spiders—arggh!"

"Come on, Grady. Don't toy with me."

"Molly, you really live right."

Her heartbeat quickened.

"The officer who made that report about the baby on August 3, 1962, was Patrolman Oscar Mendez. I checked the roster. Mendez retired in '78 and died in '91."

So it was a dead end. Molly felt a pang of disappointment. "That's living right?" she asked.

"Just wait," Grady said. "The jogger who found the baby in the cooler and called the police was one Jerry Brinker, who lived with his sister in Westlake Hills."

"Lived?"

"Yeah. I tracked the sister down. Jerry died last year. Heart attack while jogging on the hike-and-bike trail."

"Oh, shit."

"Now don't forget you are talking to one of the most indefatigable investigators in the history of the Austin PD. With a computer and a telephone there is very little I can't do. You will recall there was a witness who saw Jerry find the baby. His name is Hank Hanley."

"Is?"

"Yes, ma'am. A twenty-year-old homeless man at the time, living along Waller Creek. And guess what?"

"What?"

"Hank's now a fifty-three-year-old homeless man living along Waller Creek and sometimes, in really inclement weather, at the Salvation Army. He often takes his meals there."

"Does he have a sheet?"

"Sure. The usual class C misdemeanors—seventeen arrests for public intoxication and nine for trespass. Not too bad for a wino with such a long career. But he also has three arrests for peeping."

"How did you track him down?"

"A combination of technology and native cop cunning."

"Oh, Grady, I do love you."

"Because I'm a crack investigator?"

"That. And because you fix toilets."

"See, I'm useful around the house."

"You certainly are."

"You could have me on call twenty-four hours a day."

"Like a live-in janitor?"

"Janitor, handyman, cop, lover, masseur—you can have it all."

"Tempting. We'll talk about it sometime."

"Okay. Do you want to take over on Hank Hanley, Molly? Or shall I go roust him now, rough him up a little?"

She switched on the lamp so she could think better. "He'll know you're a cop and he might clam up. This is delicate. I think I'll take it. First thing in the morning. God, I hope he hasn't totally pickled his brains. Come over and tell me how you worked these miracles. Bring dog food, so you can feed the beast before you go back to Jezreel in the morning."

"I'm on my way."

She woke to the tickle of fingertips brushing down her spine, caressing one vertebra at a time, in circles so light it felt like butterfly wings. Then the butterflies spread out, fluttering along her ribs, under her arms, in circles around her breasts, and down her stomach, making her skin quiver in their path.

"Mmmm," she said. "Don't stop."

A voice whispered in her ear, "I could wake you up every morning. How about an alarm clock that wakes you like this?" Lips touched the rim of her ear and the nape of her neck.

"Mmmm. Yes. That would be good. But what else would it do? Show me the full range."

"Let's see, there would be two hands coming out, like this." He cupped her breasts. "Or maybe three hands." He moved his foot up her leg, running the toes slowly from her ankle up her inner thigh. "Or four." He pressed himself against her back.

Molly laughed. "No dreading the alarm going off."

"Shhhh. You'll wake him," he whispered into her ear.

She glanced over the edge of the bed at the dark shape on the floor.

She opened her mouth to complain, to tell him that it was absurd to have to keep quiet for a dog, that he should throw the beast out, but Grady stopped all complaint with his mouth.

Afterward she asked, "Any news from Jezreel?"

"Nothing. Two more days left on Mordecai's schedule. By the way, do you know the significance of Jezreel in the Bible?"

"You mean the great Valley of Jezreel where the Battle of Armageddon is going to take place, according to the Book of Revelation? Two hundred million mounted troops? Ancient serpents and giant locusts that sting like scorpions? A third of mankind killed? Blood rising as high as the horses' bridles?"

"Molly, you've been reading the Bible."

"Pretty horrific stuff, Revelation. The end of the world, directed by Oliver Stone. I suppose Mordecai picked Jezreel, Texas, to settle down in because he expects some big battle to be fought there."

"I'm sorely afraid there will be a battle," Grady said grimly as he departed.

Molly buried her face in the pillow.

She tried to go back to sleep; it was only five-thirty, but Grady had fed the dog and left him outside, and now the wretch was barking. She got up to let him in, thinking about Hank Hanley, who, she was willing to bet, didn't often have people thinking about him.

★ ★ ★

Molly had never been inside the new Salvation Army shelter. It was a huge, stark, red-brick fortress with pinched windows. *"Dedicated in 1987,"* said the plaque at the door, *"to the glory of God and service to humanity."* Molly recalled that it had taken ten years of fierce wrangling over the location before God and humanity could be served on this run-down block at Eighth and Neches. Everyone in this laid-back and liberal town firmly believed in the cause the Sally served, but no one wanted to have it as a neighbor.

At the reception desk, a young man was watching a portable television. On the screen was the all too familiar profile of the Hearth Jezreelite compound in the background and a local reporter in the foreground.

To get the young man's attention, she had to raise her voice. When he turned reluctantly from the screen, Molly asked, "Anything new happening out there?"

"No, ma'am." He flicked the sound off. "You know what I think we ought to do?"

Molly had heard countless ideas on the subject in the past forty-eight days. Everyone had an opinion. She scanned the young man's buzz haircut and earnest jaw and prepared herself for another SWAT fantasy. "What?"

"I think we ought to send in a Trojan horse." He picked up a paperback book and showed it to her. The *Iliad*.

"With a SWAT team hiding inside?"

"No. Angels. Well, really it would be the FBI, or maybe Delta Force, or Israeli commandos, but

205

they'd be dressed up like angels so this Mordecai guy would think they'd come to fight Armageddon on his side. But under their white robes they'd have grenades and Uzis and all. They'd rescue the kids quick and put 'em inside the horse, which would be armored like a tank, and then they'd kill all those crazies and take the kids home to their mamas."

"I like it," Molly said, thinking it made as much sense as anything the cops had come up with. "Is Hank Hanley on your list for last night?"

He didn't even glance at the list posted on the wall next to him. "No, ma'am. But he usually comes in for breakfast. If you want to wait, he'll probably be along because we're just starting to serve."

"Do you know where he usually sleeps?"

"No. Hank likes to sleep raw—you know, out in the elements—rather than here. He says guys in the dorm are always trying to get into his pants." He guffawed.

"Well, maybe they are," she said.

"Wait until you see old Hank," he told her. "Set yourself down over there and I'll call you when I spot him."

Molly chose a metal folding chair near the desk and watched the people coming in. Mostly men, they arrived in clusters of three or four. The majority appeared to be what you'd expect at the Sally—the truly down-and-out—but a surprising number looked like the middle class with a few wrinkles in their pants.

Three women came in carrying shopping bags, arguing in low voices. Molly watched them with fascination. She had been wanting to do an article on homeless women ever since she discovered how many women, herself included, harbored bag-lady nightmares. It seemed especially true of women who were going through a divorce or major life change. The three crones standing in the door arguing could have played the witches in *Macbeth* . She wanted to hear their life histories, see where they slept, follow them on their daily routines, photograph them. She wanted to know what they carried around in their bags.

The young man at the desk called to her, "Ma'am, here he comes."

He walked in alone—a cadaverously thin man, stooped, with a grizzled gray-and-ginger beard. Her heart sank. This was going to be a colossal waste of time. He was the walking dead, a poster boy for the horrors that alcohol can inflict on the human body. Hank Hanley looked ninety-three, not fifty-three. His sun- and dirt-stained skin was so dry and wrinkled it looked mummified. He wore Levi's that would have slid off his hips if two of the belt loops hadn't been tied together with a shoelace. His stained white gimme hat said "Hard Rock Cafe—London."

Molly rose. "Mr. Hanley?"

He reached up to take off his hat, but he missed it. On the second try he snagged the bill and lifted it off. Long ago someone had instilled in him some manners, and they were still there. "Ma'am?"

"I'm Molly Cates, Mr. Hanley. Could we sit down and talk for a minute?"

His sunken eyes darted around in confusion and his jaw quivered. "Do I know you, ma'am?"

207

"No. But I sure would appreciate it if you'd give me a few minutes of your time."

"I ain't done nothing wrong," he insisted.

"Oh, no. I just want to talk."

His darty eyes came to rest on her. "Not a cop."

Molly chuckled. "Definitely not a cop. A writer."

Hank raised a shaky hand to his beard. "A writer."

"Yes. Maybe I could take you out to breakfast," she suggested. "Is there somewhere around here you like better than this?"

He began to scratch furiously at his beard. "I like the House of Pancakes right well, but I...can't—"

"I'd like to treat you. My truck's up the street. We'll drive."

"Oh, yes, ma'am."

"Molly," she said. "Call me Molly and I'll call you Hank."

In the morning heat they walked to the truck and talked about the weather. It turned out that the weather was Hank's best subject, something he was very much in touch with. Hottest spring in eleven years, he told her. Humid, more rainfall than average. More mosquitoes and fire ants than anyone could remember. Fleas something fierce.

As they crossed Eighth Street, she felt the urge to hold on to his arm, to protect him, so precious was he—the only living link to that old event. It was hopeless, of course. This wreck of a man was unlikely to remember his own middle name, let alone the details of finding a discarded infant more than three decades ago. Even if there was something to remember that wasn't in the police report.

Inside the pancake house, the hostess took one look at Hank and bristled. She was slow in seating them, and when she leaned over to hand him a menu, her nostrils flared in protest.

After the waitress slapped down two mugs and poured them some coffee, Molly got down to business: "Hank, how's your memory?"

He gave a creaky-sounding chuckle. "My memory, ma'am? Like a piece of Swiss cheese." He took a long, loud slurp of his coffee.

"So's mine," Molly said. They both laughed, that rueful, knowing laugh people tended to reserve for the frailties of their own aging. "But there are some things that happened to me many years ago that were so unusual, so striking, that I will never forget them." Molly tried to look into his dark eyes for a response, but they looked blank. "I bet there are things like that for you, Hank."

"I remember my mama real good. And the day of my seventh birthday."

Molly smiled at him. Maybe, just maybe. "Hank, a long time ago you were down by Waller Creek when a man found a baby. You remember? A baby boy floating in a beer cooler." She watched his face.

Slowly his mouth opened, as if in wonderment. The few teeth left to him looked as if their days were numbered.

"I'd like you to tell me about that," she said.

"A long time ago," he said.

"Yes. Thirty-three years."

"But how did you know?"

"You mean that you were there?"

He nodded.

"From the report the patrolman wrote, the officer who came and took the baby. You remember that? He took your name down."

Hank nodded.

"Hank, please tell me about that day."

"I didn't do nothing wrong. I was just down there by the creek." He set his dry lips into a firm line.

"I know," Molly said. She paused, feeling herself inching out onto some thin ice. She needed to give him a reason for her questions, something to calm his anxieties. Of course, she couldn't tell him the real reason. If she told him that the baby found that day had grown up to be Samuel Mordecai, it would be public within hours. She'd seen it happen before. This man sitting across from her would be selling his story to national magazines; he'd be an instant celebrity, get a new suit, go on *Oprah* and *Hard Copy*. If this lead was to turn into something with some bargaining power, it needed secrecy.

Molly Cates tried not to tell lies. She'd been reared by a father and an aunt who came down hard on the side of truth. When she did lie, she tried to be careful to tell only lies that would not be found out later. She also tried to restrict herself to lies she could rationalize as having some good purpose. As she concocted a story to tell to Hank Hanley, she was aware of how lie leads on to lie, and that this one was likely to be only the first of many.

"The reason I'm asking," she said, "is that the baby grew up and now he's a friend of mine and he wants to find his parents, his real mother. He asked me to help him."

Hank licked his lips and said, "He grew up. How is he?"

"He's good. A fine young man." She was tempted to elaborate, but she stopped herself.

"What does he do?" Hank asked.

"He's an accountant with a wife and two daughters. But you know how it is—he's thirty-three now and he wants to find his real mama and papa." She thought about telling how he'd worked his way through college and played soccer, but she made herself quit there.

Hank's eyes began to water. "An accountant. He was just a tiny little baby, so small." He cupped his trembling hands to show how small the baby was. "He was wrapped up in this real shiny red blanket."

"Yes. I have that blanket. Actually it's a silk bathrobe."

"Is it now? How about that. Just how about that..." Hank seemed to be coming to life, getting some animation in his voice. Maybe it was the coffee. Maybe it was remembering the event.

The waitress arrived to take their order. Hank, his eyes still watering, ordered eggs, hash browns, and a side stack of buttermilk pancakes. Molly ordered French pancakes with no orange sauce.

"Hank, would you tell me how it happened? Everything you can remember."

"This ain't gonna get me in trouble, is it? I don't want no trouble."

"Absolutely not."

"Well, if it'll help that young fella. An accountant, you say?"

Molly nodded.

"I never seen such a tiny baby, so small. I think he was just born."

"That's right. When the policeman took him to the hospital, the doctor said he was only a few hours old."

"So. Well." Hank shook his head. He seemed to have forgotten he was telling a story, so Molly prodded him. "What were you doing down at the creek?"

"Oh, sleeping, I was sleeping there. See, it was early in the morning. I was just sleeping, that's all. Just sleeping."

Molly could see that if she was going to get anything out of him she was going to have to drag it out, word by word. "Tell me about finding the baby. Did you see it first, or did the other man?"

"The other man, the runner. He saw it first."

"Uh-huh."

"See, I got up to…uh, use the rest room. And he was running by. You know this is real clear. I remember this part real good. He was running by, black shorts and no shirt." He looked up at Molly. "I wonder what happened to him."

"He died last year, while he was jogging."

"Died? Oh, he looked so…healthy." His eyes watered again and this time some of it overflowed and ran down into his beard. He seemed not to notice. Molly couldn't decide if they were tears or the product of some rheumy eye condition.

Warmed up now, he went on talking without any prodding. "That man, the jogger, he stopped and made this little noise. Like 'Ooh.' And then he stepped into the water—it was real shallow there—and he grabbed up this white cooler. I remember what he said exactly. Isn't that something? After all this time I can still remember the exact words. Like you say, there are some things that happen to you in your life that are real unusual and this was real unusual. It sure was." He shook his head in amazement.

"What did he say?"

"He said, 'Holy Jesus, it's a live kid in here.' Then he said, 'Who would leave a kid like this?' and he picked the baby up and held it against his chest. He was all wet from sweating and the baby was all wet from, I guess, wetting himself. That baby didn't cry or nothing." Hank stopped and stared into space. "Didn't make a sound."

"What happened then?"

"Well, I came up and the two of us decided we needed to find some help. So we walked up to the road. He kept that baby held tight to his chest with both hands, and called out to some people at one of the university buildings to call a policeman and he got there in just a few minutes. When the cop saw that baby, he called on his radio for a lady officer to come help and she come and took the baby off. To the hospital, I guess."

"Then what?"

"Let's see. Gets a little cloudy for me here. I think we took the cop back down to where we'd left the cooler and showed him where we found the baby. That's when he wrote our names down, I think. And then he drove off."

Their plates arrived and Hank fell on his pancakes with vigor. After a few bites, he stopped. "You know something? That baby never cried once. An accountant, huh?"

213

Molly drizzled some maple syrup on her pancakes. "Hank, before the jogger came by did you see anyone else around?"

"Don't believe so," he said with his mouth full of pancakes. "No. Just the jogger." He gave a little laugh. "And the baby."

"But you'd been sleeping near there, you said."

"Yeah, but I was…you know, sleeping. You don't see nothing when you're sleeping."

"Was there anyone else there with you?"

"No. I stay alone 'cause these other bums, they always want something."

"What about during the night? Did you hear anything?"

"You know, ma'am, I drank a bit back then. When I went off to sleep nothing much could wake me up."

Molly felt the dull ache of a dead end approaching. There are some questions that never get answered. Sometimes you just had to accept that.

Hank devoted himself to breakfast with the single-mindedness of a bird going after a worm, and Molly, inspired, did the same. She paid and they left with the hostess scowling at their backs.

As they walked through the parking lot, Molly was feeling the old desperation that accompanied dead ends. "Shall I drop you back at the Sally?" she asked Hank as she unlocked the truck.

He climbed in. "I'd rather go up to the blood bank over on Twenty-ninth Street, if you're going that way."

Molly did not ask him about the blood bank; the idea of selling blood, let alone the idea of *him* selling blood, was just too much for her to tackle.

As she drove up Trinity, she got to thinking about the baby floating in Waller Creek and she wanted to be able to visualize it. That gave her an idea. It was probably desperation, mixed with her usual oxlike resistance to giving up something she wanted. "Hank, before I drop you off, will you show me the place on Waller Creek where you found the baby? It's not too far from here, is it?"

"Not far. I go there sometimes. I'll show you."

He directed her up Trinity to just past MLK. "Here," he said. "Right here."

It was on the edge of the university campus, where parking was always impossible. Molly pulled into a G permit place, wondering if she should start deducting her considerable parking fines as business expenses.

Hank led the way across the street to a stone bridge. They passed by Santa Rita No. 1, the old drilling rig that had first hit oil on land owned by the University of Texas. The rig had been moved from West Texas to the campus as a reminder of where the steady stream of money that supported the university came from. What Molly loved about it was that it talked. From a little speaker mounted on top emanated a continuous narration—the story of the miraculous gusher in 1923. This memorial was such a good idea, Molly thought, everyone ought to have something similar set up as a continual reminder of one's origins and source of revenue. It was like her keeping her daddy's old typewriter and Webster's dictionary next to her computer to remind her of where her respect for words came from.

Hank didn't even glance at the oil rig that talked.

He led her to one end of the bridge and slipped between it and a dense growth of trees that hid the path there. It was a muddy incline, steep and rough. Hank navigated it with the ease of a frequent traveler. Molly followed, sliding and grabbing tree branches for support. At the bottom, a clearing dipped downward to the creek, which was bubbling along under the arch of the bridge.

"This way." Hank turned and disappeared under the bridge. Molly hesitated when she saw how dark it was underneath, but she followed along on the gravel ridge that ran next to the water. Flattened cardboard cartons, brown bags containing empty whiskey bottles, and discarded rags indicated human habitation there.

They emerged into a bucolic scene of tall trees and dense foliage on both sides of the creek. Way below street level, they were invisible to the people passing above. It felt as if they'd dropped into some secret underworld, totally separate from the bustle of campus life above them.

Like the area under the bridge, this clearing was littered with debris. "Used to be cleaner," Hank informed her, with the air of a tour guide. "Everything used to be cleaner." He led the way to some flat white rocks jutting out into the creek. He stepped onto the rocks and pointed to an area about three feet away. "Right there. That cooler was right there stuck on some rocks." He looked up suddenly, his attention caught by the sound of laughter up at the top of the bank across the creek. Two girls in shorts and T-shirts stood laughing in a gap in the trees. Molly was surprised to see through the opening a running track and, in the distance, picnic tables and basketball hoops. It was a recreation area for students.

Hank licked his dry lips.

"Has this always been a running track and recreation area?" Molly asked him.

He was so riveted watching the girls, he didn't respond. Molly reached out and touched him on the arm. He jumped as though he'd been stung.

"It's fun to watch them, isn't it?" she said. "They're so young and full of life. And from down here you can watch without them knowing it."

He did something she'd never seen anyone do before. He took his lower lip between his teeth and pulled at a loose piece of skin there, tugging at it until he'd ripped it loose. It left a raw place on his thin lip that began to ooze a drop of blood. He licked the blood away and said, "I come here sometimes. If they're there, I look. Of course, I never...you know I wouldn't never..."

"I know, Hank. There's no harm in watching."

"No," he said. "They're sorority girls."

"Oh?"

"You can tell by the writing on their shirts."

Molly squinted and saw that both girls had Greek letters printed on the front of their T-shirts.

"Those foreign letters mean they belong to a sorority."

"Ah," Molly said.

"I see those letters around here all the time."

"Do you?"

"Uh-huh. And you know, that day you was asking about?"

"Yes?" Molly asked it carefully, not wanting to stop this flow.

"I never told this to no one, but I seen two girls with them foreign letters."

"You did? Like those two?"

"The letters were different and *they* weren't laughing." He nodded toward the top of the bank where the girls were still talking. Their laughter drifted down.

"They weren't laughing?"

He shook his head sadly. "One was bawling."

Molly's scalp was tingling. "One of the girls was crying?"

He seemed lost in the memory. "And they had letters on their shirts, but not the same as those. I should've told you before, I guess." He made a sound that strained to be a laugh. "That Swiss-cheese head of mine…"

"When did you see this girl crying?"

"Before we found the baby."

"How long before?"

"Just maybe a few minutes. When I got up to do my business that morning." Hank licked at his bloody lip again. "They was climbing the hill. One was crying and moaning, leaning on the other. That's when I saw their shirts had them foreign letters. I didn't know they left a little baby or I would've called them back. Doing something like that leads to no good for no one. You say your friend is doing good, an accountant and all, but I don't know. If he was doing so good, why does he have to send you to do this for him? And I can tell you them girls was doing poorly that day. No good comes from that. Secrets and feeling shame."

Molly was amazed by the length and emotion of the speech. "No. You're right, Hank. Do you remember what they looked like?"

"It was so long ago. And I seen so many girls since then."

This was impossible, like trying to squeeze juice from a stone. "You remember anything about them?"

"Just the letters on their shirts."

"The letters on their shirts? What were they?"

"Oh, I can't read them. I don't know no languages but English."

Molly had a sudden inspiration. "Can you draw them?"

"Well…sure." He squatted down and picked up an oval stone. He used the edge to draw in the dirt. "Both the same. Here's what them letters looked like." He drew slowly: ΠΑΩ. Pi Alpha Omega.

"Are you sure those were the letters?" Molly asked.

"Oh, yes. I still see the same shirts around. It's a sorority the girls join. When I see them letters it reminds me of that day."

"Did you ever see the two girls again?"

"No. Just that one time, that morning."

"Do you think one of them could have given birth down here?"

He thought about it. "No. I would've heard. That's a noisy thing to happen. I remember when my mama had my sister and she yelled and panted and thrashed around. I would've heard. And it would've left some mess. No. They must've brought it down here after it got borned."

Molly nodded.

"This won't get me in no trouble, will it?"

"No. I promise it won't," Molly assured him.

She offered to drive him back to the Salvation Army, but he said he thought he'd stay and sit by the water a bit. His eyes kept darting back to the girls who were still talking up on the bank.

Molly asked him if he needed anything.

"I sure did like that breakfast," he said.

She opened her purse, took out a twenty-dollar bill, and handed it to him. "For a few breakfasts."

She knew she shouldn't, and that it wouldn't do him any good, and that he would probably use it to buy booze. But she did it anyway, because it made her feel better. It made her feel she wasn't just using him and discarding him. It made her feel better about having lied to him. It made her feel better about not having asked about his mother and his seventh birthday. It made her feel that she wasn't just turning her back and walking off.

Then she turned her back and walked off.

The Pi Alpha Omega house was huge, red-bricked, and white-pillared, a formal reproduction of a southern plantation. It felt as though it were designed to intimidate, as if the architect's intent was to make everyone who wasn't a Pi Alpha, or whatever they called themselves, feel insignificant and unworthy, like field slaves with muddy shoes.

Molly stood on the sidewalk, in the throes of doubt. She'd tried the library and the university registrar to see if they had listings of Pi Alpha Omegas who were in summer school in 1962.

They didn't, and time was wasting. If she was going to follow this lead, she was going to have to take some shortcuts. And it was going to be harder than usual, much harder. She was about to tell some lies that could jeopardize her job and her reputation. And it probably wouldn't work anyway. It all hinged on her ability to concoct the right lie and act it out convincingly.

Looking at the perfectly edged grass and the blooming pink azaleas, she knew that the residents of this house would work hard at maintaining appearances. Even if she didn't need to keep the search secret, a direct approach would not work here. Pi Alpha Omegas would not willingly reveal dirty laundry, even thirty-three-year-old dirty laundry.

If she was going to do this, she was going to have to pull out all the stops, and enter wholeheartedly into the lie. She strode into the house. In the sunny living room several girls with long shiny hair were curled up in armchairs studying. A big television was on with the volume low. Molly was pleased to see it tuned to a soap opera, not coverage of the Hearth Jezreelites. One of the girls spotted Molly. "Ma'am, can I help you?" she called out.

"Yes. Where would I find the housemother or someone in charge?"

"Well, Miz Larkin is our housemother. She's usually in her office, down the hall to the right."

Molly went the way she was pointed. The office door was open. A woman with unnaturally black hair sat working at a tiny writing desk, her head bent. She looked up, showing a face far too pale and wrinkled to go with the dead-black hair. "Yes?"

"Are you Miss Larkin?" Molly asked.

"Yes, I am," she drawled. "Betty Larkin."

"I'm Molly Cates." She stepped forward and shook the woman's outstretched hand. "I write for *Lone Star Monthly* magazine and I'm hoping you might help me with a piece we are doing."

The woman's face brightened. "Won't you please sit down?"

Molly did. "Are you familiar with our magazine, Miss Larkin?"

"I surely am. But, you know, I just don't have much time for reading. The girls keep me so busy."

"I bet," Molly said. "When I think of how busy one daughter this age kept me, I shudder to think of a houseful of them."

Betty Larkin laughed.

"I'm doing research for an article on Martha Dillingham. You know, the poet, who won the Kemper Prize for Literature last year." Molly paused to see if her invention went over. Betty Larkin nodded as though she recognized the name. Molly pressed on: "Martha says one of the major influences on her career was a writing course she took right here at the University of Texas. In summer school, back in the summer of 1962. A requirement of the course was a group writing project. She collaborated on a story that summer with two girls who were Pi Alpha Omegas, but she can't remember their names and she's lost her copy of the story they wrote together. I'd like to find them so I can interview them—you know, find out what they thought of Martha back then, whether they saw her promise, and what they've done with their own writing. And I sure would like to see if one of them kept a copy of the story."

Molly settled back on the chair. "The problem is, the course list got lost, so the university registrar hasn't been able to locate the names of the people in that writing class. And the professor's been dead for many years. I'm wondering if you might have a list somewhere in your files of the girls who were here during summer school in '62. Martha feels certain she will recognize the names if she sees them."

"A list of girls who lived in the house in 1962?"

"Yes, especially the summer. I bet you thin out then."

"Yes, we do. Of course, that was way before my time."

"Mine, too," Molly said with a laugh.

"It would have been during Mrs. Stanford's tenure. She was housemother for thirty years. Beloved by generations of Pi Alphs. Now that would be an inspiring story for your magazine."

"Yes, it sounds like it," Molly said with an attempt at brightness. "Is she still around?"

"Well, barely. She's had some strokes and doesn't even know who she is now. So sad."

"Yes," Molly said, reminded that she needed to go visit her Aunt Harriet in the nursing home. She suffered a brief twinge, knowing how deeply her aunt would disapprove of what she was doing right now.

Betty Larkin said, "Of course, I have all her records here, and Franny was a meticulous record keeper."

"Was she?" Molly said.

"Yes, but I just don't know whether it would be right to show you those."

"I can see your dilemma," Molly said, "but it's information I could have gotten from the registrar if they hadn't lost it. Just a list of who was here that summer."

Betty Larkin smiled, a woman who wanted to please. "It's hard to see the harm in it. And it sounds like it might be good for the sorority. Was…you know, that writer you're doing, was she in a sorority?"

"No, ma'am. She couldn't afford it."

"Too bad. We offer scholarships now. Not enough, of course. It's such a fine thing for these scholarship girls, gives them contacts for the rest of their lives, entré into a world they wouldn't have access to."

"I imagine so," Molly said.

"Well, let me see if we can find that list for you." She picked up her phone and pressed two buttons. "Cindy," she said into the phone, "would you look in Mrs. Stanford's files for me—the light green cabinet. I need a list from 1962—girls who lived in the house during summer school that year. And bring in the directory from '62. I know we've got that in the top drawer." She listened for a minute. "Yes, now please. And make copies for me, will you? Thanks."

She put down the phone and turned back to Molly, her forehead crinkled in thought. "But you know, Mrs. Cates, you say she'll recognize the names, but how will you find them? You know how we women are. We change our names and move away."

Molly nodded. Yes, we change our names, our residences, and our hair color—often many times. How do people ever find us?

"What you'll need is one of our current directories. They're cross-referenced by maiden name and year. Also it tells who is deceased, not that your girls are likely to be. They'd just be in their early fifties, wouldn't they? Most members are in it. Some fall through the cracks, but not many. I've got a few extra directories, so I could loan you one, but I'll need to have it back."

Molly repressed the urge to kiss her. Betty Larkin had the makings of a good researcher, one who anticipated the problems. Molly wasn't sure what the duties of a housemother were, but she imagined Betty was a good one. Maybe what everyone needed in their lives was a housemother to keep track of the details and anticipate problems. Might be even better than having a wife. "Thank you so much," Molly told her. "This is such a help."

"Well, one of my jobs is to help promote networking. And this sounds valuable for the two classmates of—oh, I've forgotten her name."

Molly scrambled mentally to dredge up the name she'd invented. "Martha. Martha Dillingham."

"Yes. I've never read her, but I've meant to."

When the secretary brought in the copies of the 1962 lists and Betty Larkin lent her the directory,

Molly was out of the house like a flash. She didn't stay to chat or leave a card, as she usually did. She had gotten the information she'd wanted and more. To have gotten it any other way might have been impossible.

Molly walked back to her illegally parked truck feeling edgy, but exhilarated. This was like robbing a bank and getting away with it. There must be some moral deficiency in her that allowed her to do it so fluently and, she congratulated herself, so well. She had already gotten further than the Austin police and the Department of Public Welfare, further than Donnie Ray Grimes himself.

But so what? In one morning, she had broken most of the ASNE ethics for journalists, had taken advantage of a poor old alcoholic, and had lied outrageously to a helpful housemother. All in the hope—tenuous at best—of finding a woman who left a newborn in Waller Creek thirty-three years ago. And even if she could find the woman, unlikely as that was, would she be willing to cooperate? Would Samuel Mordecai want to hear from her? Would he care enough to bargain for the privilege of talking to the woman who abandoned him?

Probably not. But it was not going to stop Molly from trying. A serial killer she had once written about had compared her to a pit bull bitch he'd seen fight. Getting the bitch to let go of something she'd gotten hold of had required beating her practically to death.

Molly grabbed the ticket off the truck's windshield and stuffed it in her bag without looking at it. Didn't matter—she'd deduct it. Of course, that pit bull stuff was a dramatic overstatement. It was true that once she got on the trail of something that interested her, she liked to see it to the end. But she wasn't a zealot. She was not going to take this to extremes.

> *"I probably shouldn't say this to a child, honey, and if you tell your Aunt Harriet I said it, I'll deny it, but I think religious faith has done more harm in this world than the seven deadly sins combined."*
> VERNON CATES, TO HIS DAUGHTER

CHAPTER TWELVE

Feeling resentful, as though she had been coerced into taking an unwanted stepchild to piano lessons, Molly stopped to pick up the dog at Jake Alesky's. As they had unloaded his groceries the night before, Jake had offered to take care of Copper when Molly couldn't. She'd leapt on the offer and dropped him off the next morning, so she could track down Hank Hanley. But she couldn't impose on Jake indefinitely.

Pulling up to the trailer, she was surprised to see Jake sitting in his wheelchair throwing a tennis ball and Copper barreling after it with the vigor of a regular sporting dog. "He likes that," she called out the window.

Jake reached down to accept the filthy, dripping tennis ball that Copper had retrieved. "Of course he does. He's a dog."

"I suppose," Molly said.

"Did you know this breed can accelerate from zero to thirty-five in two seconds?"

"Amazing, but not particularly useful for a house pet. Thanks for having him."

"Ah, we both need the exercise." He wheeled over to the truck. "So when are we going out to Jezreel?"

"I told you. Never."

"Let me know when you change your mind. I want to go."

"Watch it on TV," Molly told him. "That's what I do. A crime scene is like football. You can see it better on the tube."

Fifteen minutes later, heading home with Copper in the back, Molly called in to the office. "There's a package and a fax for you," Stephanie said, "and some woman's been calling every ten minutes all morning and won't leave her name or number. Says it's urgent."

"Urgent? Well, what does she expect me to do about it with no number?"

"You got me."

Molly was just passing Fifth Street. "I'm coming in for a few minutes. If the woman calls back, tell her I'll be in my office in five minutes." She drove to the office and up into the parking garage. As she was getting out of the truck, the dog leaned over the tailgate and whined at her. Molly cursed softly under her breath. She'd forgotten about him.

The dog stood trembling with anticipation. "What a bother you are. I can't take you in, but—" She stopped talking when she saw a small figure watching her from the stairwell doorway. It was a woman wearing jeans, sunglasses, and a big scarf that hid her hair and some of her face. She headed directly toward Molly, walking fast, with her head down. She was tiny, about five feet tall. Certainly not menacing, but Molly clutched the pepper Mace canister attached to her keys and braced herself. She glanced around the shadowy garage, wishing someone else would appear, but the level was totally deserted.

The woman stopped in front of Molly. In a whisper, she asked, "Are you Molly Cates?"

Molly whispered back, "Who wants to know?"

The woman lifted her head and glanced around the empty garage. "I know who you are. I've seen you before. I have to tell you something. Something important." Her voice was shaky and breathless. "Something so terrible you won't believe it."

Molly felt suddenly very old and jaded. There was nothing, she was certain, nothing under the sun that was so terrible she wouldn't believe it. "Let's go up to my office," she said, "and you can tell me about it there."

"No! I can't. Let's stand over here, behind your truck."

"It's more private in my office. And much more comfortable—"

"No! I can't be seen. You don't know. Here." The woman walked swiftly to a cement stanchion behind the truck and leaned into the corner. Molly followed with grave misgivings. The woman's fear was palpable. It was also contagious.

Molly took her first good look at the young woman—the heart-shaped face and small, delicate features. She'd seen a photograph of that face just yesterday. "You're Annette Grimes," she said, keeping her voice very low and as calm as she could manage.

Samuel Mordecai's wife nodded. "I saw you before, through a window when you were out at Jezreel. He was so mad at what you wrote. He never let any of us see it. When I left there seven months ago, I looked it up at the library. That's why I came to you. You've got to tell them—the FBI and the police, the ones who are out there trying to talk to him." She leaned around the post to survey the garage again.

Molly found her anxiety level soaring; this was a dangerous situation and she needed to do the sensible thing. "Annette, I'll pass on whatever you want me to. But we need to get in my truck right now and drive to the police station. Ten blocks. We'll get protection for you, and you can tell them yourself. In safety. Come on. We'll talk on the way."

"No." For the first time the woman's voice rose above a whisper. It was shrill and feathery with fear. "I can't. I want you to tell them. If you won't do that, I have to leave."

Molly was torn. Annette looked ready to bolt at any second. The right thing, the safe thing, was to get her into police protection, but she couldn't force her, and she didn't want to scare her off. "Okay. I've got a little tape recorder here in my bag. I'd like to record what you say."

"No!" A tear rolled out from under her sunglasses. "I just want to tell you what I came to say, and get out of here."

Molly reached out and rested a hand on her arm. From the pickup came a low growl. They both jerked their heads in that direction. "Stay," Molly said to the dog. "It's all right. Listen, Annette. I think you have something very important to tell. If you let me record it, I will give it only to the FBI commander at Jezreel and the chief negotiator for the Austin police. What you say will carry more weight if I have it on tape. No one else will ever hear it. I promise."

Now the girl was trembling visibly. "Okay, but I have to hurry. They know I'm in town." She wrapped her arms around herself.

Molly already had her hand on the little recorder inside her big bag. She'd been planning to turn it on, permission or no. Now she pulled it out and pressed the "record" button. "Go ahead."

"I can't believe I'm doing this. I've been with him since I was fourteen—eleven years." Tears streamed down her cheeks. "But I have to."

"Go on."

"I saw one of the mothers—on TV—and…Oh, I feel so—" She was crying so hard she could barely get the words out. "So awful, so guilty, so… ruined. You can't know. No one can know." She put her hands over her face. "Tell them—they have to go in now and save those children. They have to. *Right now.*"

An image of eleven-year-old Kimberly Bassett came to mind and the boy with the dark cowlicks. "Why?"

Annette was sobbing so hard she could get out only a word or two at a time. "Because—he—has to—kill them."

"Has to? Why?"

"His Doctrine of Human Agency. Sacrifice is necessary."

"Sacrifice? Necessary for what?" It was Molly's worst fear, something she had avoided giving voice to for forty-eight days.

Annette took off her sunglasses. Her streaming eyes were intensely blue under black lashes. "It's the way—the Apocalypse will start—see—fifty perfect martyrs—purified—innocent." She tugged a crumpled piece of Kleenex out of her jeans pocket.

"He's only got twelve," Molly said quickly.

"Eight more is all he needs. By now maybe less." She wiped under her eyes with the Kleenex.

A surge of revulsion rose in Molly's throat. She thought she knew the answer, but she had to ask. "Where did the other martyrs come from, the other forty-two?"

"The babies—he sent them back to God direct." Tears dripped off her chin. "On the fiftieth day. Always the fiftieth day."

"The babies born at Jezreel?"

"Uh-huh. For three years."

"So it was going on when I was out there?"

Annette nodded.

"How?"

"Oh." Her nose was running in long strands. She used the back of her hand to wipe it. "This ritual—with a sickle. Handed down from prophet to prophet. Had to be done just so. At sunset. He will do it. Friday. Unless they do something to stop him…"

Molly looked down to reassure herself that her recorder was working. "Annette, to rescue them, they need to know where the children are. Where would he keep them?"

"Underground somewhere. I don't know, but the babies—" She was interrupted by gulping sobs. "They were kept in these... like underground cribs, in the barn. Earth purifies."

"The white barn?"

"Yes. With the tin roof. They were fed and changed, kept alive, but they stayed in these... boxes underground... I didn't know how awful until a few weeks ago... I had my own and he's so—" Her shoulders slumped and she sobbed uncontrollably.

Molly moved closer and put an arm around her. She looked to see what the dog was doing, but Copper was not visible in the truck bed; he must be lying down. "Annette, did you have a baby?" she asked.

"That's why I had to leave—before he knew."

"Before he knew you were pregnant?"

"Uh-huh."

"He'd sacrifice his own child?"

"It would never grow up anyway—with the world ending. That's what he taught. We believed it. This way it would stay innocent. It would go right to God without the suffering."

Infanticide—The grisliest of Molly's fears. She forced herself back to the questions she had to ask: "Annette, how would you go about rescuing the children? Mordecai says he'll kill them the second there's an attack. Will he?"

Annette took several deep breaths to calm herself. "I've been watching on TV. And thinking. He has to do it himself—in this certain, special way.

233

Rapture of Mordecai. No one else can. See, he's the Prophet Mordecai. Last of the line. And perfect martyrs of the Apocalypse—no one but him can do it, so if—" She turned her head toward the wall as a big white car came up the ramp.

Instinctively, Molly stood so her body blocked Annette. The white Cadillac pulled into an empty place near the elevator. The engine died. A woman in spike heels and a red suit got out and clicked across the cement. When she disappeared into the elevator, Molly exhaled slowly. "It's all right. She's gone.

"You were saying he's the only one who can sacrifice them," Molly said. "So if he—"

She stopped. The noise of another car coming up the ramp. A dark blue van appeared and paused, looking for a space. Then it suddenly accelerated toward them. Annette gasped. Molly grabbed her by the arm and pulled her to the truck. They reached the passenger door just as the van squealed to a stop behind the truck.

Two men jumped out and dashed toward them. Molly jerked on the door handle. Locked. She dropped the tape recorder into her bag and rummaged desperately for the keys and the Mace. One of the men grabbed her arm and wrenched it behind her. She screamed and tried to pull away. In front of her, the other man had already lifted Annette off the ground. She was kicking and screaming, but he was carrying her toward the van. An arm, hairy and huge, caught Molly around the head. It blocked her vision. She tried to bite it, but the arm grabbed her neck in a choke hold and jerked her back.

Then a freight train hit. She crashed forward, falling hard, the man on top of her. Her breath exploded from her body. She saw only gray cement. Heard violent noises—screeching and grunting and the fury of a hundred snarling demons. Panicked, she tried to move. The man on top was hot and heavy, writhing, grinding her into the cement. A deep bellow of pain from above. The thick arm around her neck relaxed. She dragged herself a few inches forward, and a few more. Until she was out from under.

She looked back. It was the dog, transformed into a blur of hissing, snarling black fury. He was on top of the man, dancing on his back, trying to rip his arm off. The man roared, tried to hit out with his other hand. Droplets of blood and foam flicked through the air.

Winded and aching, Molly pushed up to her hands and knees. She looked for Annette. The girl was being lifted into the van. A third man inside was pulling her in. "No, no. Don't! Help me," Annette cried.

"Stop! Help!" Molly called. Tried to call. Her voice was only a croak.

The van door slammed shut.

Suddenly behind her, the man rose to his knees, grunting, flailing, trying to pull away from the dog. Then he staggered to a crouching position, the dog still hanging from his arm. He screamed, "Shoot! Shoot the fucker!"

The van door opened. The bleeding man staggered toward it, but the dog pulled him back, snarling and snorting, nails scraping the cement. From the van, another man jumped out and ran toward

Copper. He had a shotgun. He held it by the barrel and lifted it over his head. Like a club.

"No," Molly screamed. "Copper!"

The dog let go and dodged to the side.

The shotgun cracked down hard—on flesh and bone. The man who'd attacked her screamed in agony, hugged his shattered arm to his chest, and crumpled to the floor. Molly managed to pull her key out of her bag, which miraculously still hung from her shoulder. She zapped the door with the remote and staggered to it. She opened it and scrambled in. "Copper. Come," she called. Her command sounded like a plea. But now the dog had the man with the shotgun by the upper arm and was dragging him to his knees. The gun clattered to the cement.

Molly slammed the door and with shaking hands managed to fumble the key into the ignition. She was blocked by the van, parked two feet behind. She started the engine and slammed it into reverse. Then she closed her eyes and accelerated. The truck jerked back two feet, smack into the side of the van. There was a crunch. She drove forward a few feet and did it again. Smash. Then she leaned into the horn. The blare was deafening, echoing off cement walls. She held it down.

She was afraid to look behind. But she did. One man was dragging the other to the van, with the dog jumping at him, trying to get hold of his arm. The arm was dripping blood. Molly kept leaning into the horn, with all her might, as if the harder she did it, the louder it would blare. Where the hell was everyone?

The men managed to get into the van. With the door still open, it took off. It headed down the up-ramp, squealing around the sharp corners.

Shaking so hard she could barely grip the wheel, Molly backed up and headed after them. She caught a glimpse of movement in the rearview mirror—a black blur streaking into the back of the moving truck.

My God, she thought, sweat running down her face. My God. That dog is a hellhound.

When she got to the entrance, a man in a brown uniform was talking into a radio. He glanced at Molly. "The police are on the way. What the hell happened up there?"

"Which way did the van go?" Molly demanded.

He nodded up Rio Grande, where there was no dark blue van to be seen. "Let the cops do it, lady. They're already on it. You wait here."

Molly did as she was told. Until she looked at herself in the mirror, she didn't know that blood was trickling from her left temple or that she was crying.

Molly kept having shivering spells, and she couldn't stop talking. "I'm not usually so mean," she said to the woman cop who was driving her out to Jezreel, "shouting like that. It's just that I need to get this tape out there to Lieutenant Traynor, and you were all wasting my time when all it really took was a call to him. So I was just trying to get you to act quickly. There's hardly any time left. What's your name again?"

"Rhinebeck. Julie Rhinebeck."

"Right. Officer Rhinebeck. Julie. I've always hated parking garages," she said, touching the bandage over her left temple to monitor the swelling in progress there. "Nothing ever happened to me before to make me hate them. I just did. I always park at meters even if I don't have enough quarters and it means getting tickets. And it's not that I'm scared of everything. It's just parking garages. I don't know, it's like—" Molly was shivering again. She kept seeing tiny Annette Grimes being thrust screaming into the van. She wouldn't let herself think beyond that, to imagine what might be happening to her now.

Officer Julie Rhinebeck reached across the seat, over the shotgun that stuck up between them, and took hold of Molly's hand. She drove with one hand and held tight to Molly with the other. "Sure, it was like a premonition you had," she said. "That's happened to me, too. And I don't like garages much either. Last year a guy pulled a knife on me in the City Bank garage. Turned out he was only twelve years old, but he looked twenty-five with that knife, let me tell you. Afterward I had the shakes like you wouldn't believe. I was so relieved I didn't shoot him. I almost did. I thought about it."

Molly glanced over at the officer's profile. With her freckled face and her glossy black hair pulled back in a ponytail, she looked like a teenager. This girl was younger than Jo Beth. When did they get so young?

"Will they let you know here in the car if they find the blue van?" Molly asked.

"Yes. They promised to call when anything breaks. Don't worry."

Molly turned to look in the back of the patrol car where Copper was sleeping on the seat. No wonder—it had been a big day. Molly had insisted he come into the station with her while they took her statement and called Grady Traynor. She had them locate a former canine unit cop, who looked the dog over and washed the blood off him. To Molly's relief, none of the blood turned out to be Copper's.

Julie Rhinebeck turned off the Interstate onto U.S. 79. "I haven't been out here before, but Lieutenant Traynor gave me good instructions." She glanced over at Molly. "He said to take extra-special care of you and the dog."

"Did he?"

"Uh-huh. And he said you both like to ride in patrol cars."

Molly laughed and the shivering subsided.

They turned onto FM 3419 and drove two miles in silence. "My God," Rhinebeck said, slowing as they passed the dirt road that led to the Hearth Jezreelite compound, "look at that. It's like a state fair or a circus or something."

Molly looked at the hodgepodge of structures rising up from the flat, treeless plain. Over the past six weeks, that landscape had become as familiar around the world as the White House. Certainly it was etched into her brain: the main building, a massive flat-topped two-story wooden box with tiny windows, and the two flanking stone towers with crenellations and little slit windows all around the top. It was geometric, unsoftened by trees or bushes.

To the right of the main structure stood several small outbuildings and a green water tank. To the left rose the huge white barn, its ridged tin roof gleaming in the sun. "Stop a second," Molly said. She wanted to look at the barn. It was a prefab structure connected to the main building by a crude plywood breezeway. In the bright sunlight, on this gorgeous sky-blue spring day, it was hard to imagine it as the scene for the horrors Annette Grimes had described.

Federal agents wearing camouflage jumpsuits and bullet-resistant vests, carrying rifles and radios, patrolled just outside the chain-link fence, which Molly knew surrounded the entire twelve acres. A corridor several yards wide had been designated as the inner perimeter by local law enforcement when they set up on the first day. No one but federal agents were allowed there. Samuel Mordecai had told the world on the day he took the school bus that if anyone—cop, federal agent, reporter, parent—set foot on Hearth Jezreelite property, the children and the bus driver would be immediately executed. From the start, the negotiators had believed him; in forty-eight days, no one but a few squirrels had set foot past the fence.

At the outer perimeter squatted two Bradley Fighting Vehicles. Beside them were two huge M-1 tanks borrowed from the Texas National Guard. Several DPS Rangers manned the outer perimeter, checking press cards and turning curiosity seekers away.

Beyond this ring was the press encampment, a

media city which had sprung up instantly after the hijacking, like an ant mound pushing up from the dirt: huge satellite trucks, news vans with antennas shooting up into the sky. There were two high scaffoldings with platforms on top for filming the compound, trailers with awnings and barbecues and lawn chairs. Campers. A volleyball net. Picnic tables. On the road behind a police barricade, tourists snapped photographs and stood around pointing. It was a bizarre combination of war zone and beach party.

At the top of each tower hung a tattered red banner about which the world had speculated. Was it a coat of arms? Some cult symbol? No one knew and Samuel Mordecai was not saying. Right now both flags hung limp, defeated, in the still air. No matter how this turned out, Molly thought, Samuel Mordecai would be defeated. But everyone else would lose, too. It was costing hundreds of thousands of dollars, burning up thousands of man-hours. And even if the children got out alive, they would have nightmares for the rest of their lives.

Molly said in disgust, "All this for a nutty eighth-grade dropout like Samuel Mordecai. Only in America. Let's go."

Officer Rhinebeck resumed speed. "Lieutenant Traynor said a mile and it'll be on the right—a white house with lots of cars in front. There it is."

It was a large, dilapidated frame farmhouse. The front lawn had become a parking lot. Cars and pickups, two Austin police cars, and several Ford Tempos that Molly recognized as unmarked units were parked at odd angles. When Molly opened the car door, Copper instantly leapt up and whined. Molly handed the leash to the police-woman. "Will you walk him, Julie?"

"You bet."

A uniformed Austin cop slouched in a lawn chair on the front porch. He stood as she approached. "Miz Cates? They're waitin' on you. Communications room—on the right."

Inside, Molly was hit by a strange mixture of smells: the mustiness of an old uninhabited house combined with the slightly burned, acrid smell of electronics. The room on the right was a Victorian double parlor with elaborate wood moldings and a tiled fireplace. So much electronic equipment was crammed into the room that it looked like a Radio Shack at Christmas, with everything inside turned on: computer monitors glowing, radios, televisions, a bunch of phones, and a fax machine churning out a heap of curled paper. One television was tuned to CNN with the sound off. Two men with earphones sat in front of a switch-board and another stood drinking coffee out of a Styrofoam cup. There was no air conditioning and they all wore dark suits in spite of the heat.

On one wall hung a huge diagram of the compound. On another wall were tacked photographs of the eleven children and Walter Demming. Around the fireplace were pictures of Samuel Mordecai, Annette Grimes, and about thirty of the other cult members.

Grady Traynor, his shirtsleeves pushed up, his collar button undone, his gray pants rumpled, was clearly not FBI. Sitting in a lopsided armchair that had tufts of yellowed stuffing hanging out of it, he was reading what looked like an endless scroll of paper.

"The seven seals?" Molly said, resting a hand on his shoulder.

He looked up. "No, a file the Cult Awareness League just faxed us. On the Hearth Jezreelites. Basically, it says they are secretive, dangerous, fanatical, and apocalyptic in orientation. Like we didn't know that already. How's my dog?"

"He's outside. Taking a walk, sniffing trees."

"So what do you think of him now?"

"Now I *know* he's a maniac."

Grady stood up, letting the papers drop to the floor. "In an eight-year career, he was injured thirteen times and made more than a thousand apprehensions." He touched the bandage at her temple and ran his fingertips around the swelling. "How are you?"

"It's just a flesh wound."

"You know better than that, Molly. An encounter like that always hits deep below the surface. Let's try again. How are you?"

"Shaky. And I can't seem to stop talking."

He kissed her gently on the lips. "Later I will listen endlessly. Let me have the tape. We'll make a quick copy before we play it."

Molly gave it to him and he handed it to a husky young man in a dark suit. "Copy it, Holihan. We'll play it as soon as Lattimore gets back from his run." He turned back to Molly. "We haven't released this information yet, but we talked to Walter Demming forty minutes ago. After we've played yours, I'd like you to listen to ours. It's exactly seventy seconds long."

A man wearing running shorts and a wet T-shirt entered the room. He was sweating profusely. He scooped up a towel from a chair, used it to dry his face and gray crew cut, then draped it around his neck. "Is this Molly Cates?" he said to Grady.

"Yes, sir. Molly, this is Patrick Lattimore, FBI assistant special agent in charge."

Molly knew his face from the nightly televised press briefings. In person Lattimore looked even more like a Doonesbury character than he did on the tube. He had a big broken nose and heavy black circles under his eyes. His creased, jowly face looked thirty years older than his body, which was lean and fit.

He shook Molly's hand. "When we finish with you here, Miss Cates, we'd appreciate your spending some time upstairs with our intelligence staff so they can show you some photos of suspected Sword Hand of God members. And we borrowed a composite artist from Dallas. Lieutenant Traynor says the Austin police will need you back at some point, but we'd like your help while you're here."

"One of them, the one who pulled Annette into the van—I never saw his face. The other two I can have a go at."

"Good." Lattimore glanced at her temple. "You've had that looked at?"

"The nurse at APD cleaned it."

He waved a hand toward the other agents in the room. "Special Agent Andrew Stein, primary negotiator—you've probably seen him on TV—Bryan Holihan, George Curtis."

Molly shook hands with them, paying particular attention to Andrew Stein, who was reputed to be the dean of hostage negotiators. He was a cherubic, unfocused-looking man with white hair that looked as wispy as a baby's.

"We're in a hurry here," Lattimore said brusquely. "Let's hear what you got. Holihan, is that tape ready?"

Holihan flipped some switches and Curtis closed the sliding door.

From speakers placed around the room came Annette Grimes's voice, shaking and weeping. "*I can't believe I'm doing this. I've been with him since I was fourteen.*" Molly found herself cringing as the tape played. When Annette got to the part about the babies, Patrick Lattimore started to talk under his breath. "Holy Christ," he muttered. "Holy Christ on the cross."

Molly had never turned the recorder off, so it caught all the sounds of the struggle: the van squealing to a stop. The screams, the snarling, the thumps, more screams and groans. Annette crying out, "No, no. Don't! Help me." Molly's croaks of protest. A man's voice yelling, "Shoot! Shoot the fucker!" The van roaring off.

When it was done, Lattimore turned to Molly. If he was shaken by what he'd heard, his face gave no sign of it. "If that dog wasn't retired, I'd hire him. Christ, that's the kind of agent we need. Now, first off, a few questions: Are you certain the woman speaking on that tape is Annette Grimes?"

"Yes." Molly walked to the fireplace and pointed at the photo. "This woman. The same woman as the photograph I saw at Dorothy Huff's house. She's very distinctive. And she took her sunglasses off, so I got a good long look. There's no question."

"Okay. Second: What was she going to say when she stopped?"

"I think she was going to tell me that if Samuel Mordecai weren't there to sacrifice the children, you might be able to rescue them. He's the one who has to do it, according to this Rapture of Mordecai."

"Yeah. We'll get to that. Third: You're a journalist. You have some sense of when people are telling the truth and when they're bullshitting. Was Annette Grimes telling the truth?"

"Yes."

A shadow crossed his eyes. He said, "I can't tell you how sorry I am to hear that. If Mordecai needs to murder those kids to fulfill his worldview, then we've spent forty-eight days negotiating for something he can't give us. We're going to have to fall back on force and I consider that a failure of major proportions."

"Have you heard anything," Molly asked, "about Annette or the van?"

"No. APD has put out a BOLO for it. They'll let us know the second they get anything. And we'll let you know. I have to tell you, though, Miss Cates, from what we've learned about Mordecai and the Jezreelites, you just don't leave them and get away with it. The Sword Hand of God see to that. That's why it's almost impossible to get any insider intelligence. Mrs. Grimes flew the coop, and she told secrets. I don't think we'll see her alive again. She will probably suffer the same fate as Dr. Asquith. You were lucky to escape that garage." He said it dispassionately.

"I know."

Lattimore ran a hand over his still-wet crew cut. "Now I want you to listen to a conversation we had this morning with Walter Demming. This is not for public consumption yet, but Mordecai gave us a minute on the phone with Mr. Demming. In return, we are giving him fifteen minutes on religious radio for his sermonizing. As a bonus, we sent him some newspapers he'd been wanting. We also stuck in the bag some inhalers for Josh Benderson. I hope to hell he lets the kid have them." He nodded. "Our minute with Demming may have been a real bargain. We just wanted to find out if they're all still alive, but I think we may have gotten a lot more. Maybe you can shed some light. Play it, Bryan."

Again Holihan flipped switches.

Andrew Stein's rich voice emerged from the speakers. "Mr. Demming, this is Special Agent Andrew Stein of the FBI. How are you?"

Walter Demming's voice was low and controlled. "I'm alive and so are the children. They said I could tell you that. We are fed, and every day Mr. Mordecai instructs us. He said I could send some messages from the children. Here they are: Kimberly wishes her mother a happy birthday. She loves her and her grandma lots. Bucky wonders if his little brother Danny is sleeping in his room since he's been gone. Lucy says her mom should give Winky a hug and she wants to come home and never leave. Josh says his mom shouldn't worry and he can't wait to get back to his dad's mashed potatoes and sugar bread. Hector says to tell his Aunt Emily and Uncle Theo that he can't wait to ride old Riddle further than the guests can gallop. Brandon sends his dad the peace of God which passeth all understanding and wishes he had a prayer book. Sandra says to tell Mrs. LaPonte, the school librarian, she's read *Stuart Little* every day and it's her favorite book now. Conrad asks the Second Baptist Church to pray for him. Sue Ellen says she loves her family a bunch. Philip says he wants to come home. Heather says hi, Mom, be good, and sends kisses.

"And here's my message. Tell my good friend Jake Alesky to send love to Granny Duck. Tell her I keep in mind what she taught me about survival, and I will live up to her example."

When he fell silent, Stein's voice took over. "Mr. Demming, we are working around the clock to get you all out safe. We haven't forgotten you. We are worried about Josh Benderson. How is he?"

"Okay. They said I could—"

A new voice sliced in. "You've exceeded your minute. We just threw our videotape out the front door. Send one of them reporters to pick it up. He should keep his hands on his head." The connection was broken.

Holihan hit the rewind.

Lattimore looked at his watch. "We've sent a car for Jake Alesky. They should be here in a few minutes. We want to hear about Granny Duck."

"Me, too," Molly said.

"Did anything strike you about the kids' messages?"

"The one from Hector was strange."

Lattimore grimaced. "You don't know the half of it. We've got all the parents corralled with some counselors at the Lutheran church over in Round Rock.

We played the tape for them. Hector's mom and dad say Hector has no Aunt Emily or Uncle Theo, and no horse named Riddle or anything else, and they have no idea what that message means. None of the other parents do either, so it isn't a question of Demming's having gotten it garbled or mixed up with some other kid's message."

"What did he say again?"

"Bryan, give Miss Cates a copy of the transcript."

Holihan handed her a sheet. Molly read it through, lingering on the message from Hector.

"Mean anything to you, Miss Cates?"

"'Tell Aunt Emily and Uncle Theo that he can't wait to ride old Riddle further than the guests can gallop'—No. Strange."

"We thought so, too," Lattimore said.

"Wait!" It came to her the way most good ideas did, like a silver fish slithering through a crevasse in her brain, exciting some neurons and dendrites as it rubbed past them. "Oh, my God. Walter Demming is in a poetry group with his neighbor Theodora Shea. Theo. It's for Theo. And they've been reading Emily Dickinson—Aunt Emily."

Lattimore slapped both palms against the wall. "Shit. The neighbor lady. We talked to her a few weeks ago. Poetry group, huh?" He turned to the man standing by the door. "Curtis, get me Theodora Shea on the phone. Do not tell me she isn't home. I want her, and I want her right now. Put her on the speaker." His voice was harsh with excitement.

Curtis sat at the computer and with a few keystrokes got a phone ringing.

A firm female voice answered.

Lattimore spoke into the speaker next to the computer. "Miss Shea, this is Agent Patrick Lattimore of the Federal Bureau of Investigation. We talked a few weeks ago. I've got you on the speakerphone here at our command post near Jezreel. There are three other FBI agents present. Lieutenant Traynor from the Austin PD is here, too, and Miss Molly Cates, whom I believe you have met."

"Yes, sir." Her voice was crisp and businesslike.

"Miss Shea, we talked briefly on the phone with Walter this morning."

"Oh, my."

"He said they were all alive and he relayed some messages from the children to their parents. One of the messages had no meaning for the parents involved. Miss Cates thinks you might know something about it."

"Try me."

He picked up the transcript. "Here it is, 'Hector says tell his Aunt Emily and Uncle Theo he can't wait to ride old Riddle further than the guests can gallop.'"

Without a second's hesitation Theo said, "Not guests, Mr. Lattimore—*guess,* with two *s*'s, no *t*. Further than guess can gallop, further than Riddle ride. It's Emily Dickinson. From the poem that begins: '*Under the light, yet under, under the grass and the dirt, under the beetle's cellar, under the clover's root.*'"

"Holy Christ," Lattimore muttered. "Under the grass and the dirt."

"I don't know the rest of it by memory, but it

250

ends with that wonderful line: '*Oh for a disc to the distance between ourselves and the dead.*'"

"I'm going to need a copy of that poem, and right quick," Lattimore snapped. "Curtis, see if you can locate it on-line. Miss Shea, what's the title?"

"Dickinson's poems are numbered, not titled. You said Molly Cates is there?"

"Yes."

"I gave her a complete Dickinson to send to Walter. It would be in there. Molly, do you have it with you?"

Molly shook her head. "No. I'm afraid I left it at home."

"Well, if you'll wait, I'll find it for you and I'll read it to you. Just a minute…"

"Tape this, Holihan." Lattimore's face was white with concentration. "But keep trying on-line, Curtis."

Theodora came back on. "Let's see if I can find it. I don't remember the number, so I'm looking under first lines. Here is it. Number 949. Are you ready for me to read it?"

"Yes, go ahead," Lattimore said. "We're taping this, Miss Shea."

Theodora read in a clear slow voice:

"Under the Light, yet under,
Under the Grass and the Dirt,
Under the Beetle's Cellar.
Under the Clover's Root,

Further than Arm could stretch
Were it Giant long,

251

Further than Sunshine could
Were the Day Year long,

Over the Light, yet over,
Over the Arc of the bird—
Over the Comet's chimney—
Over the Cubit's Head

Further than Guess can gallop,
Further than Riddle ride—
Oh for a Disc to the Distance
Between Ourselves and the Dead!"

"Miss Shea," Lattimore said, "what do you make of that message?"

"The first thing that comes to mind, of course, is that they're being held underground. He's trying to tell you where they are, so you can go in there and rescue them before it's too late. I fervently hope you will do just that, Mr. Lattimore. Without delay."

"We will do our best. Please stay home near your phone, Miss Shea, so we can reach you if we need to. Will you do that for us?"

"I certainly will."

"Thank you." The agent nodded to Curtis to break the connection. "Transcribe that right away, Curtis, so we can all have copies."

Grady Traynor turned to face Molly. "While he's doing that, Molly, this would be a good time to pass on the information you have."

Molly was startled. "What?"

"The circumstances of Donnie Ray Grimes's

birth. I already told them the general outlines this morning. Fill it in for us."

She looked at him hard.

"Go ahead, Molly. All bets are off now."

He was right, of course. With forty-eight hours left and Annette Grimes's revelation, they needed to know everything. But she was reluctant to give it up. Once she did, it might lose its potential power. "Okay." She felt suddenly exhausted. "Is there somewhere I could sit?"

Grady gestured to the old armchair and she sat in it. She looked directly at Patrick Lattimore. "All right. Yesterday I talked with Dorothy Huff."

"The grandmother in Elgin," Lattimore said.

"Yes. She told me Donnie Ray was adopted by Evelyn Grimes, as a baby."

Lattimore scowled. "I really don't understand how our intelligence group missed this."

"If you doubt it, I have the papers to prove it." Molly summarized her conversation with Dorothy Huff. Then she told about Grady's unearthing the old patrol report, about Hank Hanley and the Greek letters, and her extraction of information from Betty Larkin, the Pi Alpha Omega house-mother. She watched their expressions for disapproval, but the men all looked unperturbed, as if this was just business as usual.

"Thelma Bassett believes that mothers are a real obsession with Samuel Mordecai and I do, too. He searched desperately to find his birth mother. It's enormously significant to him. If we could come up with her identity now, I'm sure we'd have something of value to trade to him."

"Maybe," Andrew Stein mused. "God knows we haven't been able to tempt him with anything else. What were you planning to do next?"

From her bag Molly pulled out the directory and the list Betty Larkin had given her. "Well, I took the summer school list and checked to see if there were any members who were there that summer and have a current address in Austin. There are two of them, but one, Nancy Saint Claire, was a sorority officer—VP of Special Events—and might have been more actively involved in sorority life. I was planning to call her and ask if we could talk."

"What would you ask her?" Stein asked.

"Well, I hadn't decided how to proceed." Molly thought for a minute. "What I want to know is who in the sorority was pregnant in the summer of '62. I could say I'm doing a piece on how sexual morality has changed in the past thirty-five years and I've been talking to a sophomore Pi Alph who is pregnant out of wedlock and I want to compare her feelings and experiences with someone who was in that situation in '62."

The room was silent. She looked around.

"No," Andrew Stein said. "Too convoluted. Why lie if you don't have to? The best lies are as close to the truth as you can make them."

Molly flushed. Stein was right. "What if I said I was looking for the birth mother of a man who needed that information desperately and we have reason to think the mother is a Pi Alph who was at summer school in 1962. I'll ask her if she was aware of any pregnancies."

"That's more like it, close to the facts. All true,

really," Lattimore said. "We've got almost no time left. This may not be worth fussing with. What do you all think? A woman who's kept a secret this long is unlikely to give it up now. And Grimes may have moved on to other obsessions. This may be worthless." He looked around the room.

Stein shrugged. "It's worth a try. If it doesn't take away from our other efforts."

"Definitely worth a try," Grady agreed. "We could let Miss Cates do it."

Lattimore's cool eyes were assessing Molly. "Do you want to have a go at it? Or shall we take it over? I could send Holihan."

Molly looked at the broad-shouldered Bryan Holihan. The agent was probably thirty, with a square head and pug nose. "Let me. If I can't get anything, you could always take over."

Lattimore looked around at the others. Curtis shrugged and Andrew Stein said, "I think it's more likely that a woman would tell a secret like that to Miss Cates than to Holihan."

Lattimore sighed. "We haven't discussed confidentiality yet, Miss Cates. I realize you're a member of the press. I don't know what you intend to write about when this is over, but anything we've discussed in this room is strictly off-limits."

"I have no intention of writing about this," Molly told him.

Grady moved away from the wall where he'd been leaning. "Lattimore, you don't realize it, but you're lucky to be standing there with your nuts still intact. This is not a woman you dictate to."

"I'm not dictating," the agent said to Grady. He looked back at Molly. "Sorry to be heavy-handed. I just wanted to make sure you knew how we play these things."

"I'm glad to know," she told him. "But just for interest's sake, how would you stop me if I did want to write about this?"

"We couldn't stop you. But we'd deny everything. And we could make your life a living hell after the fact."

"How?"

"For starters, we'd get the IRS to audit every detail of your taxes for the past eight years." With a sly smile, he asked, "You remember what it was like when you got audited in '89?"

Molly's face must have betrayed her astonishment because he continued: "Oh, yes. It took Curtis about twenty seconds to get that. Makes you wonder if Mr. Mordecai has got some valid points about the menace of computers."

"Well," Molly said, "I survived it in '89 and I could survive it again."

"Maybe, but the audit they would do this time would make that one seem like a love feast. This time they'd ask for every receipt, every scrap of paper for every tiny deduction, every canceled check and deposit slip, going back eight years. They would find irregularities that required an even more rigorous audit. You'd be spending all your time rummaging through your records and meeting with accountants, getting friends and business associates to make affidavits about this and that business expense. We'd do the same thing to your magazine and make sure the publisher knew that you were the reason. Shall I go on?"

Molly managed to squeeze out a smile. "No. I'm convinced. Maybe the IRS is the weapon to use against Mr. Mordecai."

He didn't smile. "Oh, we tried that early on. It usually gets people's attention right quick, but Mordecai didn't even flinch. When you really believe the world is ending, taxes lose their sting."

Grady Traynor said, "If she says she won't write about it, she won't. But in light of this morning's attack and the known viciousness of the Sword Hand of God, she needs... an escort."

"Definitely," Lattimore said. "Holihan is your new best friend, Miss Cates. I hear your truck got disabled, so he'll drive you. Curtis, do your magic on that computer and find us personal data on Nancy Saint Claire. And, Curtis—ASAP."

> *"It's safer to believe. If you're wrong, well, there's nothing lost. But if you choose not to believe and you're wrong, there's hell to pay."*
> HARRIET CATES CAVANAUGH,
> TO HER NIECE

CHAPTER THIRTEEN

As Jake Alesky wheeled himself across the threshold, Molly felt a stillness descend on the room. They must have known of his condition, but Jake's presence clearly caused discomfort. It would be the very devil to have to face that reaction day after day, she thought.

257

Lattimore leaned down to shake his hand. "Mr. Alesky, I'm Patrick Lattimore. Thank you for coming. Sorry for all the rush and secrecy, but we are running against the clock here."

"I'll do anything I can to help Walter," Jake said.

"We talked to Walter on the phone this morning and he sent you a message. I want to play it for you." He nodded toward the tape player. "Holihan, make it so."

Holihan flipped the switches and the phone call played again.

Molly watched Jake's face. When it came to the part about Granny Duck, his jaw tightened and his prominent Adam's apple bobbed. "Oh, Christ." When it was over, he put his long fingers to his forehead as if shading his eyes from some glare.

Patrick Lattimore said, "We know Walter Demming has no living grandparents, or parents. So who is Granny Duck?"

Jake opened his mouth, but no sound emerged. He seemed to have no breath to propel the words.

"Could we get you a glass of water or coffee, Mr. Alesky?"

"Yes. Coffee black. Thanks."

Holihan left the room, sliding the door shut behind him.

Jake wheeled his chair to the wall with the compound diagram and studied it. Then he licked his lips and said, "Is he being held… underground?"

The five people in the room all came to attention, like dogs on point.

"Why do you ask?" Lattimore said evenly.

"Granny Duc, that's D-u-c. Vietnamese. She survived by staying underground. In 1968. Trang

Loi, this village on the Batangan Peninsula."

"Ow," said Lattimore, "bad-luck place."

"Real bad," Jake agreed. "And this village was the worst, the province headquarters of VC activities. A snake pit. Weapons and supplies hidden in hootches and tunnels, VC behind every tree, booby traps everywhere." He stopped, clearly still struggling to get his breathing under control.

Everyone was silent, waiting for him to go on.

He licked his lips again. "This old woman, this Granny Duc—she was the only person to survive the destruction of Trang Loi. A survivor. The ultimate survivor."

Holihan returned with a Styrofoam cup. He handed it to Jake.

"Thanks." Jake took a sip. "Granny Duc hid underground, in one of the tunnels under the village. Other people hid down there, too, but they came out too soon. After the main destruction, but while we were still… in the killing mode. You know?" He looked around the room.

"Oh, yes," Lattimore said, "I know. I did a tour in '69." The two men studied one another. Molly felt the flow of empathy passing between them.

Jake went on: "She didn't come out until two days after. And we…let her live. By then we'd had enough. I think Walter is sending you a message. He'll stay underground through whatever happens. I think he wants you to destroy the compound, and he'll keep the children out of the way for as long as it takes."

Lattimore started to pace the room. He stopped next to Jake in front of the diagram of the Jezreel compound. "I wish he could have told us exactly where he is. Although such precision may be a bit much to expect of someone in such adverse circumstances." He put his finger on the main building. "Mr. Alesky, the tunnel that this Granny Duc hid in—it was underneath the village?"

"Yes. The entrance was in the floor of one of the hootches, hidden under a big storage bin."

Molly's brain was racing. She hadn't been asked and she was just a visitor, but she had a hunch so overpowering she couldn't stop herself. "I think they're under the barn," she said, walking over to look closer at the diagram. "Because it's consecrated ground. He's purifying them. Like the babies. For fifty days."

Lattimore's finger moved slowly to the left and settled on the outline of the barn. "If you're right, we could increase our chances of getting them out alive by maybe ten percent. We'd target the barn and neutralize everyone there first." He pressed down on the barn, turning his index finger as though he were grinding a bug. "What do you think, Andrew?"

Andrew Stein closed his eyes and let his head fall first to one shoulder, then the other, to loosen his neck. "I'm inclined to agree with Miss Cates. If they're underground, and I think they are, it's the barn. Here's why. First, a practical reason: The Jezreelites can get there from the house without being seen because of that breezeway structure, so they've been able to take them food without our surveillance picking it up. But mainly it's the associations I get from the poem. "Under the beetle's cellar' makes me think of barns. You know—dung beetles, barns, animals live there and make dung. "Under the clover's root' suggests root cellars, storage, and I associate both cellars and barns with storage, and we know there is no cellar in the compound, and the entrance to the tunnel in Trang Loi being under a storage bin—well, it just feels right. Also, "Under the light, yet under' suggests two layers of being underneath something, and barns are dark inside. To be buried under a barn roof is like two layers of darkness. Anyway, it's the largest structure in the compound and the only one likely to have a dirt floor."

Molly looked at him with awe. That was exactly how she felt about it, but she'd been reluctant to put anything so sketchy and speculative into words. She began to see why Stein might be a superb hostage negotiator. He was fluent in feelings, intuitive, and willing to stand behind his intuition.

"Well," Lattimore said, "the English major speaks."

Grady, slouching against the wall, looking every bit the outsider he was, spoke. "I agree with Andrew. But even if it's true that they are in some underground cell in that barn, the strike force can't get across that open area fast enough to stop a determined Samuel Mordecai from getting there first and killing the hostages. Mrs. Grimes was headed toward that problem when she was so rudely interrupted."

"Can't you snipe him?" Jake asked.

Stein said, "Mr. Alesky, there is nothing we would like better. But our sharpshooters have had their rifles aimed at the front door and his bedroom window for six weeks and he has yet to walk into our cross hairs. Not once. The cowardly bastard." For the first time, Molly heard anger in his voice.

"Even without Annette Grimes's information," Grady said, "it was clear that we'd have an easier time of it if we took him out. All the intelligence coming in—the Cult Watchers report, and the interviews with the few ex-members who will talk—they all agree that there's no chain of command in there. Mordecai's the commander in chief of what he calls his destroyer angels, the militia he's got in there, and all the rest are just privates. He dictates what they'll eat and when, who sleeps with who, who does what work and how long." And who will live and who must die, Molly thought. "With Mordecai gone," Grady continued, "the Jezreelites would fall to pieces."

"Well, gentlemen, we can't snipe him if we can't see him," Lattimore snapped.

"A real shame," Stein said. "I sure wish we could figure a way to take him out." He glanced at Lattimore with an intensity that made Molly wonder what the shared secret was.

"So are we giving up on negotiating?" Curtis asked.

"I hate like hell to give up after forty-eight days of this," Lattimore said. "Until Miss Cates played that tape of Mrs. Grimes, I really thought we could negotiate those kids home to bed. But it's over. We need to get Blumberg in here now with his Ninja gear and flash-bangs. It's time to unleash them."

Jake had been listening intently. He said, "I'd like to add this: Walter knows what's going on in there better than we do. He hates violence. If he's assuming you'll attack, inviting you to, it's because he knows negotiation won't work."

Lattimore nodded. "Agents Stein, Curtis, Holihan, and Lieutenant Traynor, I am giving you a locker-room talk. This Walter Demming is a real stand-up guy. He's just a civilian, a bus driver, for Christ's sake. If he can send secret messages while he's under the gun, *and* taking care of eleven children, we handpicked, elite agents of the Federal Bureau of Investigation—and the Austin PD—ought to be able to come up with a plan to oblige the man. And not just some testosterone-surge, Geronimo attack that'll get him and the kids gloriously killed, but something elegant and controlled to give them the best chance possible under these tough odds." He looked around the room, deliberately engaging each pair of eyes. "And we've got to have that plan today."

When no one spoke, he pulled the towel from around his neck and heaved it into a corner. "So let's get the fuck going. Curtis, have you found Nancy Saint Claire for us?"

Curtis smiled. He'd been working away steadily at the computer. "Yes, sir. She's a real estate broker who owns her own company. She drives a silver Lexus, '94 model. She wears contact lenses. She's five nine, a hundred eighty-five pounds, fifty-three years old. The house she and her husband own in Rob Roy is on the market for one million eight. Last year they paid taxes on it of thirty-six thousand. Perfect credit rating. I have four phone numbers for her: home, office, digital pager, car. Shall we try her?"

"Miss Cates," Lattimore said, "you still with us

here? You've had a hard morning and you're a volunteer. You can drop out anytime you say so. But Lieutenant Traynor seems to think you're good at this and since you've taken it this far I'm willing to let you stay with it. If you want."

"Yes. I'd like to try."

"There is a condition: Agent Holihan goes with you."

"Can't it be Lieutenant Traynor?" Molly asked.

"No. I need him here. He's our reality check."

Molly was bone-weary. And she wanted to get Grady alone so they could talk all this over. But, on the other hand, she wasn't ready to let this go. She wanted to follow the strand to the very end, as far as she could take it. Her drive for closure outweighed everything else. And she hated to delegate. "Okay."

"Ring her, Curtis."

Nancy Saint Claire wasn't at her home or office phone, but she answered the first ring on her car phone.

"This is Molly Cates, Mrs. Saint Claire. I'm a writer for *Lone Star Monthly* magazine, and I have something I need to talk to you about. It's urgent. May I come see you right now?"

"What is this about?"

"I can't talk about it over the phone. Wherever you're headed, let me come meet you there."

"Well, I'm on my way to my office. You could come there, I guess. I've got a client with me, but we'll be finished in a few minutes."

She gave Molly the address in Northwest Hills and they agreed to meet in forty-five minutes.

Lattimore said, "If you can pull this off, Miss Cates, I'll hire you on."

Molly shook her head. "I hear you have to do push-ups on your fingertips. That's not in any job description of mine."

"Good luck with this," he said. "It may not be going anywhere we want to go at this point, but see what you can get."

As Molly and Bryan Holihan were leaving, Lattimore said, "Mr. Alesky, may I impose on your goodwill some more? We'd like to keep you here in case of more communications that relate to this Granny Duc business. And I'd like to sit with you and go over that incident in more detail, if you will."

Jake nodded, his face grim.

Nancy Saint Claire was a large, carefully groomed woman wearing a gorgeous suit of fuchsia silk. Her gold necklace, earrings, and watch were significant, chunky, and 18 karat. Her office overflowed with the artifacts of a long, successful career: plaques testifying to millions of dollars of sales, awards, photographs with celebrities. She was sitting behind a cluttered desk.

Molly introduced herself and Bryan Holihan.

The realtor took the ID badge Bryan held out to her and studied it. "Well, this looks like the real thing. Special Agent Holihan from the FBI?" She laughed. "What's going on? I bet it's Mr. Withers, isn't it?"

Bryan took his badge back and slid it into his pocket. "No. Who's Mr. Withers?"

She waved a plump hand with long, perfect nails. "Never mind. A joke. Sit down, both of you." She looked at her watch. "I've got twenty minutes before I have to leave for an appointment."

"Mrs. Saint Claire," Bryan intoned, leaning forward, "this is important government business, and you will—"

"Agent Holihan," Molly said, "this is woman talk. Sit back please for a minute. Thank you for seeing us, Mrs. Saint Claire. This is short notice and it's going to be the strangest request you've had in a long while."

"Don't be so sure. Just last week I had a client, a retired executive who specifically requested a million-dollar house within viewing distance of a Catholic girls' school. And he had no children." She laughed heartily. "That's Mr. Withers. I refused to do business with him; it's nice to be in a position to turn away million-dollar voyeurs."

Molly smiled. "I work for *Lone Star Monthly,* but I'm not working now, and I'm not planning to write about this. There's very little time, so I'll get right to it. A man who was adopted as a baby back in 1962 is looking for his birth mother. There is good reason to think she's a Pi Alpha Omega who was in summer school in 1962. You were there and you were a sorority officer. Were you aware of any pregnancies among your members that summer?"

She sat blank-faced for several seconds. Then she picked up the phone and pressed two buttons. "Rachel, would you bring us some coffee? And a few of those low-fat cookies, Snackwells, the ones in the red tin."

She put the phone down and smiled at them.

"That *is* the damnedest request. I've worried about the government interfering in our lives, but since when is getting pregnant an FBI matter?"

"This has to do with the hostage situation out in Jezreel, Mrs. Saint Claire. Agent Holihan is a member of the Hostage Response Team that's come to town to try to get those children out safely."

Nancy Saint Claire's smile faded. "Really?"

"Yes. We can't tell you any more than that, but this is extremely important, a matter of life and death."

"Whose life and death?"

"The hostages."

"This is crazy. How would some pregnancy—*alleged* pregnancy—thirty years ago affect the lives of those poor children? I can't see any possible connection."

"It is crazy," Molly said. "The real story is crazier than anything you could imagine, but we urgently need to know whatever you know. Please tell us."

Nancy Saint Claire was frowning. "The problem is, it's a matter of personal loyalties, and for me those have always outweighed any sense I have of public responsibility. I believe in the sacredness of keeping a secret"—she raised the palms of both hands—"assuming I had one."

"I agree with you," Molly said, "in general. But in this case, the interest of those twelve hostages at Jezreel overrides your personal loyalties. Mrs. Saint Claire, keeping secrets is a sacred responsibility. But I have just talked with Thelma Bassett, the mother of one of those children. This information could lead to something that might help her."

"Lots of coulds and mights here."

The door opened and a tray with coffee and some squarish chocolate cookies appeared.

"I forgot to ask if you wanted coffee. Well, there it is. And I recommend the cookies—zero calories from fat and pretty good in spite of it."

Bryan took one and popped it into his mouth whole.

Molly took one and nibbled on it. It tasted like all its calories came from hay.

They sat in silence while Nancy Saint Claire ate two cookies and sipped her coffee. "Back then," she said, "it was a shameful secret if you got pregnant out of wedlock, and I'm afraid I still see it like that. You're younger, so you may not—"

"Not much younger," Molly said, "and I remember it like that, too." Molly remembered all too well the panic surrounding her own unmarried pregnancy at nineteen and how telling her Aunt Harriet about it felt like her own personal end of the world.

Nancy Saint Claire set her coffee down. Suddenly a light seemed to go on behind her eyes. "Nineteen sixty-two?" she said, leaning across her desk. "Nineteen sixty-two—a baby born then would be thirty-three. Samuel Mordecai is thirty-three. But was he adopted?"

The woman was quick; Molly was impressed. "When this is all over, I'll come tell you what I can. Now you tell me. Tomorrow is the last day for those children. Please tell me what you know."

Nancy Saint Claire exclaimed softly, "I should

have my head examined. I don't know for absolute sure, but that summer—it was after my junior year—two sophomores who had been living in the house—they were roommates—left right after summer school started, and got an apartment. It was unusual at that time. And they'd paid up for the summer and it was nonrefundable. The scuttlebutt was that one of them was PG, as we used to say in those coy days, but they didn't show up at any Pi Alph functions and I never ran into them that summer, so I don't know which one. But it may be that the rumor was false—that happens, you know."

Molly got out her list. "What were their names?"

Nancy Saint Claire paused and then let out a long breath. "Let me see your list."

Molly handed it to her. She scanned the page, then took a pencil and made two check marks. She slid the paper back to Molly. "I hope I'm not going to regret this."

Molly read off the checked names. "Sandy Loeffler and Gretchen Staples."

"Yes."

"Which one is more likely to have been pregnant that summer?"

"Oh, come, Miss Cates. That's impossible. It can happen to anyone. You know that."

Molly smiled. "Yes, I do. But you have no recollection of a thickening waist or someone throwing up at breakfast?"

"Afraid not. I was immersed in my own romance that summer. Too busy trying not to get pregnant myself to notice much. I needn't have worried so much, as it turned out, since I never did get pregnant, ever, even with fertility drugs and all manner of indignities."

Molly got out her Pi Alpha Omega directory and looked up Sandy Loeffler, now, according to the directory, Sandy Loeffler Hendrick. "According to this, Sandy's in San Antonio. Have you had any contact with her?"

"No. I don't believe she was at the reunion last year."

Molly looked up Gretchen Staples, who still carried that name. "How about Gretchen, who lives in Santa Fe now?"

"She was at the reunion. She paints, or has an art gallery, or something related to art. I spoke to her briefly. That's all I know."

"Could you describe for me what they look like, or rather, what they looked like back then?"

"Let's see. Gretchen was a big girl, like me, full face, beautiful skin, glossy long black hair. Healthy-looking."

"What color eyes?"

She shook her head. "I don't remember."

"What were her teeth like?"

She thought for a few seconds. "A little snaggly, I think."

"Did her hair have any natural curl?"

"This *is* about Samuel Mordecai," the woman said excitedly. "No. Gretchen's hair was straight as a board. We were all jealous of it."

"What about Sandy?" Molly asked.

Nancy's cheeks flushed. "Curly hair, almost kinky. She used to straighten it. Dark blond, with highlights. She was very slim and fit, not an ounce of fat on her anywhere. Worked out even back then, when no one did it. Blue-gray eyes. Fine features."

"What about her teeth?"

"Perfect. Without orthodontia, I think. A natural beauty, Sandy. I'd like to see what she looks like now."

"Would you have any pictures?"

Nancy shook her head. "My yearbook got lost in one of our many moves."

Molly stood up and reached over the desk to take her hand. "Thank you. Thank you. It was a difficult decision. I'm sorry to put you in that moral quandary."

"I hope to hell this is not going to hurt those girls."

"I'll do my best to see that it doesn't," Molly promised.

When they got back to the car, Bryan Holihan complained that Molly hadn't given him time to establish his line of questioning before leaping in. Molly explained that it wasn't the questions; it was his tone. Then he objected to the dog riding in the back seat, saying he was allergic to animal dander and it was making his nose stuffy. Molly told him to open the windows.

While they sat in the parking lot, Holihan radioed the names and addresses back to Curtis at the command post. After a brief discussion about how to proceed, Lattimore decided that Molly and Bryan would drive to San Antonio right away to talk to Sandy Loeffler Hendrick. At the same time they made contact with her, an agent in Santa Fe would contact Gretchen Staples. That way the women couldn't warn one another or compare notes.

Bryan complained again about the dog activating his dander allergies. "Open the windows," Lattimore told him. Molly suppressed a grin.

The hour and fifteen minutes on the road to San Antonio was spent talking to the command post. Curtis did his computer magic. Sandy Hendrick was five feet six inches tall, one hundred fifteen pounds, owned a 1994 Jeep Grand Cherokee and a 1993 Lexus ES 300, was married to an attorney, had two daughters, now grown and not living at home, owned with her husband a house in Alamo Heights, on which the taxes last year were $12,000. She also had a record: five arrests and one conviction for DWI in the past ten years. Her license had been revoked for a year in 1990.

They stopped once, near New Braunfels, to walk Copper and pick up some food at McDonald's. Holihan had two Big Macs and two orders of fries. Molly had a chicken filet sandwich and was sorry within minutes.

As they entered San Antonio city limits, the radio crackled. It was Lattimore.

"Bad news," he said. "Real bad. Annette Grimes turned up—dead. So sorry, Molly."

Molly's stomach lurched. She'd been expecting this. "How?"

"Her throat was slit. She was hanging upside down, naked, in an empty storage unit at this place over on Burnet Road. They didn't even close the door, so someone walking by saw her in there."

"Another blood statue," Molly said.

"Lieutenant Traynor is at the scene now. The MO is identical to the Asquith killing. When we finish with you, Austin PD wants you back. First thing in the morning, if that's all right."

"I don't have anything more to tell them."

"Molly, I don't want to panic you, but Traynor says it looks like Annette was tortured some before she died. That means she probably told them what she told you. These so-called Sword Hand of God are on the move."

Molly didn't respond. The chicken sandwich she'd just eaten felt like it was coming back to life in her stomach, feathers and all. In this business it was safer not to chance eating. She was wondering how wide the Sword Hand of God were casting their net for blood statues.

"Mr. Lattimore, I'm worried about Sister Adeline Dodgin in Waco. She's the one who put me on to Gerald Asquith and the Rapture of Mordecai business. I don't want her to end up a blood statue, too."

"We've had one of our local agents watching Ms. Dodgin since you told me about her. Holihan, you stay close to Miss Cates. Don't let her out of your sight."

"Tell *her* that, sir," Holihan said.

"Miss Cates, if you give Holihan a hard time, I'll fire you."

Molly turned around to look at the dog, who was standing on the back seat hanging his head out the open window. She reached back and patted his lean rump. "Copper, I don't believe I've thanked you."

The dog pulled his head in and looked at her.

"That's right," she said. "I'm saying thank you."

Holihan sneezed.

CHAPTER FOURTEEN

"He finally did it. Old Jacksonville finally did it. He scraped through that second bar. Now there was a big enough hole for him to squeeze out. Of course, it helped that he was much thinner after nothing but water for three days. It felt so good to stand up straight and spread his wings. But he didn't have time to really enjoy it because it was starting to get light out. And he heard something that really scared him. It was a rooster crowing. Now you guys remember that—"

Walter fell silent. Josh was having a convulsive wheezing episode and most of the kids weren't really listening anyway. Kim and Lucy were whispering and Bucky was talking to his Mighty Morphin Power Ranger. Philip was sitting up straight with his hands covering his face. The others had seemed distant and preoccupied since his phone call to the outside world this morning. Now it was bedtime, and he was exhausted. He had hoped he might distract them with the story, get them to stop grilling him, stop trying to catch him in evasions.

They had wanted to hear everything about his ten minutes aboveground, every detail. He'd been talking about it all day, telling and retelling it, and still they wanted more. It was particularly difficult to keep it consistent since he had concealed some parts of it in his first version. Now he understood why cops interrogated suspects by making them keep repeating their original stories. It was difficult to lie consistently, even about ten lousy minutes, and even to little kids. They had already caught him in one lie—the one about how he'd gotten the head wound that was still oozing blood hours later. They didn't buy his original story of tripping and hitting his head on the corner of a file cabinet. And they were suspicious of the amended version, that Martin hit him because he hadn't moved fast enough.

Josh leaned over into his emergency breathing posture and gasped.

Quickly Walter got the towel from where it was drying over the steering wheel. He ran water from the thermos onto it, until it was soaked through. Then he took it to Josh. Kim had moved back to sit with him. She was rubbing the back of his neck.

Walter handed Kim the towel. She folded it, then rolled it up and handed it to Josh. He held the sopping towel over his eyes and let the drips roll down his face. It was more like some magic ritual than anything scientific, but it seemed to ease the boy's symptoms slightly.

When the gasping died down, Kim said, "Were they there, where the guy talking on the phone was? The FBI guy."

"Your parents? I don't know, Kim, but if they weren't right there, I'm sure they got the messages to them right away. They certainly have the messages by now. They know you're all okay."

"What's it like inside the house?" Conrad asked. "Is that where Martin and Mr. Mordecai live?"

"Well, you guys remember what the barn looks like, don't you? Remember the first day we walked through the double doors. It's big inside and pretty dark. No windows. The floor is dirt and at one end there are bales of hay and sacks and boxes stacked up. Then there's this wooden sort of hall-way that goes from the barn to the house, so you don't have to go outside."

"I didn't see that when we came in," Conrad objected.

"I did," Hector said.

"Me, too," Sue Ellen said.

"The house is big," Walter said, "more like a hotel, but kind of run-down and not well built. Needs painting, I think, but it was hard to see because they have sheets and blankets tacked up over all the windows. And they don't have many lights on. I told you that, didn't I? I don't know whether Martin and Mr. Mordecai live there or not. But there are other people there, because I saw a bunch of them, maybe twenty, all gathered in the center room. The phone's in a little room that looks like an office. That's where they took me, and they had me sit down at the desk."

"Was that when Martin hit you in the head with his gun?" Hector asked, his eyebrows raised in suspicion.

"No. It was later. On my way out."

"Did they point guns at you the whole time?" Hector asked. "Were there just the two of them?"

"Just the two of them—Martin and the bald guy I told you about—until Mr. Mordecai came in. Then there were three. Yes, they pointed guns at me the whole time." That was true, but he didn't tell them that it wouldn't have mattered whether they had pointed guns at him or not. He would still have done exactly as they ordered him. Martin had warned him while they were still in the barn that if he said or did anything unauthorized, anything they didn't like, they'd pull one of the kids up and shoot him in the head. So guns weren't necessary, but Martin and the other man Walter remembered from the first morning had stood behind him with their pistols aimed at his head. Just a few inches away. The whole time.

"Say it again, what the FBI guy said," Conrad demanded.

"He said his name was Andrew Stein, the same man I talked to the time before. He said our safety was the most important thing to them and that they hadn't forgotten us and they were working around the clock to get us out safe. They particularly wanted to know how you were, Josh, because of your asthma. So they are thinking about all of us and doing everything they can. I was real encouraged. There must be some progress, since they let me talk."

"But why don't they *do* something?" Sandra said. "It's been so long."

"Will they come for us?" Kim asked.

"I think so," Walter said. "I'm very encouraged. I'm sure they're working on a plan to get us out. Maybe it will be trading something or paying them something to let us go. But I think this is what's going to happen: The FBI and the police will come in and rescue us. And if they have to do it that way, there will be a fight, lots of noise and some shooting probably. You know that. So we want to

277

practice our emergency plan so we're ready. We want to make it as easy for them as we can. And that means staying out of the way and letting them do their work."

"What kind of guns do they have up there?" Hector asked.

"Well, I didn't get a chance to study them, Hector. But they have lots of rifles and they have gas masks. I told you that. So they must think there's a chance of tear gas being used. That means we have to add a step to our drill. Just in case we get some gas drifting down here. We are all going to take our shirts off and soak them in water and wrap them around our heads. Sort of like Josh does."

What he didn't want to tell them was that the house was an armory, a battle station with enough automatic weapons, ammunition, grenades, and gas masks to hold off an army. Mordecai's people had stacked bales of hay under all the windows. Furniture and sandbags were heaped against the front door, and men in fatigues knelt at the windows and paced the halls carrying AK-47s and belts of ammunition. Walter wanted the kids to expect a firefight, so they'd be ready, but he didn't want to overwhelm them with the details.

But it wasn't the weapons and hay bales and gas masks that had most upset him. What had nearly caused him to go berserk was the inhalers. When he was herded into the room with the telephone, they caught his eye immediately—four shiny yellow plastic inhalers on top of a stack of newspapers on the file cabinets. They were identical to Josh's inhaler and bore similar-looking white-and-blue prescription labels. His heart leapt. "Are those for Josh?" he'd blurted out.

Martin pressed the gun to his temple. "Sit down. We don't use drugs here, especially during purification. Those aren't for no one."

"But they look—"

"Silence. You came here to do something. Let's do it," Martin said. "You're here to talk on this phone for one minute. The Prophet Mordecai is on his way. He wants to hear this."

Walter sat on the chair. Martin and the other man stood behind him with their guns inches from his head. Walter sat motionless, but his eyes kept darting back to the inhalers. They attracted him powerfully, excited him. They were bright yellow, like sunshine, glowing with life and health, full of hope; if he could get them, they would restore breath to Josh. He wanted those inhalers as he'd never wanted anything in his life. He wanted them with such an intensity, he felt he could make them levitate and move through the air, into his hand, into his pocket. He tried to read the name on the labels but it was too far for him without his glasses. And it didn't matter. He knew they were for Josh. And he knew what must have happened. The negotiators had sent them in with the newspapers. No doubt Josh's parents had been howling about it for forty-eight days, and the negotiators had gotten tired of begging Mordecai and being turned down, so they had just sent them in.

He pulled his gaze away from them because Samuel Mordecai had entered the room and shut the door. Martin and the other Hearth Jezreelite stood straighter and stiffer. This

279

morning Mordecai was clean-shaven and his hair looked damp and he smelled clean, as though he'd just come out of the shower. It made Walter long to put his sore, filthy body under a stream of hot water.

Mordecai leaned down and picked up the phone in front of Walter. "Stein?" he said. "Here he is. You've got one minute."

Walter read the messages at the speed he'd practiced, in a monotone, trying to make them all sound alike, innocuous and trivial. But his hands had been shaking so hard he had to lay the sheet on the desk to read it.

After the call, Martin had jabbed the gun into his neck and told him to stand up. Walter turned his eyes to Samuel Mordecai, who for all his insane ravings and cold indifference seemed a better bet for compassion than Martin. In forty-eight days of being their caretaker, Martin had not given them a single kind word or glance and he had not brought them even one thing they had asked for to make their lives less miserable—no hot water or aspirin, no paper or pencils, no soap or shampoo, no flashlights, no batteries.

So he looked to Samuel Mordecai. "Prophet Mordecai," he said, using for the first time the term of address the man preferred. He did it because he wanted the inhalers and because he had no shame left. "Prophet Mordecai, please. Let me take those inhalers to Josh."

Mordecai turned to Walter. He smiled his dimpled movie-star smile. "Still hung up on earthly inconveniences, Mr. Bus Driver? You are the sort of man who in the middle of the great battle of Armageddon will be fussing over dirty laundry."

"But it won't hurt anything," Walter persisted, "and it will calm everyone down. The kids get really upset and hard to manage when Josh gets sick." Samuel Mordecai's smile stayed fixed. Walter pulled out all the stops. "The end is coming, I know. It will be easier for all of us if you just let me take those inhalers"—he pointed at them sitting on top of the cabinets—"back to the bus."

Mordecai glanced at the inhalers. Then he looked over Walter's shoulder at Martin. He gave a nod.

Walter's heart hammered. He was going to allow it.

That's when Martin slammed the gun barrel into the back of his head. Walter saw hot sparks behind his eyes. He staggered and began to fall, but caught himself by grabbing on to the desk. He didn't realize until later, after he had staggered back to the bus and sat down, that blood had soaked his hair and was dripping onto his shirt.

Now, hours after the incident, he couldn't bear to tell the children about the inhalers. He felt it would introduce them to an idea he found too evil to share with them—the idea of a world so random and uncaring, so indifferent to human suffering, that it chilled his soul.

"What else did you see in the house?" Lucy asked. "Are there mothers and children there? Kids our age?"

"I saw some women, but no children."

"Maybe they're in school," Lucy told the others. "It's a school day, isn't it?"

"Yes. Wednesday. That's probably where they are," Walter said.

"But maybe," Lucy said in a quivery voice, "maybe the children who live here are buried in a bus, too, just like us. Maybe they're in our bus that we came in. Maybe they're lambs who are chosen, too, and maybe—"

"Dummies!"

The hoarse voice came from the back of the bus. They all turned to look. Philip Trotman, who hadn't spoken a word in more than ten days, was kneeling on his seat, his nose cherry red, his eyes bloodshot from weeping. "Lucy, you're such a dummy. He's going to kill us. That's why we're here. He's going to kill us and you know it." Tears dripped down his face. "He calls us lambs. First-born. I go to Sunday school. In the Bible, lambs get killed and then burned up—burnt offerings. And in Egypt the firstborn all got killed one night."

They were all silent. Lucy looked as if she'd been slapped.

Walter had tried with all his might to avoid this discussion. How would he keep them calm now?

Then Josh began a furious high wheezing, violent and wracking. Kim slipped her arm around him and was holding the wet towel for him, crooning his name.

Walter walked to the back, where Philip was still kneeling on the seat. He sat down and reached his arms around the boy. He pulled him in tight and held on to him, rocking him slightly from side to side. Philip's slender body was rigid in his arms. Into his ear he whispered the only words that seemed to make sense. "Philip, it's so good to hear your voice again. Keep on talking. I don't know what's going to happen. You could be right. But keep on talking. Whatever happens, we'll all be together in it."

The raspy sound of Josh's tortured gasping drowned out Philip's muffled sobs. Walter closed his eyes. He pictured the yellow inhalers sitting on top of the file cabinets, four of them lined up, smiling at him, full of promise, false hope.

He let go of Philip when Josh let out a wheeze that was so high-pitched it was almost a scream. The sound was so full of distress and panic that Walter knew this would be the worst yet.

"Philip." He moved back and held the boy by his skinny shoulders. "We are in this together. I promise you. Keep talking. I'll be back right after I check Josh."

He strode up the aisle. Josh was leaning forward, his hands pressing down on his knees, his shoulders hunched up. Kim was sitting next to him, humming softly, but not touching him. Walter didn't touch him either because he knew from experience it was best not to when things got this extreme. "Josh, honey, would water help?" It was all he had to offer.

Josh made an annoyed shake of the head. He was engaged, heart and soul, in trying to get enough air through his lungs. By now they had weathered probably ten of these really bad spells, and Walter knew that Josh was already past the point of being able to speak or do much of anything other than struggle for breath. At all other times he was a kid full of goofy good humor. But when he was in the throes of an asthma attack, he was like a creature possessed. He refused to waste even a scintilla of energy on anything except drawing the next breath.

The other kids all stayed where they were, hushed and still. They'd learned, too. Crowding around him or trying to help only made it worse. Kim was still valiantly humming out of tune, her voice shaking badly.

Walter spoke in a very low voice. "I'm here, Josh. This will pass. You know what to do, how to get through it. We're all right here."

Josh gasped and threw his head back. His face was dotted with sweat and even in the dim light Walter could see that his skin had gone dead white around the nose and mouth. His eyes were wild with panic.

It was horrible to watch. Walter had seen men die in Vietnam. There had been pain and screaming, rivers of blood, limbs blown off—horrors that still haunted him. But this was worse. Watching this kid slowly choking, starving for air, drowning inside himself, was the absolute worst. Maybe because Josh was so young. Maybe because Walter felt so responsible, so completely, unforgivably responsible for allowing it all to happen. For not being able to take care of him.

Josh was panting, gulping, as if there were not enough air in the world. In the next seat Sue Ellen, whom he'd never seen cry before, was weeping quietly, her forehead pressed against the black window.

Walter felt his fury building to a hot boil. Goddamn all this—Samuel Mordecai and his Apocalypse, goddamn this bus, this pit, this grave.

Goddamn Martin, that weasel who treats us like we're already dead. Goddamn these kids. Goddamn the telephone he should never have gotten. Goddamn Josh and his faulty bronchial tubes. Goddamn those yellow inhalers. Goddamn the God who lets this happen to children. Goddamn that feckless, useless negotiator he had talked to on the phone—Stein from the fucking FBI. Why the hell didn't they *do* something? Forty-eight days! What the fuck were they waiting for? Why didn't they come in with force? If they didn't do it soon, there would be nothing to rescue but corpses, or those goddamned blood statues Mordecai kept babbling about.

Walter hadn't allowed himself to think about what the end would be, but he'd been listening. He knew what Mordecai intended. He knew what was waiting for them when that last Band-Aid got scraped off the window.

Even if they did live through this, which seemed increasingly unlikely, they'd be damaged beyond repair. His anger was boiling over. He felt like smashing the windows, ripping up the seats. He felt like tearing Samuel Mordecai apart with his bare hands, taking the Bible and stuffing it into his mouth page by page.

The raspy desperate sounds coming from Josh were nonstop now, full of panic. They drowned out Kim's feeble humming.

Walter paced the aisle and found the children looking up at him with round, frightened eyes. God, you couldn't do anything here without it upsetting everyone.

He grabbed the towel from Kim and soaked it

again with water. Desperate for something to do, anything, he held it above Josh's head and twisted it gently so water dripped on his head. "Imagine it's a shower, Josh, steamy and hot. That's what it is. Yes. Yes. Feel it. The steam is rising. Breathe it in. Into your throat. Into your nose. Way back in your head. It's so warm. Opens everything up." He twisted harder, making rain. "You're soaked. In the shower. Steam's rising, all around you, hot water pouring down."

Kim was looking up at him wide-eyed, terrified.

Now Josh was gasping, his head flung back. His chest had grown big and barrel-like, as if it were ready to explode. He had air, lots of it, but he couldn't get it out. His hair was plastered to his head, and he was trembling all over. He was going to explode.

Walter wanted to put his mouth on Josh's and breathe for him, to suck the trapped air out and breathe new air in. He wanted to take hold of him, work him like a bellows, force him to breathe. He'd asked Josh after one of the attacks if it might help for him to try CPR. Josh had just laughed.

Now he was making a sibilant rasp that didn't sound human.

"Josh, listen. Can you smell the bread? The bread you and your dad make in his machine. That white bread, all hot, with butter and sugar melting into it. Mmmm. Let the smell come in. Open your nose. It's right in front of you, honey. Open up for it. Take it in. Smell it, Josh. Let it flow."

Josh was making a rattling way in the back of his throat.

God, who could tolerate this?

They had to have help.

He dashed to the front of the bus, out the door, and into the pit of black earth. He looked up at the wooden slab covering the hole. He reached up and beat his fists on it. "Help! Martin, we need help down here. We've got an emergency." He tried to keep the panic out of his voice. "Martin," he called louder, "Martin, come here, please. Pull the slab back. Please!" He looked back to the bus to see if he was panicking the kids, but without his glasses, he couldn't see that far.

"Open up," he called. "Prophet Mordecai, come here. Please." His voice was rising in spite of his efforts to control it. "God would want you to. At the end of the world or any other time. Josh is real sick. Please come help. We need you down here. Help! Help!" He found himself screaming, his throat raw with it.

He stopped to listen for a response.

Nothing.

He looked back to the bus. Now they knew. The situation was hopeless. And he was worse than useless. A man with a long history of letting people down in the crunch, a man of no use to anyone, a man who made mistakes when it really counted. Images fired through his head—Jake, long-legged and whole, as he had been before Trang Loi, before Granny Duc. Before their lives got ruined. The kids getting on the bus that morning laughing and singing that ditty he hated—*"the worms crawl in, the worms crawl out."*

Tears spurted from his eyes. He couldn't hold them back anymore. They poured out of him— twenty-seven years of stored-up remorse.

He reached up and beat against the wood again. "Please, please, come down here!"

From the bus, he heard Kim calling. "Mr. Demming! Mr. Demming!"

He raced back.

When he got close enough to see Josh, he felt like screaming in horror. The boy's head lolled back. His eyes were twitching and popping out of his head. His lips had darkened to navy blue. His mouth was wide open, his tongue protruding. A dark wet spot was spreading outward on the front of his jeans.

Sitting next to him, Kim was shaking, her arms wrapped around herself.

Walter Demming could think of nothing in the world to do.

His lips started to move. From the past came some words that had once given comfort to friends of his. "'The atmosphere of Titan,'" he said aloud, "'the atmosphere of Titan is like the atmosphere outside the back door of an Earthling bakery on a spring morning.'"

The kids were all staring at him, their wet eyes wide with shock.

"Say it along with me," he said. "Come on. "'The atmosphere of Titan is like the atmosphere outside the back door of an Earthling bakery on a spring morning.'" Several of them joined in the third time, falteringly. "'The atmosphere of Titan,'" more voices joined, "'is like the atmosphere outside an Earthling bakery'"—they were all in chorus—"'on a spring morning.'"

He looked down at Josh. His head lolled back

on the seat. His face was pale blue, his eyes closed. He'd gone silent.

Walter fell to his knees in the aisle next to the boy. He started to say it again: "'The atmosphere of Titan…'" but he stopped. It was inadequate. Utterly inadequate.

A prayer he didn't even know he remembered came to his lips instead. "Our Father"—the words forced themselves out like a groan—"which art in heaven." He didn't believe it, any of it, but it seemed to be coming from somewhere beyond him. "Hallowed be Thy name."

The children joined in: "Thy kingdom come, Thy will be done, on earth as it is in heaven."

He had forgotten the next line, but the children took it over. He listened and then joined them at the end: "But deliver us from evil, for thine is the power and the glory forever and ever. Amen."

He leaned over and rested his forehead on Josh's leg. The wetness had spread down. Walter felt the warmth of the soaked denim on his forehead.

Deliver us from evil. Please.

And then he tried Jake's old mantra one more time, very low, just for Josh and for himself: "'The atmosphere of Titan is like the atmosphere outside an Earthling bakery on a…'"

He stopped because he imagined he smelled, not urine, and terror, and death, but fresh bread baking somewhere.

"This thing of darkness I acknowledge mine."
PROSPERO, *THE TEMPEST*

CHAPTER FIFTEEN

They arranged to meet Sandy Loeffler Hendrick at six-fifteen in the snack bar at her health club on San Pedro. Bryan Holihan had done the talking on the phone, saying it was an urgent and confidential FBI matter. He suggested they meet someplace other than her home. Before they went into the spa, Holihan called Santa Fe to tell the agent there that they were about to make contact.

Molly spotted her right away, sitting at a table with a lipstick-stained coffee cup in front of her—still blond and lithe at fifty-two in a shiny black Lycra sports bra and tights. She greeted them warily and, when Bryan Holihan flashed his ID, she took it and laid it on the table in front of her. She stared at it for such a long time Molly wondered if she'd gotten stuck. Eventually she stood and asked them if they'd like juice or coffee. Both declined.

"This seems very strange," Sandy Hendrick said. "The only really private place to talk is one of the personal exercise rooms. We might as well do that." She picked up her cup and headed toward the door. They followed her upstairs, through a huge room carpeted in purple and filled with shiny chrome-and-black machines and no people. She showed them into a small room. One wall was mirrored from floor to ceiling and the opposite wall had a ballet bar. Sandy Hendrick closed the door, turned on the overhead fan, and un-rolled three plastic mats. "Sorry there are no chairs, but you said this required some privacy and this is really the only place." In one graceful, continuous motion, she lowered herself into the lotus position.

Molly assumed an identical position.

Bryan Holihan looked down and turned around once like a dog looking for the right position. Then he went down to one knee on the mat and stayed like that, looking as if he were going to make a proposal of marriage.

"Does this have anything to do with my latest DWI?" Sandy said, looking at Bryan.

"Oh, no, ma'am," he said. "Nothing like that."

"Mrs. Hendrick," Molly said, "this is a most delicate and difficult matter. I believe in a woman's right to privacy around matters of reproduction, but we have some extraordinary circumstances here. I'm going to tell you something that only a few people in the world know and, except for me, all of them are in law enforcement. Whatever you tell us will be shared only with those few, very discreet people.

"Thirty-three years ago, in the summer of 1962, when you were in summer school at the University of Texas, a newborn baby was abandoned. A male baby. Now a grown man. He needs to know the identity of his mother." Molly paused and watched the woman's face. "I have reason to think you might be his mother."

Sandy Hendrick's face had lost some color, but her expression remained totally impassive. Not a muscle twitched anywhere. Her skin had suffered the ravages of the years, the Texas sun, and alcohol, but her features had survived intact: her full lips, slanted blue eyes, and her delicately sculpted nose, which rose at the tip and seemed to pull the upper lip along up with it, revealing even white teeth.

"That's it?" she asked. "That's what you came for?"

Molly nodded.

"I'm sorry y'll have come all the way from Austin for this," she said. "I could have told you over the phone. This has nothing to do with me." Under her black jog bra, her breast heaved as if she'd just run a marathon. "I *was* in summer school in 1962. That's a matter of record. I failed French III, and"—she had to stop for breath—"I had to take it over. I had nothing to do with any baby. This is all so bizarre." She picked up her coffee cup, but her hand was shaking so violently she had to bring the other hand up to help hold it steady. Even using both hands, she was unable to get the cup to her lips. She set it down.

"Mrs. Hendrick," Molly said, feeling a stab of compassion for the devastation these questions were causing, "you and your roommate, Gretchen Staples, moved out of the sorority house even though you'd both paid through the summer and couldn't get a refund. Why?"

"That's none of your business. This has nothing to do with me. Let's finish up here."

"Mrs. Hendrick, when I was nineteen, I got pregnant. I wasn't married and my parents were dead. I remember the panic like it happened this morning. It can happen to anyone,

292

and it's very scary. I still find it difficult to talk about."

"I'm sorry for your misfortune, Miss..." She shrugged.

"Cates. Molly."

"As I said, this has nothing to do with me." She started to get to her feet. "And I'm going to be late for—"

"Wait a minute," Molly said. "Please sit down for a minute more. I want to tell you about this baby—who he is now."

The woman remained standing.

"Please sit."

With a grimace of annoyance that was the first real expression she'd shown, she sank back down to the mat.

"Now I'm going to tell you something that you may find upsetting. The baby that was abandoned that summer is now the cult leader who's holding a dozen people hostage in Jezreel."

Sandy Hendrick kept her expression frozen, but her face paled, making the black eye shadow and liner around her eyes stand out like soot smudges on parchment. She looked like a woman who'd just had all her blood sucked out.

Molly moved in for the kill. "Have you been following that situation in Jezreel, Mrs. Hendrick?"

The woman spoke, barely opening her mouth. "Yes. Of course." Her breath was coming raggedly. Molly was fascinated by the contrast between her attempt at impassiveness and the upheaval her body was caught in. We think we have our bodies in check, but our breath and blood, our tears and tics—those involuntary functions have a life and will of their own, Molly thought. They betray us every time. All the exercise in the world will not bring our bodies under control.

Sandy Hendrick was saying, "Everybody knows about that. I think about those children all the time."

"Do you?"

"Yes, of course. It's terrible, just terrible."

"He's planning to kill them. The negotiators have not gotten anywhere. If they knew the identity of his birth mother, they might be able to use that information to bargain with him. When Samuel Mordecai was twenty-one he searched for his real mother, desperately, but he never found her. It's very, very important to him."

"I'm sure it is, but there's no reason to be telling me this. You're wasting your time, and mine. I'm not the woman you think I am." She turned her head and looked at herself in the big mirror.

Molly studied the woman's profile, giving special attention to the finely molded uptilted nose and the upper lip that pulled up slightly to reveal her teeth. Molly had spent two hours watching Samuel Mordecai, and she'd had ample opportunity to admire his profile. She had always found it astounding when a genetic code imprinted itself on an offspring in some exact reproduction of a parental feature: mother and daughter with identical tufts of hair between their eyebrows, father and son with indistinguishable chin clefts. What bad luck for this woman that she had produced and abandoned a child whose upper lip was the mirror of her own, an undeniable link between them.

294

The resemblance took your breath away.

"Have you seen photographs of Samuel Mordecai?" Molly asked.

"Yes. I suppose. In the paper."

"I wish I had a good, clear photo to show you, Mrs. Hendrick. No one could miss the resemblance. I believe you could tell us the date you gave birth that summer and where you left your baby and what he was wrapped in. Mrs. Hendrick, have you listened to what he said on the radio? He talked about being wrapped in the mantle of the Beast. I think you could explain that."

Sandy Hendrick leapt to her feet, her slender body vibrating. "This is ridiculous!" Her voice shook with rage. "I don't have to stay here! I'm leaving."

"There's a grandchild," Molly continued. "A boy. His mother was murdered today. His father will not come out of this alive. That baby will be an orphan. You wouldn't have to get involved, but you could if you—"

"No! I never had a baby until my Sarah was born in 1967, and I'd been married for two years. I was a virgin when I got married! I never—"

Bryan Holihan spoke up. "We could do this privately, Mrs. Hendrick. No one would have to know."

"Listen!" she cried out. "I'm not the woman you think I am."

Molly studied the taut, high-strung body, the tense, self-preoccupied, ravaged, humorless face. The woman was about to break. Sandy Hendrick was right—she was not the woman Molly thought she was. She was certainly Samuel Mordecai's biological mother and a DNA test would prove it, but she was not the right woman. It would do no good to continue tormenting her, or to try to coerce her to speak to her son. And, anyway, it didn't matter. She had come to the end of the strand. She had found what mattered.

Molly stood. "Sorry we bothered you, Mrs. Hendrick. You're right. This is a misunderstanding and I apologize."

Bryan Holihan reached up and grabbed her arm. "But—"

"Agent Holihan, it's clear Mrs. Hendrick is not the woman we thought she was. We need to let her get on with her evening."

He struggled to his feet.

Sandy Hendrick looked incredulous, as if she'd received a last-second reprieve from certain disaster.

Molly handed her a card, her usual practice. "If you want to talk to me, later on," she said, "give me a call. Thanks for your time. We'd appreciate your not talking about this matter to anyone." No danger of that, Molly thought.

They returned to the car in silence. As they pulled out of the lot, Holihan demanded, "Have you lost your mind? That's her. Even I could see the resemblance to Mordecai. And she was just starting to break down. All the signs were there. You had her where you wanted her. In two more minutes she would have admitted it."

"Probably," Molly said. Copper was leaning into the front seat resting his head on Molly's shoulder and she was scratching behind his good ear.

"Then why—"

"Because I saw that it doesn't matter."

"Doesn't matter! Then why have we wasted all this time?"

"Nothing is ever wasted, Bryan. Haven't you learned that? How old are you?"

"Thirty-one."

"Well, see, you're too young." Molly leaned back and closed her eyes. "I need five minutes of silence to think some things through before we call in. Okay?"

The dark landscape whizzed by. One good thing about Bryan Holihan was that he drove like a bat out of hell. Another was that he didn't feel he had to make conversation. That made for perfect thinking conditions. Molly sat cross-legged in the passenger seat and contemplated deceit and homicide. Or, more accurately, she decided, ingenuity and assassination.

The dog slept on the back seat, occasionally making little whines and twitches in his sleep. Molly glanced back at him and wondered if police dogs had worse dreams than other dogs. According to Grady, this one had had his fair share of nightmare experiences during his career. But this morning, when he'd gone after the attackers in the garage, he had seemed joyful in his ferocity, totally alive, an animal doing what he was born to do. Bred and trained for such action, he would kill easily and without remorse if the occasion required it.

Just like most people.

Molly had never had the slightest problem understanding why people killed one another. There were times in her life when she had been angry enough or scared enough to commit murder; if the conditions had been right, she probably would have. On the *Patriot* police beat, she had seen the results of countless murders—murders for money, revenge, love, drugs, and in one memorable case, murder for bottle caps. Her reaction had never been surprise or outrage, but a grim acknowledgment that it happens because that is the kind of animal we are.

Now she was going to do something she'd never done before: try to persuade others to commit a homicide. "Bryan, I'm ready. Let's call the command post. I need to talk to Lattimore and Stein."

He glanced over at her and grunted an assent. When he got Andrew Stein on the radio, he handed the mike to Molly. She asked, "Who else is present, Mr. Stein?"

"Curtis, and Borthwick."

"Would you get Lattimore in and Traynor, too, and ask Borthwick to wait outside? I want to tell you what happened, and I have an idea I'd like to talk about."

"Traynor's still at the Grimes scene and Lattimore's on his way to the airport in Austin."

"He's not leaving?"

"No. Just picking someone up. Jules, could you wait outside. Go ahead, Miss Cates, it's Curtis and me."

"Is this frequency secure?"

"It's supposed to be. Go ahead. Have you found Mom?"

"Oh, yes. Sandy Hendrick is the mother all right. She didn't admit that she was, but she looks so much like him you could pick her out from a hundred other women. Also she was so stressed by our questions, she was ready to explode. She's really tried to repress the event. If we'd stuck with it, we could have broken her down, but I could see that it doesn't matter."

"Doesn't matter?" Stein sounded impatient.

"I needed to complete the line of inquiry to see what the point really was. This is probably immoral and unethical, but I've got to tell you what I'm thinking now, while we still have time."

"We're all cynical adults here," Stein said.

"Here's what I'm thinking. Mr. Stein, I've heard the FBI has agents who are trained as assassins."

"Miss Cates, I—"

"No. Don't respond to that. I know that you do, but you probably call it by some other term, like rearrangement specialists or mortality adjusters. Here's my real question: Have you got any middle-aged women, around fifty, who have that kind of experience? Who can go into dangerous situations and take someone out? That's the way you say it, isn't it? Take them out?"

There was silence at the other end.

"Do we all agree that launching an assault on the Jezreelites without taking Samuel Mordecai out is likely to give us dead hostages?"

"Miss Cates, where are you going with this?"

"First answer me. Do we agree?"

"We could get dead hostages even if we did figure out how to take him out," Stein said evenly.

"I know, but we would have a better chance with him out."

"We're all nodding," Stein said curtly.

"Okay. You said Mordecai always watches the Channel 33 news at six, right? And you've used that to feed him information."

"Uh-huh."

"Suppose they carried a news item tomorrow that Samuel Mordecai's birth mother had been located and that she wanted to talk to him before the end."

"Uh-huh."

"And suppose he bit on it and contacted you and said he wanted to talk to her, too. And suppose she said it had to be face to face and private, and she wasn't afraid to come in where he was. And suppose she went in there, into the compound."

"Yeah."

"And suppose she gets him alone, away from where the kids are, sort of diverts him. And suppose she kills him. And right then you start the maneuver, take the barn, and swoop down to protect the agent."

"That's a lot of supposing."

"I know."

"We're a civilian agency, Miss Cates. We don't kill people."

"Bullshit."

"Maybe you watch too many movies."

"Maybe I do."

"Where are you now?" Stein asked.

"San Marcos just zoomed by. With Bryan driving, we're forty minutes from you."

"Come back right now. Do not pass go. Do not collect two hundred dollars. Bryan, do not stop at McDonald's. We're all dining here."

"But what do you think?" Molly persisted.

"I think you need to come here. Grady will be back shortly and Lattimore should be back in an hour or so. We'll talk about it then."

Grady Traynor, Andrew Stein, and a slender bald man Molly hadn't met were standing around the computer monitor eating fried chicken and watching George Curtis type words onto the screen. The bald man wore jeans and orange suspenders with palm trees on them over a lavender T-shirt.

Bryan Holihan immediately went to the bucket on top of the fax machine and took out a piece of chicken.

Grady kissed Molly on the cheek. Then he embraced her, holding on longer than usual. She looked up at him. His face seemed grayer than it had a few hours ago and the circles under his eyes looked engraved into the skin. "Bad scene?" she asked.

"One of the worst."

Andrew Stein said, "Miss Cates, this is Jules Borthwick, just flew in from New York. Molly Cates."

Molly shook hands with the bald man. His hand was fine-boned and soft. She'd never seen anyone who looked less like an FBI agent. "Are you an agent?" she asked.

"Don't you just love those dark suits?" he warbled in a falsetto. He lowered his voice to a normal pitch. "I'm a consultant—makeup and special effects."

"Mr. Borthwick is a celebrity," Andrew Stein said. "He created the Elephant Man on Broadway, the Mantis Pieta, lots of movie and rock video monsters. He's said to be a genius."

Molly studied Borthwick with interest. "Is this true or are they playing with me?"

"Oh, it's true, especially the genius part. I got an Obie for Methuselah the Dread."

"What are you doing in Jezreel?"

Andrew Stein said, "It will all come clear. Wait until Lattimore gets back."

She looked around. "He's not back yet?"

"Plane was delayed," Stein said curtly. "Just twenty minutes."

"Who's coming in?" Molly asked.

"The woman you were talking about—the fifty-year-old agent—Loraine Conroy." Stein checked his watch. "They should be back here by eleven."

Molly was breathless with surprise. "You had already—"

"Great minds," Stein said. "But your idea of breaking it on the TV news is excellent, original with you. We were planning to call Mordecai with it direct, but this is much better because he'll see it and call *us*. That way, it feels like his idea. Go ahead and print that out, Curtis, so she can read it."

Curtis hit a key; the light on the printer began to blink.

Molly tried to keep her voice even. "When did you decide to do this?"

"Early this morning, right after Lieutenant Traynor told us Samuel Mordecai was adopted and how far you'd gotten in searching for the mother. We've been sitting around here for days trying to figure out how to get someone inside there to take Mordecai out, and then you came into our lives and gave us the answer. Hallelujah. Lattimore called Quantico right then to ask if Rain could fly down. We had to get a green light on Mordecai, but the real problem is that we have a policy against risking agents' lives to get hostages out." Seeing her expression, he explained bluntly, "Hostages are considered to have one leg in the grave already and you don't risk a fully alive person for them. But when children are involved, everyone goes all mushy."

The printer spit out a single sheet.

"So," Molly said, feeling hot anger building up, "you knew all along it didn't matter whether we found the mother or not, but you let us make the trip to San Antonio."

"Oh, no. We hoped you'd come back with a bona fide mom. It would be nice to have her in our pocket, just in case. But you know as well as we do this negotiation's at a dead end. Mordecai's just been leading us on, buying time. Any bargaining chip is worthless. He never intended to let any of the kids go."

Molly looked at Andrew Stein's plump face in wonder. She'd been considering herself ruthless. But these guys were way beyond her.

Stein picked the paper up from the printer and handed it to her. "Read it out loud."

Molly read: "MOLLY CATES: *I was working on a story about Samuel Mordecai for my magazine when I learned he had been adopted as an infant. I went back and researched it. It was difficult, but I finally located his birth mother yesterday. She lives in Houston now and had no idea that Mordecai was her son until I talked to her yesterday.*

"NEWSPERSON: *How can you be sure that the woman you found really is his mother?*

"CATES: *Because I was careful not to give her any of the details I knew about where the infant had been found and when and what was found with him. She was able to tell me all that, every detail. There's no question—this woman is Samuel Mordecai's real mother. She wants more than anything in the world to speak with him, explain things to him.*

"NEWSPERSON: *What are the circumstances of his birth? You said he was found?*

"CATES: *At this point in time I'm not at liberty to talk about that.*" She stopped reading and said, "I'd never say "at this point in time.' I'd—"

"Just read it," Grady said.

Molly shrugged and continued: "NEWSPERSON: *Have you passed all this on to the FBI negotiators?*

"CATES: *Yes, I have. I gave them copies of my notes and tapes.*

"NEWSPERSON: *What do they intend to do about it?*

"CATES: *I don't know.*"

Molly finished reading and looked up. "Why me?"

Grady said, "Have some chicken. We've got plenty."

She shook her head. "Why me?"

Andrew Stein said, "First of all, it has the advantage of being as close to the truth as we can stay. This version is true up until the last step. Makes for less lying, more chance of it being believable, less chance of getting caught. But the main reason you're the one to do it is that he's talked about you in our conversations."

"He has?" She looked at Grady; he hadn't told her this.

Grady shrugged.

"He trusts you," Stein said.

"Trusts me! Oh, no. You've got your wires crossed." She walked to the fireplace and studied the selection of photographs they had managed to find of the estimated hundred and fifty Hearth Jezreelites believed to be inside the compound. At the top was Samuel Mordecai standing with Annette Grimes outside the compound. He was smiling, golden-haired and radiant, a sun god on top of the world. Next to him, Annette looked tiny, pretty and shy.

"No," Stein said. "He sees you as ungodly, unfeminine, wrongheaded, and doomed. But he also sees you as ruthlessly honest and struggling to tell the truth as you see it. More honest than the people who call themselves Christians and do nothing about it. He thinks your interest in exploring faith is more religious than most people's watered-down or fake belief."

"He said that?"

"Yup. Curtis, find her the transcripts of the relevant phone tapes, please. Mordecai says you didn't try to misrepresent yourself and you quoted him accurately. He says you tried to get at the truth, but it was impossible because your magazine, your audience, and the world you live in are hopelessly materialistic and corrupted. So you had no chance."

"Well, that may be true," Molly said. "There are days I think that myself. But how did my name even come up?"

"At one point we approached him about outside, neutral people to serve as possible go-betweens. Mordecai insisted you are the only one he'd trust. But like everything else we've tried with him, that collapsed."

Molly was flabbergasted. She'd assumed Samuel Mordecai had hated her as much as she hated him. It was pathetic. If he had no one he trusted more than her, then he was truly alone and besieged in this world. "Well, he couldn't be more wrong, could he? I'm clearly an inveterate liar and now I'm collaborating on fraud and murder."

Andrew Stein said, "The problem here, Molly— may I? I'm tired of saying Miss Cates."

"I wish you would."

"The problem, Molly, is what we in the business call divergent worldviews. Mordecai sees what he's doing as leading the world to its glorious, millennial rendezvous with God, and you see what he's doing as butchering innocent children. In divergences this extreme, normal morality doesn't apply." He looked at Grady. "Lieutenant, Mr. Borthwick and I have some work to do. We need Bryan, too. Could you take Molly through the script idea?"

"Sure," Grady said. "Can we use the computer in here?"

"Yes. And it would be nice to have a draft before they get back from the airport. Curtis, you man the phones, please. Come on, Jules." The three men left. Curtis slipped a pair of earphones on and sat at the hostage phone control panel.

Grady pulled out the chair in front of the computer. "Sit down, Molly. We need to get some notes and tapes put together. We want evidence that will convince Samuel Mordecai that you did in fact track down his mother."

Molly looked at her watch. "This sounds too much like a term paper, and it's ten-thirty, Grady. I was planning on taking my dog home to bed."

He patted the chair. "Sit down here and rest your weary self. Your shoulders look all tense. Let me work on them."

Molly sat. Grady stood behind her and rested his hands on her shoulders. Slowly he began to knead the tight muscles at the base of her neck. She closed her eyes and relaxed into his familiar hands. "Good thing the dog's outside," she murmured.

"Yeah, it would be nice if Curtis were, too."

"Mmmmm," she said, letting her head fall forward, "that's good, right behind the bones there. Ooo. Perfect."

"This job is right up your alley," he said into her ear. "A bit of writing and a bit of acting." His thumbs were working their way down her spine. "We want you to write a script, Molly. An interview between you and Samuel Mordecai's mother. You come in and tell her what's led you to her and then she tells you—eventually—the details of his birth and abandonment and you get convinced she is the mother. She ends up saying she's regretted leaving him every day of her life and wants to tell him about it and why she did what she did. Make it convincing and make the mother contrite and loving." He used the heels of his hands to press into her lower back.

"When Agent Conroy gets here, we'll want to record the two of you reading your parts into your little recorder."

He took his hands off her back, picked up a file folder and opened it. "Her name—the mother—is Cynthia Jenkins. She lives in Houston, on Terrace West in the Memorial area. She's a third-grade teacher, a widow with no kids. She has spent her life mourning the infant child she abandoned. The interview took place last night, around eight, at a restaurant near Hobby Airport. You flew in to talk to her." He handed her the folder. "We've got a driver's license and a passport for her right here. The photo on them is Loraine Conroy's."

Molly picked up the passport and opened it. The woman in the photo had gray eyes with thick, dark eyebrows, short brown hair going gray, a straight nose, wide mouth, and sallow skin.

"What's her story?" Molly asked.

"Apparently she's legendary. The best marksman in agency history. She once shot two possibles in a morning."

"What's a possible?"

"I guess it's like shooting off a gnat's eyelash; it's theoretically possible, but rarely done, and never twice in a row. Conroy's a former nun, quit the Church and joined the agency in '72, when they started taking women. Speaks three languages, has been everywhere in the world—foreign counterintelligence, all kinds of undercover assignments. Now teaches at Quantico. She's done this sort of thing before, although it never gets any press—very hush-hush. A real stand-up guy, they all say."

Molly looked at the photo again.

"Can I get you anything to prime the creative process?" Grady asked.

"I lie better with a Coors Light on the desk."

"It shall be yours."

Molly raised her hands to the keyboard and started to type:

M.C.: *I have something very difficult and very urgent to talk to you about, Mrs. Jenkins. I believe in a woman's right to privacy about matters of reproduction, but we have some extraordinary circumstances here. It has to do with a baby boy who was abandoned in the summer of 1962.*

C.J.: *Oh, my God. My God.*

M.C.: *Mrs. Jenkins, I hate to cause you distress, but I have to ask if you are the mother of that child.*

C.J. (with a sob): *What happened to him? I have wondered about him every day of my life.*

M.C.: *I'll tell you about him, Mrs. Jenkins, but first would you tell me the date and some of the circumstances surrounding the birth? So I can verify it.*

Grady was reading over her shoulder. "Don't you think C.J. should stonewall a little? She collapses awfully quick."

Molly took her hands off the keyboard. "You promised me a beer, Grady. Go fetch it. You can critique when I'm finished."

"Okay, but don't forget to include—"

"Grady!"

The scene flowed out of her fingertips into the keyboard and surfaced as a line of words moving across the screen. Molly moved her lips, saying the words as she typed them. In the scene, the tough but empathic journalist pushes for all the details. The miserable and tender repentant mother tells about the birth, the panic, the need for secrecy, the two bewildered and terrified young girls not knowing what to do, the beer cooler, the robe, the creek—vivid details only the mother could know.

When the journalist is satisfied that this is the woman she seeks, she tells her about Samuel Mordecai's adoption, his searching for his real, birth mother.

She finished the scene like this:

C.J.: *Do you think he might talk to me? You say he searched. That must mean he wants to find me. If the world is coming to an end I want to see him, speak with him first. I want to tell him what happened, how I've felt. I want to hear about him, everything about him. Do you think he might talk to me?*

M.C.: *I don't know.*

C.J.: *I'm not afraid. I'd like to go there. As long as I could speak to him privately, without lots of other people around. I need to talk to my son. You understand?*

M.C.: *Yes. What I'll do is give all this to the negotiators. They'll have to decide what to do about it. Thanks for talking to me, Mrs. Jenkins. I need to catch my plane in a half hour. Here's my card.*

Molly glanced at her watch. Eleven. She'd done it in a half hour. This scene was so much more satisfying than the real one in San Antonio. It had the right emotion and it came to closure. It felt wonderful to channel her lying urges into something constructive. You could make things turn out the way you wanted, make people feel the way you thought they ought to feel. You could improve on life.

She told the computer to print and stood up to stretch.

By the time Pat Lattimore finally returned from the airport, Molly and Grady had gone over Molly's script, refined it, and printed out three copies. To Molly's delight, Andrew Stein had declared it ready for opening night.

Lattimore, looking even more exhausted than usual, introduced them all to Agent Loraine (Rain) Conroy, a tall, lanky, handsome woman. She wore gray slacks, low heels, and a blue blazer. A heavy-looking canvas duffel hung from one shoulder. Conroy stowed the duffel carefully under a table and gave Jules Borthwick a long hug. Then she stood back and regarded him with a grin. "I know you've got a show opening, sweetie, but when they asked me to do this, I said only if you'd do my body. You're the best, and for this we need perfection."

"We need to start right away on the body cast, Rain," Jules told her. "It will take me all bloody night to do it. I've got the alginate ready in the kitchen." He opened his arms wide. "Baby, is your body ready for me?"

"Wide open," she said.

"I need the weapons now. You brought your own?"

"Of course," the agent said, pointing to her bulky duffel. "The reason the plane was delayed. I don't check, ever, and the security guys were new and didn't know the procedure."

They went right to work on recording the scene Molly had written. Rain Conroy read it over to herself once, and when they started the tape turning, she gave a perfect, tear-jerking performance.

Molly was astonished; the woman should be on Broadway. She brought the words on the page to throbbing life. She could even cry on cue. To simulate the restaurant, Grady and Andrew clattered some plates in the background and turned a radio on low.

By the time Molly and Grady left at 1 A.M., they had assembled a folder containing the tape, the adoption file, the police report, Molly's genuine notes, plus some fabricated ones, and the Pi Alpha Omega directory—a complete record of the successful search for Donnie Ray Grimes's mother.

They drove home in Grady's unmarked car, with the dog hanging out the window, sucking in the smells of the spring night.

As they passed the entrance to the Hearth Jezreelite compound, Molly leaned her head back and closed her eyes so she wouldn't have to look at it. She told Grady once again about the encounter in the garage, about Annette Grimes being lifted screaming into the van. "Grady, she had a new baby and her face was like a flower."

"I know. And what happened to her was the worst possible way to go. If you have the slightest reservation about your contribution to the plan to take Mordecai out, shake it off." He kept his eyes on the road. "Molly, I'm grateful you escaped it. I don't think I could bear it if something happened to you. How are you feeling?"

"Exhausted, but I've never felt more alive, more... whatever the opposite of a blood statue is."

"Escaping death is the ultimate aphrodisiac." Grady put his hand on her leg. "You know that."

She moved closer to him, hoping the dog wouldn't notice. "Yes, but don't you feel it's inappropriate somehow? A betrayal?"

"Oh, no. I've always felt it honors the dead." His light touch progressed slowly up her thigh.

"Mmmm, I like that. We'll go home and honor the dead."

"Home—that sounds good. Have you thought any more about my lease problem?"

"No." After a silence, she added, "Yes. I have thought about it. I'm worried. It attracts me and repels me at the same time. Grady, I've gone feral. Like an animal who would love the warmth and affection that comes from being a house pet but can't give up its bad habits. I'm not housebroken anymore. I eat when I feel like it. I read all night when I want to. I never cook. I still do vigils. I don't hang up my clothes. I keep some bad company. I follow my obsessions. I work all the time—it's what I love."

"Ditto, ditto, ditto," Grady said. "We're a match made in heaven."

"Maybe, but I live like a man, and in my experience, that works better for men than women. There is something about domestic life that, over time, makes women feel guilty and stressed when there's no toilet paper."

"How about a prenuptial agreement whereby I pledge never to ask 'Where's the toilet paper?'"

Molly laughed. She snuggled into his side and snaked her arm around his neck.

A menacing growl emanated from the back seat.

She pulled her arm back. "Let's do this, Grady. Let's hold off on a decision, see if the world ends on Friday. I filed for an extension on my taxes. I don't want to waste the time and agony if it's not necessary."

"Are you equating my moving in with paying taxes?"

"Oh, no. More like an audit where all your vices and faults and sloppy record keeping are laid bare."

"Molly, Molly," he said, sliding his hand between her legs, "the only thing I want to lay bare is your body, and the sooner, the better."

She glanced in the back to see if the dog was sleeping. "*That* is fine by me," she whispered.

> *"They shall hunger no more, neither thirst any more; neither shall the sun light on them, nor any heat. For the Lamb which is in the midst of the throne shall feed them, and shall lead them unto living fountains of water; and God shall wipe away all tears from their eyes."*
>
> Revelation 7:16–17

CHAPTER SIXTEEN

It had been the hardest night.

After the kids all understood that Josh had died, Sandra had suggested some singing, but the songs she tried to start were church songs that none of the others knew, so it fizzled out. Walter couldn't think of any songs either, so he suggested each of them talk about Josh, tell a memory that they would like to keep alive. So they took turns. Each of them told something. Hector told a school memory that made them laugh and cry at the same time. He imitated Josh trying to get out of PE, which he hated, by telling the teacher that he felt his heart had been programmed for only a certain number of beats and he didn't want to waste them on playing touch football because he didn't see the point of it. Walter told about Josh saying that he'd discovered one day, while Samuel Mordecai was preaching, that the Book of Revelation would make a great Saturday-morning TV cartoon—the Revelation Roundup, Josh called it. After that, Josh had entertained himself during the longer sermons by imagining Mordecai as one of the characters—Mr. Preachy Prophet. When they were all finished, Conrad had closed with a prayer. Walter thought it was as good a memorial service as he'd ever attended.

Then he had carried Josh out of the bus into the pit and settled him there, intending to go back to spend the night with the living children who needed him. But he couldn't do it. His legs would not let him leave. It defied all common sense, but he needed to stay with Josh, keep him company. So he sat down on the dirt and took Josh's head into his lap so it wouldn't be resting on the damp earth. He leaned back against the crumbly side of the hole and closed his eyes. It reminded him of the first night he had sat with Jake in the field hospital, after Jake's legs had been amputated. It had felt then, and it felt now, that morning could never come because he couldn't imagine life just going on about its business after so cataclysmic an event.

He dozed, off and on.

During the night, the kids kept waking up, crying and calling out. They would get up and pad out to the pit to see if it was really true or just a bad dream. Around 3 A.M. Philip came out and sat down close to Walter. He rested a hand on Josh's head. "I never saw anyone dead before," he said. "Did you?"

"Yes. I was a soldier in Vietnam. When I was ten years older than you are now. I saw lots of people dead."

"Did you kill people?"

"Yes, I did. I thought it was my job to do that. I was trying to stay alive."

"Where do you think Josh is now?"

"I just don't know about heaven, Philip. I believe Josh is alive in our memories. In our hearts. In his family's memories. He's here whenever one of us is thinking about him. Or like now, when we're talking about him."

They sat silent for a while.

Walter said, "Philip, I feel really bad about something and I want to apologize to you."

Philip looked up at him.

Walter slid his arm around the boy. "I think you couldn't talk because you thought I didn't want you to tell the truth. And you were right. I didn't want anyone to talk about why we're down here. I didn't want you kids to talk about it and I didn't know how to. I guess I was afraid we'd all panic and wouldn't be able to take it."

"What do you think now?"

Walter looked down at Josh. "I think we can take anything that comes our way," he answered softly. "And it's better to talk about it, so you say anything you need to, anything that is true. You can keep me honest."

Philip leaned against him and let his fingers play with Josh's lank blond hair. "What will happen to him?"

"His body? I don't know. I suppose when Martin comes down in the morning we'll figure it out."

"He's not scary."

"Josh? No, he's not scary at all."

Philip's eyelids were lowering. "I know that Jacksonville's going to get away," he said in a drowsy voice.

"How do you know that?"

"He's the good guy. And in stories the good guys get away."

"But in real life, it doesn't always happen that way."

"I know," Philip said, "but Jacksonville's a story."

"Yeah."

When Martin dropped down into the pit in the morning and saw Walter sitting with the dead boy across his lap, he sucked his breath in, but that was all. No expression of grief or regret or even annoyance crossed his face. He called for help and two men in fatigues appeared with a paint-splattered plastic tarp.

Walter took it from them and wrapped the small body. They tried to take over then, but Walter calmly asked them to go above and let him hand

317

the boy up to them. They pulled themselves up the hole and reached down. Walter lifted the body and let them pull it up. Even as dead weight, Josh was a lot lighter than he was forty-nine days ago when Walter had lifted him down and staggered under the weight. Now he was leaving. Walter watched dry-eyed as Josh disappeared and the wooden slab slid into place.

He knew one thing now for sure: He would not stand here and watch another one of these children leave dead. Whatever horrors might be ahead, that was one he would not allow to happen again.

It had taken Walter a few weeks to recognize the advantage of having the bus seats so easy to unbolt. The Jezreelites must have started to take all the seats out as they had done with the back ten rows, and then changed their minds. The bolts had been loosened, so that even the kids could unscrew them with bare fingers. In the third week, he'd started thinking about using the seats to barricade themselves in an emergency.

The seats were heavy and awkward to move, but with Walter and several kids lifting together they could do it. They'd picked their times carefully. When they were pretty confident neither Martin nor Mordecai would come down, they had done some fast experimenting.

One seat on end could be braced in the doorway to block it. When they dragged another seat behind it, and wedged that one against the driver's seat, it made a formidable barrier that would prevent anyone from getting inside the bus for a long time. And it was solid enough to prevent someone from shooting at targets inside the bus. The Jezreelites could fire through it, but they couldn't get the necessary angle to hit people in back.

To make another barrier, in the back of the bus, they had figured out how to build on top of the last seat in each row. They unbolted one seat and lifted it on top of the back of a fixed one, and tied it in place. Then they unbolted another seat and tied it to the fixed seat, to make the structure twice as high and twice as thick as one seat alone. Walter thought bullets would not make it through. It wouldn't save them indefinitely, but it might buy them time, give them ten minutes of protection, which could be critical in an assault. All they had to do was survive until the federal agents could find them. The trick would be getting the barriers in place quickly when the action started.

So they'd worked out the teams and had held regular practices. Hector was the captain of the Bong Tongs, who would take shelter on the right side of the bus behind the barricade. Kim was the captain of the Jacksonville Six, who would take shelter on the left. When Brandon pointed out to Kim that, with Josh dead, they were now really the Jacksonville Five, Kim punched him—the only physically aggressive act Walter had seen her make. She said they were still the Jacksonville Six and always would be.

Walter had assigned team members to try to balance physical strength and speed. Two from each team were stackers, whose job was to unbolt a seat and, with Walter's help, stack it on one of the fixed back seats. Two others were tyers, who would secure the two seats together with belts and friendship bracelets and sweaters and jackets.

One from each team, Sue Ellen and Conrad, were to help Walter unbolt seat number one and tip it on end in the doorway. Hector and Walter would then brace it with seat number two.

Bucky, who was a Bong Tong, had the job of getting the water to the back of the bus when the alarm was given, and making sure everyone soaked his shirt in it. In case of tear gas.

As he watched them going through the drill on the forty-ninth day, Walter knew this would be their last practice. It needed to be a damn good one. Every move had to be automatic so they could do it in the dark if they had to, even with the noise of combat going on above them. This time they were doing their jobs with their eyes closed. They had done this many times before, but it had never gone well.

"This is impossible," Heather complained, eyes scrunched closed, getting ready to unbolt the wrong seat. "It makes me dizzy."

Walter took hold of her hand and moved it to the correct seat. "Keep your eyes closed. Your seat, old number R-nine, has this huge rip in the top of the seat back. Feel it. That's how you'll know if we have to do this in the dark. Then you'll run your hand down the back and the leg to the bolt. Good. Yeah, that's real good. Now unscrew it fast. Yeah. It's possible they'll turn off the electricity or it will just go off. We've got to be as quick in the dark as in the light.

"Kim," he said, "where is your team keeping its ties? Will you be able to find them in the dark?"

Kim was sitting on the floor with a belt in her hands. She seemed not to have heard him. She had spoken little in the twelve hours since Josh's death. The life force seemed to have drained out of her.

He leaned over and tapped her on the shoulder. "Kim, honey, where are your team's ties kept?"

She looked up. "Oh... They're in this plastic bag under the seat." She reached under and got the bag. "We've got"—she dumped them out—"three belts, two sweaters, two long bracelets, and a jacket. Oh, and Josh's belt makes four belts." She looked up at Walter. She and Walter had taken the belt out of Josh's pants before the Jezreelites took his body away. "His is best because it's longest."

Walter smiled at her. "He'd be happy to be of service."

Kim's eyes filled with tears and Walter found his doing the same in response. He fought it because they needed to work. They couldn't afford to mourn.

He looked at the belt she was holding. It was thick, strong leather, but flexible, with a sturdy brass buckle. "Kim, let me have that belt. You have enough without it and I might need it."

She handed it to him.

He made a loop and slipped it around his forearm and then jerked it tight. "They should all stay in the bag under the seat from now on, so they're ready. Your tyers are Sandra and Philip, right? Let's see you two do it in the dark. Come on."

Philip was quick with his hands and eager to catch up since he had not participated in the earlier practices.

They all ran through the drill twice more, both times with eyes closed, until they had it down pat.

"That looks good," Walter told them. He glanced at his watch. Both Mordecai and Martin had made their morning visits, but he worried Mordecai might come back because he had not done his usual marathon sermon. Instead he'd scraped off one of the two remaining Band-Aids and said it wasn't worth worrying about death since they'd all be reunited tomorrow at sunset. Death was nothing more than a pinprick in the great scheme, an earthly inconvenience. Then he had left quickly, without his usual fanfare.

Walter put a finger in his mouth and let out a shrill whistle. "Okay, Bong Tongs, let me see you all in position now."

The five Tongs knelt down in the back on the right side, behind the last seat. With their heads pointing to the back they assumed the yoga pose of the child, their torsos folded up on their bent knees, their backs curved and their foreheads resting on the floor. "Good, Tongs. But get a little closer so you're touching each other. Good. Arms crossed over your heads. Yes. Now tell me, Bucky, when do you get out of this pose?"

His voice muffled against the floor, Bucky said, "When you say, 'Tongs, fall out,' or when someone shows us an FBI badge."

"Good. Nothing else will get you to move. Nothing. What do you do if you hear shooting and explosions, Heather?"

"Stay in position," she said with a giggle.

"Right. What do you do if you hear someone outside telling you to get out of the bus? Hector?"

"Stay right here in position."

"Good. What do you do if something happens to me, if I'm injured, Philip?"

"Stay in position, like this, no matter what."

"Exactly right," he said. "Okay, Jacksonville Six, assume your positions."

The five children knelt down in the back on the left side and folded up.

"Okay. Get a little closer together. That's perfect. And remember, we're all going to be really scared. It's normal—being scared happens to everyone. But what are we going to do when we get really, really scared?"

Lucy said, "Pretend we're armadillos and roll up tighter."

"Yes! What else are we going to do when we get scared? Sandra."

"Sing," she said. "'The Wheels on the Bus' and 'A Hundred Bottles of Beer on the Wall.'"

"Good selections, Sandra, and you're going to lead the singing. How are we going to sing, Brandon?"

"Loud!" Brandon barked out. "Loud as we can."

"Loud is the most important thing—so they can hear us aboveground. So they can hear us in Austin. Okay, fall out, Tongs. Fall out, Jacksonville Six, but stay here a minute. There's one more thing we haven't talked about."

He hunkered down in the back. "I have to tell you this. Martin or Samuel Mordecai or some of the others may come down here to get us. We won't go. We will refuse to go. I may have to fight them. I have a knife. And this—Josh's belt. And I've done this before when I was in the army. So I don't want you to worry. I can do it. Now if I should be hurt or knocked out or something, you are to keep on doing the plan. Your team leaders, Hector and Kim, will take over. This is going to be difficult, but we can do it. We can do it because we have to. You guys have any questions?"

"You forgot to ask about the wet shirts," Bucky pointed out.

"Oh, thank you, Bucky. When are we going to cover our heads?"

"After we do the stacking and tying. Before we get into the child pose. We all take our shirts off"—he giggled—"even the girls, and we soak them in the jug and we put them over our heads."

"Good. Do we wait for gas to appear first?"

"No. We just do it."

"Yes. All right. That was a terrific practice. I think we're ready. Let's put everything back to normal. It's too neat. We need to mess up our areas a little. We don't want Martin getting suspicious. When you're finished, we'll do a set of push-ups, and then we can have some story."

"No more push-ups!" Heather howled.

"I agree," Kim said. "They hurt."

"You guys are getting soft," Walter said. "We're soldiers now. We'll do the push-ups."

While they were putting things back to normal, Walter played with the larger of the two knife blades on Hector's Swiss Army knife. It was small, only three inches long. He wished it was much, much longer. He caught sight of his reflection in the knife blade. It was the face of a stranger, an old stranger, with a scraggly gray beard and dry flaking lips. He snapped the blade shut and looked around to see if any of the kids were watching him. Then he pulled the belt off his arm and slipped the loop over his head. From behind he pulled it tight around his neck. That might be useful. He took it off and slipped it into the back of his pants.

It was time to think about the story. He hadn't really decided how it was going to end, and he was worried about it. He didn't want it to end on a downer. That was the last thing any of them needed. Things were bad enough. On the other hand, kids as brave and resilient as these kids would not be satisfied with a facile happy-ever-after ending.

So he just wasn't sure. He hoped the answer would come to him as he was telling it, when he got into the flow. So far it had worked like that. He hoped it would continue.

He put the knife in his pocket.

The kids were in their seats, watching him expectantly, hoping he'd forgotten the push-ups. Out of habit, he did the head count. When he came up one short, he could have wept. But he stayed silent, watching the ten faces in front of him, waiting for the story to be pulled out of him.

"So," he said. "So Jacksonville was out of the cage. Free. And the rooster was crowing. The sun was starting to come up. He was ready to motor. But first he had to get Dr. Mortimer out. He couldn't leave without him. So he crept across to the other cage. The old guy was lying all curled up. Jacksonville tried to open the door, but it had a big padlock on it. There wasn't time to use the vegetable peeler on the bars. It had taken Jacksonville all night to peel through his own bars. He had to try something else. But he didn't know where the keys were kept."

"Where's Lopez?" Hector asked. "He was there before. I hope the guy's not off boozing and drugging again."

"That's a good question, Hector. And I'm afraid that's just where that armadillo is. After he got the anteaters to make rain, they insisted he had to keep his promise right then. Remember, he said if they helped him, he'd buy them some more wine. So Lopez kept his promise, and one thing led to another and before he knew it, it was almost morning. He managed to talk two of the anteaters into going back with him. Just as they were sneaking back into the Tong village, Jacksonville was getting out of his cage.

"So when Jacksonville was trying to figure out how to unlock Dr. Mortimer's cage, here comes Lopez and the two giant anteaters. Jacksonville's happy to see them, but they don't have time for a reunion or anything. They all know they have to get out real quick, so they take a look at Dr. Mortimer's cage door. The lock is pretty big. One of the anteaters gets a thick stick, and he tries to pry the lock open. But it won't budge. Then Lopez has this idea. See, Lopez is pretty bright when he's not eating slumber bugs or drinking wine. And even when he is drinking wine, he's pretty bright."

Walter paused because he hadn't figured this part out yet. "What do you kids think his idea is to get the lock open?"

"Maybe they could try to find the guard who has the key," Lucy said.

"Yeah, but they're in a hurry," Sandra said, "and they'd have to look inside all the—what do you call them?"

"Hootches," Philip contributed, surprising everyone. "Maybe they could wake old Dr. Mortimer up and ask him, since he's the genius."

"Yeah," Heather said. "That's good, Phil."

"I think they use the vegetable peeler to pick the lock," Conrad said.

Walter pointed at him. "Yes. That's exactly what they did. And one of the anteaters had done some burglaries back when he was younger, and he knew exactly how to do it. He had that lock open in less than a minute.

"Now, during all this, Dr. Mortimer hadn't moved or said a word. Jacksonville was afraid he might be dead. But they pulled him out and they could see he was breathing. He was pretty weak, but he was alive. And he could even walk—kind of—with an anteater on each side to support him. As they were leaving the village, Dr. Mortimer got real upset. He said he couldn't leave yet because of the Galaxy Peace Ray. He'd buried the model, the only one there was in the world, right near here.

"The problem was, it was really getting light now and the roosters were crowing all over the village. Jacksonville asked Dr. Mortimer why not just make another peace ray when they got back home.

"Dr. Mortimer said he couldn't make another one. He'd lost his instructions and it had taken his whole life to make this one. It was his lifework. And it could make the whole world peaceful. He had to go back for it."

"They should split," Hector said. "I don't think the peace ray works anyway. People are not going to suddenly get all sweet and peaceful."

"Hector," Lucy said sternly, "they have to stay. They promised the President. They need to finish the mission."

"Well," Walter said, "Jacksonville was thinking they should split. They'd found Dr. Mortimer, and they could escape if they left right away. And those two anteaters were not about to stay around. They saw the sun coming up and said they heard their mothers calling and off they ran. That left just the three of them—Dr. Mortimer, Lopez, and Jacksonville.

"Both Lopez and Dr. Mortimer wanted to go for the peace ray, so Jacksonville agreed. They helped Dr. Mortimer walk and he pointed the way—back across the town square, then to the right near the pond where the Tongs took baths. They walked about halfway around the pond to some woods. Dr. Mortimer took them to a big tree and started looking around. He scratched his head and said, 'It's somewhere around here, but I'm not sure quite where. My memory is not what it used to be.'

"You might think that the situation was kind of hopeless. But remember, Lopez is an armadillo and armadillos have some unusual abilities. Now here's one you may not know about. Armadillos can smell things below the ground. They can smell things as far as eight inches below the ground."

"Wait a minute," Sue Ellen said, "is that really true or are you just making it up for the story?"

"It's really true," Walter said. "They can smell

things below the ground. Often animals can do things, have these special abilities, because it helps them get food. And that's true here. Remember what armadillos like to eat best?"

Philip said, "Beetles, ants, and worms."

"Right. And those all live below the ground. So it's really useful for armadillos to be able to smell them down there. Then they know where to dig. So what Lopez did now was to start sniffing, his long pink nose snuffling along the ground. He went back and forth, up and down.

"Of course, Jacksonville was jumpy as a cat standing there waiting as it got lighter and lighter. A dog barked and he could see the sun. And there was some noise coming from the village. Any second the Tongs were going to discover that their prisoners had escaped.

"Then Jacksonville had a real scare. He heard someone coming. Around the pond—someone in white was coming. It was the old lady Tong who had given him the vegetable peeler. She was carrying something. It was a shopping bag. And when she got closer, he saw that it said 'Bloomingdale's' on it. Now he didn't know what—"

Walter stopped because the wooden slab was scraping away from the hole and he heard voices above.

"I have trouble believing in what I can't see.
But I have trouble not believing in it, too."
MOLLY CATES

CHAPTER SEVENTEEN

"So, Mom, how does it feel to lie your head off on national TV?" Jo Beth Traynor was a little breathless from doing fifty push-ups.

"It was just the local news." Molly had stopped at twenty-five. She was stretched out watching her daughter. She'd been trying to keep up a pretense of normal life on the afternoon of the forty-ninth day, but with the news today of Josh Benderson's death, she felt despair nibbling at her. More disaster was right around the corner. "Anyway," she added, "it was taped."

"Yeah, but it will get picked up nationally."

"I suppose."

"So how did it feel?"

"Honey, I've never spoken words that felt more sincere, more on the side of the angels. Those lies just rolled out of my mouth smooth as velvet. I'm sure I could have passed a lie detector test."

"Scary."

"Yeah." She rested her chin on her hands and thought about trying a few more push-ups. But she couldn't make the effort, even though the song playing was "La Bamba," which usually energized her, and even though she knew that sweating hard was an antidote for depression, and even though there was nothing else in the world she wanted to do.

330

"Okay," Michelle screamed out over the deafening beat of the music, "we're going to work those abs now! Turn it over. Lower backs into the floor. Squeeze your glutes, pull your abs in tight. If you don't suck in, you're just doing all this work to make it pouch out. So suck it in. Ready? Up, up, up!"

"Depressing," Molly gasped. "To do something this painful, and end up with pouchy abs."

"What if he doesn't take the bait?" Jo Beth asked, moving her upper body up and down with ease.

"If he doesn't call by seven-thirty, they'll call him and ask if he wants to see her."

"What if he doesn't?"

Molly paused, head and shoulders up. The queasiness sit-ups always produced flooded her with a vengeance, worse than ever. "Then they'll just go ahead with the maneuver and hope for the best."

"Oh, Mom. All that work and it comes to this.... Poor Dad. It's such a defeat. Losing little Josh Benderson, giving up on negotiating."

"It's been excruciating."

"They could just as well have stormed the place on the first day and saved us all an ordeal."

"Not really," Molly said. "The theory is the longer you can stretch these things out the better. The longer a perp holds a hostage, the less likely he is to kill him. And this new development is worth trying." She paused to catch her breath and fight down the nausea. "I think they've done the right things all along, honey. But it may have been impossible from the beginning."

Jo Beth's eyes narrowed, skeptical at twenty-four that anything was impossible. They continued their sit-ups in silence.

"How's your dog?" Jo Beth asked, as they stretched out.

"Copper? The same demented creature. The Terminator of the canine world."

"I hope you're treating him like the hero he is."

"As a matter of fact, I am. On your recommendation I went out and bought him a bag of Science Diet, and some rawhide bones. And a chew toy, which he devoured, squeaker and all, in fifty seconds flat."

"Sounds like he's moved in. Now how about Dad? Is he moving in, too?"

Molly stopped doing sit-ups and stretched out on her back. She lay silent, feeling frayed and jangled. This wasn't something she wanted to talk about.

"Well?" Jo Beth said. "It's good parental practice to be open with your children about these things. Is Dad going to move in?"

"Honey, I don't think so."

"Why not? He's there most of the time anyway."

"I know, and I love that. I love it when he comes over. I love it when he stays the night. And I love it when he goes home. It's unnatural and immature, I suppose, but I like that better than the continual togetherness of marriage."

Jo Beth kept on moving up and down. "Mom, you're such a bad example."

Molly felt the familiar rush of parental guilt. "I know. I'm sorry."

"How am I ever going to get married and have babies when I have in front of me a mother who's so happy on her own?"

"Honey, that's just my idiosyncrasy. It's not healthy. You are healthy. And when the time is right for you and the man is right, you will get married and have babies. It's a wonderful way for most people to live, the best, the most satisfying. Having you was the best thing I ever did. I wish I could do the rest of it. But I've tried three times and each time I've been miserable, just waiting for them to go home."

"But I know you love Dad."

"Yes, I do. Your father's the love of my life. But I already tried living with him."

"But that was when you were too young. It would be totally different now."

Molly felt hot fear welling up in her chest. She felt cornered, pressured. "I really don't want to talk about this now, Jo Beth."

"Mom, this is so perverse."

"I know." She found herself tensing.

"I think you should rethink this. Dad is—"

"Jo Beth, stop it." She couldn't keep her voice from rising. "You're pushing me. I try not to do that to you and I don't think you should do it to me. I'm scared, really scared about this. You need to back off."

Jo Beth went silent.

In the front of the room, Michelle was demonstrating crunches in which she pulled her knees in to touch her elbows while doing sit-ups. Molly and Jo Beth followed suit.

After a while, Molly said. "I'm sorry I shouted.

I'll let you know when we decide something on this, but it's best for you not to ask for a while. Okay?"

"Okay," Jo Beth muttered.

"How's work, honey?"

"Fine, but it's pretty much all there is. When you work fourteen hours a day, there's not much time for anything else."

"No, there isn't. This firm seems to demand a lot."

"Yeah, but it's a family tradition, anyway—workaholism."

"I think it's a choice, baby. You don't have to do it if you don't want to."

They finished their sit-ups in silence.

As they were walking down to the dressing room, Jo Beth said, "You aren't going out to Jezreel tonight?"

"No. Wasn't invited. My part's finished, thank God."

"What are you going to do?"

"Tonight? First I'm going to get rid of Officer Valdez, an unfortunate young man who was born with no smile muscles. He's enough to make me yearn for Bryan Holihan. Then I'm going to wash my hair, read a little, go to bed early."

"Oh, sure," Jo Beth said. "I know what you're going to do. You're going to sit in the dark and stare at the window all night. I see it coming. God, that used to scare me when I was a kid. Why don't we go to a movie? We'll take Officer Valdez along. I bet I could make him smile."

"Thanks, honey, but I promised Lattimore I'd stay close to the phone. And I wouldn't know what to do with the dog. I've got to pick him up. Poor Jake's been stuck with him all day."

There were two empty cans neatly aligned at the foot of Jake's wheelchair; he held another in his hand. The dog was sprawled nearby chewing on the nublike remains of what this morning had been an enormous rawhide bone.

Molly got out of the police car she'd been driven around in all day. Copper jumped up and greeted her with a swaying tail. She leaned down to pat him.

"He's glad to see you," Jake said, "and you look glad to see him."

"Do I? Well, there is a tendency to feel grateful to someone who saves your life."

"Is there?" Jake said. "It depends on the circumstances, I think."

Molly dragged a chair over and sat down. "What are the circumstances in which you wouldn't feel grateful?"

Jake shrugged and looked down into his beer can.

"You told Lattimore about it yesterday, didn't you?" Molly asked.

"I had to."

"Why?"

"Because there was more to the Granny Duc story than what you heard. It didn't end there, and I wanted to be sure we interpreted Walter's message right."

Molly leaned down to pat the dog, who'd settled at her feet. He'd gotten some sticker burrs in his ears; she should buy a brush. "So what happened to Granny Duc?"

"Walter killed her with his bare hands." He said

it in the same tone he would have used to say, "She's living in Cincinnati with her son."

It was like a hammer blow to the chest. Molly felt she'd come to know Walter Demming over the past three days and this didn't fit. "Why?"

"I told you when you first came here that I wasn't going to talk about it, and I'm not. I told Lattimore because I had to. Anyway, he was there. He has the context for hearing it."

Molly wanted to shake him. He was so stubborn. Eventually he was going to tell her—why didn't he just get it over with? She looked at her watch. "It's almost six, Jake. I'm going to be on the news in two minutes. Do you have a TV we could watch?"

"Yeah. All the amenities chez Jake. I've even got cable." He looked toward Officer Valdez in the car. "What about him?"

"He'll wait out here. I think he prefers it."

"Come on in." Jake wheeled to the trailer and situated his chair on the lift. The dog bounded up the steps and Molly followed.

The trailer was orderly and compact, with bookcases and a soft-looking sofa. Jake switched the little TV on with a remote.

Copper went to a dish on the floor and started to drink. He seemed right at home.

"Channel 33," Molly said.

Jake got the channel. "A beer? It's Shiner, much better than that sissy stuff you drink."

"Sure. Thanks."

He navigated the tiny kitchen with efficiency, using one hand to turn his chair, the other to work. He grabbed a can out of the fridge, popped the top, and handed it to her. "Want a glass?"

"No." The news was starting. Ellen Sussman, the stiff-haired blond anchorwoman, began: "Today, two new developments in the forty-nine-day-old terrorist standoff in Jezreel, where the lives of twelve hostages have been threatened by an extremist religious cult. In a tragic turn of events, negotiators learned today that eleven-year-old Joshua Benderson has died in captivity." A photograph of the plump, blond boy flashed on the screen. "According to FBI spokesman Patrick Lattimore, authorities had been especially worried about the boy because of his chronic asthma, which required regular medication. News of the boy's death was given to negotiators in a phone call from Walter Demming, the bus driver who was taken hostage with the children. Demming told negotiators Joshua had died of breathing problems during an asthma attack sometime last night. The boy's body, wrapped in a plastic sheet, was carried out of the compound by two cult members and laid at a point midway between the cult compound and the gate. Two television news reporters were allowed to enter the property to pick up the body. Here is that scene at Jezreel at two o'clock this afternoon."

Footage aired of the two newsmen entering with their hands in the air. They picked up the small bundle. They carried it out through the gates and put it into the back of a waiting ambulance.

The camera returned to Ellen Susman in the studio. "In another development, Molly Cates, associate editor of *Lone Star Monthly* magazine here in Austin, says she has learned that Hearth Jezreelite leader Samuel Mordecai was abandoned as an infant and later adopted by Evelyn Grimes. Cates says she's found the birth mother who abandoned him. In a taped interview earlier today Miss Cates talks about her search."

Molly, looking earnest and worried in a black pants suit and prim white blouse, sat in a chair facing Ellen Sussman. The newswoman asked the questions that had been scripted for her and Molly answered, also as scripted. "Yes," Molly said at the end, "there's no question the woman I talked to in Houston is his birth mother—his real mother. And she wants very much to see him, talk to him." Molly supposed that Sussman and her bosses at the station didn't know the story was a fabrication. Lattimore had set it up, faxed KTAX the questions, and Molly had merely arrived as scheduled and done the interview.

The news report then went into a summary of the long history of the standoff and ran a few seconds of the previous evening's briefing with Pat Lattimore. It ended with photographs of the remaining ten children and Walter Demming.

Molly picked up her beer and took a long cold swallow.

Eyes on the screen, Jake said, "You're one hell of a good liar."

"I know."

"If I thought it would help Walter," he said, using the remote to turn off the television, "I would sell my soul."

"Because Walter saved your life?"

"Walter didn't save my life. He made a mistake

338

that ended up getting me injured. Then he forced me to survive as a freak."

Molly felt the tears creeping down her cheeks before she even knew she was crying. Then it came over her full force—the torrent of grief and sorrow she'd been holding at bay. Now it simply surged up from her chest, where it seemed to reside, and pushed through her eyes. "The beer was a mistake. It lowered my resistance. I don't know," she said to Jake through the tears. "You'd think at my age I'd know something for sure, but I don't. Maybe the world *is* ending, dying around us, and we just don't know it. Have you noticed how everything's speeding up? Samuel Mordecai sure is right about that."

Jake sat quietly, watching her cry. Every so often she took a sip of beer. When she finished it, he got her another, and one for himself.

Two beers later he told her about it.

"Geronimo Joe Barbour and me—I never knew why they kept us rather than killing us the way they did the others they ambushed at the river. Three days in a bamboo cage so small I couldn't sit up. Bowl of water, a little rice. Hot, hot sun. People walking by laughing, poking at us with sticks, like we were zoo animals." He spoke with no emotion, as if he were talking about a day at the office.

"One thing got me through—a book, a paperback I'd had in my pocket. For some reason they let me keep it. An old girlfriend from Milwaukee had sent it to me. The whole time, for three days, I read and reread that book. Sometimes to myself, sometimes out loud to Joe."

"What was it?"

In reply, he wheeled to the shelves that lined the end wall of the trailer and went right to the place on the shelf. He pulled a book out and handed it to Molly—an ancient paperback, faded and torn, crinkled as though it had gone through the washing machine. *The Sirens of Titan* by Kurt Vonnegut.

She opened it carefully, afraid it would crumble under her fingers. "I've never read this."

Jake took a sip of his beer. "There was this one sentence I memorized and kept saying over and over. It got to be like a prayer, or a mantra. Joe started saying it, too. He was in screaming pain from the gangrene in his foot, and when things got unbearable, we just kept repeating this silly sentence."

"What was it?"

"Page 265," he said. His eyes closed, he recited, "'The atmosphere of Titan is like the atmosphere outside the back door of an Earthling bakery on a spring morning.' Another one I liked is on the same page: "There are three seas on Titan, each the size of Earthling Lake Michigan. The waters of all three are fresh and emerald clear.' I liked that because I grew up on Lake Michigan, but Joe was a redneck who didn't even know where the Great Lakes were, and he was a chow hound, so the bakery worked better for him. You'd be amazed how well it works. I got so I could say it twice and I would be transported to that bakery door, Heinemann's bakery in Milwaukee, on an early spring day just after the snow has melted, and I could smell the kuchen just out of the oven. With Joe, it was cherry pie at a bakery in Memphis, where he grew up."

He took a long swig of beer. "That's where he was when he died, I think. At the end of the second day. Geronimo Joe Barbour, the most gung-ho GI you ever saw. And dumb as a rock—ten months in 'Nam and he still believed we were saving the world for Democracy, winning the hearts and minds of the people. They just left his body in the cage. Didn't notice he was dead, I guess. The flies sure noticed—two hundred fifty pounds of dead Joe kept them busy.

"I knew our platoon would come. Trang Loi was in our orders. I just didn't know when, or if I'd still be alive. My goal was to live long enough to see every person in that fuckin' village die." He crushed his empty beer can with one hand. "And I did."

"On September 1, 1968. At dawn. Our guys swept in so fast and in such force—that's the only thing that saved me. The village was overrun before the VC knew what hit them. It was Walter who found me and opened the cage. For a while we just watched the killing swirl around us, but then Walter found me an AK-47 under one of the hootches so I could join in. I could barely walk, but I could kill.

"The orders were to wipe the village off the map, and by God, that's what we did. According to the intelligence, there were no civilians in Trang Loi. And really that was right. They were all trying to kill us, even the kids. We just killed them first. Although even that's complicated, who killed who first.

"See, in the six days before I was captured, we had nineteen dead and twenty-eight wounded. They mutilated our dead. They set booby traps for us everywhere. They sent small children along the trails with grenades. And their center of operations and supply was Trang Loi.

"So when we got a chance, we did unto them as they had done unto us, but we did it to them more, worse, longer, harder. There was nothing they had done we didn't do back that morning. Our blood was boiling."

He wheeled to the refrigerator and got himself another beer. "You ever seen those paintings by Heironymus Bosch? Trang Loi when we got finished makes those look like a church picnic. Heaps of bodies rotting in the sun, flies everywhere—more flies than you thought were in the whole world. At the end of the morning, we were too tired to talk. The only sound was that buzz, the flies. We pushed the bodies into a ditch and left them for the flies. That night three old men came out of the tunnels, waving a white flag. We took them to the ditch and shot them.

"The next morning we set fire to the hootches and their food stores, and we exploded all the weapons that we couldn't carry with us.

"It was then she came out. We were putting C-4, this plastic explosive, into the holes to close off the tunnels. So she had to come up. All alone. In this immaculate white ao dai, like a small ghost. She was tiny, not more than seventy, eighty pounds, wrinkled like a prune, teeth brown with betel nut, bowing and praying. "GI, you no shoot Granny Duc. No VC, no VC.' Stanley

Jones, Geronimo Joe's best buddy, the one who had taken Joe out of the cage, aimed his rifle at her, but Walter stopped him. He said we'd done enough and that we had to stop somewhere.

"But I recognized her. She was old, but a powerhouse. I'd seen her working with the men, ordering everyone around, distributing grenades and AK-47s as the units came to pick them up. I said to Walter, wait, maybe we should kill her. She is VC. She worked on weapons supply. I saw her. I recognize her. And our orders were to wipe the village out."

Jake shifted around in his chair, as if he couldn't find a comfortable position. He rearranged his pant legs, folding some of the extra material and tucking it under his stumps. "But Walter did some dope in those days, just pot mostly, and he was feeling mellow. He said to let her go. She was an old woman, and we had to stop somewhere. If we killed her, we'd have to kill the whole damn country. And he was right, of course. That's really how it was. If we were going to win, we'd have to kill them all, every fucking one of them, and the babies, too.

"Everyone else wanted to waste her. We all stood around arguing about it, while she stood there bowing and whining, 'You no shoot Granny Duc. No VC.' It was actually kind of humorous. But Walter's real persuasive and we'd all done so much killing that the lust had passed."

Jake had been looking at Molly as he talked, but his eyes shifted away now. He seemed to be looking into space. "Anyway, Walter carried the day and we ended up not shooting her, even though there seemed to be something messy about leaving her, a nagging loose end.

"We moved out that afternoon. She was sitting alone on the ashes where her hooch had been, next to a stack of Lurps, this dried food we'd left her. That old lady looked like a lost child. Walter and me were the last ones to leave. I went back for something that I'd forgotten. It was stupid, but I did. Then I was jogging to catch up with the unit." He paused to take some deep breaths as if he had been jogging. "Granny Duc ran up behind me and tossed something at me."

Jake took a long drink from his can. "Who would have thought that old mama-san would have perfect aim? A throwing arm like Nolan Ryan. The grenade exploded right at my feet. Talk about the world ending. That's what I thought had happened. It felt like the earth exploded and threw me into outer space.

"Granny Duc was running for the trees. She almost made it, but Walter ran her down, screaming all the way. He tackled her. He got an arm around her neck and he just pulled back and she snapped. She just…snapped. Then he lay there on top of her crying. I saw all that happen. And then I was gone, blessedly out of the world for days."

"What did you go back to get?" Molly asked softly.

He nodded toward the book in her lap. "That."

Molly ran her fingers over the stained and wrinkled cover. "So what did you and Lattimore decide the Granny Duc message meant?" she asked.

"Like we first thought—that he's underground and he's going to hunker down and wait till it's safe to come up. But I think there's another message there: He'll kill if he has to."

Molly must have looked stricken.

"Here," Jake said, "you look like a woman in need of a mantra. Try this with me: 'The atmosphere of Titan is like the atmosphere outside the back door of an Earthling bakery on a spring morning.'"

Molly said it along with him a few times and by the end she was laughing.

"What's your bakery?" Jake asked.

She used her sleeve to wipe her wet face. "The Upper Crust, on Burnet Road. Cinnamon rolls."

"We shake our heads in amazement over people falling prey to communal cults like the Hearth Jezreelites. They walk away from their families and their middle-class lives, sign over their worldly goods to the cult, and submit themselves to the harsh authority of a despot who dictates every detail of their existence. Why, we wonder, would anyone subject himself to that abuse? Cult experts say that those of us who express the strongest aversion are ripest for the picking."
MOLLY CATES, "TEXAS CULT CULTURE,"
LONE STAR MONTHLY, DECEMBER 1993

CHAPTER EIGHTEEN

After she had settled Officer Valdez in front of the house, Molly took a very hot bath and washed her hair. It was painful because the slightest pull on her hair made the cut at her temple sting. Getting out of the tub, she noticed a purple bruise on her hip. It must have happened when she'd been knocked down on the garage floor. As soon as she saw it, it started to hurt.

She wrapped a towel around her wet hair and went downstairs in her terry-cloth robe. She didn't open the mail. She didn't survey the contents of the refrigerator. She didn't look at the newspapers. She didn't check her fax. She didn't even listen to the messages on her phone machine.

Instead she did something she'd been thinking about all day. She rummaged through the stacks on the kitchen counter and found the book

Theodora Shea had given her to pass on to Walter Demming—*The Complete Poems of Emily Dickinson*. Ever since Theodora had read that poem over the phone yesterday, it had been calling out to her.

She found it—poem 949—and read it through several times, first silently, then aloud.

It could have been written for her.

It spoke directly to her lifelong preoccupation with the dead. As a child, she'd had recurring nightmares about people she loved being buried in the black, cold earth. It seemed like the ultimate banishment, exile to a dark realm, under the light, under the grass, under the dirt. *'Under the beetle's cellar'*—that's just the way she had always seen it—a frightening, lonely, primitive place, cold and distant, at the bottom of the food chain. To consign the bodies of people you loved to the beetle's cellar was hideous.

Her mother, who had died when Molly was nine, was buried under brown dirt in a small family cemetery east of Lubbock, and her father, who had been murdered when Molly was sixteen, was buried under the rich black earth near Lake Travis. After each of them was buried, Molly felt they were impossibly far away, beyond conjecture, beyond light. So far that the longest arm in the world couldn't reach out to them, so far sunlight could never warm them.

But it was the last two lines of the poem that had really caught her interest:

Oh for a Disc to the Distance
Between Ourselves and the Dead!

She had no idea what Emily Dickinson meant by a Disc to the Distance, but what she pictured was a flat Earth with the dead at the dark, far side, in the shadow of the Moon. If Molly could just turn it, or tip it, or if she could change her position slightly, she could bring them closer into view. That was what her vigils were about, she thought now—trying to find a disc to the distance between herself and her dead.

Each time she stared into the dark window, she was trying to bring the dead into focus, rotate them closer, communicate with them. There was something about this Apocalypse business that seemed to accelerate the process. It was useful to have a constant reminder that one tilt of the disc we live on will send us flying into eternity.

Tonight there was a growing crowd to commune with. She wanted to tell Annette Grimes how valiant she'd been in risking her life for the hostage children. She wanted to commend Gerald Asquith for his premonition about being blown toward God. She wanted to ask Geronimo Joe Barbour if he really had died outside the bakery door in Memphis with the scent of cherry pie in his nostrils. She wanted to tell Granny Duc that she understood how obsession and the desire for revenge could make you do horrible things. She wanted to sing a lullaby to young Josh Benderson, and tell him about places where the air was so sweet and easy you could take it in through your pores. And she wanted to tell Vernon Cates that he was present still, every time she used his old Webster's dictionary, every time she started up her Chevy truck.

She turned off all the lights. Vigils came easier in the dark. She settled into the wing chair and stared at the huge black picture window. Slowly she began to sink into the darkness beyond the glass.

She was called back up by the sound of nails clicking against the wood floor. The faint jingle of dog tags and the swish of a tail announced Copper's presence. He stood in front of her, a dark shape with two glowing eyes—a wild beast who'd wandered in toward the campfire. Molly recalled the snarling demon he'd become that morning in the garage. If he got it into his demented head to attack, she was lost.

The dog rested his head on her bare knee. His breath was hot on her leg. His head was heavy, as though the entire weight of the dog were behind it. She sat still, feeling the solidity of his head and the warm wetness of his jowls. After a few minutes she felt saliva slowly pool and dribble down her knee.

Molly rested her hand on his head. "Of course. You have your own dead to sit for, don't you? It's been only a few months and you're still waiting for him to come home." Molly looked down at the dark shape. "Join me. We'll make a night of it."

The dog turned around in place a few times, then thumped down at her feet.

Molly didn't know if it had been hours or just minutes until the phone rang. She ran to catch it before the machine took over.

"Molly, thank God. Patrick Lattimore here."

Her breath caught. "What's going on? Did he call?"

"Yes. But we've got a major snafu, and it has to do with you. Could you come out here right now?"

"Why? What is it?"

"I'd rather wait until you get here to discuss it."

"It will take me a few minutes to get dressed."

"Molly, would you wear a skirt and a T-shirt, something that fits pretty close to the body? Nothing baggy. And flat shoes." There was a jumbled conversation at his end of the speakerphone. His voice came back. "Oh, yeah, and panty hose."

"Why?"

"We can talk about it when you get here. Bring the dragon robe, too, please, and let me talk to your officer. What's his name?"

"Valdez. David Valdez. He's outside. I'll call him."

Molly beckoned the officer inside to the phone and ran upstairs to get dressed. This was so crazy, to go running out there to Jezreel. But she'd let herself get sucked up in it. It was too late to say no. She pulled on a short, straight denim skirt. She could think of only one reason for the dress code—to show someone she had nothing concealed. This was dangerous, out of her area. She was no Rain Conroy. She grabbed a white T-shirt from the pile of clean laundry. Her hands were shaking. She should not be doing this. She was a writer, an observer. Her job was to chronicle, not get involved. But how could she possibly turn her back on this?

She pictured Thelma Bassett and her pink-haired daughter who was having difficulty with long division. She thought about Walter Demming, who had taken a vow of noninvolvement. She thought about the little boy with the cowlicks—

Bucky DeCarlo—she'd learned his name in spite of her efforts not to. She didn't want all those names added to her vigil list.

That list was already too long, and Samuel Mordecai was adding to it daily. She thought about Josh dying with no medical care and no family to comfort him, the look of terror on Annette's face as she was wrested into the open van. She thought of Gerald Asquith and what his last minutes must have been like. She pulled the T-shirt over her head and looked in the mirror. Those were compelling reasons to get involved, but they were not the reason she was going out there, the reason she would end up doing whatever they asked her to do. It was something else. She didn't know what to call it, but it seemed to lie somewhere between obsession and acquiescing to fate.

She slipped her feet into black loafers, then stuffed a pair of panty hose in her bag.

Downstairs, she switched on the kitchen light and added the book of poems to the jumble in her bag. She picked up the box Dorothy Huff had given her and looked around. Copper was still lying in the dark living room, faithful to the vigil. Maybe after all these years she had found a partner as devoted to his dead as she was to hers.

Valdez greeted her with his usual lack of expression. They sped up I-35 at eighty miles per hour with the lights whirling. No siren.

When they turned off the Interstate, he turned off the light bar. A quarter mile before the compound entrance, they came to a new roadblock that was diverting traffic—a sign that things were on the move. The policeman manning it had their names and descriptions in his book and waved them through. As they passed the Hearth Jezreelite compound, Molly took a good look. The huge portable searchlights outside the front gates and all around the perimeter flooded the compound with a stark white light, bright as a baseball stadium. In the slit windows at the top of the stone towers, she thought she could make out gun muzzles. The covered windows of the boxy main building showed only faint light inside. Early on, the negotiators had threatened to cut off electricity to the compound, and Samuel Mordecai had replied they could do that, but if they did, he would send them a child's finger each day they kept it off. The electricity had stayed on.

All around the complex, for hundreds of yards in all directions, the ground was flat and barren. There was no place to take cover. How would the tactical force make its approach? Molly wondered. Maybe they'd crash through the fence in tanks or personnel carriers. It was ten-thirty. They must be getting ready to move in, but there was no indication of it. The only sign of life was the usual DPS and FBI contingent standing guard. And the press, of course. On the outer circle, they sat in groups outside their vans and trailers drinking and talking. Her colleagues of the Fourth Estate keeping their own sort of vigil, waiting for disaster.

A mile down the road, there were more cars than usual parked in front of the old farmhouse. All lights were blazing.

The communications room was packed with people, and it was hot, vibrating with tension. Grady Traynor leaned against the wall with his arms crossed tight over his chest, glowering at the activity. Molly knew that body language well; it meant he was totally hostile to something going on. She thought she could anticipate the issue.

Curtis was working at the computer. Holihan and Stein stood in front of the diagram of the compound, talking to two burly men dressed in full night-assault gear—black jumpsuits, black balaclavas and ballistic vests, holsters worn low on their thighs, gas masks hanging around their necks. Stein kept his left index finger on the barn and his right one on the main building just to the left of the front door. Molly's stomach dipped. They were really going to do it. She stopped to glance at the photographs of the children whose names she had tried not to learn. Someone had updated the label under Josh Benderson's photo. Under his name and age was typed: "Deceased."

Pat Lattimore was watching Rain Conroy, who stood in the middle of the room. She was naked except for a pair of black bikini briefs. Molly was transfixed by a body that gave only a grudging nod to her sex. Small breasts and the slightest suggestion of flare at the hip marked her as female. But the rest of her seemed beyond gender. Broad shoulders and a flat belly that had never even thought about pregnancy. Long legs with pronounced muscle definition down the thigh— runner's legs. Her arms were long and muscled, ropy with veins—the arms of a woman who could do push-ups all day.

She looked less naked than most people would in such a setting, maybe because her skin was olive-colored, maybe because she seemed to have a total lack of self-consciousness.

Jules Borthwick was squatting next to her holding a bizarre object that looked like a vest or a teddy made out of her own skin, but several sizes too big.

Lattimore was saying, "The bulk isn't a problem. It's an asset. Just look around you at the mall, Jules. Don't you ever go to the mall? Most women of this age are broad as barns. It's expected. This is a woman with a thirty-three-year-old son. She's had a hard life, eaten lots of junk food. She's fat, frumpy, and nonthreatening, the absolute last person in the world who might be carrying a concealed H and K P7 automatic. We want her to look solidly middle-aged."

"Middle-aged is no problem," Borthwick muttered. "It's making her look like a woman that's hard." The makeup artist was scowling.

Rain smiled down at him fondly. "It would be easier for us to make you look like one, Jules."

"Yeah, but I'm not sufficiently nuts. You, however, are going to walk through that gate with a gun and explosives concealed where your boobs would be if you had boobs! Ah, sweetheart, what a job you've got." He wrapped the vest around her torso.

Patrick Lattimore said, "If only you could figure out how to add a Kevlar layer, Jules, it would be perfect."

Borthwick paused for a few seconds. "Patent pending," he said.

Rain studied Molly with level gray eyes. When they had met the night before, the agent had barely glanced at her, but now she looked Molly over, assessing her, as if she were choosing up sides for some very important athletic event.

Pat Lattimore approached her. "Molly. You're here." Crisis, she noted, had got them to first names. His face was gray with tension. "Molly Cates, meet Blumberg and Kroll." The two men in fatigues turned and nodded impassively at her. "This is such a zoo. Let's go in the other room so we can talk. I need to tell you what's happening."

Grady pushed away from the wall. "I'm coming, too."

Lattimore shrugged. He led the way to the back of the house, through a kitchen that looked and smelled as if it had been turned into a laboratory. The counters were covered with gallon cans of gooey-looking substances, jars, tubes, rolls of gauze, clumps of clay, brushes, knives and spoons, and tools she couldn't identify. The room reeked of turpentine and Elmer's glue. On the linoleum table sat a statue that looked like it was made of gray cement. It was clearly an exact life model of Rain Conroy from crotch to shoulder.

Lattimore took them into a small room that contained a few file cabinets, four folding chairs, and a telephone on the floor. "Sit down," he said.

Molly sat at the table. Grady leaned against the wall and folded his arms over his chest. Lattimore pulled a chair close to Molly and sat knee to knee with her. "It worked perfectly. You did good. He called before the news was even over, at six-twenty. Said he wanted her to come see him. Molly—his voice was shaking. We got him by the short hairs."

Watching a tic at furious work in Pat Lattimore's

cheek, Molly wondered who had whom by the short hairs. The agent was wired.

"Here's the problem: He wants proof. We anticipated that, of course. Stein told him no problem, we'd send it in. But that's not enough for him. Mordecai says he wants *you* to bring it in and walk him through it."

A chill swept through Molly. "I can do that over the phone, can't I?"

"That was our first suggestion. No go."

"How about a videotape?"

"Our second suggestion. He said he wants to look in your eyes while you tell him about it...in person."

Molly's arms were prickling with goose bumps. She wished she'd thought to bring a jacket.

Grady was staring down at the floor. Molly could feel his anger radiating out. She tried to will him to look at her, but he refused.

Lattimore said, "We told him that sending a civilian into a hostage situation was against all agency rules and regs. He said then the deal was off. He needs you to guarantee that this woman is his mother. He wants you to take him step by step through your search.

"Lieutenant Traynor got on the phone to say that he had done most of the work in tracking her down, and he could come in and show him the documentation. Mordecai just laughed. He wants you, Molly. He thinks you will tell him the truth. And he sees you as someone on the edges of the power structure, not part of it. Also, he knows we have allowed members of the press into some situations in the past. There is some precedent."

Molly rubbed her arms to warm them. "So, Pat, you want me to go in there?"

"I'm not asking you to do it because—"

"The hell you aren't!" Grady sprang up from his slouch. "This is so fucking *dishonest*. Of course you're asking her. You're putting her in an impossible situation." A man who rarely lost his temper and never shouted, Grady was shouting now. His face was darkening.

Lattimore held a hand up to stop the outburst. "Hold on a minute, Lieutenant. Molly, you need to know we've been going back and forth on this for"—he checked his watch—"four hours. Lieutenant Traynor dissents from everything I'm going to say. If he will wait until I am finished he can have his say and I know he has an inside track with you. So if he will just let me finish."

He shot Grady a harsh look, then turned back to Molly. "Ordinarily I wouldn't even consider letting you do this. It's risky. But I am convinced that the only way we have a prayer of getting the children out alive is if we take Mordecai out first. If we buy what Annette Grimes told you, and I do buy it, he's the one who has to do the killing tomorrow. If he's out and we get in there quick, we could grab the kids before the others decide what to do. Also it will make things easier for our strike force. All available intelligence agrees there's no chain of command in there, just Mordecai at the top. If we neutralize Mordecai, their resistance will flag. The assault could be over quicker, with less loss of life.

"Molly, we've been brainstorming this for six weeks, and the only way is Operation Mom. Our only chance is to get Rain inside and give her a shot at him. The problem is he insists on you to authenticate her."

Molly was overwhelmed. She looked up at Grady. "Do you agree with that reasoning?" she asked.

He continued to stare at the floor as he answered. "In dealing with someone as wacko as Mordecai, reasoning is beside the point."

In a low, gruff voice, Lattimore said, "If you were to take the evidence in to Mordecai, here's how it would work. He agreed that you could do it right at the door. It has to be inside the door, though, because he won't show himself. He suspects that we're trying to snipe him. Imagine that."

"Pat," she said, finally giving in to a gnawing fear, "that article I wrote about him. You've read it?"

"Yeah. Several times."

"It worries me. I know from past experience that when people read things about themselves that contradict the image they want to project, they never forgive it. There is something about the printed word that stings worse than spoken words. Mordecai may be harboring a big grudge. I know this sounds paranoid."

"Molly, if you aren't paranoid, it's because you aren't paying attention. These are all things we've thought about, believe me. We certainly considered that possibility. We just listened to the old tapes where he talks about you. Even Lieutenant Traynor here agrees with this: Mordecai thinks you're as honest as it's possible to be given the corruption of society. You did skewer him, but I don't think he realizes that. The man has a sixth-grade reading level and that article was too so-phisticated for him. He doesn't read or think well enough to pick up on your underlying theme."

"Another thing," Molly said. "What about Annette? Maybe he knows she told me about the babies and everything."

Lattimore shook his head. "He can't know. We sent in some papers yesterday and he listens to the news, but we haven't given out anything about Mrs. Grimes or Gerald Asquith. And there's no communication in there other than our hostage line. We changed the other phone numbers. No one can call in but us, and he can't call out to anyone but us.

"I believe his killings need to be ritual, and only after fifty days of purification. I don't think he presents a danger to you in a situation like this. The Sword Hand of God is another matter. They are loose cannons, beyond his control, on their own and probably scared as shit since we've ren-dered him incommunicado. But I actually believe him when he swears to us by his God that he won't harm you. Now, Molly, I can't ask you to do this. I'm just telling you what's been said."

Grady spat, "That's bullshit, Lattimore. You've set up a situation where if she says no she con-demns those hostages to death. You're manipu-lating her to do something no sane civilian would do." He hunkered down next to her chair so his eyes were level with hers. "Molly, say no and get the hell home. This is spontaneous combustion just waiting for the spark. We could get a Waco-like conflagration here tonight. People could die."

Molly reached out to him, took his head in her

hands, and kissed him on the lips, long and lingeringly. As always she loved the feel of his mustache against her upper lip. "I love you, too,
Grady," she whispered. "Always have."

She turned back to Lattimore. "How would this
work, Pat?"

Lattimore glanced up at Grady, to check out
his reaction, then said to Molly, "Like this. You
walk in through the gate, with Cynthia Jenkins in
tow. No show of force anywhere, just two women
alone. The two of you approach the door. They
let you in. You go no more than four steps inside.
He closes the door. You introduce him to Cynthia.
But here's what we worry about: a body search.
We hope they won't do it. And they probably
won't. They'll see that you have no place for a
weapon and anyway you're both unlikely prospects
as assassins. Even if they do decide to frisk you, it
won't be much of a search. The guys who train
cops say the hardest people for beginners to frisk
are women in skirts because it's embarrassing,
especially—excuse me—older women, because it
seems so impolite.

"Even if they do frisk you, it's not a problem.
The prothesis Rain is wearing will feel like the
real thing. But if they strip you down, we could
be in trouble. Though she might even pass that if
they don't insist on underwear coming off."

"Why panty hose?" Molly asked.

"Oh, because Rain will be wearing support hose
to hide the prosthesis hip seams and if you do,
too, it will look like the norm."

"Then what?"

"You show him the documents and tapes and

tell him how you tracked down his mom. Five minutes. Then he'll let you walk out. Your part is done. You leave, Rain stays. He's asked for a private hour with her. You walk back the way you came. We pick you up outside the gate. Rain will delay what she's going to do until you've had time to get clear. And that's it."

"What does Rain say about this plan?" Molly asked.

"Well, of course, she—"

Grady interrupted. "She says she'd rather face a firing squad than go into a situation this volatile with an amateur like you, and she thinks you'd be crazy to agree to it. Also, she thinks you look like someone who can plan an assassination but would faint if you saw the reality close up."

"Nothing personal," Molly said, managing a smile.

"Well, she does have her reservations," Lattimore said. "None of us like it much. This is not ideal."

"What if I don't do it?"

"We'll tell him it's out of the question for you to come in and hope he'll back down."

"Do you think he will?"

"He hasn't backed down once in forty-nine days. Oh, there's one more complication."

"What's that?"

"He wants Thelma Bassett, too. The three Marys, he calls you. He says he's been impressed with her and he'll let her speak to her daughter once more before the Apocalypse."

"She's more than willing," Molly said.

"I know, but we can't allow it. If she were to go

361

in, he might bring some of the kids up from where he's keeping them. That's the last thing we want to happen. We need them to stay underground until we've got the whole situation under control."

"When would all this take place?" Molly asked.

"In an hour or so."

"An hour! I just went by the compound. How are the HRT guys going to get close without being seen?"

"They're already there. They've been in place since six. By now they're peeing in bottles and getting the twitches."

"Where are they?"

"I can't tell you. If you don't know, you won't be tempted to look in that direction." He rested his palms on the table, as if to show he'd dealt all his cards. "We need to get this show on the road. It's your decision."

"Say no," Grady said. "This is not your fight, Molly. Go home."

"Grady, it *is* my fight. I can't say no. You know that." She looked at him and tried to get him to smile.

He closed his eyes for a few seconds. When he opened them, he said, "So be it. But, Lattimore, you and I know that these Wild West maneuvers never go as planned. Let's work up some contingency plans for what she does if this goes ballistic."

Lattimore nodded. "That's exactly what we're going to do now. Come on." He put a hand on Molly's arm. "Oh, one last thing—when this is over, it never happened. Rain will disappear. There will be no record of her having been here. We will never acknowledge any

362

part of it. We will say Samuel Mordecai was a casualty of our tactical maneuver, shot while firing on government agents."

"Is that a prophecy?"

"Yes, one that can't miss. Mordecai won't live through the maneuver," Lattimore said. "We just got the ME's report on the Benderson boy. He died of asphyxiation. There wasn't a trace of medication in his body. That contemptible bastard didn't even bother to give the kid the inhalers that would have saved his life. When I saw that, I knew that Donnie Ray Grimes was bought and paid for."

> *"They were not given power to kill them, but only to torture them for five months. And the agony they suffered was like that of the sting of a scorpion when it strikes a man. During those days men will seek death, but will not find it; they will long to die, but death will elude them."*
>
> REVELATION 9:5-6

CHAPTER NINETEEN

Samuel Mordecai leapt down first, in a shower of earth. Martin thudded down behind him.

It was unusual for both of them to come down at the same time. It had happened only once before. Walter gripped the open knife in his pocket and watched them closely. It might be time.

Martin reached up to bring down a large cardboard box. He had already brought them dinner an hour ago. He looked around at the kids. They had all stopped what they were doing and were sitting motionless.

"Lambs, Lambs." Samuel Mordecai stepped onto the bus. "We've got something for you. Tomorrow is your special day. And for a special day we have special things for you to wear." He reached into the box Martin was holding and pulled out a white garment. He held it up for them to see. It was a long white robe, in a child's size. "Come here," he said, pointing at Heather. He never called any of the kids by name. He hadn't learned them.

Heather looked up at Walter for help. Her bottom lip began to tremble.

Walter nodded encouragement at her.

"Come here, Lamb," Mordecai said.

She stood up and walked slowly to the front.

Mordecai held the white robe up to her shoulders, and studied the hem, as if checking the length. "That's about right. For a pretty little blond girl. Our women made these of pure cotton just for y'all. When you get up tomorrow, cast off your old clothes and put these on. Put on the pure white raiment of the purified. Then I'll come and tell you some wondrous gospel, the good news to end all news."

He raised his hands in the gesture Walter had come to loathe so intensely it made his teeth hurt. "*They were dressed in white,*" Mordecai intoned, "*and had crowns of gold on their heads. From the throne came flashes of lightning, rumblings and peals of thunder.*' Tomorrow, Lambs of mine, tomorrow." With that, he stepped out of the bus and pulled himself up through the hole. Martin dropped the box and left without a word or a backward glance.

Walter watched them go and thought that if he had the opportunity to kill them, he would do it without hesitation. He closed his eyes and indulged himself in a fantasy he'd been having lately. His current fantasy combined the Power Rangers scenes the kids acted out with Samuel Mordecai's images from Revelation. He pictured the kids and himself bursting up from the hole and morphing from meek victims into fearsome giant scorpions. They would inflict horrible pain on the Jezreelites, so that they would long for death. The more vividly he could picture it, the more satisfying it was. If he ever got out of here, he decided, he might start drawing insects: beetles and scorpions.

"I'm damned sure not gonna wear no dress," Hector said.

"Me neither," Brandon said.

"Oh, don't worry about that." Walter picked up the box and tossed it into the pit. "None of you are going to wear those."

Bucky and Lucy were both starting to cry, and Walter felt general panic building up. They knew the end was near. It was impossible not to know.

"Mr. Demming, tell us the rest of the story," Philip said. "Before we go to sleep."

"Is that something you'd all like?" Walter asked.

The kids all agreed and settled into their seats.

If ever there was a group that needed escape from reality, Walter thought, they were it. He hunkered down in the aisle and faced the kids. He counted heads, anticipating the stab of pain when he came up one short. Then he waited for the end of the story to come to him.

"The old Tong woman," he said. "She's coming along the path with her shopping bag. Lopez is still trying to sniff out where the Astral 100 Galaxy Peace Ray is buried. The sun is rising. Now here's what happens. Lopez stops sniffing, and he starts digging—furiously. Armadillos have these long front claws that are great for digging. Pretty quickly he makes a hole, and he hits something hard. He pulls it up. Whatever it is is wrapped inside a green plastic garbage bag. Dr. Mortimer says, 'That's it. That's it—the Galaxy Peace Ray. We've found it.'"

Bucky said in a slow, sleepy voice, "He wrapped it in a garbage bag so it wouldn't get wet in the ground."

"That's right," Walter said. "It's a very fragile machine, and it shouldn't get wet."

"I forgot why he buried it," Heather said.

Hector said, "So the Tongs wouldn't get it and destroy it. Open your ears, feather-head."

Heather's face got red and she stood up. Walter was afraid a fight was coming.

Philip stood, too, and raised his hands in the air. "He who has an ear, let him hear what the Spirit says."

It was something they had all heard Samuel Mordecai say scores of times, and Philip's impersonation caught his twang and his theatrical intonation. They all laughed—even Heather, who sat back down.

"So," Walter said, "finally they've got it—what they came for—and the sun is up and they hear people shouting in the village. They need to get away. Just one Peace Ray wouldn't be enough to defend against hundreds of Tongs. But Jacksonville doesn't know what to do about the old lady. She's calling out to him and waving. And she's hurrying as fast as her short legs can go, and she's smiling at him. She's calling out something in Tonganese.

"Lopez is saying, 'Come on, come on. Let's go.'

"But Jacksonville's real polite. You know how he is. He doesn't like to offend anyone or hurt anyone's feelings. And he remembers that she brought him the vegetable peeler, and was so kind to him and everything. He feels he ought to say goodbye. And thank you. So he walks toward her. She's hurrying, but the bag looks kind of heavy. Jacksonville wonders if it's a gift for him or maybe she's bringing something for them to eat on their way home. Or maybe she wants to kill him. He doesn't know.

"She finally gets to where he is, and she smiles and bows. She puts her bag down and reaches inside."

Walter's legs hurt from hunkering, and he was feeling dizzy. He sat down in the aisle and leaned his back against the seat. He felt like he was at some point of no return; he'd gotten the story to this point and the only way out was to keep on going. He looked around at the children. In the dimness, their white faces seemed disembodied. They had gotten so pale their skin seemed to glow in the dark.

"At this point Jacksonville hears Lopez and Dr. Mortimer running up behind him. They're both pretty slow, but they're hurrying because they're worried about what the old Tong woman is going to do. Dr. Mortimer has the Peace Ray, and he raises it to shoot her. Lopez says, 'Wait. She's just a harmless old lady.'

"Jacksonville says, 'I don't know. Maybe we should.'"

Kim interrupted. "But it wouldn't hurt her, would it? It would just make her nice and peaceful if she wasn't already that way."

"But shooting at someone is so rude," Lucy said, "and she's an old grandmother."

"They ought to do it," Hector said, "just to be sure."

"Well, that's how Jacksonville felt," Walter said. "And Dr. Mortimer did, too. Anyway, he just felt like shooting someone with the Peace Ray, and she was there.

"So Dr. Mortimer takes aim at the old woman and pulls the trigger and all these sparks fly out and land on her. And she twinkles—you guys know how the Galaxy Peace Ray works. It looks like she's covered with these tiny fairy lights. And she gets this peaceful sweet look on her face and she hands the bag to Jacksonville. He looks inside, and he's totally shocked and amazed by what he sees."

Walter stopped to let the suspense sink in. He thought they might come up with guesses about what was in the bag, but they were silent, watching him with tense expectation.

"What?" Bucky said. "What?"

Walter lowered his voice to a whisper. "It was a bomb. A powerful bomb that would make a hole in the earth the size of an Olympic swimming pool. It would blow everyone around into smithereens."

"No!" Kim said, her voice shaking with passion. "She *saved* him. She wouldn't want to hurt him."

"But, Kim," Sandra said, "maybe she wasn't planning to hurt him. Maybe she was going to give it to him to take along. You know, for protection."

"Shit," Hector said, "I say she was going to blow him up and make herself a hero."

"You *would* say that," Lucy said.

"So, Mr. Demming, what was she going to do with it?" Brandon asked.

Walter shook his head. "I don't know. And they never found out for sure. Because once she was shot with the Peace Ray, she couldn't imagine doing anything mean or hurtful. She couldn't even remember anything violent she'd ever done or thought."

"That's not fair," Brandon said. "It can't end like that."

"Well, it hasn't ended yet," Walter said. "Let me finish."

"Let him finish," Bucky said.

"All right. They were leaving now, but the old woman went with them. She had to because she couldn't live with people so warlike and aggressive as the Tongs now that she'd been shot with the Peace Ray. They took the bomb with them in case they needed it for their escape. But they didn't, so eventually they threw it in the ocean.

"The old Tong woman followed them, all the way back to Austin. She'd never been to Texas before, but she loved it, and she was used to the heat because it was even hotter in Tongaland and much more humid. She moved in with Jacksonville and Lopez, and she did the cooking. She made these wonderful spicy noodle dishes for them. Of course, they didn't like noodles much, but all the neighbors did."

"Noodles and what?" Sandra asked.

"Oh, various things. Shrimp, vegetables. Sometimes, as a treat for Lopez, she'd do spicy noodles with beetles, or spiders, if she could catch them."

"How about the President?" Hector asked.

"He was real happy to get Dr. Mortimer and the Galaxy Peace Ray back. The mission was accomplished, and he had them all to lunch at the White House. He gave them medals and plaques and certificates saying they were heroes."

"What did they eat at the White House?" Sandra asked.

"Well, in honor of Jacksonville, the President had one of the White House butlers go out and find some good ripe roadkill—it had been a possum, I think—and scrape it up into a pizza box and—"

"Arggh," Sue Ellen said.

"And for Lopez some delicious gourmet beetles on a silver plate. They don't allow slumber bugs at the White House, but Lopez had given them up anyway. And for Dr. Mortimer, a steak, to build up his strength, because he had lost so much weight while he was in prison."

"A rare steak," Conrad said. "With A-1 sauce and french fries."

"Yeah," Walter said. "That's right."

"So they lived happily ever after?" Philip asked in a skeptical tone.

Walter looked to the back of the bus where the boy lay on his seat with his head sticking out in the aisle. "Well, they certainly weren't happy all the time, Philip, and they didn't live forever. Jacksonville still worried about being ugly and Lopez had to fight off the craving for slumberbugs all his life. But they did have some very happy times together. Jacksonville read many good books and Lopez had the best garden in the county. So you decide for yourselves. If that's living happily ever after, then they did. Now you guys need to go to sleep. Before you do, I want you to close your eyes and practice in your mind your part in our emergency plan. When I give the signal, you need to be able to go right to it. Okay? I think we're going to have to do it for real tomorrow."

Kim came up and sat on the seat Walter was leaning against. She lifted his ponytail and took the rubber band off it. Then she started combing his hair. He protested softly, "Kim, honey, it's so dirty."

"Yeah, so's mine. It doesn't matter. You can't help it. I like to comb hair. I'll make it look nice."

Heather, curled up on the next seat, said in a sleepy voice, "Me, too. Maybe when I grow up I'll be a hairstylist like my Aunt Cheryl. She's real pretty. You'd like her, Mr. Demming." She lifted her head up suddenly, as if something had just occurred to her. "Do you have a girlfriend or anything?"

"I did," he said, "Carolyn. But she married someone else and moved to Dallas."

"Oh, she shouldn't have," Heather said.

"I know." He was getting tired. Having his head touched always did that to him. It was so relaxing, so soothing. Kim had even managed to get a bad snarl out without pulling. He closed his eyes.

Finally she got the hair combed out to her satisfaction. "It's gotten long," she said. "Are you going to cut it when you get home?"

"I don't know. Do you think I should?"

"No. I like it long. Heather, let me have one of those scrunchies you've been saving."

Heather sat up and reached in her pocket. She pulled out a red fabric-covered band and handed it to Kim. Gently Kim combed his hair back tight and gathered it into a bunch. She slipped the band on and secured it. Then he felt something soft against his forehead. It tightened. She was tying something around his head. "What's that?"

"It's that old blue handkerchief of Josh's I always kept for him. I washed it out yesterday," she said, "so there's no boogers on it or anything."

He reached up and felt it. She'd twisted it into a narrow band and tied it in the back. He was stunned. It was what he'd always done in Vietnam. To keep the sweat out of his eyes. "Why did you do that, Kim?" he asked.

"I don't know. I thought it would look good. Don't you like it?"

"Yes, I do like it," he said. "I think it will bring us good luck." And God knows, he thought, we are due some. Please, God, if You could grace us with just a little luck down here, we will make the rest of it ourselves.

"There is no reason why good cannot triumph as often as evil. The triumph of anything is a matter of organization. If there are such things as angels, I hope that they are organized along the lines of the Mafia."

WINSTON NILESRUMFOORD
FROM *THE SIRENS OF TITAN,*
BY KURT VONNEGUT

CHAPTER TWENTY

When Molly, Patrick Lattimore, and Grady Traynor returned to the communications room, Rain Conroy was fully dressed. She sat on a desk chair with her face tilted up toward Jules Borthwick, who was daubing pink lipstick on her mouth. He'd used face powder to whiten her complexion and applied a streak of rouge along each cheekbone. He had done something amazing to her hair, which had been short and sleek, to make it frizzed and dry-looking, for all the world as if she'd had years of bad perms.

Molly stared in wonder at the transformation.

"Stand up," Lattimore said.

Rain waited for Jules to finish blotting her lipstick, then she stood.

It was astounding. She was now a bulky, tired, fifty-two-year-old elementary school teacher with a round-shouldered hunch and a look of amiable confusion. She wore a green cotton-polyester suit and large round, fabric-covered earrings that matched. The skirt was A-line; it hit her mid-calf in the most unflattering way, and managed to make her legs look heavy. The jacket hung open to reveal a white rayon blouse with lace trim. Her legs had the orange cast that comes from support hose, and her long feet looked comfortable in sturdy black pumps with low heels.

The body was what was really amazing. The thickness around the middle looked like the natural postmenopausal thickening, and the low-slung breasts, just discernible underneath the white blouse, looked soft and real.

"Wow!" Molly said. She studied the blouse, which seemed to fasten down the front with a hidden placket and a lace edging. "But how do you get to your weapon?"

Rain stepped toward her and smiled sweetly. Before Molly could smile back, Rain turned into a blur of motion. She ended in a crouched shooting stance with a pistol gripped in both hands. It was aimed into the fireplace.

Jules stepped back. "Hot damn! We got Velcro for our pistol-packing mama. What would we do without Velcro?"

Rain laughed. "We'd have to do décolleté."

"Miss Cates is going in with you, Rain," Lattimore said. "Just as far as the door, to hand over her materials and testify to your identity."

"I thought so. That's why I wanted her to see that move." Rain looked at Molly. "If things go wrong and you see me start to do what I just did, get the hell out of the way. Hit the floor and crawl under something. Hostages and pain-in-the-butt innocent bystanders get shot because they don't stay down." She slid the gun back inside her blouse, sucking her breath in to reposition it in the space inside her fake torso. Then she ran a hand over the placket to close it and smooth the fabric over the bodice. "We need to talk."

"Yes," Lattimore said, "we surely do. Holihan, put that house plan up here on the board, please."

Holihan tacked a large sheet of paper next to the diagram of the compound. "This is the first floor of the main building," he told them. "We got this from a local builder the Jezreelites consulted about some structural problems in the building three years ago. He made this from the sketches he did at the time. You've been inside, Miss Cates. Does this track with your recollection of it?"

Molly looked at it. There was the big central room you entered into directly through the front door. To the right was the kitchen and behind that was the huge mess hall with long tables. To the left was the office where she had spent two harrowing hours with Samuel Mordecai.

"This is the way I remember it."

Lattimore said, "Well, this time you shouldn't see more than the area around the front door. Look. Here's how it goes." He stepped over to the compound diagram and planted his middle and index fingers just outside the gate. "We drop the two of you off here. Lieutenant Traynor will take you in his unmarked unit. We're going to do it so fast the press won't know what's happening. You'll be inside before they can react.

"You're going to take the lead, Molly. You get out of the car. Cynthia—we're going to call her Cynthia from now on—will follow along. You'll open the gate. It's a simple lift latch like on a tennis court. No lock. You'll push it open and close it behind Cynthia. You'll be solicitous of her because this is painful for her. You're carrying the folder under your arm." He snapped his fingers. "Curtis, get the folder, please."

Curtis handed him the brown accordion file with Molly's handwriting on the tab identifying it as 'Samuel Mordecai.'

"Everything's in here," Lattimore continued, "including your little tape player in case he wants to play the tape and doesn't have one that size. We'll go over it all in a minute." He handed the file to Molly and put his fingers back at the gate. "So you walk in. You'll lead the way, Molly, with Cynthia just a step behind you. We want you to look all business. No hesitation. Move briskly and deliberately. You're the confident one, Cynthia's timid and a little stunned by all this."

He walked his fingers through the gate to the front door. "The lights are bright. You know we have these searchlights set up. You'll be blinded by them. Keep your eyes down on the ground. Don't look behind you. There will be guns pointing at you from the towers and from some of the windows in the main building. Ignore them. You walk to the front door. They'll have been watching you, so they may open it for you as you approach. If not, knock. They'll open and let you in."

He moved over to the house diagram. "Molly, you go in first. This is real critical right here. You say, 'I'm Molly Cates and this is Cynthia Jenkins,' and you wait. If Samuel Mordecai is there, you address this to him. If not, wait for him. When you see him, Molly, don't greet him or make any small talk. Don't smile. Keep it cool and impersonal. Don't argue with him. That's what our psychologists advise. Don't get involved in any discussion about what's been happening. Just stick to what you came for, which is to give him the folder and summarize it.

"Now, the place you want to stand to do this dog and pony show is right here to the left of the door." He walked his fingers there.

"If they say they want to search you, you let them, but don't make it easy. Make them work for it. Frown and look embarrassed, offended.

"If he tells you to come into the office or somewhere else, say this: 'The agreement was that I'd show it to you here. I can leave it with you, but I'll show it to you here.' Take the lead and show him the police report with the names. Tell him it led to Hank Hanley, who was one of the witnesses on Waller Creek. That led you to the Pi Alpha Omegas, which is how you eventually tracked Cynthia Jenkins down. You flew to Houston last night to talk to her. She acknowledged right away she was his mother and was able to fill in all the details. You brought your tape of that discussion. You always tape interviews.

"So hit the highlights, like that, and hand him the file. Ask if he has any questions. All we want you to do is vouch for her and validate it. Then you get out of there. Ask Cynthia if she's all right, pat her on the arm, and say that you'll see her later. And you walk out." He switched back to the compound diagram and walked his fingers from the front door back to the gate. "Walk at the same rate you walked in. Brisk. You'll feel like running.

Don't do it. And don't look around. Just keep your eyes on the ground. Lieutenant Traynor will be waiting with the car. You hop in and he'll bring you back here."

He gave Molly a pinched smile. "And that's it."

"That's it if everything goes perfectly," Grady said.

"Okay," Lattimore said, "let's talk about contingencies. Number one is the body-search issue. If they just frisk you, it's all right, even if they really feel you both up. If they want to do a strip search, Cynthia is going to have a fainting spell. Molly, we've practiced it already. She will feel poorly and all you need to do is be solicitous. She'll carry it."

Rain said, "The whole idea is for me to get Mordecai in a room alone. Everything I do or say will be aimed at that."

"The second problem," Lattimore said, "is if he wants you to come with him and Cynthia, to have you show him the stuff privately. You want to resist that. Let me repeat: The goal here is for Cynthia to get him alone. If it's necessary, and you have to go along with it, then be sure you stay out of the way. Rain will take him out at the first opportunity. You'll hit the floor and stay there. We'll hear the shot for sure because we have our electronic ears on, and the first shot's our cue to move. If she can, she'll blow out the window of the room she's in with a frame charge. You can count on our coming through that blown window within sixty seconds, even if it's on the second floor. The lights will go off, inside and out, as soon as we hear the shot. They have a generator, but we don't know if it works and anyway it'll take a while for it to kick in, so you may be in the dark. And there's no moon tonight. Cynthia has a tiny laser light."

Grady uncrossed his arms for the first time. "Tell her what happens if they get made, Lattimore."

"If thirty minutes pass with no shot and no blast, we're going to assume you got made and we'll come in. Molly, if there's some delay other than that, ask Mordecai if you can call me. Say you don't want me to worry. All you have to do is pick up the phone and I'll be on the other end," Lattimore said. "At worst, this will be a diversion—to mask our assault."

"Have you ever seen an explosive entry, Molly?" Rain asked.

"No."

"And she's not going to," Lattimore said.

"But if you get unlucky," Rain said, "and get to see one tonight, you should know what to expect. We go in fast—screaming like Banshees, black hoods, gas masks, Ninja gear, flash-bangs blinding you and deafening you, assault rifles blazing."

"Sounds like a Rolling Stones concert I saw recently," Molly said.

No one laughed.

Rain said, "I don't know what effect Mick Jagger has on people these days, but our entries make most people piss in their pants the first time. I did. You've got one thing to remember: Stay down. That's how you survive."

"Okay," Lattimore said, "if no one has anything else to add, let's give the ladies some time to powder their noses and get their seams straight." He looked at his watch. "Fifteen minutes, ladies and gentlemen. Then come back here and I'll make the call to Mordecai. Curtis, get me Blumberg."

Molly found the bathroom, but her bladder was much too nervous to give anything up.

Walking past the little room off the kitchen, looking for Grady, she saw Rain Conroy sitting alone inside. Her head was lowered, her eyes closed. Her lips moved silently. Her fingers were busy with something in her lap and at first Molly wasn't sure what she was doing. Molly took a few steps into the room and saw that it was a rosary. Rain was moving her fingers slowly from bead to bead.

Molly stood quietly and watched her pray. She knew she ought to leave, but she couldn't.

When Rain finally opened her eyes, Molly was still watching her.

"Old habits die hard," Rain said. "And this business makes you superstitious. You tend to do exactly what you did all the other times you survived."

"Are you still a Catholic?"

Rain smiled. "Are you still a woman? Are you still a member of your father's family?"

"But you quit being a nun."

"And I bet you quit being a virgin."

Molly smiled back at her.

Rain said, "I don't mean to be flippant. I don't go to mass, haven't for twenty years. I did once commit my life to the Church, but it proved un-worthy of me. Sexist. Corrupt. Rigid." She shrugged. "But so is every other organization I've seen since then."

"Well," Molly said, "I'm interrupting you. Sorry.

But one more question—just now…what do you pray for?"

"For courage. And luck. For my reflexes to keep their edge just a little longer. For the soul of Samuel Mordecai. For the hostages." She ticked them off on her fingers—"Hector Ramirez, Lucy Quigley, Sue Ellen McGregor, Brandon Betts, Bucky DeCarlo, Heather Yost, Kimberly Bassett, Conrad Pease, Sandra Echols, Philip Trotman, and especially Walter Demming."

"I'm impressed that you learned their names. I haven't wanted to get that close."

Rain nodded. "I usually pick one name to concentrate on. I think it will be Philip Trotman this time. To center myself when things get messy. It calms me." She studied Molly. "You might need one tonight. Why don't you take Heather Yost? That sounds like a lucky one to me." Rain closed her eyes. "But do it in the other room, please. I need a little time alone."

But Molly hesitated. "Rain," she asked, "do you have any other advice for me?"

Without opening her eyes, Rain said, "Make sure you pee before we go, and, for God's sake, stay down."

Molly found Grady in the kitchen studying the cast of Rain Conroy's torso. When he saw Molly, he wrapped his arms around her and hugged her close. "Molly, go in and get out quick. No heroics."

"No danger of that," Molly said.

He nodded at the statue. "She's paid to do it. And trained for it—a professional. You're not."

"I know."

"It will all be over tonight."

"Yes."

"I was thinking it would be fun to go out tomorrow night—it's Friday, you know—and drink some beer under the stars. We'll take our dog along. What do you say?"

"I say it's a date. After my exercise class."

"Skip it."

"No. I've vowed to be able to do fifty consecutive push-ups by the end of the year. Did I tell you that?"

"No, but Jo Beth did." He chuckled. "She said you haven't got a prayer."

Molly studied his face. "Did she?"

"Uh-huh."

"Well, she's wrong. Grady, do you ever pray?"

"No. Well, maybe. Sometimes lately when I'm suffering over something, worrying about it, I find myself just stopping, and I say, 'So be it.' And then I let go of whatever it was that was eating at me, and I feel as light as air. All it seems to take is saying the words: So be it."

"Thy will be done?" Molly said.

He leaned down and kissed her lightly. "I guess."

*"The first angel sounded his trumpet, and
there came hail and fire mixed with blood,
and it was hurled down upon the earth."*
REVELATION 8:7

TWENTY-ONE

The night was cool and moonless. Molly had forgotten how dark it got out in the country, and
how shrill the cicadas were.

They passed through the roadblock without
slowing down. At the checkpoint, Grady flashed
his badge and the DPS trooper immediately waved
him through.

In front of them, the Hearth Jezreelite compound rose from the flat plain, flooded with white
light like a stage set, surreal and dramatic. The
first time Molly had seen the compound it had
been just a ramshackle bunch of buildings hous-
ing an obscure religious group. Now, surrounded
by spotlights and media attention, the crenellated
stone towers flanking the flat-topped central structure loomed like a sorcerer's castle in a grade B
horror movie. Surrounded by tanks and personnel carriers, satellite trucks and press vans, it compelled attention. The whole world was watching.
Molly couldn't take her eyes off it.

But the most bizarre, nightmarish part of the
scene you had to supply yourself—the underground part—ten children and a bus driver buried alive under the barn. She tried to conjure up
the picture so she could hold them in mind.
Aboveground, the floodlights had banished the

darkness. But belowground, it would be eternal night—just dark earth and the creatures that crawled through it. Under the light. Under the grass. Under the dirt. Under the beetle's cellar. Buried alive. It raised goose bumps on her skin. She wrapped her arms around herself. Dear God, how could they survive it?

Grady pulled up close to the gate. He checked his watch and turned to Molly in the back seat. "Look at your watch. The time is nine minutes past eleven. By the time you get to the front door it will be eleven past. You have until eleven forty-one."

Molly looked down at her watch. "Okay. Eleven forty-one."

"Right. I'll be here waiting, Molly. Get in and out quick."

"I will." She slid out of the car and opened the passenger door for Rain, who struggled out, groaning as if she were slightly arthritic.

Rain smoothed her skirt around her hips and looked around at the weedy grounds and the glaring lights. "My goodness gracious but those are bright."

Molly turned to look at her. The voice was brand-new—a soft, shaky twang with a whiny edge to it that was totally unlike Rain Conroy's low, clipped Boston voice. Molly was awed. The voice, the dowager's hump she'd managed to contort her back into, the meek body language—Rain had become Cynthia Jenkins.

They were a troupe of actors arriving on this bizarre set: Rain Conroy with her new voice and her rubber torso, Molly with her folder of lies, federal agents with weapons hidden somewhere.

But the agents were not pretending; they were ready to kill in earnest.

"Here we go." Molly opened the gate and walked through. She held it open for Rain, who said, "Oh, Lordy." She looked dazed as she passed through. "Lordy mine."

Molly closed the gate and started up the weedy gravel drive that led to the main building. Rain was having a hard time walking on the gravel. No one watching this middle-aged woman, with her heels sinking into the gravel, her breathing labored after only a few yards, would ever dream she was a professional assassin. The sound of their shoes crunching the gravel seemed very loud in Molly's ears; it drowned out the cicadas and the steady hum of the generators outside the fence.

Molly wanted to look back at Grady's car, to touch base, make sure he was waiting. And she longed for some evidence that the entry team was close behind them, ready to storm to their rescue. She wanted to reassure herself that they were backed up by all the firepower the law could muster. She resisted the temptation to look back, but couldn't stop herself from glancing up at the towers, first the one on the left, then the one on the right. Something was missing. She looked up again. The tattered red banners were gone, the banners that had been flying, one from each tower, throughout the standoff, the banners over which there had been so much speculation. Whatever image they bore had been too faded and indistinct for anyone to make out, even with sophisticated telephoto lenses or binoculars. She glanced once more. Definitely gone. Was it a sign of some sort?

They passed the derelict green truck sitting up on cinder blocks and the two cars that had been parked in the driveway for forty-nine days. They had become part of the landscape, much debated by the press. The black Corvette was registered to Samuel Mordecai, his personal vehicle. The white Toyota had no license plate, and no one knew who owned it.

Trying to follow orders to look straight ahead, Molly let her eyes flicker over the white barn, the huge double doors, the tin roof.

As they neared the front door of the main building, Rain sucked her breath in.

Up close Molly was surprised at how shoddy the construction was. The siding had separated; gaps showed the insulation in places. The gray paint was peeling. It was a run-down godforsaken place with no plumbing, no privacy, no beauty, and no comforts, and yet more than one hundred and fifty people had chosen to come here. To sit and listen to Samuel Mordecai preach. To follow him, even though he was leading them into the valley of death. It was incomprehensible. Beyond reason. She'd researched it and thought about it, and still it was a total enigma. She had written an article which purported to shed light on the cult phenomenon, which contained observations that appeared perceptive and wise, but it was a bogus wisdom. She wasn't even close to understanding. What made these people give up everything and come to this godforsaken place?

And here she was, too, in spite of all her vows to keep her distance.

When they were ten yards away from the door,

it swung open. Rain grabbed Molly's arm and held on tight, as though she needed support. Molly patted her hand.

The single cement step was cracked and crumbling. Molly's heart was thumping so hard she was sure it must be visible under her T-shirt.

She stepped up and Rain followed, still clinging to her arm. They walked through the doorway into the dim interior of the big room. After the bright lights outside, Molly had trouble seeing. When her eyes adjusted, she saw the room was filled with men in tan camouflage fatigues and ballistic vests. All held assault rifles. At every window several leaned against hay bales. They were watching out through holes in the sheets that covered the windows.

The reality of it stopped Molly in her tracks. This was a war zone and they had walked right into it, right into a fortified bunker. She stood still and felt the prickle of sweat under her arms. It would be all right, she told herself, if she just followed the plan.

The three men nearest the door kept their rifles pointed at Rain and Molly. One pushed the door shut and another stacked some sandbags against it. All escape was cut off now.

Molly looked from face to face, seeking Samuel Mordecai. She didn't see him.

She needed to do her part and get the hell out. She recited her lines: "I'm Molly Cates and this is Cynthia Jenkins."

No one responded.

Molly's eyes darted around the room. The men were lifeless automatons, their faces indistinguishable in the bad light. Only a single bulb hung near the center of the huge room. The corners and edges were in deep shadow, but she could make out dozens of boxes lined up against the walls. Several long wooden boxes looked like boxes in which guns were shipped. If the other boxes were full of weapons and ammunition, the Jezreelites were equipped to hold off an army. She wondered if the entry team knew how much force they were up against.

They stood in silence for what seemed a long time. Molly forced herself not to shift from foot to foot. All she had to do was say her piece and get out. While she waited, she rehearsed her script in her head.

Finally from above came a rapping noise. It seemed to come from the stairs at the back, but it was too dark to see to the top.

One of the gunmen took a few steps toward Molly. He pointed with his rifle. "Upstairs."

Molly glanced at Rain, whose cool gray eyes were slowly sweeping the room.

Molly said, "The agreement was I would show Samuel Mordecai my notes here, at the door."

The man touched the gun to her spine.

"You don't understand," Molly said. "I'm supposed to—"

He jabbed the gun into her back.

Molly had a moment of panicky fear that it might accidentally discharge.

"Upstairs," the man repeated.

She moved toward the stairs, with Rain still holding her arm. Panic lapped at her in hot little waves. This was not going according to plan. Not at all.

Two of the men walked behind with their rifles just inches from the women's backs. Molly was sweating. Her legs felt weak, undependable. Her body was undisciplined, not trained for this. She was starting to shiver. Again she wished she had worn a jacket.

When they got to the rickety wooden staircase at the back, Molly hesitated. This might be her last chance to get the plan back on track. She opened her mouth to protest. A gun pressed into her lower back, hitting a knob on her spine and sliding off. There was no choice now. She'd abandoned the luxury of choice when she agreed to enter this madman's lair.

She put her foot on the first step and looked up into the darkness. There were no lights on the stairs or at the top. She had to feel for the steps with her foot. As she mounted them, she counted. One. Two. Three. Four. Next to her, Rain's breathing was labored.

A voice from the darkness at the top said, "We need to go *through* the blood. Can't climb over it, ladies, can't go around it. Got to go right through it. Like in childbirth. Y'all will understand that."

Molly and Rain stopped climbing.

At the top of the stairs a light flicked on.

Samuel Mordecai stood there waiting for them. He wore black jeans, boots, and a ballistic vest Molly recognized as similar to the ones the Austin police wore. That would make him harder to kill. Molly hoped fervently that Rain Conroy really was the crack shot she was reputed to be.

Mordecai was staring intently at Rain.

Molly started to repeat her lines: "I'm Molly Cates and this—"

"I know," he said, without even glancing at her. "I know." His eyes were fixed on Rain. He looked long and hard, greedily studying her gray eyes and wide mouth, as if her features might hold some familiarity for him.

Rain took another step up to get in front of Molly. "Miz Cates just came to introduce me. She needs to leave and I want very much to talk to you alone."

"Both of you will come up," he said in an even voice.

Molly continued to climb, reluctantly. Every step she took away from the front door carried them closer to disaster. She stopped at the top of the stairs and made another try at salvaging the plan. "The agreement was that I would stay at the door and show you how I found your mother. My break was in finding this homeless man, Hank Hanley, who—"

"Enough," Mordecai said.

She held the folder out toward him. "Then let me leave this with you. I have to go. They are expecting me right back."

He pushed the folder back at her. "They are expecting lots of things that won't happen." He turned and headed down the dim hallway toward an open door.

Molly felt the rifle against her backbone again. She followed him down the hall.

Samuel Mordecai waited at the door for one of the guards to enter first. The other guard prodded Molly with his gun. She stepped into the room. Rain followed, then the second guard, and finally, Samuel Mordecai. He shut the door.

The two guards positioned themselves on either side of the closed door. They held their rifles ready and stared into some middle space like servants who were expected to be in attendance but not hear the discussion.

Molly's heart pumped in huge bursts. Grady was right. Things were going south here pretty damn fast. Rain couldn't take three of them on and survive. They had to get rid of the two guards, and quick. And she had to get the hell out.

Rain stepped forward. She said, "I feel bad about Miz Cates being here. Please let her leave."

Still studying Rain's face, Mordecai said, "Leave? She's got work to do."

Molly held up the folder again. "Let me—"

He held up a hand to silence her. "Not that. Here's what I'll let you do. I'll let you tell me—is this woman my mother?" He pulled his gaze away from Rain and approached Molly, invading her space, stopping just inches from her. He bent his head down to hers. "Is she?" His breath was hot on her face.

Molly felt the corner of her left eye quivering. She tried to stop it and couldn't. This lie would be her death if he knew anything to disprove it. She met his eyes. "Yes, she is." Her voice came out nice and steady.

"Do you swear it on your eternal soul here on the eve of Apocalypse?"

Molly nodded. Right now the survival of her body felt paramount; she would worry about her soul when the time came. "I swear it."

He looked at Rain and sighed, shaking his head sadly. "You had to come," he said. "It was prophesied."

Molly glanced around the room. The only illumination was a small gooseneck lamp on a desk. Scattered around the unvarnished wood floor were barbells of various sizes. At the end of the room stood an unmade king-sized bed piled with a jumble of sheets and blankets. A belt with a holstered pistol lay on top. Above the bed was a small window that must open to the front. If she looked out, she'd see Grady's white Ford Tempo parked in the shadows near the gate.

One of the gunmen said, "We should search them now, Samuel."

Mordecai looked at Rain, who had a hand pressed over her heart, still trying to catch her breath. Then he ran his eyes over Molly, from head to toe. He looked at the man and shook his head.

At least one thing had gone as planned.

Molly said, "They are expecting me to walk out now. And Cynthia needs some time alone with you." She nodded toward the guards at the door. "Could they walk me out?"

A smile played briefly at the corner of Samuel Mordecai's mouth. "You aren't finished. You have a job to do." He walked over to his desk. "The most important writing job since the Bible was wrote down." He stared down at some red fabric that was draped across the desktop. He picked it up and shook it out. It was an old banner. Molly recognized it immediately as one of the banners that had flown from the towers. He stretched it out in front of his body, extending

392

his arms to show them the image on it. Molly was not surprised to see that it was a coiled dragon. Painted crudely in black, it was nowhere near as detailed or resplendent as the embroidered one on the silk robe that had served as his swaddling cloth, but the circular design was identical. Like a child's clumsy attempt at copying the other.

"This is my mascot," he said, glancing down at the dragon. "My defender, my rock of ages, my parent." He looked hard at Rain. "It protected me when others left me to die."

Rain took a step toward him. "Let me tell you about it." Her voice was tremulous. "I have so much I want to say, Samuel—so much." She took another step forward. "But it's painful to talk about. I need to do it in private—just the two of us." She reached out and touched him gently on the arm.

He looked down at her hand on his arm. A vein pulsing along his jawline frightened Molly. The man was a time bomb. He could detonate at any moment.

He took the banner he had been holding outstretched and lifted it up and over Rain's head. He brought it down behind her and draped it around her shoulders like a shawl. "There. Now *you* can feel it. The presence of the Beast. How do you like it?"

Rain didn't move. "I'm so sorry for the pain I caused you," she said.

"Well, that's as it should be. It's prophesied." He turned away from her and walked to the desk. He picked up another red banner and held it out. "You haven't seen the other banner, Miss Cates. Look."

This one bore a crudely painted picture of two hands with the fingers stretched up. From each finger a yellow ray extended up, and on each finger some words were printed, but the letters were too faded and too small for Molly to read them from where she stood.

With the wide-eyed, exhilarated look of a child who has been anticipating revealing a surprise he is certain will dazzle everyone, he said, "I made this when I received my first rapture and became the new Mordecai. Twelve years ago. The ten prophecies of Mordecai are here. All have come to pass, or are about to."

Molly glanced at her watch. Eleven-nineteen. They'd been here eight minutes already, and he was just warming up.

"Miz Cates," he said, "it don't make any difference what your watch says. Time is ending."

"Yes, but—"

"I want you to read this out loud."

Molly stood where she was, unsure of what to do. She glanced over at Rain, who was standing in the middle of the room with the banner draped around her.

"Come on," he said. "Come closer so you can read it. Read so my mother can hear. It's our story. Yours, too." He held the banner out closer to her, flicking it like a bullfighter enticing a bull. "Read."

Molly took a few steps toward the banner until she could just make out the crude letters that ran vertically down the fingers. She tipped her head to the side so she could read easier.

"Go on," he said, his breathing coming quicker. "Start with the thumb on the left hand. That's where the story begins. Read it out loud."

Molly read the five words: "*'The mother sins in blood.'*"

Without looking at Rain, he said, "Hard to believe any mama would give birth to a baby and just throw it out like it was garbage." His lips were tight with anger. "The mother sins in blood. Yup. That's sure true." The muscle in his jaw twitched.

Rain said, "I want to tell you about your father and the rest of—"

"Too late! It don't matter now." He spat the words out with venom.

"But there are things—"

"Shut up." He whirled and draped the banner over the desk, so the words on the fingers lay on top. He smoothed it out flat and turned back to Molly. "Read the next one."

She took a few steps closer to the desk so she could see it better. She read the words on the second finger: "*'The prophet moves through blood.'*"

"Well, that's true, too, ain't it? I got born and left to die, but I managed to survive. I managed." Molly could feel the man's barely controlled anger radiating off him in heat waves. It was an anger that could justify burying children alive, sacrificing infants, inflicting pain and death on others. His anger was so powerful, he believed he could destroy the world with it.

"Go on." He nodded to Molly.

She read the middle finger: "*'The Beast watches.'*"

"You bet he does," Mordecai said. He

looked at Rain. "Tell me, what does that mean in our story?"

Rain looked up at the guards. "It's so hard to talk about it with them and Miss Cates here. I'm shamed. I wish we—"

His voice sliced through hers. "Answer me!" he thundered. "The Beast watches—what does it mean?"

Rain sighed. "I suppose that old housecoat of mine I wrapped you in, the one with the dragon on it."

Samuel Mordecai appeared suddenly stricken. His shoulders stiffened and his forehead wrinkled in pain, as if he hadn't really believed it until that minute, as if the pathos of that abandoned infant were just now hitting him. "Read on," he said to Molly.

"*The prophet touches heaven,*'" Molly read.

In a sudden manic shift of emotion, Samuel Mordecai smiled his dazzling movie-star smile that involved only his mouth. Looking at Molly, he said, "The tips of the prophet's long slender fingers are his nexus to heaven."

Molly tensed in surprise. The wording was familiar. It was from her "Texas Cult Culture" article.

"That's right," he said. "I had to look up that word. Nexus means connection or tie or link. I love your words. Go on."

Molly read: "'*The words fill his hands.*'"

"Uh-huh. Tell us what you wrote about my rapture."

Molly tried to remember the passage. "I don't know it by memory," she said.

He reached down and opened a desk drawer

and pulled out a folded magazine. He handed it to Molly. "Read from where it's marked."

Molly found a penciled X and began to read from her article: "'*The tips of Samuel Mordecai's long slender fingers are his nexus to heaven. In what he calls his rapture, he raises his bare arms above his head and spreads his fingers wide like a satellite dish seeking the right signals from on high. He stretches them higher as if reaching into heaven itself for inspiration. Even the blond hairs on his fingers seem receptive. You can see his fingertips vibrate; then his fingers tremble. He cups his hands to capture the message, his face radiant, as if a shower of gold has sprinkled down on him. He lowers his cupped hands to his open mouth. Whatever he has received, he seems to be incorporating. Then he begins to speak.*'"

"Right on," Mordecai said. "*The prophet touches heaven. The words fill his hands.* Molly, don't that amaze you? These words get raptured to me twelve years ago and you come along and put that sacred vision in your worldly words, for your corrupt magazine. Like it was so powerful it broke right through to you."

Molly was stunned. She had written that description of Samuel Mordecai as part of what she considered a devastating portrait of a dangerous, self-deluded prophet. The paragraph she just read could be taken out of context and interpreted as the description of a man having a genuine vision, but you'd have to ignore the rest of the article that detailed his endless sermons, his incoherent theology, his tyranny over the group. Didn't he understand that?

"Read the other hand," he said. "The right hand tells what's needed to start the Apocalypse. Then you'll understand what I'm doing. Start with the little finger."

She read: "'*Fifty perfect martyrs.*'"

"See, God demands it. It is the only way. Tomorrow they will be complete." He nodded at Molly to continue. She had forgotten to breathe and found herself short of oxygen. She sucked in some breaths and read the words on the next finger: "'*Earth to purify.*'"

"Yes. Earth purifies in fifty days. Read the next one."

Molly forced her lips to say the words. "'*Earth to accept blood.*'" Staring down at the red fabric, Molly pictured Kim Bassett smiling into the camera and Bucky DeCarlo with his unruly cowlicks. She glanced up at Samuel Mordecai. He was nodding sadly, as if mourning the inevitability of it all. He said, "The blood has to soak into the earth. It's the only way, the ancient way of the Mordecai Prophets. You understand that now. Go on. We're getting to y'all's part."

"'*The mother's repentance,*'" Molly read softly.

Samuel Mordecai walked to where Rain stood with the red banner around her shoulders. "Tell me you repent your sins."

"Yes," Rain said in an even voice, "I do repent. Every day of my life. I regret with all my heart what I did to you, and if I could undo it, I would."

Samuel Mordecai's eyes filled with tears. "I can almost believe that. But it don't matter. Before this day is done, you *will* repent in earnest." He walked over to the bed and lifted the belt with the holster and pistol attached. "You surely will. The worm has turned. I'm in control now, the Alpha and the Omega, the Mordecai Prophet."

Rain seemed to come to life. She reached her hands out toward Mordecai. "Then help me to repent. Pray with me. Show me how to seek forgiveness. I don't know how. But you know these things. Help me."

He turned to face her. *"Help* you?" he said in an icy voice. "Help you like you helped me when I was a helpless babe?" He slung the belt around his hips and buckled it tight. "Should I wrap you in the mantle of the Beast and set you adrift? In a beer cooler? Like a piece of garbage?" He stood inches away and looked down at her. "Like a piece of garbage."

"But you're much better than I am," Rain said. "I want to pray with you, in private, just the two of us." She reached out again and touched his arm.

He struck with the speed of light. His arm whipped up and caught Rain on the side of the face with a crack. She crashed sprawling to the floor. "Private!" he hissed. "The two of us!" He stood over her. "Oh, yes, ma'am," he said, his jaw throbbing, "like it was private when I went through the blood?"

He reached down and grabbed the front of her jacket. He jerked her to her feet and dragged her to the bed. Then he put both hands flat against her chest and shoved. She landed sitting on the unmade bed. Her eyes were startled and her cheek was darkening from his blow.

The guards both took a step forward and aimed their rifles at Rain.

Molly held her breath. Had he felt the gun? Did he know? If he did, they were dead.

"Stay there," he spat, "you loathsome whore of destruction."

He walked back to Molly. He was breathing hard and beads of sweat had popped out on his forehead. "Now, where were we?" He looked down at the banner on the desk. "Oh, yes. The tenth one, the last. It's for you. Read it."

Molly read: "'*The scribe's gospel.*'"

"When I read what you wrote about me reaching up and getting the truth from heaven, I knew the scribe I'd been waiting on was you. And when you found my mother, I knew for sure. It was prophesied, and here you are. You have good words, but nothing worthy to write about. Now you do. Tonight you're going to write down the new gospel, the rapture of the fifth and last Mordecai. For the righteous who will survive the coming end."

Molly sneaked a look at her watch. Her heart sank. Eleven twenty-four.

"I get my words from heaven," he continued. "But a scribe is necessary to write them down."

He stretched his arms out and closed his eyes. "The scribe is here. The mother will be made to repent. And tomorrow the purified martyrs will offer their blood to the earth. We are ready for Your coming, Lord."

God. She'd known he was crazy, but she hadn't known the extent of it, and she hadn't known that she had a role in his insane fantasy. She looked at him with his big golden head thrown back and his eyes closed. If only the guards were gone. This would be the perfect chance to kill him.

He opened his eyes and jerked the banner off the desk. He walked over to the bed. "This is for you, you baby-murdering whore." He thrust it out to Rain. She started to rise, but again he put his hand against her chest and gave her a shove. "You stay right there." He tossed the red banner on her lap.

Then he returned to the desk. "Sit down," he said to Molly in a businesslike tone.

Molly looked at her watch. "First I need to let Patrick Lattimore know I'm delayed. He was expecting me back by now. I want to talk to him on the phone. So he doesn't panic."

"Time is ending. Delay don't matter." Samuel Mordecai pulled a stack of white paper and some ballpoint pens from the desk drawer. "Sit down. You use a computer at home, I bet."

She nodded.

"That's what corrupts your words. The Beast that lives in the computer. You start so nice and pure, like telling how the rapture comes to me. Then you go on to them other things that are false." His face took on a stony tightness. "All warped by that Beast in the computer."

He set the paper and pens down on the desk. "Here you go. Everything a scribe needs."

She hesitated.

He took a step closer and looked down at her. "Sit. Seize the chance for salvation."

Molly glanced at Rain, desperate for some clue. But Rain just sat watching, her gray eyes sweeping the room.

Molly sat at the desk.

Samuel Mordecai squatted down next to her. "I'm going to tell you the words, and you're gonna write them down. By hand." He took the cap off a pen and held it out to her. "Start like this. Write at the top: "The Heaven in Earth Vatic Gospel of the Jezreelite, as raptured to Samuel Mordecai, the fifth and final Mordecai Prophet.""

Molly picked up the pen. Her hand trembled. She tried to hold it steady, but it was beyond her control. The rest of her body was trembling, too. It gave her an idea. She glanced at the guards and back at the blank page in front of her.

She put the pen to the paper and started to write the heading he'd given her. She concentrated on tensing her right shoulder and arm to make her shaking even worse, like the wild shaking her arms did during push-ups.

It worked. Her pen hand shook like fury.

She tried to write "The" and made only some messy squiggles. She turned her face toward Mordecai, whose head was on a level with hers. "It's them," she whispered, nodding at the guards at the door. "They scare me. I need good conditions to write. Calm and supportive. I can't do it with them watching." She gave him an anguished look.

Mordecai reached out and wrapped his hand around hers. He forced her hand back down to the page. "Sure you can. Try."

When he let go, the pen shook as if she had palsy. She wrinkled her brow, as if trying to bring her hand under control. She used her left hand to brace the right. But she was unable to make a single recognizable letter.

"I'm trying," she told Mordecai. "I want to be the scribe, and I can be. If they leave. They send bad vibrations. Let them wait outside, or downstairs."

He was silent for several seconds.

Then he stood and looked at his guards. "Wait outside," he told them. He patted the pistol on his hip. "I'll be fine."

They nodded and left, closing the door behind them.

By the time they were out, Samuel Mordecai had squatted down again, close to her.

"Now," he said, "at the top: 'The Heaven in Earth Vatic Gospel of the Jezreelite.'"

Slowly, Molly printed it. "It's easier to read if I print," she said. "My handwriting isn't good."

He let out a bitter laugh. "The Beast in the computer does that—makes you dependent. A writer who can't write by hand anymore—that's how the Beast takes us over."

Breathless, Molly glanced over at Rain. It was time, but Rain was still sitting on the bed. Close enough for a good shot. But with no direct line to her target because Molly's body was between her and Mordecai.

Molly could lean away and drop down to the side. But she didn't want to do anything to alert him to danger. He could draw his gun.

Rain raised her hand to her heart, as though she were feeling ill, about to faint.

Molly turned in the chair and appealed to Mordecai. "Your mother looks ill. Help her."

Without even glancing up, he said, "We got work to do."

"Okay," Molly said. "I'm ready now."

And she was ready. Ready to help him offer himself up freely. She said, "When I write, it has to be inspired. We want these words to be direct from heaven, every word raptured. Let's do it right. Show me how the prophet touches heaven and gathers words in his hands. Show your mother how the words come in through your fingers. She's never seen it."

It was so corny. So shameless. No one would fall for it.

But he did.

He stood up. And, slowly, he raised his arms, and his eyes, toward heaven. Molly leaned to the side, away from him. As she did, Rain Conroy stood and drew her gun in one smooth motion. The sharp pop came simultaneous with the move.

Samuel Mordecai staggered back a step and stared at the woman he believed to be his mother. His mouth and eyes opened wide with shock and betrayal. It had happened again. But he didn't make a sound. Just like the newborn baby Hank Hanley described, the baby who hadn't cried or made a sound.

Then he crumpled to the floor.

Rain shouted, "Down!"

Molly dropped off the chair to the floor and scrabbled under the desk.

Then the world erupted around her.

Explosions, screams, shots, and roars burst in from outside.

Banging and shouting at the door.

Two more shots in the room.

The lights went out.

Then an explosion shook the whole building. The floor vibrated under her hands. The desk rattled above her.

Molly huddled under the desk, arms over her head. In the darkness, she smelled cordite and smoke. Bangs and thuds inside the room. Sudden bursts of light flashed so bright she saw them through her closed eyelids. Another shot. And another. A scream.

All around her the rapid fire of guns, punctuated by explosions and cries.

She smelled more smoke and had a sudden vision of the buildings in Waco going up in flames. If that happened here she would never get out. She'd die like all those people who died at Waco. She'd burn to death huddling under this goddamned desk.

Voices screamed from everywhere.

She was cold, shivering.

Suddenly the room was filled with screeching and stomping that shook the floor all around her. More bursts of light. From underneath the floor, bangs so loud her ears hurt.

The building was shaking, rocking on its foundation. It was going to collapse and burst into flames.

This was Samuel Mordecai's Apocalypse. The battle of Armageddon. And he was missing it.

Molly was freezing cold, shaking wildly. She tried to hold herself together by curling up tighter. Why had she done this? It was insane. She repeated to herself, "Heather Yost. Heather Yost.

Heather Yost." Then, unbidden, the others came into her head: "Kim Bassett, Philip Trotman, Hector Ramirez, Lucy Quigley, Bucky DeCarlo, Conrad Pease, Brandon Betts, Sandra Echols, Sue Ellen McGregor." She had learned their names in spite of herself. She pictured them curled up safe somewhere, waiting for the madness to end. And when it was over, Walter Demming would lead them out. They'd come out blinking and smiling. "Heather Yost," she said aloud, "Heather Yost." In the moments between bursts of gunfire, she could hear her own voice droning.

A hand touched her back. A voice close to her ear growled, "That's right. Keep praying. And, Molly—stay the hell down."

When the lights finally came back on Molly opened her eyes. Inches from her, Samuel Mordecai lay with his arms stretched over his head. Even in death his eyes and mouth gaped open in betrayal. In the exact, precise middle of his forehead was a neat third eye, wide open and dark red.

She closed her eyes and went back to the litany of names—the names she hoped, and prayed, would not need to be included in her next vigil.

"When he opened the abyss, smoke rose from it like the smoke from a gigantic furnace. The sun and sky were darkened by the smoke from the abyss. And out of the smoke locusts came down upon the earth and were given power like that of scorpions of the earth."

REVELATION 9:2-3

CHAPTER TWENTY-TWO

Walter Demming woke in total darkness.

He was sweating and disoriented. He sat up, thinking he heard distant gunfire and bombs. Around him kids were starting to whimper.

It was happening.

"It's time," he said.

He leapt to his feet. "Kids, get up. It's time! Bong Tongs! Jacksonville Six! To your posts."

Breathless, he pulled Hector's knife from his pocket. "The lights are out, but that's okay," he called. "We don't need lights. We know what to do. Sue Ellen and Conrad, get number one unbolted now. I'll be right back to lift it."

He slipped Josh's belt from the back of his pants and looped it over his left shoulder. In the pitch dark, he felt his way to the door. Kids brushed past him, bumped into him, into each other. It was chaos. Some were crying, but they were up and moving.

He stepped into the pit and stumbled over something. The fucking box of robes. He pressed himself up against the side of the pit and waited. The Jezreelites would be coming for them, he was sure.

407

It was only seconds before the wooden slab scraped back from the hole. Dirt filtered down.

Two more seconds of sleep and he'd have been caught.

From above, a flashlight beam flickered. Voices whispered.

Walter gripped the knife and tried to keep his breathing silent.

The light beam wavering above gave enough light for him to see the outline of legs descending.

He tensed, prepared to kill. This time he would not hesitate.

The smell of stale sweat hit his nostrils. The beam flicked down on the figure about to drop. Not Martin. Shorter, thicker. A bald man. The one from yesterday's phone call.

Walter timed his move. An instant before the man's feet hit earth, he lunged. He grabbed him from behind, around the chest in a bear hug that kept the man suspended in air with his arms raised. Something thudded to earth. The flashlight. It shot a sickly yellow beam across the pit floor.

Walter brought the knife blade to the man's throat. He sliced.

The man screamed and gave a mighty twist. He tried to bring his arms down. The knife blade slid out of his flesh. It was like trying to kill someone with a fucking nail file. The man had his feet on the ground now and he was fighting back, bucking and grunting, kicking. Walter held on, his arms locked around the man. He was heavier than Walter and strong. Walter could barely hold on to him.

From above came a whispered "What the hell? James!" A light flashed down on them.

Walter pushed him into the side of the pit and leaned hard against his back to pin him there.

He raised the knife to the man's throat again and stabbed. The man screamed and wrenched his body. It sent the knife flying and nearly broke Walter's hold.

"Martin, help." The man grunted it out. "He's got—"

Walter struggled to regain his grip. He lowered his left shoulder so the belt slid down his arm. He caught it in his hand. Then he tried to slip the loop over the man's head. But he was thrashing around, arching his back, struggling to break out of Walter's hold.

Walter tried again to force the belt loop over his head. This time he managed it, got it around his neck. He grabbed the loose end with both hands and jerked it tight. The man bellowed and squirmed, tried to get his hands under the belt, but it was too late. Walter had it digging into his neck. The man scrabbled at it with his fingers. Walter pulled it even tighter, grunting with the effort. Harder, tighter, more. No mistakes this time.

A light flashed down from above.

Walter gave the belt another jerk. The man was choking, flailing with his arms.

A voice from above barked, "Get out of the way, James. I'm going to shoot."

Walter pulled back on the belt with every last ounce of strength. He pictured decapitation.

The man gurgled.

Walter gritted his teeth and pulled. To finish it.

From above came the scuffle of someone coming down. Then a thud behind him. Holding tight to the belt, Walter glanced around. In the light from the fallen flashlight, he saw Martin. With a pistol in hand.

The choking man collapsed back and fell to the ground, taking Walter down with him.

Walter felt a stab in his side, like a rib cracking. Good. The pain goaded him on. The man was lying on top of him. Giving him some cover. With both hands he dragged back on the noose. To kill.

The man spasmed and went limp.

A gunshot cracked—a thunderclap and flash of light in the enclosed space.

Kids were wailing from the bus. "Mr. Demming! Mr. Demming!"

Walter was on his back with the dead man lying on top of him. He shoved the corpse off and tackled Martin around the knees.

Martin fired a wild shot as he fell. Walter leapt on him and grabbed his gun hand. He forced Martin's hand to the ground and brought a knee up hard into his groin. Martin screamed. Walter made a lunge for the gun and ripped it out of his hand.

He put the gun to Martin's head. Martin was crying, "No. Don't."

Walter fired. He put the gun to Martin's other temple and fired again.

Then he crawled to the dead man and put the gun to his head and fired.

From the top of the hole, someone called, "James! Martin! Talk to me." Walter aimed up toward the sound and fired.

On his hands and knees, he backed out of the pit. To the safety of the bus door. He was gasping when he got there.

A gunshot kicked up dirt at his feet.

He looked at the flashlight lying against the pit wall, next to the two dead men. He might need it.

He inched back toward the pit, aimed up and fired. Then he darted in, grabbed the light, and darted out. A gunshot followed him.

Several kids screamed from the darkness, "Mr. Demming! Are you all right?"

He called back, "Keep working! I'm fine."

Aboveground the unmistakable sounds of automatic gunfire and grenades continued. They had finally come. And he had a gun and a flashlight. He looked down at the pistol—an automatic that probably had ten more shots in it, if Martin started with a full clip. All he needed to do was hold on, keep the Jezreelites from coming down.

Another shot boomed down into the hole. And another, kicking up dirt.

He turned and flashed the light back into the bus. Now the problem was to help lift the seats and still keep them Jezreelites at bay.

He called back, "Sue Ellen, Conrad, is it unbolted?"

"Yes."

"I'm coming."

He focused the flashlight on the first seat. Sue Ellen and Conrad had already tipped it on its back.

He turned the flashlight back into the pit to check. No one coming. But the light drew two shots.

He flashed the light into the back of the bus. Chaos. One of the seats hadn't been unbolted yet. It didn't matter. He wouldn't have time anyway to go back there and help them lift. The plan had changed.

He called out, "Listen. Kids in the back. Stop working. Leave the seats alone. Hector, Brandon, and Kim, come to the front. New assignment." He lighted the way for them. "The rest of you, stay back there."

Then he flashed the light back into the pit. No one coming. He stuck the pistol in his waistband.

"Change of plans," he said. "I've got this gun now. I can hold them off from the pit. But I need to be outside. I'll get the seat in the doorway, but I won't be able to wedge it with number two. The five of you can do that without me."

Kim looked at him in horror. "But, Mr. Demming, you—"

"Don't argue," he said. "This is an order. Let's go."

He ran to the door to flash the light around the pit. He fired up once to hold them for a while. Then he ran back onto the bus. He handed the flashlight to Kim. "Hold this." With Sue Ellen and Conrad, he dragged the seat to the door. "Okay, I'm going to get outside and pull. You guys push from in here."

He helped them get the clumsy barricade on end, then stepped to the other side and pulled it with him as he backed out the door. Before they closed off the doorway, he said, "Give me the light back, Kim. I'll need it."

She handed it to him with a look of despair. He set it down in the pit. They wrestled the heavy seat into place in the doorway.

A volley of shots rained down into the pit. He pressed up against the seat.

"Okay, you five, drag number two and wedge it

in really good. Then get everyone into position in the back. I'm right here."

He turned and looked up at the hole. An occasional light beam flittered by, but nothing else. The stuttering of automatic gunfire continued from above. Behind him the kids were dragging the seat into place, grunting and whimpering with the effort, but he heard it moving. They were doing it.

It was the first moment of stillness for him and he realized he was soaking wet and shivering.

The lightbulb overhead flickered suddenly and came back on. Walter switched the flashlight off. Conserve batteries. In the back of the bus the kids cheered the return of the light. Behind him, he heard the clanking and scraping of the seat as they wedged it into place.

"Mr. Demming, it's done," Hector called. "And it's real secure."

"You did good. We're in business. Get everyone into position now," he said. "On the double."

From up above a voice called, "Bus Driver, come out now. Or we're coming down." In answer, Walter fired up at the sound.

Walter's shivering was out of control now and he felt so wet.

He looked down and saw that he was covered with blood. His shirt and his jeans were soaked through. His arms were smeared and his hands were slimy with it. Who would have thought James and Martin had so much blood in them?

At the square of light overhead a face suddenly appeared and a gun fired. He shot back. There was a scream and the face disappeared.

Then he felt it. The drained weakening, the

light-headedness. And in his right side, a stab of pain so deep it shook him like a rag doll. He lowered himself to the ground shaking. He leaned back against the barricade they had made.

He didn't pull up his shirt to look. Whatever was there would wait.

He looked at the two corpses bleeding into the earth. The shooting above was dying down, he thought. That battle could go only one way. They just needed to hold on. He tried to keep the gun aimed up, at where he'd heard the scream, but it was so heavy. He let it rest in his lap for a minute.

He heard the kids rustling and talking, bickering in the back. Finally he heard Sandra's voice, faint but clear and sweet. "Okay, y'all. We're singing. Here we go." Her sweet soprano voice trembled. "The wheels on the bus go round and round, round and round, round and round."

He yelled, "All of you, sing!"

More voices joined, faint and shaky, at first, but they were singing. "The wheels on the bus go round and round."

"Louder!" Walter called. "Louder."

The voices intensified. "Round and round, round and round."

"Good," he said, his voice weaker. "You all did so good." He tried to raise his voice so they could hear him over the singing. "I'm proud of you all." But his words were slurred and soft. And it took so much energy.

"The wheels on the bus go round and round, all over town," the children boomed out.

Walter was feeling so sleepy. He needed to stay awake, to keep watch, but his eyes were too heavy.

He tried to fight it off, but it curled around him and smothered him with dark, wet, heavy blankets. He sank down and rested his cheek against the cool earth. Sleep claimed him.

> *"These are they which came out of great tribulation, and have washed their robes, and made them white in the blood of the Lamb."*
> REVELATION 7:14

CHAPTER TWENTY-THREE

Molly Cates kept her eyes fixed on the open double doors of the white barn. A cluster of ambulances were parked in front with their back doors open and a crowd of EMTs standing ready.

Bryan Holihan took her by the elbow. "Come on," he said for the third time. "They want you back at the post. Traynor has some news for you."

She shook his hand off her arm. "Go on, Bryan. I told you. I'm staying until they come out."

"You can watch it on TV back at the command post," he said.

She glanced over at him. For the first time since she'd met him he wasn't wearing a suit jacket; that was because she was wearing it. When she had emerged from the compound, she couldn't stop shivering, and he had put it over her shoulders. "I wouldn't leave here now," she said, "if you had a subpoena for me. I want to see them walk out. In person, not on TV. It can't be much longer." She looked at her watch. Twelve-twenty-six—just an

415

hour since she and Rain Conroy had walked through the door.

One of the fire trucks revved its engine and headed straight toward where they were standing at the gaping hole in the chain-link fence. The tanks had mowed down whole sections of the fence when they stormed the compound. Molly and Bryan stepped aside to let the truck pass. Three more fire trucks and a pumper remained, keeping an eye on the smoldering first floor, where a fire had erupted in the kitchen.

No one was saying how the fire had started, but it had been very convenient for the entry team; it had helped end the confrontation quickly. When it came right down to it, the Hearth Jezreelites did not want to burn to death. And since their leader, the Prophet Mordecai, was dead, there was no one to stop them from surrendering when the flames got serious. Those who had not been killed or wounded had come running out of the burning building with their hands raised. It saved both sides from taking more casualties.

Molly looked at Bryan Holihan, who had his radio pressed to his ear. "Bryan, tell me something. Was that fire set deliberately?"

He looked down at her for a few seconds without taking the radio from his ear. He shrugged. "Stun grenades and ammunition are highly flammable. Fire is always a possibility in these dynamic entries."

"Oh, Bryan" she said, "stop being such a prick. Was it deliberate or not?"

His smile did not reach his eyes. "You can ask Lattimore, but he won't know either."

Molly glanced over to the gate where Patrick Lattimore stood talking with one of the entry-team commanders. "I *will* ask him." She headed toward the gate, stepping over a section of crushed chain link. Now, in the aftermath of the carnage, the compound looked like a carnival. In addition to the fire trucks and ambulances, there were still two tanks and two personnel carriers parked close to the building. Scores of Austin police cars and transport vans and DPS units with lights whirling surrounded the compound.

FBI agents in black, with rifles ready, were still patrolling the compound looking for stragglers—cultists who might be hiding in the outbuildings or on the grounds.

The press was being kept back behind the outer perimeter, but cameras were whirring everywhere, and reporters were running around accosting anyone going in or out of the compound.

It was a spectacle. In all her years of reporting, Molly Cates had never seen anything to equal it.

But the main event, center ring, the focus of all attention, was the white barn. Everyone was watching, waiting, praying.

For the past eighteen minutes Holihan and Lattimore had been getting radio updates from the team inside the barn. The children were still underground, barricaded inside the bus, and the agents couldn't budge the seat they had wedged in the door.

Molly was so wrought-up, so jittery, she couldn't stand in one place. She'd been pacing back and forth between Holihan at his post and Lattimore at the gate, bugging them for updates. She had actually found herself wringing her hands. Now, as she approached Lattimore, an agent from the entry team jogged out of the barn and joined him. Molly hurried so she could catch what he was saying.

The agent had pulled his black hood down so it dangled around his neck along with his gas mask. He was very young with a sand-colored crew cut and mustache. "Yes, singing," he was saying with a grin. "I swear to God. They're all huddled in the back singing. Some annoying song about a bus. And we're calling out to them, "It's all over, kids. Come on out. Everything's fine. Your families are waiting for you.""

He unzipped his vest, revealing a sweat-soaked black shirt underneath. "One of the kids says they aren't coming out until Mr. Demming tells them to or they see a badge that says FBI on it. Kroll tells them Demming is on his way to the hospital in a helicopter, but he's got a badge to show them. He can slip it between the seat and the doorframe if one of them will come get it. Well, the kids have to talk this over, lots of yammering and arguing." The agent tapped the fingers and thumbs of each hand together to pantomine jabbering mouths.

"Finally this kid comes to the barricade at the door and says, "Do it, man.' Tough little kid. So Kroll slides his badge through and the kid has to take it back to confer with the other kids. And I guess they finally agree it's authentic 'cause he comes back and says okay, they'll come out. But then they can't move the seat that's wedged against the seat that's blocking the door. And, from outside, we can't do it either."

"Amazing," said Bryan Holihan, who had joined

them. "The kids must have done it themselves. Demming was outside the bus."

"Yeah. But you'd swear that barricade was done by a bunch of engineers. Anyway, we told 'em, "Don't worry. The fire department is here. They've got the gear to get you out.' While we're waiting for the fire guys to come, Kroll asks them if they're all okay, and yeah, they're okay, but they're worried about Mr. Demming. What happened to him? We say we aren't sure, but it looks like he's got a gunshot wound." His grin faded. "Of course, we don't tell them there's a pool of blood an inch deep seeping into the dirt at the bus door, or that the guy barely had any life signs when the paramedics put him in the copter." He wiped his sweating face with his sleeve. "I guess they can hear about that later.

"So now the firefighters are down there in the hole, bending the bus door back like they're opening a can and—"

Lattimore held a hand up for silence. "Here they come." Everyone turned toward the double doors of the white barn. They were coming out. At last.

Molly hooked her fingers in the chain link and watched. Her mouth felt dry as ashes.

The first one out was a blond girl, closely flanked by two agents. Molly thought it was Heather Yost. The little girl held a hand up to shield her eyes from the glare of the lights. "One," Molly said out loud. "That's number one. Walking under her own steam."

The second was a tiny dark-haired boy in shorts. He was holding an agent's hand and carrying a white doll. Bucky DeCarlo, the youngest, the boy

419

with the cowlicks. His hair was much longer now, the cowlicks flattened down. "Two."

The third to emerge was Kim Bassett, her face pale as skimmed milk, her pink hair darkened with dirt. She stopped in the barn door, seemingly stunned by the lights and commotion around her. The agent next to her put his arm around her shoulders and encouraged her to keep walking. "Three," Molly said.

The next was a black-haired kid with huge dark eyes talking animatedly to one of the agents. His hands moved rapidly as he talked. Hector Ramirez. "Four."

The next three came in a group and her view of their faces was blocked by the beefy agents surrounding them. She continued to count aloud: "Five. Six. Seven."

Two more came out. A thin dark-skinned girl wearing glasses and carrying a book clutched to her chest. Sandra Echols. "Eight." Next to her walked a shorter boy who was covering his face with his hands, crying, Molly thought. She wasn't sure which one he was. "Nine."

And the last one—a small pixielike girl with curly brown hair. Lucy Quigley. "Ten."

Molly let out the breath she didn't know she'd been holding.

All of them accounted for. All alive and walking on their own. All except Josh Benderson, of course. And Walter Demming.

Molly had seen Demming rushed out on a stretcher. By the light of the flames of the burning compound, she'd glimpsed the face of the man on the stretcher speeding by—a man with scraggly gray hair pulled into a ponytail, a grizzly beard, and a blue headband.

They had whisked him off in the Star-Flight helicopter that had been standing by with its engines running.

The report she'd pried out of Bryan Holihan was that Demming was critical, with a gunshot wound in the back. He was in shock from blood loss. They were flying him to Brackenridge Hospital in Austin, which was equipped to deal with serious gunshot wounds.

Molly watched the children gather and stand huddled together in a tight, silent group behind the ambulances.

The plan was to take them to Memorial Hospital in Georgetown, where their families were waiting. Molly wondered what the families would find when they finally took their children home. Whatever it was that had happened to them during these past forty-nine days, these children would not be the same children their parents had sent off to school on February 24; they would never be the same children again. Of that she was certain.

Molly squinted to try to see better. There seemed to be a problem at the barn door. The kids were not getting into the ambulances. They were standing around, and it looked like they were arguing with the agents and the EMTs. Molly was too far away to hear their voices, but she could tell from their body language that they were arguing.

Lattimore spoke into his radio. "Tell them it's just a ten-minute ride. And there's an attendant in each ambulance."

Molly tugged his sleeve. "What's going on?"

He kept the radio pressed to his ear as he answered her. "Oh, the kids want to ride together in one ambulance. But it's against the ambulance service's policy, so they're arguing about it."

Molly felt hot indignation rising in her throat; it was the first time all night she'd been warm. "Pat! Those kids have been crammed together like puppies in a litter for weeks. To separate them so suddenly is outrageous. You're the ASAC. Use your power. Tell Kroll to let them ride however the hell they want."

"Molly, calm down. It's being taken care of. Kroll is trying to work out a compromise to divide them into two ambulances. They won't fit in one. Poor Stan. I've never known him to get rattled before. He's used to handcuffed bank robbers at the end of a maneuver, not opinionated little kids."

After a few minutes, three of the children climbed into one of the ambulances, but the others seemed to be hanging back. And they were arguing again.

Lattimore said into the radio, "But their parents are waiting at Memorial Hospital. Do they know that?" He listened and then said, "He'll be going right into surgery. They won't be able to see him anyway. Tell them that." He waited.

Molly watched Stan Kroll leaning over and listening to Hector Ramirez, who was shaking his head forcefully.

"Okay, okay," Lattimore muttered. "Hold on, Stan. I'm coming in. *I'll* talk to them."

He lowered his radio and said, "The kids insist on going to the same hospital where Demming is.

I need to talk to them. Come on, Holihan. You've got kids that age."

Molly stepped to his side. "I'm coming, too."

He shook his head. "No. It's better—"

She said in a low voice, "Pat, you owe me. Big time. I'm coming." The intensity of her need to see the children up close surprised her. Now that she was involved, she wanted to know everything about them.

Lattimore shrugged, and walked through the gate. Holihan followed. It was not a graceful acquiescence, but Molly took it as a yes. She had to jog to keep up with the two men as they strode across the weedy packed-dirt path that led to the barn. Stan Kroll was still leaning over talking to the kids. As Molly neared them, she could see he was looking red-faced and unhappy. Lattimore was right: Apparently this was proving more stressful to him than the assault.

The three kids inside the ambulance were crowded into the open rear door with their heads sticking out. Bucky DeCarlo had his thumb stuck in his mouth. The other seven were huddled around them. They were very thin and very dirty, and they kept blinking at the lights. Surrounded by black-clad agents, they looked as pale and vulnerable as featherless birds fallen from a nest.

Hector Ramirez took a step to meet Molly and the two agents. "Who's in charge?" he asked, raising his chin aggressively.

Lattimore looked down at him. "I am. Patrick Lattimore, assistant special agent in charge." He smiled. "You must be Mr. Ramirez."

Several of the kids giggled.

Hector glanced back at them, then turned to Lattimore. "Yeah, that's me. We want to go to the hospital where Mr. Demming is. They said he was going to Austin and we were going to Georgetown. We want to go where he is."

"Your families are waiting for you ten minutes away from here," Lattimore said gently. "In Georgetown. They've been waiting for you and worrying about you for forty-nine days. Let's not keep them waiting any longer."

Hector turned around and looked at Kim. She set her lips tight and gave a single shake of her head.

Hector turned back to the adults. "Mr. Demming might need us. We want to go there."

From behind him, Kim said, "Our parents can come there—to the hospital where Mr. Demming is. That way, we can see them and be there for him, too. You could call them now and tell them to meet us."

Several of the kids nodded at that.

Molly studied Kim Bassett's dirty, freckled face and the firm, stubborn chin that was so similar to her mother's. She felt a flood of relief. Terrible things had happened to this child, but she seemed to be...intact.

"But everything's set up for you in Georgetown," Lattimore said. "The doctors are all ready to take care of you there. We just talked to them on the phone."

"Man," Hector said, with a dismissive wave of his hand, "we don't need no doctors. We ain't sick. Just hungry. Sandra has the runs, but she's okay."

"Well, I—we need to have you looked at," Lattimore said, appealing to the whole group. "It's all—set up. You can't just—" He stopped when he saw the kids' lack of response. This was the first time Molly had seen him not in control of the situation. She looked at Hector with admiration—a formidable person, standing his ground against the awesome authority of the federal government.

"Come on now, kids," Lattimore said. "Just hop in the ambulances, and we'll talk about this some more when we get to Georgetown."

Bryan Holihan, who had been watching the interchange with his radio to his ear, suddenly tensed and moved away several yards. He turned his back and said something low into his radio. Alarmed by his expression, Molly walked back to join him. He listened with his eyes closed. "Okay," he said. "Ten-four." He lowered the radio and looked at Molly. His eyes were wet with tears.

She put her hand on his arm and whispered, "What is it, Bryan?" But she knew.

"Demming. He died before they could get him on the operating table." A tear broke loose and trickled down his cheek. He used his radio to swipe it away. "Goddamn. If we'd gotten in just a minute faster—"

The news sucked Molly's breath right out of her lungs. Her whole body felt deflated with loss and disappointment. She didn't even know the man, had seen him only once, as he was dying, but the loss felt huge and very personal.

Patrick Lattimore appeared behind Molly. "What is it?"

Holihan glanced toward the children. "Demming's dead," he said in a low voice.

"Oh, dear God," Lattimore said, "what are we going to do about these kids?"

Molly glanced over at the children, who were whispering and arguing among themselves. Kim Bassett broke away from the group and walked toward them. "Is it about Mr. Demming?" she asked.

The three adults looked down into her pale, smudged face without answering. Molly felt her mouth dry up. She was relieved to leave this to Patrick Lattimore.

Kim's shrewd, calm glance moved from face to face. "It *is* about him, isn't it?"

Hector hurried to join them, his black eyebrows raised in alarm. The other kids started to drift forward.

Kim turned to Hector and said, "Oh, Hector, he died and they don't want to tell us."

Hector looked up at the adults. "He *died?* Is that right?"

Patrick Lattimore nodded. "He died just now, at the hospital. I'm so sorry to have to say it. I know that you kids—"

"Is there someone there with him?" Kim asked, dry-eyed. "Or is he alone?"

Bryan Holihan said, "His old friend Jake Alesky is there with him."

Kim nodded and turned to the other children. "Something bad has happened," she told them. "Let's go back to the ambulance, y'all." She pointed to where Sandra, Bucky, and one of the other boys were still hanging out of the back. "Then we can hear it all together."

Lattimore turned to Molly with a look of anguish. "What do you think? Should we leave them alone? I wish one of the psychologists was here. I want to get them to their parents."

Molly watched as all ten children huddled together at the back of the ambulance. Kim put an arm around Bucky and started to talk in a voice so low Molly couldn't make out the words. The kids leaned forward to hear.

"I think it would be an intrusion for us to interfere right now," Molly told Lattimore. "Let's give them some time alone." She lowered her eyes, feeling that it was an intrusion even to watch.

One of the children let out a wail, and others began to cry.

Lucy and Heather leaned together weeping on one another's shoulders. One of the boys sat on the ground and wept soundlessly.

Molly watched them hug and comfort one another. Whatever horrors they had endured during their captivity, she realized, something remarkable had happened down there underground to knit them together.

After a while, Hector called out to Lattimore. "Okay, man. We'll go to your hospital now."

Kim stood at the back of one ambulance and Hector at the other. Quietly the children divided themselves into two groups and climbed in.

Then, with no sirens or lights, the ambulances drove out of the smoldering compound and headed west toward Memorial Hospital in

Georgetown, where the children's families and a team of doctors and social workers were waiting for them.

Molly looked at her watch. It was forty-two minutes past midnight, April 14. The fiftieth day, the day Samuel Mordecai had expected the world to end. She glanced at the ruins of the Hearth Jezreelite compound. He had certainly inflicted a great deal of damage on the world, this abandoned infant turned angry prophet. And the damages hadn't all been reckoned yet.

But life on earth was pretty resilient. She recalled the stubborn expression on Kim Bassett's face. Lord, wasn't Thelma Bassett going to be glad to see that expression again. The thought made Molly smile and, at the same time, it brought hot tears to her eyes.

Back at the command post, lights were blazing. Grady Traynor threw an arm around Molly. "We caught the three Sword Hand of God perps."

"Oh, Grady! How?"

"Your friend Addie Dodgin, in Waco, helped. She's been calling, Molly, and wants you to call her, no matter what the hour."

"Tell me," Molly demanded.

"They were in a stolen van outside her office, waiting for her to come out. She spotted them and called the feds. They'd told her to call if anything didn't look right. They swooped down and caught them with all the paraphernalia for turning people into blood statues. We'll need you to take a look at them, Molly. Tomorrow will do."

"Okay. I need to talk to Rain Conroy. Where is she?"

"Long gone," Grady said.

"Gone?"

"On her way back to Quantico. She got debriefed by Andrew Stein, grabbed an ice pack for her face, and was on the way to the airport less than fifteen minutes after you two came out."

"She didn't stay to see the kids," Molly said.

"No. But she left you a message."

"What?"

Grady grinned. "She said, 'Tell Molly Cates she's the only stand-up writer I ever met.'"

Molly's face felt flushed with pleasure. It was a compliment she would carry with her to the grave.

Molly watched as Patrick Lattimore released the evening's final tally to the press:

In what he referred to as a highly successful tactical maneuver, all ten of the remaining hostage children had been rescued from the buried bus where they had been kept during the forty-nine days of their captivity. All were alive and apparently healthy, although two of them, Sandra Echols and Philip Trotman, were being kept overnight at Memorial Hospital in Georgetown for observation. The rest had been released to their families.

Eleven cult members had been killed in the assault, including Samuel Mordecai, who was shot in the head by the HRT entry team while he was in the act of firing on them.

Fifteen cult members had been wounded.

Two federal agents had been killed in the

line of duty, and three had been wounded, one critically.

One hundred and twelve cult members, including sixty-three women, had been taken into custody and charged with murder and attempted murder. Other charges were under consideration. A search of the compound revealed forty-two neat graves, believed to be the forty-two infants murdered by the Hearth Jezreelites.

The bus driver, Walter Demming, had been shot by the cultists during the assault. He had died of his wound shortly after arriving at Brackenridge Hospital.

Patrick Lattimore did not mention the existence of Special Agent Loraine Conroy, who had killed Samuel Mordecai and three other cult members.

He did not mention Molly Cates.

When questioned about the two women seen entering the compound twenty minutes before the assault, Lattimore said he had no comment.

It was a version of the events that stunned Molly. He had turned the story of the devastation at Jezreel into a football score, a cool postgame recitation of dry statistics. He had managed to censor out of it all the juice—all the fear, all the loss and tragedy, all the loyalty and devotion, and all the courage.

The press, of course, would sniff out the drama. Herself included. She was already thinking about the story she wanted to tell. It had been taking root in her brain for days without her knowing.

★ ★ ★

It was 3 A.M. before they were finished at the command post and Molly and Grady could head home. Molly rested her head on the seat back, beyond exhaustion. They passed the compound, which was still ablaze with lights. The acrid smell of charred wood still hung in the air. But only one fire truck, three DPS cars, and a small group of agents patrolling the fence remained. It was over.

"So, Molly. How do you feel?"

"Awful. Wonderful. Exhausted. Weepy. Seeing those children walk out alive was a high point of my life, Grady."

"Mine, too. How about your own adventure tonight?"

Molly closed her eyes and thought. She hadn't had time yet for summing up. "I would never do it again. I used up whatever luck I have allotted to me for this lifetime. From now on, I'll have to be careful."

He grinned at her. "I know that feeling."

"How about you, Grady?"

"Given the odds against us, I think we pulled off a miracle. Those kids were as good as dead. We dragged them back from the underworld. With Walter Demming's help. And yours, Molly."

He might have said more. There was lots more to say, but she didn't hear any of it because she was asleep.

CHAPTER TWENTY-FOUR

Grady Traynor was waiting when Molly and Jo Beth walked out of the Sports Spa. He was sitting on the tailgate of Molly's repaired pickup drinking a beer. Copper was lying at his feet.

Jo Beth leaned over to give her father a kiss, but she stopped halfway when Copper lifted his head and growled at her.

"He'll get over that," Grady said.

Jo Beth stood back and studied the dog. "Maybe you should send him for retraining."

"Military school," Molly said. "He could board."

Grady stroked the dog's head. "Don't pay any attention to what your mother says. Actually, she's smitten with the animal. This morning she bought him a bed."

"I thought a bed of his own in the kitchen might keep him out of my bedroom," Molly said, with a meaningful glance at Grady.

"We'll see," he said with a smile. "How are your push-ups going?"

"I haven't actually started the new program yet. It's only April. But by the end of the year I'm going to have arms like Rain Conroy's."

"Jo Beth," Grady said, "how about joining us? We're going out to the lake to watch the sun set. If the world's going to end at sunset,

432

we thought the lake would be the best place to watch it happen."

"Thanks," Jo Beth said, "but I've got a date. And I'm late. Got to run."

They watched her walk across the parking lot in her black tights and long gray sweatshirt. Before she got into her car, she turned and waved at them.

"We do good work together," Grady said, throwing a kiss at his daughter.

"Yes," Molly said. "We certainly do." She ran her fingers over the repaired rear fender. "Thanks for getting this fixed."

He patted the tailgate, and she hoisted herself up to sit next to him.

"I've been thinking, Molly."

She tensed. Here it came. There was no putting it off any longer. "What?"

"About my lease and all."

"Uh-huh."

"Barbara Gruber called me."

"Oh?"

"She's going to Washington for six months to learn how to set up a DNA lab. But since she's a good buddy of yours, I suppose you know that."

"Uh-huh."

"She's looking for someone to sublet her house. It's got a fenced-in yard, she says."

"A perfect dog yard," Molly said.

"That's what she said. And the rent's exactly what I've been paying. A real coincidence."

"Yeah."

"I told her I'd take it."

Molly turned to look at him. His pale aqua

eyes had always reminded her of Oriental Avenue on the Monopoly board. She took his face between her hands. "Oh, Grady! What a good idea. It's only about a mile from me. I could help you with the dog."

He laughed. "It *is* a good idea."

She pulled his head down to kiss him, but Copper growled low in his throat.

Grady said, "Wait. Hold that thought." He jumped down from the truck, took the dog by the collar, and led him up front and into the cab. He slammed the door and ran back to resume his position on the tailgate. "Now. Where were we?" He leaned down and kissed her, first chastely on the cheek, then lingeringly down her neck, his mustache tickling like butterfly wings, and finally on the mouth—a long, deep exploration that left them both breathless.

Afterward, he reached back into the cooler and took out a beer. He popped the top and handed it to Molly. "It will give us six more months to contemplate the eschatology of cohabitation," he said.

"A new countdown." Molly took a long sip of her beer. "Have you noticed how time tends to organize itself into a series of countdowns? As soon as one ends, another begins. Two weeks till your lease is up. Seven years till I'm fifty. Eight months till I can do fifty push-ups. One day to taxes. Fifteen days till my article is due."

"Yes, and when they aren't built in, we make them for ourselves." He tipped his head back to take a long swig of beer. "What *are* you going to write about Jezreel? The story about Special Agent Rain Conroy and how Samuel Mordecai really met his maker is pretty sensational. Too bad you can't tell it."

"Not really. That's not the story I want to tell. There's a much better one."

"Walter Demming?"

"Yeah. Walter Demming and his eleven kids. Don't you wonder what happened down there underground for forty-nine days, Grady? You saw what it was like. Can you imagine living there for that length of time with all those children? I talked to Kim Bassett today. The first day they were down in the hole, the Jezreelites turned the lights off and left them in the dark. They were all terrified, she said, crying and screaming. To calm them down, Demming started telling them a story and he kept it going, an installment or two a day, during their captivity. Kim said he finished the story last night, just a few hours before he was killed. The characters were animals—a turkey vulture and an armadillo—and they had adventures that sound to me a lot like some of his and Jake's experiences in Vietnam.

"And the way he let the FBI know where they were is remarkable—the poetry and the Vietnam reference. That cries out to be written about. And, Grady, there's no question that what he did last night saved their lives."

"Sounds like you're a little in love with him," Grady said.

Molly sighed. "I suppose I am, a little. All the children are. And they're eager to talk about him. I'm planning to go to the memorial service on Tuesday; a few of the kids are going to give eulogies. And I want to see how they do over time.

Kim had trouble sleeping last night, and her mom says several of the other children woke up screaming. I think they're in for more than just bad dreams."

"It's a hell of a story," Grady said, nodding.

"It is. I think what I love about Demming is his natural courage, the unselfconscious kind that just emerges out of character and the situation."

Grady took hold of her hand. "Molly, that's the reason I had to take Copper."

She looked up, surprised. "It is?"

"Yes. I watched him work once, and he struck me as a creature who just couldn't stop himself from being brave when the situation required it. He didn't choose courage, it just bubbled up from his nature. I couldn't stand to see that snuffed out. There's so little of it around."

Molly nodded.

"Oh-oh." Grady pointed at the orange ball of the sun that was just beginning to flatten against the horizon. "It's setting. We're not going to make it to the lake."

"I like it right here in the parking lot," Molly said, sipping her beer and savoring the way the clouds on the horizon got suffused with orange and pink and gold.

"Me, too. Looks like the world's not going to end today." Grady lifted his can. "Here's to the world continuing," he said, "just as flawed and imperfect as it has always been."

Molly smiled. "I'll drink to that." She tapped her can to his. Then she held it up in a salute to the dog, who was watching them intently, his nose pressed against the back window

EPILOGUE

Excerpt from "Under the Beetle's Cellar," by
Molly Cates, *Lone Star Monthly,* June 1995

*... They don't really hang out together much, they
say. But sometimes they gather out on the playground
and talk. They talk about the nightmares and the
moments of panic when the school bus comes to a sudden stop or when the lights go out. They talk about
how Bucky's thumb-sucking has gotten out of hand,
and about how Sandra's persistent stomachaches are
mostly in her head. They joke about going to therapy.*

*They talk about Josh and what it was like to
watch him die.*

And they talk about Walter Demming.

*They say that in the beginning he didn't seem to
like them much, but, later on, when he walked the bus
aisle at night checking on them, they would sense his
presence and feel taken care of. They say he wasn't
someone you would think of as funny or entertaining,
but the story he told became their all-time favorite;
sometimes now they talk about Jacksonville and Lopez
and argue about the ending, and they laugh. They say
he didn't like religion much, but he ended up praying
anyway. They say he's hard to describe, hard to pin
down as this thing or that.*

*And that's true. After all, he was a man who broke
all his vows. When he came home from Vietnam, Walter
Demming had planned, like Candide, to stay home
and tend his own garden. He had vowed to avoid in-
volvement, but he ended up intimately involved in the
lives of eleven children. He had vowed to avoid violence, but he died in an explosion of apocalyptic vio-*

lence. He had vowed to maintain his privacy, to attract no attention, but he became headline news around the world, and was awarded posthumously the Presidential Medal of Honor.

Fate, or whatever force it is that delivers people to that very place they have been avoiding, devised for Walter Demming a situation that compelled him to transcend his rules and act instead from his heart and his true nature.

IF YOU HAVE ENJOYED READING THIS
LARGE PRINT BOOK AND YOU
WOULD LIKE MORE INFORMATION
ON HOW TO ORDER A WHEELER
LARGE PRINT BOOK, PLEASE WRITE
TO:

WHEELER PUBLISHING, INC.
P.O. BOX 531
ACCORD, MA 02018-0531